MINE TO LOVE

PROTECTION SERIES
BOOK 6

KENNEDY L. MITCHELL

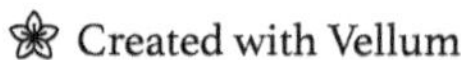 Created with Vellum

To my amazing alpha readers. Thank you for putting up with all the texts, voice messages, and tears while writing these stories. I couldn't do it without you.

PROLOGUE

The slow cadence of dripping water in the corner of the dilapidated shed added to the ominous feel that engulfed the small space. Just the way he liked it. With a deep inhale, he closed his eyes, savoring the familiar scent of blood, decay, and fear. That fear pulsed off the small woman who sluggishly awoke moments ago from the drugs still coursing through her veins, surprised and terrified to find herself strapped to the metal chair bolted to the plywood floor. Observing from a shadowed corner, he watched her fight against the tight restraints. Her eyes widened when they scanned the room and landed on the rusted bedframe and stained mattress that sat just a few feet away from where she was bound.

She struggled even harder to break free, increasing his interest to near obsessive levels.

He enjoyed the ones who fought back. Loved being the one who broke them until they were a husk of who they were before meeting him. The woman before, the FBI agent his partner requested he handle, fought hard the first day, but then her true weak nature rose to the surface, and the insistent begging began.

His lips curled into a snarl. He didn't want the pleading or offers of sexual favors for a reprieve from the pain and terror he enjoyed inflicting. It was taking what they weren't willing to give, pushing them to the brink of what their body could handle before pulling back that he craved.

This urge, the desire to inflict as much pain and torment as possible, had been a part of him for as long as he could remember. The need to strip women of their worth, to make them realize they were nothing but a tool for his wants and desires, was ingrained in him from an early age.

With the new partnership, the way he abducted his victims was easier, with much less risk than how he hunted before. The collaboration between himself and his partner not only kept his pleasure sheds full but his many accounts growing as well. Though he knew it wouldn't last much longer now that the partner had his special puppet in his sights.

"You won't get free," he rasped.

Her attention snapped to where he hid in the shadows. After pressing the Record button, the small red light on the camera above him now blinking, indicating everything was in working order, he tugged the hard plastic mask down over his face, hit the spotlight above her head, and stepped forward.

The tiny woman's features hardened, only her eyes exposing the sheer terror that flowed through her system. Behind the mask, he grinned and inhaled again, savoring her unique smell of terror. One step, then another, he drew closer, though he stayed out of the spotlight's bright beam.

Shouted curses echoed off the metal walls as she struggled with renewed earnest to break free.

Pausing beside her restrained arm, he trailed the tip of a gloved finger up her inked forearm, enjoying the panic his touch caused his little bird. That was what she was. A tiny, insignificant bird who was caught in his cage and at his mercy.

Just how he liked it.

"Get the fuck away from me," she sneered with false bravado.

A humorless chuckle rumbled in his chest. This bird *was* unique. Almost as if she were not only fighting for herself but for someone else. He tilted his head to the side, staring at her hardened features.

"Who do you fight so hard for, little bird?" he asked, surprising himself. He never talked while the camera recorded his every move.

A flash of panic flicked across her features, eyes widening and lips parting with a gasp.

Interesting.

"You won't get away from me," he said, trailing that single finger higher along the column of her neck before tracing it along her petite face.

Faster than he could detect, her face whipped to the side, trapping that single finger between her teeth. His barked curse rattled the metal walls.

With a hard pull, the single digit reluctantly shifted from her clamped jaw, almost tugging his glove off with the sharp movement.

A rage-induced haze clouded his vision and thoughts. Not holding back, he curled the injured hand into a tight fist and sent it sailing toward her smirking face. Her head snapped to the side, spit and blood flying out of her mouth, adding to the other dried fluids on the ground. Chest heaving, he restrained himself from striking her again, knowing he wouldn't stop until she was nearly dead and broken. No, he wanted to savor her fight, craved to take his time breaking this one. She would be the most fun he'd had in a while.

When his vision cleared, he couldn't believe what he saw.

Instead of cowering, sobbing like all the others had at the first touch of pain, she sat straighter than before, eyes locked on him. Blood dripped from her busted lip, and already her eye was swelling, but that didn't take away from the defiance in her icy glare.

"You hit like a girl," she said. Sucking that busted lip, she gathered up a mouthful of blood and spit it in his direction, landing beside his boot. "Why don't you let me out of these and make this a fair fight? Or are you too scared you'll get bested by a girl? Fucking coward."

Oh, she was special.

His heart raced, and all his blood drained straight to his cock.

Breaking her would be his greatest achievement.

"You will eat those words, little bird," he said with a chuckle. "We will have fun, you and I." Gripping her hair in a tight fist, he yanked her head back until a sharp hiss whistled past her clenched teeth, yet still that defiance poured out of her jade-green eyes. "Though I will be the one having all the fun."

Unable to stop, he shifted closer until his hard cock rubbed against the side of her head, the zipper of his jeans adding to the friction. His lids fluttered closed as her silky, soft hair slid beneath his movements.

"Fucking sick bastard," she seethed. "Who fucked up that tiny brain of yours?" Each word was strained, as if speaking was a struggle with her neck arched back. "Let me guess. Your mommy was mean to you."

His movements faltered.

All desire vanished, leaving ice lacing his veins.

Her responding chuckle said she noticed her words had struck home.

"Typical narcissist asshole, blaming their mommy for their fucked-up view of women."

His hold tightened, pulling chunks from her scalp, but still she laughed.

Laughed at him.

Just like she did.

Just like they all did.

The earlier ice turned to fire as his anger fanned into a blazing inferno.

With a hard shove, he released her head, the force causing her neck to snap forward. Her grunt of pain did nothing to cool his need to show her who he really was, how wrong she was to laugh at him.

Striding over to the play bucket, he grabbed the first tool his gloved hand could wrap around and turned.

Those green eyes widened, the fear from earlier overtaking her fake bravery.

He flicked the switch, the electric prod crackling from the high voltage.

A wide evil grin bunched his cheeks behind the mask, moving the hard white plastic up his face.

"Ready to break, little bird?"

Each step closer drove his anticipation higher until a sharp bark from outside the shed paused his advance. Tilting an ear toward the sound, he cursed when another bark sounded, this time slightly farther away. His dog was the only warning system he allowed this far out, having trained him to make him aware of any unwanted visitors while he worked.

A knowing feeling settled in his gut.

Betrayed.

The motherfucker got his special puppet and betrayed him to tie up loose ends.

Two could play that game. But first he needed to escape without being caught; then he'd exact revenge. Maybe even take the bastard's special puppet for himself as payment.

Dropping the cattle prod, he glanced around, knowing his DNA covered every inch of the space—not that it mattered, as he always kept the most identifiable part of himself covered with gloves—before landing on his little bird.

He wanted to take her with him to finish what they started, but he couldn't risk it.

Yet.

Forcing his feet to move, he shifted a metal panel aside and slipped out into the cold December night. The surrounding trees and cloud-covered moon were perfect for a clean escape. Waiting for another bark to gauge which direction not to run, he kept his back sealed to the corrugated metal.

He'd find his bird again.

Then they would play until her end.

This was just the beginning.

1

TALLON

The soft silk of the thin black tie slid beneath my fingertips as I secured the snug knot. After smoothing it along the buttons of my pressed light blue dress shirt, I turned from the mirror, not bothering to look at my reflection. The too-pale skin and dark circles beneath my bright blue eyes pissed me off every time I looked in the mirror. Hell, I didn't even acknowledge the constant tremble of both hands from the near ketamine overdose.

Four days ago, the bastard who stalked my sister, Tinley, got the drop on me, which added fuel to my ever-present anger, resulting in me nearly dying and unable to keep her from being abducted and nearly ripped from my life forever. Thankfully, my best friend, Special Agent Bryson Bennett, was there for her while I fought for my life in the hospital and brought Tinley home safe.

The unmade bed shifted as I perched on the edge to slip on a pair of black dress socks. Before last week's events, the sight of the disheveled mess would've bothered me until I made it with military precision. Though the mess in here and everywhere else in the apartment didn't even appear as a blip on my give-a-shit radar anymore. Too many other actual issues to handle first.

Tinley survived and was now safe in Louisville with Bryson. The sick fucker who wanted to keep her for himself, who'd orchestrated and filmed the murders of dozens of women over the past several years, was dead. Yet, the case wasn't closed. Not until we caught the partner, the one who actually committed the murders, the one on film torturing and raping women for his sick enjoyment and shit-tons of money.

I shook my head in disgust. Of course there were two of them out there. For almost two years, I and the FBI task force I put together chased the bastards, though until last week we had assumed it was only one unsub, not a team. That was the only upside of what happened with Tinley. Now we knew there were two—well, now one with the brains of the partnership dead.

Though, from my perspective, the more dangerous of the two was the one still breathing. Based on a basic profile provided by Special Agent Rhyan Riggs, this fucker got off on inflicting maximum pain, enjoyed taking what was not freely given, and ending an innocent victim's life.

It was only because of the partner's coordinates that we even found the local location where the unsub kept, tortured, and videoed the victims. When the tactical team overtook that shed, they found the woman he'd most recently abducted, computer specialist Remington Dotson, and the unsub gone.

Securing the thin laces of my dress shoes, I stood and grabbed both guns from the bedside table, securing one to my hip and the other in my ankle holster before swiping my FBI credentials off the dresser. I wasn't expecting any threats where I was headed with Nashville Detective Jameson Bend, an old friend and—

Fuck, that relationship was too complicated to think about before coffee. I'd done a good job the last decade of forgetting about my past to focus on saving innocent people from the evil in the world.

I shook my head to clear it of the memories trying to force their way forward. Since that night ten years ago, I hadn't participated in the lifestyle I took part in with Jameson, instead throwing myself and all my energy into the job. I'd risen through the ranks at the FBI, and was now leading my task force and had received many accolades and awards. The side effect of all the time and effort put into tracking and capturing killers left me with zero personal life, which was fine.

At least that was what I'd convinced myself of until I saw *her* last night.

Remington Dotson.

When she walked into the apartment to see Tinley, beaten and just as pale as me, I was too shell-shocked to do anything but gape. Jameson too. What were the odds that the last woman we shared, a woman I distinctively remember despite the decade that had passed, was the woman rescued from that damn psychopath's torture shed in the woods?

And then she turned and walked away.

From me.

From us.

She saw me and Jameson, a flash of fear, shock, and anger flipping across her petite features before she turned and left, leaving us both reeling. It was clear she remembered us just as well as we remembered her. Maybe as clearly as I did. There was something about her that night, a vulnerability yet strength that never let me forget her. Plus that fucking mouth of hers and the way she submitted beautifully to all my demands.

When we chased her down outside my apartment building along the downtown Nashville street, she refused to talk, stating they got everything they needed at the hospital before she was discharged, and we needed to leave her alone. Though that was yesterday. Last night, I was too surprised to do anything but let her leave. Today, however, after recovering from the shock of seeing her, of her being our only witness, I was ready to demand she talk with us about what happened in that shed.

And convince her that protective custody was necessary. I'd seen the damage this bastard could inflict. I couldn't stomach the idea of her being the next body I had to view on a coroner's steel table.

The loud phone ringing snapped me back to reality. Blinking, I looked around, realizing I'd randomly paused between the living room and kitchen, too lost in my mind. I should take a few days of leave to recover, but that wasn't a luxury I could afford.

Rolling my shoulders, I stretched out my neck and shoved a trembling hand into the pocket of my slacks, tugging out my ringing phone.

"Harper," I barked, not bothering to check the screen.

"Good morning to you too. You sure this is a good idea?" Jameson's voice poured through the earpiece as I forced my feet to move. "She seemed hell-bent on not talking to us last night."

I shoved the plastic cup filled with coffee grounds into the machine and hit the Brew button. "It doesn't matter if this is a good idea or not. It has to happen. She's a witness now, and this fucker is still out there. We need her official statement and to emphasize the danger she's in. I'm hoping we can talk her into protective custody."

The following awkward pause had my muscles tensing beneath my suit. Things hadn't been easy between us since I approached him last week, needing help with Tinley's stalker case. Though I didn't have time to make things right between us. The case took precedence, not his feelings or frustrations about me.

"Maybe we should hand this over to someone else," he grumbled.

"No," I snapped. Pulling the now steaming coffee mug from the machine, I took a tentative sip, burning the tip of my tongue. "This is my case. I've been after them for almost two years. I'm not letting this... whatever this is keep me from being the agent to finally catch this bastard."

"I get that, but she clearly wants nothing to do with us. Hell, she ran from us despite having just been drugged and held by a fucking deranged serial killer. What does that say about how she feels about us?"

"It was one night ten years ago," I snapped. "She can move past it just like we are. It's about saving her life and other potential victims, not about what happened in the past."

"I get that it's easy for you," Jameson said, an edge to his tone. "But remember, just because you can forget the past so easily doesn't mean everyone else can."

"What the fuck does that mean?" My grip on the mug tightened, my fingers slipping along the hot ceramic.

"Nothing. You're right. No one from your past matters." I winced at the accusation in his tone. "We'll go at this just like we would any other witness. Meet you at the station in an hour."

After ending the call, I tossed the phone on the counter and glared at the black screen.

Sealing my lids shut, I inhaled deep through my nose and held it for five counts before releasing it slowly. Fuck, this was complicated. I didn't do complicated. Control, details, and facts—that was what I thrived on since I got that call ten years ago that changed my life forever. If I was in control, then there was no surprise, nothing to catch me off guard.

Though it seemed with the unexpected return of the beautiful woman from my past and teaming up with Jameson to solve the case that my control on everything was already slipping.

Swallowing a mouthful of coffee, I focused on the bitter taste and slight burn along my throat. All I had to do was get through this case; then I could go back to being the asshole workaholic I'd developed into in order to survive the abundant guilt and self-loathing.

I couldn't let my guard down.

Not for him, not for her.

This was business, not personal.

It had to be.

2

REMINGTON

"What's your name?"

My response clogged in my throat as I blinked like an idiot at the two most attractive men I'd ever seen in person. The two came to my rescue just seconds ago, when an aggressive drunk refused to accept the word no.

Holy hell, I was really doing this. Finding not one but two or even three partners for the night was why I dressed up and came to a specific bar. Word around town said this was the place for the more daring of hookups, and that was exactly what I needed.

After years of seclusion and abuse, I craved a night of fantasy.

And these two hot men with their full focus on me, well, that was exactly what I came here to find.

"Remy," I whispered, finally able to speak. The two men smiled and shared a knowing look. "My name is Remy."

The nickname was as close to my actual name as I felt comfortable giving them.

"Well, Remy," the hotter of the two with bright blue eyes said, "I'm Tallon, and this is Jameson. Would it be okay if we bought you a drink?"

We.

I shook my head, and the man's hopeful smile fell.

"No, I don't want another drink. I want to get out of here."

That smile returned slowly, curling the corners of his lips. "Alone?"

Finding the backbone I'd worked the last year to find, I shook my head again. "No. With you two."

Smacking my forehead to the edge of the desk, a low groan rumbled in my throat as the memories from that damn night flashed behind my eyes for what felt like the hundredth time today. And it was only ten in the morning. I tried to convince myself that the erotic memories playing on constant replay today were because of seeing them last night in Tinley Harper's apartment, but I couldn't lie to myself. The panty-melting memories of that night, maybe some embellished after so many years had passed, flicked through my mind all the time.

What did that say about me that my last memorable sexual experience was a decade ago? It said I was lame, that's what. Sitting at home on a Friday night watching crime show documentaries by myself was not the best way to really put myself out there.

My lack of social skills with the opposite sex had to be the reason I bolted from that apartment last night the moment I recognized their faces instead of confronting them like the mature almost forty-year-old I apparently was not. Then, to prove myself even more awkward, I basically told them to fuck off and sprinted to the car as fast as my short legs would allow. I'd just been drugged and had woken up in a torture shed with a fucked-up psychopath, yet I ran from two men who I knew from experience wouldn't hurt me.

Well, except maybe being hurt again by their rejection if they knew I was still holding on to the memories of that night, but what was the sting of being forgotten after a one-night stand compared to a painful death by a serial killer? Yet, still I bolted, even though the fear of what would happen next still ran deep. Fear for my safety *and* Crew's. Only knowing that the bastard, who was seconds away from torturing me before the cavalry arrived, didn't have my name or a way to gain my personal details kept me from truly freaking out.

The high-pitched ring of a desk phone in the cube close by cut through the endless click of keys as the row of coders worked on their daily tasks. Closing my eyes, I inhaled slowly to get my shit together and focus on my damn job. I probably should've stayed home one more day to recover, but that wasn't in the cards because of the unexpected days I took off last week when I was in the hospital. When I showed up with my face a bruised mess, I told everyone a cover story that I was in a terrible car wreck. Explaining what *actually* happened felt too personal to share with a bunch of people I barely knew.

Straightening my back, I rolled both shoulders and turned to the computer screen, intending to refocus on the lines of code I'd spent the last hour writing. The asshole manager over this project would be by shortly to remind me again of our tight deadline.

Adjusting my focus to my blurry reflection in the screen, I studied the cut along my lip and swollen, black eye. Unease rolled through me, twisting my stomach, remembering a time when this beat-up reflection was the norm.

The mouse slipped in my clammy hand beneath my tightening grip. I shook my head to dislodge the dark direction of my thoughts. I couldn't focus on that today, not when

I was already distracted. Jett was in the past, and that was where he would stay. Just like the memories of the two hotties from last night. Sure, my life was boring, too busy, and occasionally overwhelming as a single working mom, but just because they were hot didn't mean....

Fuck, they're so hot.

Wait. Where was I going with that?

As much as I wanted to deny it, the idea of seeing them again, now that the initial shock had worn off, was intriguing and nerve-racking considering how it ended. But it wasn't like any of us promised the others more than that. It was a one-night stand, a hookup. Though I had wanted to see them again, but they clearly didn't find the night as soul-altering as me, considering I never heard from or ran into them again.

Despite my attempts to find them.

"It was ten fucking years ago, Remington," I whispered low enough that the developer in the next cube couldn't hear me talking to myself like a lunatic. "They showed you how good sex could be." Though no one else had ever come close to worshipping me like they did together. "And then they went on with their lives. Move on and stop pining for them."

Though *they* didn't have a daily reminder of our night together like I did. Just thinking of my nine-year-old son, Crew, had my gaze sliding to the only picture on my small desk. Held in a basic black frame was a picture we took almost a year ago of us laughing at something as I snapped the selfie. Love and happiness clear in my bright green eyes while joy and complete innocence shone in his bright blue ones.

Bright blue, just like his father's.

His father who did not know he existed.

I swallowed against the lump in my throat and turned back to the screen.

"How far behind are you?" My shoulders tensed, almost hitting my ears, at Carl's—my douchebag project manager—grating voice. He stepped even closer, boxing me inside my tiny cubicle.

I hated men like him. Who used their size to intimidate me. Which it didn't take a big man to do, considering I was on the petite side at five foot three.

"I'll get everything done just like I always do," I gritted out, teeth clenched to keep from cussing him out for all the office to hear.

"You better. Your speed and accuracy are the reasons we hired you. Don't forget that."

"I'll get it done," I said, forcing my fingers to type out the next line of code despite the urge to swivel the cheap office chair around and punch him in the balls. If it wouldn't ensure I'd be fired, resulting in me not being able to pay my mortgage, I totally would. Being an adult sucked sometimes. "I've never failed to deliver what's asked of me."

"True, but you're distracted." A weight settled on my shoulder, the heat from his hand seeping through the thin material of my blouse. My movement stiff to keep from throwing that punch, I twisted my head and glared at his offending appendage, wishing I was a superhero and could catch his hand on fire with my eyes. "Are you sure you're okay after the *accident*?"

The way he emphasized the word suggested he didn't believe my excuse for my injuries or absences. Thank goodness it was normal for me to wear long sleeves covering up my tattoos so it was easy to hide the marks left on my wrists from the tight restraints.

"I'm fine."

His hand tightened, squeezing my shoulder in what I assumed was supposed to be a comforting gesture. My lips curled into a snarl as I turned back to face the computer screen so he couldn't see my clear disgust. Now was not the time to rock the boat. I had to play nice.

"Good, because I'd hate for you to work through Christmas in order to get everything finished, being a single mother and all."

Oh, he was a manipulative cocksucker.

"Thanks for the reminder." That hand slipped away, and I could almost feel his smirk. The bastard enjoyed getting under my skin. "Now if you don't mind, I need to focus. I'll already be working through lunch as it is, and you know I can't work late, being a single mother and all."

"I don't know how you do it."

Unable to stop, I shoved off the desk, swiveling the chair around until I faced him. Tipping my chin, I put as much ire and contempt into my glare as I could muster.

"I don't have a choice. That's how. Now leave me alone so I can get this done on time for QA."

Without another word, he turned and disappeared around the tall cube wall, his annoying voice filtering through the office as he spoke to another developer, but this time without questioning their progress or commenting about their personal life.

"Asshole," I grumbled. Using the stiletto ends of my black heels, I swiveled the chair back toward the screen and sighed. "Get your shit together, Remy. They've probably moved on, just like they did before."

My heart sank at that thought. Which was dumb.

I was being dumb.

Just as I centered my focus on what I needed to get done next, the desk phone lit up with an incoming call, the loud ring startling me. I eyed the blinking red light and the extension written above it on the small screen. I never got visitors or calls, so why in the hell would reception call me? My mind immediately went to Crew, but if it had something to do with him, the school would've called my cell, which sat silent on my desk. Tentatively, I gripped the gray plastic handle and lifted it from the base, silencing the piercing ring.

"Yeah?" I said, brows furrowed.

"This is Linda up front. I have two gentlemen here who say they need to speak with you." My stomach dropped and lungs froze. "They say it's a police matter," she whispered conspiringly into the phone, making the words tickle in my ear.

"Okay, I'll be right there."

After placing the phone back into the base, I stared at it like it could solve all my problems. *Fuck. Fuck. Fuckity fuck.* Apparently, me telling them no last night to another interview to give my statement wasn't acceptable. They had to figure out where I work and come here.

I pursed my lips into a thin line. *How dare they? How fucking dare they!*

Irritation flared partly because I told them no to a formal interview last night, and secondly... well, maybe I wasn't really over them never calling even though I'd left my number on the hotel desk after I snuck out while they slept.

Shoving to my feet, I smoothed the black material of the snug pencil skirt over my round hips and resituated my silk blouse into the waist. Inhaling deep, filling my lungs with oxygen-fueled courage, I shook out my hands and turned on the balls of my feet.

The office space that housed this branch of the massive software corporation wasn't large, only enough for about twenty developers shoved into tiny cubes and a few offices for management. I sensed Carl's disapproving gaze tracking my movements as I strode past his office. It took almost all my energy to not flip him a double bird; only the reminder that this job paid twice what I made before kept me moving and my hands clenched at my side.

One day, when I had something else lined up, something better than this place, I'd tell him everything I'd held back the last six months. But until then, I needed to play nice in the corporate sandbox and dress in the constricting business professional attire instead of my normal... unique flare. Crew needed braces, his private school tuition was due for the following school year, and, well, I wanted more Doc Martens to add to my collection, so I needed this job, or rather the decent pay.

Even though I mentally braced myself for seeing the two men again, I stumbled, the toe of my heel catching the carpet when I rounded the corner. All the breath rushed from my lungs the moment Special Agent Tallon Harper—whose full name and title I'd learned just last night—turned from the ugly abstract painting hanging in the lobby and locked those blue eyes on mine.

Well over six feet, blond hair shaved tight on the sides and longer on top, square jaw dusted with scruff, and a straight nose that he was currently staring down as he seemed to catalogue my face as I did his. He was beyond attractive. Smoking hot was a better way to describe his good looks. My heart hammered against my chest as I took in his features. Features that were so similar to the ones I saw daily. There was no doubt Crew was his son.

Swallowing down my rising panic, I swiped the palms of both sweaty hands along the front of my skirt and cleared my throat.

Do not think about that night.

Do not remember their roaming hands working completely in sync with the other's. Or the way they edged you to the brink repeatedly before thrusting you over the edge to bliss so many times you lost count before passing out from sheer bliss and exhaustion.

Jameson—Detective Jameson Bend per the business card he shoved in my hand last night—studied my every move as I restarted my progress toward the two. Shorter than Tallon, yet still way taller than me, he had more of a leaner athletic build. Top that with his light brown, almost floppy hair, easy smile, and honey-brown eyes, and he was way more approachable than Tallon.

Offering a small professional smile and nod to the receptionist, I paused in the middle of the lobby and clasped both hands behind my back so they wouldn't see the nervous tremble. I refused to acknowledge Tallon's blatant once-over until his attention paused on my chest. Glancing down to ensure all buttons were secured, concealing my full chest, mortification bloomed, blasting heat throughout my body, at finding my nipples hard, pointing straight at him, betraying the rush of desire that awakened from simply seeing him.

Damn my traitorous body.

Who got horny from just a single look?

A sex-deprived woman, that was who.

Me. I was the who.

My cheeks flushed. Desperate to cover the evidence of my attraction, I crossed both arms over my chest.

"May I help you two?" I asked, not even attempting to mask the bite in my tone. Let them know I was annoyed. They had no right to show up here.

The two men exchanged an unreadable look before

turning their full attention back on me. And just like that, they transported me back to the hotel room when their full, lust-filled attention was trained on my trembling body as they planned what to do next.

Oh fuck, is it hot in here? I shifted my weight as a wave of dizziness hit me.

Damnit, why didn't I take care of the throbbing need they stirred up with one of my many toys when I got home last night?

"Is there somewhere we can talk in private?" Tallon's deep, commanding tone seemed to echo around the small lobby.

With an eye roll, I gestured to the small conference room to our right and waited until they passed to follow. With my attention on Tallon's ass, I almost smacked into his back when he pulled the glass door open and moved for me to enter first.

"So chivalry isn't dead," I said in jest as I passed. "Thank you."

Heavy silence instantly filled the small space as the three of us settled into chairs, me on one side of the oval conference table and them on the other.

"Before we get started, I want to make sure you're okay with this," Jameson said. Tallon shot him a side-eye glare as if that wasn't the opening line they discussed. "Since we have a past, even if it was a long time ago."

I studied them as I internally gauged my feelings.

Though it made things awkward, having a somewhat relationship with them actually made all this easier, oddly.

"It's fine. The past is in the past, right?" I remarked a little stiffly. "We're all adults here, but really, there isn't a reason for you two to be here. I have a job to do, and since I missed a couple days last week because of this mess, I really need to get back to it. Like I told you last night, the hospital collected the evidence, and I gave my statement. There's nothing else to say." Pushing to my feet, I stared them down, though it lost some of the impact considering even though they remained sitting, we were eye level.

"You're in danger. Do you not care?" Tallon snapped.

"Why do you?" I said before I could stop myself. Closing my eyes, I inhaled deeply to keep shoving down the conflicting emotions these two seemed to drag up. "The man who abducted me never called me by name, and I asked my friend Agent Bekham about it, who assured me I was a victim of opportunity and that the man who took me didn't have a way to find me."

"But he's still out there," Tallon said, those blue eyes boring into mine. "You're not safe. Let us put you into protective custody—"

Fear raced down my spine, sending a chill shooting through my veins, cooling the heat these two created. "No." His eyes narrowed in obvious annoyance while Jameson appeared quite entertained by our heated banter, glancing back and forth between us like we were some kind of sideshow. "I will not uproot my life because *you* think I'm in danger. If that changes, then I'll reconsider."

"You can't reconsider if you're dead." The chair rolled back, slamming to the wall as Tallon stood, towering over me even from across the table.

"And why does it matter so much to you?" I countered.

He started to respond, no doubt with something else arrogant and demanding, but Jameson cut him off. "Protective custody is out, understood. What about we meet in the middle, and everyone can get what they want?"

"Like what?"

"An unmarked car with an officer in front of your

house." I eyed Tallon while I considered Jameson's offer. Nostrils flaring, face red, Tallon was clearly not a fan of this recent development. "And sorry about Tallon. Clearly he has control issues." Jameson winked, making me smile at the attempt to lighten the mood.

I pressed both hands to my hips and snorted. "Yeah, now *that* I clearly remember." My eyes widened the second the words were out of my mouth. *Did not mean to say that out loud.* Clearing my throat, I broke off Tallon's intense stare. "Unmarked in front of my house is fine. But they cannot interfere or report anything unless it's case related."

Tallon's brows furrowed. "Meaning?"

I lifted a single shoulder, faking nonchalance. "My personal life is not to be reported. It's none of your business. Listen, a few nights ago, I went to an apartment because Agent Bekham asked me to check it for cameras, and I ended up drugged, abducted, and held against my will. Yes, I understand the seriousness of this, but I walked into this mess and have no intention of sticking around to see how it pans out. I'm glad your sister is okay. She seems like a good kid, but I'm stepping away from all this while I still can. Please respect that."

"I don't understand why you're fighting this," Tallon gritted out. "Why won't you let us protect you?"

"And why are you trying to force me?" I said, sounding just as pissed as he did. "Just because I'm a witness doesn't mean I don't have rights." I shot a questioning look at Jameson, who looked like he could use a bucket of popcorn to further enjoy this dominance show between me and Tallon. "Right?"

"Correct," he stated, grimacing when Tallon shot him a glare.

"Are you this overbearing with every witness?" I demanded.

"Yes," he hissed.

It took everything in me to not flinch.

Well, fuck. I thought his persistence was because I was different, maybe special because of our past. It seemed I was just like everyone else in his eyes, though. Just another witness, another victim for him to control until he got what he needed for the FBI.

Suddenly, the weight of everything sat heavy on my chest, making it difficult to take a full breath. I shouldn't be disappointed—hell, seconds ago, I was pissed that they tracked me down at work—but I was.

"Well, then, I'm sure you're used to getting pushback," I remarked, my voice weaker than just moments before.

"Not really. You're the first to not want protection from a fucking serial killer."

My hackles rose at the arrogance in his tone.

Fuck him.

Fuck them both for walking back into my life and reminding me of... everything.

"Unmarked car," I said, pointing at Tallon. "And that's it."

Gathering my courage, I turned, putting my back to them, and strode for the doors. Tears gathered in my lower lids with the swell of emotions warring inside me. Fear, longing, more fear, though that had nothing to do with the psycho who held me captive and all to do with Tallon. A large part of me was terrified of what would happen if Tallon found out about Crew. What if he tried to take him from me? I knew nothing about the man other than he was amazing in bed and apparently an arrogant dickhead.

My throat sealed at the thought of Tallon taking Crew.

My sweet son was my life, my reason for living. I wouldn't let Tallon take my baby from me.

It wasn't like I didn't try to find either of the two men after I discovered I was pregnant. I tried. But with no way to contact them—hell, I didn't even have their full names—I could only return to that bar where I met them night after night after night, but it was as if I'd imagined them, never seeing them again.

Chin lifted, I marched back toward my cubicle, ignoring the heat from their stares burning into my back.

This was for the best.

For everyone.

3

TALLON

"Well, that went well," Jameson said at my back as I stormed through the glass doors. Turning toward the bank of elevators, I thundered down the hall and punched the call button. "She looked good. Definitely not what I was expecting after her crazy outfit last night. The stuffy corporate look—"

Whipping around, I slammed the heel of my hand against his shoulder, catching him off guard. A flash of surprise flickered across his face as he stumbled to the side, morphing into annoyance.

"You're talking about a witness," I hissed and took a menacing step closer before shaking myself out of the unexpected rush of anger. "Fuck, sorry."

His forehead furrowed as he studied me with clear caution. "What the hell has gotten into you? Is this the way you've treated other witnesses and survivors in the past? Because if it is, I have to say, your tact needs fucking work. You basically called her an idiot for refusing our help."

I opened my mouth but snapped it shut when I didn't have a decent response. She'd asked me the same thing, if this was how I treated all witnesses. And I lied. I fucking lied to her face that yes, this overprotective urge was normal. It most certainly was not. Sure, I was considerate of witnesses and victims, wanted them to be safe, but this was a hundred times fucking more than that.

This was borderline obsessive in the insistence to keep Remy safe.

What was wrong with me? Ever since I saw her in my apartment, I'd been agitated, on edge, and seeing her just now made it a thousand times worse. Add in the fact that she refused to listen to me, not giving two shits about her own safety, and I was trembling with restraint.

I wanted to shake her for being so damn stubborn about the seriousness of what she was now in the middle of while at the same time yank her close and seal my lips to hers. It had been ten years since I'd seen her, ten years since that night. The best night of my life, which turned into a morning that changed my life forever when I got the call about Tinley's initial abduction.

The fact that my sister was abducted not once but twice by the same delusional bastard fueled the constant guilt I carried around to oppressive levels.

"I don't fucking know. What I know is she's in danger, and I've dedicated my life to protecting those who need it."

The elevator arrived before Jameson could respond. We stepped inside, and he tapped a knuckle against the button for the lobby.

A question had eaten at me since we sat down in the conference room, where it was clear she was more at ease with him than me. "Did you ever see her again? After we... that night?"

He shot me a weary side-eye glance. Which I guessed I deserved, considering my volatile temper at the mere mention of Remy. "Nope. When you walked away from it all, so did I. I never even went back to that bar where we picked—"

I held up a hand, cutting him off. Guilt and shame hit me like a sucker punch in the gut. It always did when I thought about where I was, what I was doing the night my sister was taken from the downtown Nashville streets.

"Then why is she more comfortable with you than me?" I practically growled.

A tall woman in the corner peeked up from her phone at the sound and scooted deeper into the corner.

Fucking hell, I needed to get my shit together.

"Maybe she's more comfortable around me because you're acting like a possessive asshole, pissed that the object of his obsession won't bend to his demands." He didn't even try to soften his booming tone, uncaring about the woman clearly listening to our conversation. "You're the one who said it this morning. The past doesn't matter, so you need to treat her like you would anyone else."

But clearly it *did* matter.

"To her, I think it does." And maybe to me, or else I wouldn't be this worked up over her. "Why else would she refuse protection, and put herself in danger?" I groaned. Reaching up, I pinched the bridge of my nose.

"Which I could understand if it was last week, or hell, even six months ago, but ten years? I remember it was a fun night, but come on, move on."

The woman beside me huffed at Jameson's comment and rolled her eyes. Obviously, she didn't agree, yet I felt the same as Jameson. Everything was consensual, and we didn't make any promises of more than one night. We didn't even exchange information, for God's sake. I had hoped to see her again, that I remembered, but then Tinley was taken, and my life flipped upside down.

"What do you think the deal is with her not wanting the officer to get involved or report back to us on her private life?" I questioned before I could stop it from leaving my lips. "Makes me think she's hiding something. Maybe she was married, or is now, and doesn't want us to know. That would make sense on why she was cagey about us."

Jameson smirked, and I knew he read through my mood now that I let that question slip.

"Would that bother you?"

"No," I said too quickly.

He burst out laughing, though there was an edge to it. "Clearly it does. Because you care if she cheated on someone back then, or because you want to fuck the sass out of her mouth now?"

The door dinged, signaling our arrival in the lobby. The woman shouldered past Jameson, calling him a pig under her breath before stomping off.

Once we were outside, he paused. "Though I don't think that's why she was cagey around you."

"So what's your theory?"

"Even though we just hooked up with her that night, you're being a controlling asshole. She's not your girl, yet you're barking orders like she is. And just so you know, I somewhat agree with her being angry with us."

"The hell?" I said, surprised. "Why? We're just trying to protect her."

Fuck, maybe if I said it another few hundred times, I might believe this sudden obsession was just about her safety.

He swung the keys to his town car around his finger several times before he caught them in a tight fist. "I understand why you dropped everything, especially now after meeting your sister, but Remy wasn't the only one you ditched and never looked back on after that night. And now you're back barking orders, acting like nothing happened. It sucks being left behind with no goodbye, no warning."

Jaw slack, I watched him stride toward the car, movements stiff. Still processing his words, I climbed into the passenger side and slammed the door shut. The drive back to the police station where my FBI-issued Tahoe waited was long and tense, the silence between us nearly vibrating with unspoken words.

Whipping into an open parking spot, he shifted the car into Park but kept the engine running.

"Like I said, I don't know if that's why she's being difficult considering it was one night for her, but for me, we were friends. Sure, you had your sister to find, then took the world on to save others from the same fate." I pursed my lips to keep from cutting him off. "But you ditched me like our friendship meant nothing. No explanation, no calls or beers after work like we'd done before." Shifting in the seat, he lasered me with an intense stare. "One day we were friends, and the next not. So yeah, I understand her hesitancy that comes from being ditched. And now you're back because you need something from us, acting like nothing happened."

Fucking hell.

He was right, but admitting I was wrong wasn't my best quality. Grinding my jaw back and forth, I shoved down the urge to tell him how fucking brutal it was for me to walk away too. How I still kept everyone on the outskirts of my life, even my best friend, and how fucking lonely that was. How the shame of our lifestyle and guilt from being with them when Tinley was taken was almost too much to bear. But admitting to all that made me feel like a damn pussy.

What could I say? Handling emotional shit was another nonexistent quality of mine.

Hell, maybe it was best for everyone if I just stayed in this guilt cell I'd constructed to keep everyone at arm's length. If no one was close, then I couldn't be devastated again, wouldn't have that soul-crushing helpless feeling constrict so tight I almost couldn't breathe.

"I handled it badly," I said after a minute. "But my sister was missing, and then she was found and hurting." Turning to look out the window, I tightened and flexed my hands. "I was with you two when she was taken, and the guilt of that just ruined me. Hell, it still does." I wouldn't go into detail about how that night was the last time I truly let go. There had been women here and there over the years, but I always kept my guard up, never allowing myself to fully give in to the moment. "I vowed that if we found Tin, then I'd change. Stop being so damn selfish, to not let myself be caught with my fucking pants down again while someone I loved, someone I swore to protect, was left vulnerable, and focus on saving people instead of—"

"Living your fucking life? You realize what you're saying is crazy, right? You've punished yourself for the last decade for something that wasn't your fault, that you couldn't have prevented, no matter where you were that night. That man was obsessed with her. If he hadn't taken Tinley that night, he would've found another."

I huffed a laugh. "You sound like Tinley. But yeah."

He hummed, acknowledging me, thumping his thumb along the steering wheel. "So now what?"

I swallowed hard. There was so much in that question that I wasn't sure where to unravel answers.

"Now," I said. "Now we find this sick fucker who's torturing and killing women, keep trying to get that little spitfire Remington to cooperate, and go from there. This case is a priority. Even with that fucker Vincent dead, my task team is still focused on this. It's not closed until we catch this partner."

Jameson nodded. Shutting off the engine, he reached toward the door. "Come in, and we can go over the evidence we found in that shed. I'd also like to be brought up to speed on these two as a team from your past investigations. Knowing what each handled in the partnership could help us alter the profile of this bastard."

With a confirming nod, I shoved open my door and stepped out into the chilly December wind. Though others shuffling down the sidewalk had their coats wrapped around them, I welcomed the cold, loving how it seemed to temper my simmering agitation. Though the second I pushed through the glass door into the station, a wall of arid heat smacked me in the face, immediately drying out my throat and lungs. I followed Jameson as we weaved through the few civilians and officers milling about, making our way toward the side door that led to the detectives' bullpen, where only two others occupied the large space, barely paying us any attention as we headed to Jameson's desk other than giving a simple nod.

Jameson collapsed into his chair with a groan and leaned back, interlacing his fingers behind his head. A sharp squeak of metal sounded as he rocked back and forth. "Do you?" he asked, smiling like he was in on some secret.

"Do I what?" I grunted, half paying attention to him as I shuffled through a stack of files on his desk, searching for the one that held the evidence report from the shed. I paused on the one with the findings from the hospital.

Knowing they poked and prodded her to death after everything she'd just been through shot a bolt of anger through my system. Grabbing it and the other file, I tossed both on top of the stack.

"Want to fuck her again?"

One corner of my mouth curled into a smirk, which was an answer in and of itself.

"Thought so." A bang rattled through the space when he slammed his hand on the metal desk, emphasizing his point. "There's nothing wrong with that. You know that, right?"

My half smirk fell.

I didn't know that. In fact, I was almost positive that it was wrong to want Remy considering the danger she and others in this city were in.

"Let's focus on the case," I grumbled, not sure if my frustration was directed at him or myself.

As I skimmed over the report, nothing registered, my mind too distracted by the tiny brunette who wanted nothing to do with me. Which was odd. Not saying every woman fell to their knees around me, but finding a bedmate had never been a problem. I remembered her, though. Especially remembered how, after that night, before I got the call that they couldn't find Tin, I wanted to see her again. One night wasn't enough. Though I could never pinpoint what it was about her that made her unforgettable, just that she was.

A few times while on the road hunting down yet another sick bastard, I found myself alone in a hotel room thinking about her. More times than I wanted to admit, I tried to find her, but all I had was her first name. Hell, now I knew that wasn't even her first name but a nickname.

Remy.

My lips moved as I silently said her name.

There was still that vulnerability behind her tough exterior, a kitten with tiny claws. My heart raced thinking about having her again, of getting to enact the fantasies I'd played out in my mind while jerking off to her petite face for the last several years.

Short button nose, heart-shaped face, lips that were meant to be licked and fucked. Covering my groan with a fake cough, I shifted on my feet, hoping to keep my half-mast cock from being too obvious.

"Do you miss it?"

Peering over the rim of the manila folder, I studied Jameson. I knew what he was referring to but didn't want to open that line of conversation about our past with others listening. "Sex?"

His eyes widened. "Please tell me it hasn't been ten fucking years since you last got laid."

Since I last had anything meaningful? Yes.

I flipped him the bird and shook my head. "We don't all have the life of leisure like a detective, asshole. I'm fucking busy. Here." The file with the results collected at the hospital flew toward his face. He snagged it midair before it could slap him like I intended. "Look through that and let me know if you see anything interesting."

Refocusing on the file in my hand, I held it close and read as I paced around Jameson's desk, the heels of my dress shoes clicking against the concrete floor in a steady beat with my quick steps.

Inside the shed, the CSI team found some dog hair from the mutt restrained at the scene, plus blood and other fluids that matched two female victims. I swallowed at seeing Agent Burton's name listed in the report. We didn't even know she was missing while the sick bastard tortured and killed her on film.

Squeezing my eyes shut, I then blinked a few times to clear the wave of guilt that wanted to drag me under, and directed my full attention back to the report.

Foreign male DNA but no hits in CODIS. No familial match in the system either. Though there was a note to see a tech about connecting cases that pulled up as a DNA match from years ago.

"Huh," I said, pausing my steps as I read that line again.

"You seeing what I'm seeing?" Jameson said from where he was hunched over the file opened on his desk. "No prints, but the DNA left on Remy matches evidence from cases from about fifteen years ago."

My heart stopped. All thoughts of the case fled my mind, unable to process past what his words insinuated.

"What DNA?" I rasped. The folder in my hand crinkled beneath my tightening grip.

"There was some found on her, probably transferred from when he carried her into the shed." He paused and huffed a mix of a laugh and disbelief. "The report says she admitted to mouthing off to him, and he reacted, which is how she got the busted face." He snorted like it was funny. "Somehow, that doesn't surprise me." He blanched at whatever he read next, making my stomach sour. "It says there's a recording of it all. The fucker recorded it all."

"Did he...?" I swallowed, unable to say the words. Why? Why was I so wrapped up in this woman? I'd worked many cases that involved the demented shit men came up with to hurt innocent women, but this felt different—personal, almost. Maybe it had to do with the recent assault and murder of a female acquaintance?

Because really, that was all this Remington Dotson was

to me. I barely knew her for even twelve hours a decade ago, yet somehow she was more.

More than I wanted to admit.

"No, he didn't sexually assault her," Jameson responded. I forcefully expelled my held breath, easing the dull burn in my lungs. *Thank fuck for that.* "The connected cases piece is interesting. We need to get a look at those notes, pictures, and reports as soon as possible."

Nodding in agreement, I slid my phone from the side pocket of my black slacks. Staring at the blank screen, I debated how to proceed. If I went through the proper channels, all that damn red tape that would need to be cut in order to view the cold case files, it could take forever. Or I could ignore the rules, which I never did, and skip all that to get the answers we needed now.

With each slow blink as I weighed my options, Remy's injured face flashed behind my lids.

No, this couldn't wait. Not with her tangled up in this mess.

Hitting my best friend, and fellow FBI agent, Bryson Bennett's number, I pressed the phone to my ear, resuming my anxious pacing as it rang.

"I need Agent Charlie Bekham's number," I said the moment Bryson picked up. This guy could get me the files quick. As an FBI agent and hacker who helped us recently to find the clues that saved my sister, he was exactly who I needed now.

In the background, I heard Tinley's voice ring out. The sound of her laughter soothed some of my growing impatience.

"You sure about that?" Bryson responded. "He doesn't seem to be a huge fan of yours."

I stumbled, thigh nailing the corner of the desk. What

the hell was that about? Not that it mattered. The Bekham guy could hate me all he wanted as long as he got me what I needed for the case.

"I need his help. The DNA found at that shed matches DNA from a few cold cases over a decade ago. Going through the proper channels...." I didn't finish, knowing he knew all too well how slowly everything ran at the bureau.

"You'd have those files this summer instead of tonight." His heavy sigh blew over the mouthpiece. "If it has to do with finding the fucker who hurt Remington, I'm sure he'll be all over it."

I worked my jaw back and forth, debating asking the question that had run on a loop since Remy mentioned she knew Agent Bekham. "How does he know her, anyway?"

"Not sure. He offered her as local help when I needed it. I didn't question it."

"Why do you say he doesn't like me?" Sure, I was an asshole, but the guy was in Texas, for fuck's sake, and I'd only spoken to him on the phone a couple times.

"Not sure. Doesn't matter. He'll get you what you need. How is she, anyway, Remington?"

I huffed and pinched the bridge of my nose between two fingers, hoping to calm my throbbing headache. "Still refusing protection, even though I demanded she needed it."

"Hmm," Bryson said. "That's interesting."

"What's interesting?"

"You. The way you're acting. It feels awfully... familiar."

"In what way?"

"How I acted around Tinley when she was in danger. Obsessive, demanding, overbearing. Just an observation of how you were last night when she ran from you and now this. Whether you want to admit it, this Remy means something to you."

"She's just a witness."

"Right." He dragged out the word, clearly not believing me. "Keep lying to yourself and see how that goes. I hope I'm there when you realize you're being a dumbass and it's before you lose her. You deserve a life outside the FBI, Tallon."

"Do I?" I muttered.

"You're a fool if you think otherwise. I'll text you Bekham's contact information."

"Thanks. And tell Tin hey for me. After all this is done, I'd like to come up and stay for a few days."

"Sounds good. Now go catch that fucker, and stop being a dumbass about your obvious feelings for Remy."

Grinning from ear to ear, I stared at the phone screen, waiting for the contact information to come through.

Like me or not, this Charlie guy better get me the information we needed, and fast. My gut told me we had little time to piece the clues together. Though my gut also told me Remy was hiding something. About the case or something else, I wasn't sure.

But I would uncover her secrets.

Whether she wanted me to or not.

4

REMINGTON

"I understand you're worried, but the crazy man has no way to find me, remember? And that was almost three weeks ago," I said into the empty car as I talked to Charlie through Bluetooth while I inched through the carpool line outside Crew's school. "You said the technical one is dead, right? So I'm good."

"I did, and he is, but that doesn't mean this fucker isn't smart in other ways." Charlie's voice poured through the speakers of my late-model black Ford Explorer, the concern and tension clear in his voice. "I'm worried about you. I don't understand why you won't trust the FBI guy and the detective, but whatever. Your enemy is my enemy, though I wish you'd let them offer some kind of protection."

Chewing on the corner of my lip, I studied the back end of the Mercedes in front of me. Charlie was a good friend. He knew what I ran from all those years ago and clearly still felt the urge to protect me. Which was nice, considering he was the only one I had in my life who gave two shits about me and Crew. The moment we virtually met, Charlie took on that role of protector, and I'd been grateful ever sense.

Deep down, I knew it was dumb to refuse more protection, but what choice did I have? I had no one to rely on locally for help, and the fear of Tallon taking Crew away once he found out about him kept me from going to them directly for protection.

There were zero good options for us. The story of my life. It was as if the moment I agreed to go on that date with Jett in high school, my life veered down the roughest path possible. But if I hadn't dated Jett, I wouldn't have married him. I wouldn't have run years later for fear of my life, which landed me in Nashville and at that bar when I met Tallon and Jameson, which gave me Crew.

So yeah, the on-the-run, single-mom life was tough, but I wouldn't want it any other way because it all led me to him.

"I'll be fine," I said, shaking myself out of the daze I'd slipped into. "We'll be fine. I'm extra vigilant at home, and we have that officer out front." Which I hated, yet knowing someone watched the house helped me sleep a little easier at night. "If something happens that makes me question our safety, then I'll react. Until then, I don't want to disrupt Crew's life for a what-if. Or my job."

"I thought you hated that job," he huffed.

"I don't hate the pay or the dental benefits," I said with a smile. "Remember, we're not all computer gods like you. Some of us are just lowly developers."

"You're more than just a developer, and you know it. I can't give you details of what we've uncovered since it's an open case, but this fucker is bad news, Remington. Just be careful."

Crew's tall frame and profile came into view as I drew closer to the front of the school. *Fucking finally.* It felt like I spent most of my life in this damn carpool line.

"Listen, I'm getting Crew now. I gotta go. Thanks for calling."

"Let me know if things change. You don't have to do everything on your own. Let me and Rhyan help."

I snorted. "From Texas?"

"For you, we'd figure it out. Rhyan knows everything and is eager to do whatever we can to keep you and Crew safe." My stomach churned. He didn't even know everything, so how could she? "Check in every day just to put my mind at ease that you're okay."

"Fine," I grumbled. "Unnecessary, but okay. Thanks, Charlie."

The line went silent just as the back passenger door swung open. With a wide smile, I shifted to face the back as Crew lumbered into the cramped space. "Hey, buddy, how was your day?"

"Good."

Brows raised, I waited for him to elaborate, but as usual, I didn't get any additional details. After he settled into the seat and buckled up, I turned, sighing at this new way-too-early preteen attitude he'd formed the last few months.

We were halfway home when the quiet filling the car became too much. With my fingers poised over the volume knob, his voice had me pausing in case any movement startled him back into the sullen silence.

"Hey, Mom," he said.

Glancing in the rearview, I found him staring out the window, chin resting on his palm.

"Yeah?" Oh, this was good. He was opening up. Maybe I wasn't completely failing at this parenting thing after all.

"Why would a cop show up at school and ask for me?"

Not thinking through my reaction, I gripped the wheel with both hands and jerked it to the right, whipping us into a parking lot while still going about thirty miles an hour. Crew's shouted curse filled the car along with the screech of tires along the asphalt.

"What the hell, Mom?" The shake in his voice made me wince.

Fucking hell, I scared him.

And the Mom of the Year award goes to....

Not me.

Flying into a parking spot, I slammed on the brakes, making him curse again when the seat belts caught. Muscles trembling from the overload of adrenaline, my foot knocked against the brake pedal as I held on tight to the wheel, desperately trying to calm myself down enough to speak without yelling.

"Watch your language," I snapped. Shifting the SUV into Park, I twisted fully in the seat to face my stunned nine-year-old. "What cop?"

Eyes still wide, he shrugged. "I don't know. Gray was in the nurse's office, which is by the front desk, when the guy came by asking to see me and flashing some kind of badge." I swallowed down hot fear-driven tears. It was happening. Tallon knew about Crew and was coming to take him away from me. Without even warning me. "Gray said the security guard told the cop he couldn't do that without parental approval."

After a beat of silence, I motioned impatiently for him to keep going. "And?"

"And nothing. The cop left. Gray came back since he was faking being sick anyway to get out of the spelling test and told me what happened. Why are you making a big deal out of this? Are we in trouble?"

"We're fine," I said, feigning confidence I sure as hell didn't feel. Turning back around, I stared unseeing out the windshield. "We're fine. I'll find out what's going on, okay? Just give me a second to call Uncle Charlie. Do your homework while I step out and make a quick call."

Instantly the cold, damp January air chilled me to the bone, my lightweight work clothes doing nothing to keep me warm. Fisting the edges of my jacket, I pulled it tighter around me to ward off the chill. Ass against the closed driver side door, I withdrew my phone from the side pocket and clicked to the missed calls. Hitting the one I knew was Tallon's cell phone number, based on the sheer number of missed calls, I held the trembling device to my ear.

"Harper," he barked the second the ringing stopped. Whether it was the gravity of the situation or hearing his voice, I couldn't find my own to respond. "Who the…?" His voice trailed off before coming back. "Shit, sorry, Remy. I didn't check to see who was calling before I answered. Is everything okay?"

I swallowed. "What the hell were you or Jameson doing at my son's school today?"

"What?"

Tightening my free hand into a fist, I shoved it into my jacket pocket and dug it into the corner. "I said, what the hell were you or Jameson doing at my son's school today? That's low even for—"

"Hold up. You have a kid?" My next words vanished. "Remy?"

"You're lying. You were at his school—"

"How could I be at his school when I didn't even know you had a kid? What the hell is going on?"

"He said someone came by his school wanting to talk to him." I stared at the cracked blacktop, trying to piece the mismatched pieces of the puzzle together. "His friend said the guy flashed a badge. It… it wasn't you?"

The fear of Tallon taking Crew diminished only to be replaced with confusion.

"Give me a second," Tallon commanded. That firm voice sent a shiver of desire down my spine. I seriously needed to get laid if just his voice made my core tingle. Though that was a problem for another day. "I texted Jameson to see if it was him, but I don't think he knew you had a son either."

My brows furrowed. "What does that mean?"

"Okay, he just responded. It wasn't him who came by the school either. Remington, I need you to listen to me. You and your son are in danger." Using my backside, I shoved off the metal door and yanked it open. "My sister said a guy came by the bar she worked at one night claiming to be a detective and tried to get her alone. We assumed it was the Vincent guy's partner, the same one who you, according to the reports, taunted in that damn torture shed. It means he's found you and your son."

Ice filled my veins, stealing my breath. Glancing into the back seat, I studied Crew's pinched features as he concentrated on his math homework.

"I gotta go." Tallon's shouts for me to come directly to his apartment for protection filtered through the speaker as I pulled the phone from my ear and hit the End Call button. Immediately tapping on Charlie's number, I blew out a shaky breath.

"I didn't mean you had to check in today—"

"Charlie." I swallowed, unshed tears burning down my throat. I couldn't cry. Not in front of Crew. It would scare the shit out of him even more than I already had with my *Fast and Furious* driving. First, I needed to get Crew somewhere safe. Then I could break down.

"What happened?" His tone shifted to all business. No

longer was I talking to my friend but rather Special Agent Bekham.

"I need your help."

GETTING Crew out of harm's way was a priority. Thankfully, that was the straightforward part. Charlie and Rhyan saved my ass by being open—more like ecstatic—to housing Crew for however long was needed. After purchasing a last-minute one-way plane ticket to Dallas, packing us both enough clothes for a couple weeks, and one very teary goodbye at the Nashville airport, it was close to ten, and I'd missed no fewer than a hundred calls and texts from Tallon demanding I fill him in on what was going on.

With Crew now safely in the air and Charlie already at the airport waiting for the flight to land, I felt somewhat calmer and ready to tackle this shit show head-on. Though the idea of that bastard knowing how to find me still had me on edge, at least it was just my safety I had to worry about.

Which was odd. For over nine years, I'd put Crew first, always worrying more about him than myself. Panic, worry, and unease all shifted through me as I processed the idea of not having another life to keep safe for the first time since those two pink lines showed up on the stick.

At a red light, I eyed the single stuffed duffel in the passenger seat, wondering, not for the first time in the last few minutes, if I was making the right decision.

Though all in all, this was my only option if I wanted to stay alive—which was high on my priority list. Going to Tallon and Jameson for help was the last thing I wanted to do, considering I could barely think clearly with them around, but desperate times and all that. And if I were being honest, it still hurt a little—more my ego—considering I left my number, and they never called. Wanting someone to call you and them not doing so really, really sucked.

It was fun, and there were no promises of more, but the connection I felt with them—with Tallon especially—made me hope for more than just that one night. I'd hoped they'd felt that too, so when I never heard from them again, nor could find them to tell either I was pregnant, I was beyond disappointed.

There had been a few men in my life since, though nothing really stuck out in my mind like that night with them. Their firm bodies, the way they worshipped mine with their hands and mouths....

The blare of a horn made me jump an inch in the seat, sending my heart racing. With a small "sorry" wave, I pressed on the gas to hurry through the green light. Two more blocks to go. Minutes away from what I knew would change me, alter the stressful yet free life I'd lived these past several years.

Would this change be for the better or worse? I wasn't sure, but there was no doubt in my mind that after tonight, nothing would ever be the same. At some point, I'd need to tell Tallon about his son. It was the right thing to do, even if I was terrified of what would happen after the truth was revealed.

Worry and nerves churned my stomach as I worked through various ways to bring it up. Telling someone they were the father of a child they hadn't even known existed wasn't your usual conversation starter.

Forcing a smile on my face, I turned down the radio to practice. Hopefully then I wouldn't get too tongue-tied and butcher the conversation.

"Hey, Tallon, I know we have our hands full with finding

this crazy fucker, but surprise, you're the father of a nine-year-old boy." I grimaced and tightened both hands on the wheel to stop from slapping myself. "Hey, want to see a picture of my son? He looks a lot like you because you're his father." With a sharp shake of my head, my dark, long-bob-length hair slid along the back of my neck. "Oh, my son? Yeah, you're the father. Surprise!"

Dread settled like a lead weight in my gut as his apartment building came into view. Fingers crossed he was home. Before I hung up earlier, I heard him say something about his apartment so this was my first stop. Pulling into an open street parking spot, I cut the engine and took a deep breath, hoping to quell the rising nausea.

"You've survived worse," I muttered to my reflection in the rearview mirror. "Just tell him and be done with it. You have bigger worries, lady." For emphasis, I pointed at my still-healing eye. "Focus on not dying a terrible death and not"—I flicked my eyes away—"potentially having to share custody of your sweet boy with a man you don't really know anything about."

My chest tightened.

What if Tallon was a bad guy?

What if he was abusive, like Jett?

What did I really know about Tallon besides what I'd learned recently?

His sister seemed nice the few minutes I talked to her—before the drugs that were slipped into the bourbon by the sick fuck stalking her took me under. Maybe Tallon came from a wonderful family, and Crew would just fit right in.

I wouldn't know until I got my ass out of this SUV and found out.

Though my hesitation didn't just come from knowing I needed to tell Tallon about Crew. Just being in the same room with him did things to my body; a single intense look made me desperate for his touch. There was an attraction to Jameson too, though I felt greedy even thinking that I could have them both again. Could I control myself around Tallon if we were stuck in proximity for too long?

Hopefully a safe house was available so I didn't have to test my resistance to the hot, arrogant agent every hour of the day until the case was closed.

Shit. I forgot to pack my vibrator.

Rolling both shoulders to dislodge the tension building there, I gripped the duffel's rough canvas straps and shoved the door open. The thin hot pink leggings, black crop top, and long bulky sweater did nothing to keep me warm as the night's winter wind cut through the downtown streets. Shivering, I hurried to the lobby doors, but once I was a few steps inside, my feet turned to stone. Frozen in the middle of the lobby, the sense of déjà vu swept over me as I eyed the vacant space.

Twice I'd entered this building.

The first time, they wheeled me out on a stretcher, unconscious from the ketamine-spiked alcohol. The other time, I ran out like my ass was on fire, too shocked at seeing Tallon and Jameson to handle the situation like a damn adult.

Pushing my feet to move, I pushed my elbow to the elevator button and waited. Anticipation of what was to come pressed against my chest, turning my breaths shallow. Heart pounding, sweat slicking my hands, I forced myself onto the elevator and hit the button for Tallon's floor.

This is it.

No turning back now.

5

TALLON

I weaved around the stack of boxes littering the living room, my bare feet slapping against the fake hardwood floors as I moved from one side of the apartment to the other while glaring at the blank phone screen. This woman, who I barely knew, was under my skin, and not knowing where she was or the full details of what happened earlier caused unfamiliar worry to gnaw at my stomach.

Guilt I was used to. This overwhelming worry about someone's exact whereabouts was new.

I desperately needed to know more about her. I hoped uncovering the unknowns about Remy's life would help, but I was still waiting on her full file from the normal FBI tech since that fucker Agent Bekham wouldn't send me anything personal on her. In fact, the asshole was now avoiding my calls, which pissed me off more than her hanging up on me. Remy had yet to return my few dozen calls and texts, demanding she get back to me and explain herself. The desperation I hadn't felt before grew as the minutes ticked by with no word on where she was or even if she was safe.

Fuck, I needed a drink.

If I had more details, then I could make a plan and be in control of what happened next.

Control kept me fucking sane. It was something I always needed after my unstable childhood, but after Tinley was abducted, the need to control everything around me became more necessary than air to survive. After that night, I swore I'd never allow myself to be caught unaware again.

Then Remy showed up in the apartment I shared with Tinley, a woman I hadn't seen in ten years, beaten to shit by the psychopath we were chasing, throwing my whole life off-kilter. I wasn't sure I'd ever been more surprised than when I first saw her, and I'd been desperate to get my feet back under me since.

Facts, evidence, details were what I needed to settle the insistent urge to control the outcome of the future. That was impossible, yes, but still, feeling like I was in control helped me function.

Pausing to look out the floor-to-ceiling windows, I sealed a hand to the glass, my palm instantly cooling from the cold surface as I reveled in the view one last time. Tomorrow was finally moving day. Same building, though a one-bedroom instead of two now that Tinley lived in Louisville with Bryson. I couldn't stay here knowing that dead fuck Vincent had set up cameras to watch Tinley.

If it weren't for the risk of burning the place down, I'd set the entire apartment on fire.

Moving my hand, I flexed my fingers, relieved to find the tremble had eased; what remained I blamed on my sky-high blood pressure. Too much had changed the last few weeks between seeing Jameson again, finding out Tinley and Bryson were together, and then Remy showing up. I couldn't get my shit together long enough to relax.

And now I couldn't find Remy, and—

A knock pulled my attention from the bright lights on the other tall downtown buildings to the door. Brows furrowed, I checked my phone. No new calls or texts indicating I should expect someone. Shoving the device into the pocket of my mesh gym shorts, I strode through the living room and gripped the knob, twisting it to open the door without looking through the peephole.

All the air rushed from my lungs in relief at finding Remy standing just on the other side of the threshold. I took in the petite woman shuffling from one foot to the other, from the stuffed duffel she carried to the black Doc Martens, hot pink leggings that curved along her defined legs and higher to a toned stomach, exposed by a black crop top that seemed shorter because of her large tits. My slow perusal paused at her slightly parted lips.

All the blood rushed to my cock, leaving me light-headed as I stared at those lush lips, remembering what they felt like wrapped around me. Sure, it had been years since we were together, but a man didn't forget the best fucking head he'd ever received, no matter how much time had passed. When I finally drew my gaze up, I found hers glued to my bare chest as she licked her lips.

"Seriously," she said, voice pitched higher than normal. I smirked and leaned against the doorframe, crossing my arms, flexing a little just to be an ass. Her gaze jumped up to mine. "We need to talk."

Edge of the door gripped in one hand, I stepped to the side and gestured into the apartment. "Agreed, Remington."

With an eye roll, she weaved under my outstretched arm, careful to not touch a single section of bare skin, and hurried into the apartment.

After closing and locking the door, I turned, eager to

finally get the answers to my never-ending questions. "I see you finally came to your senses."

"Oh, get off your high horse," she retorted before pausing just a few feet away. My brows dipped when she didn't move, standing as still as a statue.

"What's wrong?" I asked, moving to stand in front of her. Searching her features, a frown pulled at my lips. "You okay? You look a little pale." My mind raced, desperate for a solution to fix whatever had put the look of unease on her face.

"Give me a second," she rasped, swallowing hard. Her green eyes flicked to the kitchen, and she visibly shuddered. "This was where it all started, you know? It's just a little overwhelming being back in here."

I almost smacked myself. Of course this would be difficult as hell. The woman was drugged in this apartment. Yet another reason I needed to move.

"Right, sorry. Do you want something to drink?" When she blanched, I shook my head at my dumb ass. "Water. I have bottled water that you can open yourself." I paused and studied her face for any hint of hesitation. "I know we have a unique past, but you know I wouldn't do anything to hurt you, right?"

The need to hear her confirm I wasn't a threat was overwhelming. Balling both hands into tight fists, I waited for her answer, not moving until I got what I needed to calm the absolute fucking guilt eating me alive. When those green eyes drifted to my hands, she winced.

Confused by the strange reaction, I forced both hands to relax and inhaled a deep breath to ease my tense muscles. Within seconds, her own breath whooshed past her parted lips, and she visibly relaxed too.

Interesting.

"I don't think you would hurt me on purpose," she said

after a second. Closing her eyes, she pulled the duffel around, using it almost as a shield between us. "A water would be great. Thank you."

With a nod, I went to the kitchen, careful to keep her in my line of sight. Her dark hair shifted with the subtle movements as she took in the apartment.

"You moving?" she asked. Setting the bag down, she turned and followed me into the kitchen.

I gestured toward a barstool for her to sit. "I couldn't stay here. Not after... everything."

She nodded, face pulled in a grimace. "Understandable. Where are you moving?"

Ignoring the insistent urge to shift the conversation to why she was here and what the hell happened today, I reached inside the fridge and grasped two bottles of water. If she needed small talk first to get comfortable, I could give that to her. For now. I owed her that much. Plus the idea of her running because I pushed too hard like that day at her office made my heart clench.

What the hell was that about?

"A few floors up, a one-bedroom."

Her dark brows rose along her smooth skin. "What about your sister?"

There was no way I could fight the growing smile. "She moved in with my best friend and his daughter." The bottle I was handing her slipped between her fingers, the plastic clattering when it hit the island. I frowned at the bottle but picked it up and tried again. "I think you met him while you were here looking for the cameras."

Remy cleared her throat and took the bottle, this time able to keep it in her hand. Maybe it slipped because her hands were so tiny. Maybe she could only handle those miniature bottles. The urge to grab my phone and order a case to be delivered tomorrow was fierce.

"That's nice. He seemed like a good guy. Overprotective, but nice."

I nodded in agreement. "He's a great guy. Great father too. I know he'll be good for her. They both will."

"What about you?" she asked.

I studied the way she avoided my gaze, now picking at the thin plastic label around the still unopened water bottle. "What about me?"

"Do you have any kids?"

Odd question, but okay. I leaned a hip against the island and twisted the lid of my water. "Nope."

"Do you want kids?"

I frowned, utterly confused at the strange topic. "Based on the demented shit I've learned about those who I call family"—my brows rose as a slight tremble started along her hands, making the water shift in the bottle—"plus all the evil I see, it makes me not want to condemn a kid to growing up in this world." When the plastic crinkled beneath her tight grip, I cringed. *Probably the worst thing to say to a mother. I'm a fucking idiot.* This woman had me tripping over my damn tongue. "But to each their own. Do you only have the one? A son, if I remember correctly before you hung up on me?"

Her breathing picked up as those green eyes met mine, her face now even paler than before. Not thinking about anything other than keeping her from passing out, I lashed out a hand to open her bottle and force some water down her. Before I understood what was happening, pain radiated up my forearm as it was twisted, my wrist slamming to the granite counter.

I stared wide-eyed at my twisted arm, the angle and

pressure forcing me to shift my upper body to ease the sharp pain radiating up to my shoulder. Knuckles white, Remy's tiny hand held a death grip around my wrist. Cheeks flushed, she now stood, the stool shoved a foot behind her.

"Um," I started, needing a moment to figure out what the hell to say to this strange turn of events, "I was trying to open your water bottle for you." Seeing as she'd just disarmed me with those tiny hands, the idea of little bottles and her not being able to break the plastic seal had me chuckling.

"Sorry, sorry. I'm...." Slowly peeling her fingers off my skin, she quickly stepped back, her backside hitting the stool and sending it toppling to the floor. The loud bang made her jump, then shift to put the downed stool and me in her line of sight. "This was a bad idea. Fuck."

I'd seen this kind of panic before in survivors, which sent me shifting to full agent mode. Hands up, I scooted back until my ass hit the fridge, putting as much space between us as possible.

She studied me, never looking away, standing in a defensive position that only came with hours of training. The hold she used when I moved too fast and now the perfect stance made me study her without the cloud of our past coating my vision.

Something or someone had happened to Remington. Considering she wouldn't have had time to get this level of skill down in the last month, I had to assume someone hurt her before, which made her train in self-defense.

Hot anger boiled in my veins as I waited for her shields to lower. Whoever made her this afraid deserved to have the same level of fear and panic instilled in them.

An array of emotions flashed over her face while I waited for the panic to recede. After a minute, something like resignation settled over her features, softening the pinched look of panic. Her rigid stance eased, and those raised hands, ready to block a hit, slowly lowered to her side. Something inside me let out a heavy breath, seeing that sliver of trust that she knew I wouldn't hurt her.

She cleared her throat. "Sorry. I don't do well with quick movements."

The taste of copper coated my tongue as I bit down to keep from demanding to know what happened to her. Maybe it was because she was a recent victim that provoked my protective side to the point of being irrational.

I dipped my chin and slowly lowered my own hands.

Silence engulfed us as we stared, neither of us knowing how to move past the awkwardness.

Thankfully, the startling ring of my phone broke our standstill. Not looking away, I slowly reached into my pocket and pulled it out, answering the call before pressing it to my ear.

"Harper," I clipped.

"Did you find her?" Jameson asked, sounding as tired as I felt. "The judge didn't sign off on tracking her phone."

"Actually," I said, raising a brow at the woman studying me, "she found me. As in she's here, at my apartment, and about to explain what the hell is going on."

His heavy exhale filled the phone. "Fuck. Okay. Do you want me to head over there?"

I slid my eyes to her duffel. She followed the movement.

"I can't go home," she whispered, a slight tremble in her voice. "I... I need a second." I started to tell her she could use my room for some space, but she turned on her heels and strode toward Tinley's old room.

"I've got this," I said into the phone while tracking her every step. "You sound fucking exhausted. Get some sleep.

We can recap in the morning after I figure out what the hell is going on with her."

"We need to convince her to stick with us until this is over," Jameson said, reiterating what we'd discussed after reading the cold cases that were linked to the sick fucker who abducted her. "I can't go through this freak-out if she's okay or not again. It's the only way we can keep her safe."

Gaze locked on the duffel she'd dropped, I snatched my water bottle from the counter and took a long sip. "I don't think that will be a problem. Whatever happened today changed her mind about needing our protection. My guy still hasn't gotten me the full file on her. Can you ask someone at the station to pull a basic background?"

"Why not ask Agent Bekham?"

I snorted. "I think he's Team Remington and not giving me shit on her. Though I got the impression he'd do whatever it takes to help us catch the bastard who took her, so there's that. I'll call you tomorrow."

There was a pause, keeping me from ending the call.

"What?" I asked. Slumping back, I pinched the bridge of my nose, the stress of the last few weeks hitting me like a semitruck. Now that she was here, safe with me, the fear- and frustration-filled tension drained, leaving my muscles and mind weak.

"You sure it's a good idea to leave her with you, alone?"

"What's that supposed to mean?" I gritted out.

"It means you act like a controlling asshole around her. I'm afraid without me as a buffer she'll run. Again."

My lips curled into a snarl. "She will not run from me again. I'll lock her in here if I have to."

"Fucking hell, man, you sound like one of the psychos you chase. You realize that, right? Do we need to go over all the reasons holding a woman against her will in your apartment under the guise of protection is still considered kidnapping in the eyes of every damn judge?"

I instantly deflated, hating the concern in his voice. "I would never jeopardize the case or her safety. But you're right. I'll calm the fuck down. This isn't personal, it's business. She's just a witness, nothing more."

Without saying another word, I ended the call and tossed the phone to the counter. Movement in my periphery had me looking up. I blanched at finding Remy standing in the doorway of Tinley's old room, lips pursed, clearly having heard my side of the conversation.

Good. Her understanding the obvious line I was drawing between us would help her and me keep whatever this was between us contained. I could do this. Move past this strange urge to possess her like I did that night with Jameson in the hotel room.

Business, not personal.

For years, I'd put myself second to the job. Now it was time to do it again. To forget how I felt for her, ignore the way my body reacted every time she was in the room.

Denying myself what I wanted had to happen to keep her safe.

Giving in wasn't worth the risk.

It never was.

6

REMINGTON

Maybe I needed a CAT scan or MRI to ensure there was no lingering brain damage from the drugs or beating that asshole delivered in that shed. Why else would I be this... off? I wasn't an emotional person, yet here I was on another emotional roller coaster.

No less than thirty minutes ago, I was terrified to tell Tallon about Crew, so there was no reason I should feel this way. Fucking disappointed. And downright sad, like my heart hurt after hearing his take on not wanting children of his own. But I was. And I wasn't sure how to deal with this sudden change of emotion or the need to defend Crew. To tell Tallon how amazing my son was, that he was brave and strong and such a damn good kid. Make him regret those words and the nine years he'd lost out on knowing his son.

The son he didn't know existed.

Fuck, this was messy.

And then there were his last words to who I assumed was Jameson on the other end of the line.

Business, not personal. I was just a witness, nothing more.

Fine. I could deal with just being a witness, a survivor to him. It would make denying this pull easier, knowing he didn't feel this charge between us. I thought maybe the over-protective asshat-ery was him feeling something deeper for me, but apparently, I was wrong. Him trying to control and hover was him just being a good FBI agent.

FML. Look at me. I was upset about them not wanting me then, and now I'm in the same position, feeling fucking sorry for myself. Why was it the one man I wanted, the one I was attracted to, wanted nothing to do with me? Only saw me as a job?

I could use a drink right about now—except I gave it up after the last one I had was laced and almost killed me.

I forced my features to soften to keep the internal war raging inside me hidden and then stepped into the box-filled living room. At least it looked different this way. Not sure how I would've reacted if it looked the same as it had when I was here last month to help Tinley and nearly died.

"You good?" Tallon questioned, a weary look on his features. I studied his face, noticing the tight lines around his eyes and the scruff-covered jaw. He looked as tired as I felt. Which made me feel bad, considering I was probably the source of his exhaustion.

"Yeah, I just needed a second before we dove into the reason I'm here and my life is completely uprooted." I offered a hesitant smile, hoping he'd take the bait and break the tension between us. When he didn't, I blew out an exaggerated exhale. "Okay, how about we just start over? From scratch."

A line formed between his light brows, making him look serious. *Damn, does he ever let loose?* "Start over?"

"Yeah, like introduce ourselves—real names this time—and forget about what happened back then. This is business, not personal, right?" I kept my tone light so he wouldn't take offense to me throwing his words back at him. "Maybe that will settle whatever this—" I waved a hand between us, "—tension is."

Or we could just fuck it out.

Though I would not say that out loud and set myself up for that rejection, even if that route sounded way more enjoyable.

Shit, I was turning into a hussy. I'd never had sex on the brain this much—well, minus those odd few months during pregnancy when I was literally horny from the time I woke up, and none of my toys seemed to relieve the need. Though I was an almost forty-year-old single woman; why shouldn't I have an active libido? Twentysomething-year-olds shouldn't get to have all the fun. I deserved dick too. Good dick.

Not the half-hard cock I'd been subjected to the last time I attempted intimacy. There was something wrong if you had to wonder if it was in yet, and even worse if you asked out loud. That never went over well.

"Right."

I jerked at his voice, somehow getting lost in my sex-deprived brain. Maybe I should take my chances with the serial killer. Being this close to Tallon would no doubt end messy.

Scrubbing a hand along his jaw, he shoved off the counter and slowly strode to where I stood. Keeping his movements smooth, he held out a hand between us. "Special Agent Tallon Harper."

I took his hand and did my best to suppress the shudder that slipped through me at the skin-to-skin contact. His engulfed mine, those thick fingers nearly wrapping around my entire hand, yet there was a gentleness in his grip.

"Remington Dotson. Developer for Technical Solutions, mother of one, and current target of a man with a preference for abducting women and holding them against their will."

His lips pursed.

He obviously didn't find that last part as funny as I did. There went the hope of keeping things easy between us. Guess he'd just keep that stick firmly lodged in his ass.

"You ready to share what happened today, Remy?"

Rolling my eyes, I flopped down on top of the leather sofa, tugging the edges of my sweater together to cover the expanse of bare skin showing. Not that I was self-conscious or anything, more because it was fucking cold. Either he was too cheap to turn the heat on or, like most males, ran a thousand degrees warmer than me.

Chewing on the edge of my lip, I debated my answer. I could stick with being a smartass if he was planning to be the hard-ass FBI agent, but honestly, I was too exhausted to keep up the tough act. It was one I wore most days, only being my real self around Crew or while I was home alone. Hell, I couldn't even let my defenses down around the moms at the private school that I almost needed to sell an organ to afford. They were like fucking sharks in the water, waiting for a drop of blood before devouring you whole for showing any sort of personality outside their Stepford wife standard.

I already broke that mold being a single mother; add in the tattoos and unconventional style and I was the black sheep of the school. Not that I cared, but I heard the whispers, what they assumed happened between me and Crew's father. Thankfully, none of them were even close to the truth. If they found out I got pregnant during a wild ménage night and never saw the father again, they would push me out of their prestigious all-boys academy in a heartbeat.

"Remy?"

"Hmm?" I said, pulling myself out of my head and tipping my chin up to search his face.

"You zoned out there for a second. Are you still struggling with the effects from the ketamine?"

Was that it? Was that the reason I'd been so off-kilter these past few weeks, and not the resurgence of these two men in my life?

"Um, maybe, but I think I'm just tired." Just saying it out loud made the weight of exhaustion push harder on my shoulders. Snuggling deeper into the couch, I covered a wide yawn. *What I would do for a blanket right now.* "Exhausted, really. I haven't slept well since that night."

With a look of concentration, he slowly slid his gaze down my body, more assessing than sexual, much to my disappointment. "Okay, we can talk about everything tomorrow." The surprise must have registered on my face, because he blew out a breath and looked at the ceiling. "I'm not an asshole." I arched a brow. "Fine, maybe I am when it comes to keeping others safe, but not too much to not let you get some sleep before you explain what happened today. But I need to know one thing so I can get some rest tonight too."

"What's that?" I asked hesitantly.

"Your son." *Fuck. Here it comes.* My palms grew sweaty and my heart raced, wondering where this question was going. "Is he safe?"

I blinked at him. That was not what I expected. "Huh?"

"You said someone came to his school, and clearly he's not here with you right now. Is he somewhere safe tonight until we figure this out tomorrow? Or do I need to send an officer to where he is to bring him into protective custody?"

For some unknown reason, his question made irritation

itch beneath my skin. "I'm a good mom," I snapped defensively.

Well, "good" might be an overstatement, most days I considered myself subpar at the mom thing.

Now it was his turn to blink, not understanding. "I'm not questioning that. I'm saying I need to know for my peace of mind that some kid isn't out there in harm's way. I won't be able to sleep until you confirm he's safe. You don't have to tell me where he is, just tell me you've taken the precautions to keep him away from this sick asshole."

Well, now I feel like shit.

See, roller-coaster emotions.

I totally have lingering brain damage.

Emotional damage?

Or is that something different?

Either way, he obviously didn't mean his question as an accusation like I took it. Shit, maybe we couldn't start over. There was too much of a mess—most of which he didn't know about or understand—between us.

The sincerity in his voice, the passion in the need to know my son was safe, had me answering honestly. "He's safe. The second I realized he was in danger, I put him on a plane to Texas."

"Family?"

I shook my head, then nodded and shrugged.

Yep, that totally cleared *that* up for him.

He huffed a laugh, the corners of his lips twitching upward in an almost smile. Hell, had I seen him smile once. I remembered those sexy smiles coming easily before, as if it was more natural for him to smile than not. But now... it felt awkward, strained almost.

And enter yet another dip in the emotional roller coaster.

The thought of him not smiling made me sad.

Why in the hell did I care this much? Why couldn't I just see him as a hot piece of ass and not... care?

"Family to me, I guess. I sent him to stay with Charlie and Rhyan." That almost-smile fell, making me wish I had said nothing. "Charlie's been there for me for years. Even though I've never met his girlfriend, I know I can trust her. Trust them with his safety."

"What about his father?"

I swallowed hard. I could take this moment and tell him the truth. But I was too scared. Too much of a chickenshit. So I gave him a half truth.

"He wants nothing to do with him."

Tallon just nodded as if that made sense, and fucking hell, did that dig the rusted knife of desolation deeper into my heart. He really wanted nothing to do with kids. It should make me feel better knowing that if he found out he was a father, there wasn't a risk of him taking Crew, but instead I wanted to cry.

Like ugly cry.

Add in the fact that I forgot my vibrator to cure this insistent throb between my thighs and a complete breakdown was almost certain at this point.

"I think I should go to bed." Shoving off the couch, I maneuvered around him to get to my duffel. "If you have extra blankets, I can sleep on the couch." I'd ask to stay in Tinley's old room, but it was bare, all the furniture gone.

"Not a chance, Remy." Without another word, he strode off toward the other bedroom next to what used to be his sister's. "I'd kick my own ass if I let you sleep on the couch while I hogged the bed." I had to basically jog to keep up with his long strides, almost bumping into his bare back when he stopped just over the threshold. "You'll sleep in here. Let me get some fresh sheets."

"I don't want—"

"The fact that you're here will give me the best night's sleep I've had since the shit went down." My heart thundered at his admission. I desperately wanted to ask why but bit my tongue to keep the words from slipping out. "The couch will be fine for me, but...."

"But what?"

"I'm not sure how long it will take to catch this fucker. Maybe I should cancel the move and keep this two-bedroom. Get more—"

"No, don't do that. Not on my account. I'll sleep on the couch—"

"How many bedrooms does your house have?"

I almost asked how he knew I lived in a house, then remembered he'd been the one to set up the unmarked car.

"Um, two," I responded, scrunching my nose, trying to figure out where he was going with that line of questioning. There was no way he was thinking what I thought he was... right?

His solid chest rose and fell with an exaggerated breath. "We'll discuss tomorrow. But we'll keep it as an option."

"Says who?"

"Says the man you came to tonight to keep you safe."

Well, shit. He had me there.

"Fine." I sighed and rubbed at my dry eyes. Pressing on the still tender flesh made me wince. "Can I grab a shower? It's been a long day."

"Sure. Use mine. Let me get the sheets out of the linen closet first."

He followed me into the adjoining bathroom. The space was bigger than the other room's bathroom, with enough room to not feel too crowded with us both inside. Though if Jameson joined the party....

Warmth built beneath my cheeks at the dirty direction my mind went. That was not happening. We were solving the case, and then I'd go back to my normal, slightly boring, busy life.

While I unzipped my bag to dig out fresh underwear and pajamas, I studied him from the corner of my eye. Movements stiff, he retrieved a set of sheets and a towel from the small linen closet.

Did he feel the same pull? Or was this all one-sided?

"I'll leave you to it," he said, not meeting my eyes. "If you need anything, let me know. Otherwise, I'll see you in the morning."

Licking my lips, I simply nodded and took the offered towel, squeezing it close to my chest. "Good night."

The moment the door clicked closed, I released my held breath through tight lips. Turning to the mirror, I studied the pink flush of my cheeks, knowing full well it was from his proximity and the memories of us three together.

With a frustrated groan, I stripped out of my clothes and tossed them in a pile on the floor before turning on the shower. When steam billowed out of the glass enclosure, I stepped beneath the spray, hissing at the scalding temperature against my nearly frostbitten fingers and toes.

Unfocused stare on the subway tile, I methodically washed off the remnants of the long, emotionally exhausting day while keeping my hair dry. Making today an unexpected hair wash day would be the final straw to push me into a blubbering mess.

Unease grew as I watched the suds swirl down the drain. Tomorrow would be another long day if this discomfort between us kept up. Clearly, starting over wasn't the answer. We needed to clear the air.

Which meant talking about that night like adults.

Then our focus could be fully on the real threat—the man who shouldn't know who I was or how to find me, yet did. Despite the hot water, a chill ran down my spine, and goose bumps sprouted along my arms. I swore when I ran from Jett that I'd never allow another man to hurt me, and I'd kept that promise since the day Remington Sawyer ceased to exist.

If I had to open myself up for rejection from these two again, to keep that promise to myself and keep Crew safe, I'd do it. Whatever the consequences, I knew I had to tell them the truth.

About everything.

7

TALLON

An insistent muffled vibration beneath the pillow pulled me awake, an annoyed groan rattling in my chest. Forcing my eyes open to thin slits, I dragged the phone free and blinked at the screen.

Jameson: Be there in ten.

Fuck, what is he doing coming over here so damn early? My eyes widened at the time in the right-hand corner of the screen. Nine in the morning. After rubbing the sleep from my eyes, I typed out a quick reply.

Me: Door's unlocked.

Every muscle protested as I swung both legs over the edge of the couch, the cold floor a shock to the bottoms of my bare feet. With both arms stretched high over my head, a groan slipped from my lips as my spine popped and cracked when I twisted one way, then the other, attempting to ease the tightness. Fucking hell, getting old sucked. There was a time when sleeping on the couch didn't affect how I functioned the next day. Clearly those days were gone.

After running an eye over my emails to ensure nothing pressing needed my attention, I stood and unlocked the front door. While making coffee, my gaze kept flicking to my closed bedroom door. With Jameson close, she needed to get up so we could figure out this mess and come up with a plan. Leaving the coffee brewing, I crept toward the bedroom, ears perked for any signs of life behind the door.

Hand on the doorknob, I waited, breath held, straining to hear her moving around, but only the sound of the coffee hissing from the kitchen cut through the silence. Twisting the knob, I slowly pushed the door open.

"Remy," I said in a hushed tone. I sucked in a quick breath when I fully stepped into the room.

Curled into a tight ball on the very edge of the bed, only the top of her silky dark hair peeked out from beneath the covers, pulled tightly over her head. Worry gnawed in my gut as I crept closer. It looked like she was making herself as small as possible in her sleep.

But why?

That worry shifted to anger. Between the way she reacted last night to my quick movements and now this, it was clear she'd been hurt in her past. By whom, I had no fucking idea, but I sure as hell would find out. A fire burned in my chest at the need for vengeance, to hurt the bastard who hurt her.

"Remy," I muttered, now standing beside where she still lay unmoving. My eyes softened, the urge to comfort her and tell her she was safe hitting me like a punch to the heart. "Remy, it's time to wake up."

The form beneath the covers still didn't move. Hell, how was she even getting enough oxygen under there?

Heart racing, I reached down and gripped where I thought her shoulder was. Just like last night, her quick movement was so unexpected that I didn't have time to process what was going on until I was on my back, pinned to the mattress, blinking at the ceiling.

Dark hair sticking up in various directions, Remy hovered, her bony knee pressed to my bare chest and hands gripping my biceps, keeping them pinned to the mattress. It would be easy to flip her, considering she weighed half of me, but I knew better. That would only make this situation worse.

Green eyes widened as they flicked between mine. Staying completely still, I gave her as long as she needed to fully wake up and realize I wasn't a threat.

I knew the moment she realized what she'd done and where she was. Those dark brows furrowed before shooting up her forehead.

"Fuck," she squeaked.

"It was my fault. I was trying to wake you up," I murmured. "Give yourself a second."

Where this calm side of me came from, I had no fucking idea. Normally I was too tightly wound to waste a single second on emotional shit. Yet here I was, staying as still as a statue despite the ache radiating through my muscles and discomfort where her knee pressed against my sternum.

"Shit, I'm sorry," she whispered, lower lids growing watery.

"It's okay," I said back. Realization of the reasoning behind what happened all those years ago smacked me in the face. "That's why you left."

Her hair shifted as her head cocked to the side. "I'm here."

The firm hold around my biceps slipped, and the knee on my chest shifted so she was now straddling my chest. My teeth ground with the effort to not focus on her warm center pressing on my bare skin. The large T-shirt she slept in had ridden up, now bunched around her hips. It took all my restraint to not grip her thighs and shift her lower to sit on my throbbing cock.

Who knew being pinned beneath a beautiful woman did it for me, but it fucking did. My dick twitched beneath my gym shorts, eager to remind her how good we were together. I swallowed hard.

Shit, did she say something?

This was bad. I was too distracted by her tempting pussy to even carry on a conversation, much less protect her.

"That night," I stated, finally coming back to the train of thought before my dick distracted me. "That morning, rather. You were gone. You didn't want to sleep with us."

Her throat worked as if the words were stuck there. "Couldn't sleep with you." Easing back a little, she carefully extracted her hands from my bare arms. "It took me a long time to be where I am now, though I think... what happened in that shed stirred up some memories I'd worked hard to forget. When normally I don't even think about him, now it's right there... all the bad memories."

"Who?" I asked before I could stop myself. "Who do you try to forget, Remy?" Reaching up, I cupped the side of her face, brushing my thumb along her cheekbone. Barely restrained anger at the bastard who created those bad memories flowed through my veins, making me itch for a fight. "Who hurt you?"

"Is this a group activity?"

Two things happened at once. Jameson's voice registered, snapping me out of my intent focus on the beautiful woman on top of me, and bone-shattering pain radiated from my crotch when her knee smashed against my cock and balls as she scrambled to extract herself from me.

Face twisted in agony, I cupped my now-throbbing cock,

the blood pounding through my ears distorting her curses and Jameson's laugh. Sharp breaths hissed through my clenched teeth as I sucked down gulps of air to keep from throwing up.

When hands gripped my forearm, shoving the person off to keep them away while I got my shit together was second nature. It wasn't until a loud thud and Jameson's curse filled the room that I unsealed my eyes. Remy sat a few feet away, on the floor, blinking up at me in horror.

Then it clicked.

I didn't push Jameson away.

I shoved her.

"Remy," I groaned, my voice raspy. Forcing my body into action despite the way my muscles were locked up, I pushed an elbow into the mattress, attempting to sit up. My stomach dropped when she scurried back, putting more distance between us. "Sorry. Thought... Jameson." Hopefully she understood what I was trying to say between deep breaths. "Won't hurt you."

What little color was left drained from her face. "That's what he said too."

"What the fuck is going on here? Who hurt you?" Jameson turned to me with a murderous look on his face. "Did you fucking hurt her last night?"

"No," I cursed.

"My ex," she squeaked.

Well, that was one way to distract me from the pain still shooting little shock waves through my balls. Swallowing down the string of curses that wanted to slip, I sat up, my feet firmly on the floor.

"You want some ice?" Jameson said cautiously.

"I'm good," I said, releasing a controlled breath. "I'm good. Did you say ex?" I directed at the woman now standing, looking ready to bolt out the door. "Ex what? Husband? Boyfriend?" She blanched, eyes flicking to the open door. "Don't you run away. Not again."

"Again?" she snapped. "I didn't run away the last time."

"Oh yeah, you were gone," Jameson muttered more to himself. "Now I remember. I was wondering why I was drawing a blank on the awkward morning-after conversation."

Slowly standing, I winced as I stood to full height, though now the sharp, soul-sucking pain was only a low throb. "I'm getting some Advil, and then we're talking about this. All of this. If we can't work together, then this fucker will keep killing, starting with you." I pointed at Remy. "I will not let that happen."

Putting my back to them, I limped to the bathroom, hoping I hadn't packed the pain meds yet.

Fucking hell, today was going to be a long day.

"That was painful to watch." Jameson's voice filtered into the bathroom.

"It was painful to experience," I grumbled. Grabbing the bottle of painkillers, I shook four into my palm and popped them into my open mouth, swallowing them dry. I glanced at the mirror. Jameson stood on the threshold between the bathroom and bedroom, his normal smirk gone. "What's wrong?"

He turned to look over his shoulder. "You know, what we did together was just fun." I nodded. Turning on the faucet, I splashed some cool water on my face and took a sip from my cupped hand. "Just making sure we agree."

My stomach dropped. Shit, was he saying he wanted to pursue Remy on his own?

"On what?" I asked after patting the water drops from my face with a clean hand towel. Out of habit, I hung it back on the towel ring, ensuring it was pulled through equal distance and folded so the ends matched up. Seeing the slight tremble in my hand had me grabbing the edge of the granite vanity with a white-knuckle grip.

"That if something happens between you and Remy, I'm good with it."

I met his gaze in the mirror. "Who says something will?"

He scoffed. "If you can't see it, you're a fool. There's something between you two. It's volatile. I noticed it when we visited her that first time, and just now, you two were fully absorbed in each other. You'll end up fucking or fighting."

I ground my teeth, not wanting to confirm his observation. He was right, though. And I sure as hell wasn't jonesing to fight her. Fuck, this was bad.

"Are you saying you're not interested in her?" I asked.

A smile crept up his cheeks. I wanted to smack myself for basically confirming his observation by not denying my attraction to her.

"I'm not saying that. If you two want company, I'm still on board with 'the more the merrier.'" I huffed at that. Turning, I leaned against the edge of the vanity and crossed my arms as he continued. "Just don't feel guilty if something happens with only you two. You already carry enough of that shit anyway."

I could only offer a clipped nod in return.

He was right. And the weight of all this guilt was slowly drowning me. What I wouldn't give to just be free from it for a few hours. To not remember how I failed Tinley ten years ago because I was a selfish fuck and missed her performance that night. How my mother blamed me for not being there for my sister and layered more guilt on saying Tinley would blame me too if she knew where I was instead of with her.

Though I'd spoken to Tinley, the air now cleared between us, I still couldn't shake the feeling of shame that came with remembering my old lifestyle.

"You know you shouldn't, right?"

"Easier said than done," I muttered as I ran a hand over my face.

"It would be easy if you had someone to share that weight with. Sounds like she has some shit in her past too. Maybe you two can help each other."

I narrowed my eyes. "Stop profiling me."

"It's funny. I never knew I naturally did that until Agent Rhyan Riggs mentioned it. I've always just enjoyed figuring out the reasons, putting the pieces of the puzzle together."

"It makes you a good detective."

"And hopefully a good profiler," he said with a shrug. "I'm taking the job in Texas." I blinked at my friend, not sure what to say. I was excited for him, yet I wasn't sure he understood what he'd be giving up by joining the bureau. "I told Agent Riggs that I wanted to get through this case first, help you find Vincent's partner, and then I'd get on the schedule for training."

Pushing myself off the vanity, I grabbed his shoulder as I passed and gave it a squeeze. "You'll be a great addition to the team. I have no doubt. Though make sure you know what you're getting yourself into."

I yanked open the top dresser drawer and pulled out a clean shirt.

"And what's that?" he asks behind me.

"Long nights, no relationships, constantly on the road." I snagged a pair of clean boxers from another drawer.

"Yeah, I figured it wouldn't be an easy transition, but I'm

ready to move on from this town. Nashville is my home, but it's time to take my career to that next step. I'm ready. What do I have to lose, you know?"

I paused, clothes clutched tightly in my hand. "Years of your life spent waking up in unfamiliar hotel rooms chasing different killers because it never ends. They keep popping up and coming up with new ways to hurt an innocent victim." Inhaling deep, I glanced over my shoulder. "Looking back, I don't regret what I've done, but a part of me regrets not putting my life first." I motioned toward the door that led to the living room. "I'm going to grab a quick shower. Then we sit down with Remy."

Not waiting for an answer, I strode into the bathroom to give myself a second to get my shit together to be ready for the long day ahead of us. After stripping off the loose gym shorts I slept in, I turned the shower lever all the way to the right and stepped into the cold spray.

As I scrubbed down, I tried to redirect my focus back on the threat and case. But Jameson's comments ran on a loop in my mind.

What if he was right? What if whatever was brewing between Remy and me was inevitable?

Could I protect her, do my job, and allow myself to indulge in her?

Or would me letting my guard down put her life at risk?

And my heart?

8

─────────

REMINGTON

I took a cautious sip from the coffee mug just to have something to do while avoiding their pointed stares. Jameson's brown eyes held a softness to them while Tallon seemed on edge, his stare burning a hole straight through me.

Not sure what his deal was. The intensity that radiated off him at all times was attractive and intimidating. The casual look he wore today with dark jeans and a snug T-shirt made him less authoritative than the suits, but it was just as amazing on his fit frame. I licked my lips, staring at the defined chest now covered by soft cotton.

He really was perfection.

Well, his body and good looks, anyway. His attitude needed a little help, and he could stand for someone to yank that stick out of his FBI ass, but even with those two things, I couldn't help but want him. I couldn't remember the last time I'd been this attracted to someone, so much so that I fought to not squirm in the chair to ease the low throb between my thighs.

The throb I didn't quell last night because I literally

passed out the moment my head hit the pillow. The amazing mattress combined with his intoxicating all-male scent lingering on the fresh sheets instantly lulled me to sleep.

Holding the mug between both hands, I relished the heat soaking into my chilled fingers. "Where do you want to start?" I asked tentatively.

Jameson's gaze darted to Tallon. This I remembered between the two from that night. Tallon was the one in complete control while Jameson followed his commands. The coffee nearly sloshed over the side of the mug with my full-body shiver.

Shit, I had to get that under control. There would be none of that. Especially once Tallon found out about Crew. Hell, maybe he'd just leave and let the serial killer take me as punishment. I swallowed down a burst of panic at the thought.

Surely not. Right?

"From the beginning," Tallon stated. His knees bounced up and down, jostling his upper body where his elbows pressed on the tops of his spread thighs.

I'd considered what all to tell them while getting ready earlier. I could explain the general synopsis of my past, giving no details that could come back and bite me in the ass.

"Okay, but just so y'all know, I fully expect the same from you two," I said with a pointed look to both. "This isn't a one-way street of information."

Jameson nodded. Tallon just stared.

"Start with the ex," Tallon said, shifting to the edge of the couch.

I shrugged. "He's an abusive asshole. Though it was gradual, and the physical abuse didn't start until after years of mental and emotional shit." Swallowing hard, I studied the stacks of cardboard boxes filling the room. "The sleeping, that was... well, he liked to wait until I was completely unaware, vulnerable, then startle me awake. It was a fun game for him."

My heart hammered in my chest as the memories flooded in, almost like I was reliving those moments of panic when he would jerk me awake, forcing me to do his bidding. If I didn't, that was when the punishments came into play.

"How long?"

"Ten years," I whispered, shame coating me from the inside out. Shame that I wasn't strong enough then to leave sooner, strong enough to see how with each year, things escalated in his treatment toward me.

"Where is he now?" Tallon asked. My attention snapped up at the coldness in his tone. I cocked my head to the side as I studied the way his fists tightened and flexed. "What I mean is, are you safe from him now? Or do I need to handle the situation?"

My responding nod was slow, still confused on why he seemed so pissed on my behalf. I was just a witness, right? Part of the job, so why would he care if Jett was still out there? "Yes, I'm safe. For now."

"Did he ever hurt your son?" Jameson asked quietly, but there was an edge to his tone that sent a shiver down my spine.

The ends of my hair swished along my neck with my headshake. "No, he wasn't born yet. I got out before that. I ran from the bastard when I found some courage and got the chance. That's how I ended up in Nashville."

"That night we met you," Tallon's blue eyes flashed as if he was also fighting the onslaught of memories at just the mention of that night, "did you know what that bar was known for before stepping inside?" Some of the color faded from his cheeks as a grimace wrinkled his handsome face. "Or did we ambush you—"

I sliced my hand through the air, cutting him off. "I knew exactly what I was getting into. It's why I went to that bar that night."

"How in the hell could you trust men after your ex?" Jameson asked, a hint of awe in his tone. "Two strangers at that?"

I blew out a steady breath while gathering my words to explain that the need for a connection that night outweighed the dangers. "When I met you guys, it had been a year since I left my ex." I debated going into more detail. Ultimately, Jameson's worried look pushed me to continue. If they knew all the details, then they'd know I wanted everything that happened that night. There was no reason for them to think they forced me to do anything I was uncomfortable with. "So at that point in time, the night we met, I'd had no type of intimate contact, no emotional connection, in over six years." I pressed my fingers to my lips, holding back a giggle at the shocked look on their slack faces at that revelation. "And yes, I was nervous, but I also knew to trust my gut. I was desperate for a connection, for physical touch. For some reason, it felt safer, easier maybe, knowing if I went to that bar, there would be two or more involved in the night, better than just going to a hotel room alone with a single stranger. Before you two showed, I'd already turned down a few offers." Tallon's back went ramrod straight. I eyed him warily but continued. "I was actually about to leave when you two came to my table, and I just knew. There was something about you that made me feel safe."

Jameson nodded. "Thanks?"

I huffed a laugh, though the lightness of the conversation vanished, and a frown pulled my lips down. "I had fun that night. A lot, actually. You two made me feel seen, and... I don't know, cherished, maybe? Or maybe it meant more to me since it had been so long since I'd had anything like that, and that's why I took your rejection so hard. You didn't promise—"

"Rejection?" Tallon barked, the single word clipped almost like an order. "You're the one who left, Remy."

My dark lashes fanned up and down as I slow blinked, trying to understand why that made any difference as to how they rejected me by not calling. "Yeah, I left, which you now know why, but neither of you ever called. That's what I'm talking about."

"How could we have called? We didn't even know your real name."

I bristled, shifting against the seat to sit up taller. "Don't give me shit about that, considering you didn't give me your full names either. Understand that I still have to protect myself from being found by my ex. So no, I will not go off and tell every random person my name."

"So that brings me back to my initial question. How could we have called?" Tallon demanded.

My stomach dropped as I searched their faces for a hint of deception, finding only confusion. "I left you my number," I stated a little more hesitantly now that I was second-guessing myself. The two men shared a look before turning back to me. "On the notepad at the hotel."

Tallon squeezed his eyes shut, almost like he was in pain. Jameson studied his friend cautiously.

"That next morning," Jameson stated. "Tallon got a call that his sister, Tinley, was missing."

"Tinley?" I questioned. "The one who was just stalked and kidnapped last month? That sister?"

Tallon offered a solemn nod. "The man who abducted her recently had done it before. The morning after we were together, I got a call from her dance company saying she didn't show up for rehearsal. I knew immediately something was wrong. Tinley stuck to her commitments. I got Jameson up, and we ran out of there to find out what the hell was going on. The next three weeks were literal hell as we searched for her, then the following months after, while she recovered and we had zero leads."

His chest rose and fell in quick succession. I tucked my free hand beneath my ass, nails scratching the leather chair to keep from reaching out to comfort him. There was this pull to him that urged me closer, to feel safe tucked against his side. Jameson was just as attractive, but there wasn't that intense tug to him as there was with Tallon.

Though I had to wonder if they were always a package deal or if they ever did one-offs. I sure as hell wouldn't want to ruin their friendship if something happened between just me and Tallon. These two were keeping me safe from the bastard after me.

Not that anything would happen.

Hypothetically speaking.

You know, asking for a friend.

"So, needless to say," Jameson said, pulling me out of my random internal debate, "we saw nothing that morning when we raced out of there. Hell, I think I was only halfway dressed when we bolted from the hotel."

Some of the lingering resentment for the two men lifted at their explanation. Releasing a slow breath, I leaned back in the chair, the tight tension leaking from my muscles.

"That makes sense," I said after a few seconds of

processing this new revelation. Though another question forced its way out of my mouth before I could stop myself. "That explains why you didn't call, but why didn't either of you ever go back to that bar where we met?"

The way Tallon's intense gaze studied me made me think he read through the innocent question. "How do you know we didn't?"

"I went back," I reluctantly admitted, feeling like a damn obsessed groupie. "I wanted to see you two again. Finally, I stopped going by the bar, waiting for either of you to show up. It just made me look desperate." I pursed my lips, remembering that one bartender who told me to give up and stop pining for the two men who clearly didn't want to see me as badly as I wanted to see them again. I hated her truthful words but appreciated them just the same. I never went back after that. "I eventually stopped and moved on."

Which I guess was partially true. I moved on with someone else, a baby boy who needed all my time and attention.

Jameson ran a hand along his jaw. "Believe it or not, but three weeks ago was the first time I've seen or talked to Tallon in nearly a decade." He shifted on the couch and rested an ankle on top of his knee. The way he was leaned back gave him the perfect angle to monitor both me and Tallon. "After his sister was found, this guy vanished."

"I didn't vanish." Tallon scoffed. "I was working double time to find any evidence to identify the bastard who took my sister."

"And after?" Jameson questioned, raising a single brow.

My gaze volleyed between the two. Clearly this wasn't the first time these two had had this conversation.

Tallon shoved off the couch with a grunt and stormed to the kitchen.

"Is he always this angry?" I whispered conspiringly to Jameson.

Granted, it was a decade ago, and hot sex made everyone happier, but this Tallon in front of me seemed different. More tense and irritated than the man who lingered in my memories and sometimes met me in my dreams.

"Nowadays, yeah, but cut him some slack. You weren't the only one who got dosed up with ketamine by that fucker Vincent." A shocked gasp filled my lungs. My gaze snapped across the kitchen to Tallon's back as he fixed himself another cup of coffee. "The bastard got the drop on him at the hotel we were staying in. It's how he got his hands on his sister the second time. I don't think he's been good since, not that he was a ball of cheer before that."

"I'm fine," Tallon grumbled, and turned to face us. "Just fucking tired of evil-ass motherfuckers."

Picking off a stray hair from my zebra-striped leggings, I focused on that while admitting something I hadn't told anyone. "Well, I don't know if it's the ketamine after-effects or all the stress lately, but I'm having a hard time remembering things. Like this cup of coffee." I held it up, and their eyes narrowed on the mug. "It's clearly in my hands, but I don't remember making it or one of you handing it to me. It's happened a few times since—" I waved a hand, "—everything."

"Have you told your doctor?" Tallon asked. The near panic in his tight tone caught me off guard. Okay, what was his deal? His reactions toward me were way over the top, almost like he cared. Which made zero sense. "Or gone to the ER for a brain scan?"

Funny, I'd just asked myself that same question, yet it sounded ridiculous coming from him.

I couldn't help but snort. "You act like I have all the time in the world to go wait for a doctor to tell me I'm fine and it will just take time for me to get back to normal. I'm a working single mom. What little time I have is spent at the gym or sleeping."

"That must be tough," Jameson said quietly. "I was raised by a single mother, and I remember being so damn impressed by how she juggled everything with me and my five sisters."

"Five?" Tallon and I exclaimed at the same time.

"And I thought one was exhausting," I grumbled. "Your mom must be one amazing woman."

Pride radiated from Jameson's wide smile. "She was. Still is, to this day." His brows furrowed as he glanced around the room. "Where is your son?"

"Safe," I stated with confidence.

"How old?"

Tallon continued typing away on his phone, not paying attention to us, but Jameson arched a brow as I physically recoiled from his innocent question.

"Third grade."

If he asked me outright, right now, I wouldn't lie to them. But this was not the time or way I wanted them to find out when Crew was conceived. It made me a coward, but I wanted to kick that big revelation down the road to handle another day.

Avoidance was a beautiful thing.

"There." I turned my attention to Tallon, thankful for his interruption. "I made an appointment for you with my doctor," he stated, gaze still glued to the phone in his hands. My jaw dropped. "We'll wait for the movers, then head that way."

"You can't just—"

He just stood and walked off to pace, dismissing me.

"Jackass," I grumbled. "So damn bossy."

Jameson shot me a knowing grin. "If my memory serves me correctly, I remember you enjoying his bossy side."

All the chill from the room evaporated as hot arousal raced through my veins. A slow burn crept up my neck to my cheeks.

Gaze never leaving mine, Jameson smirked, knowing his words invoked a pleasurable response.

"We also need to discuss the living situation," Tallon said.

"Living situation?" Jameson questioned with a barked laugh. "We haven't even come up with a plan yet on how to catch this guy."

"I'm moving in less than an hour to a one-bedroom apartment. You've said before that your apartment isn't an option for whatever reasons. She has a home—"

"That would be difficult as fuck to secure with all the points of entry," Jameson countered.

"Where we can all stay," Tallon continued like Jameson hadn't spoken. "With us and the officer stationed out front, we can keep her safe."

"I don't think—" I said, but Tallon cut me off.

"Either we go to your place or we move into my new one-bedroom apartment, but I can tell you right now I'm not sleeping on the couch again. I'm too old for that shit."

Old? He didn't look old. Neither of them looked—

Oh shit. What if they're significantly younger than me? Yep, totally don't know the age of my baby's daddy. That's normal, right?

"How old are you?" I blurted. Setting my mug on the floor, I pressed two fingers to my temples and massaged the tender skin in tiny circles. Shit, what if he was one of those young guys who just looked older because of his confidence? Or an old guy who looked young because he was blessed with great skin? "This is so backward."

"Thirty-eight," Tallon answered, tone light with humor.

"Thank fuck," I groaned. When neither said anything, I peeked an eye open, finding both of them staring at me, clearly confused. "I'm thirty-nine. I was worried for a second that I'd moved into cougar status a decade ago and didn't even know it."

Jameson's full laugh rumbled throughout the apartment. The corners of Tallon's lips curved upward like he fought a smile.

"I think your house is the better scenario," Tallon stated. "It'll give Jameson and me space since we'll be working on this case 24/7 until we catch the unsub. But we can make that call after the doctor's appointment. If we need to stay in my new place for a night or two before making a final decision, that's fine." He pointed at me. "Just a heads-up. I'll be in the bed with you. Are you okay with that?"

I swallowed hard.

Was I?

In the bed. With me. Arm's distance away.

Maybe we should just go back to my place. I was already struggling with my overwhelming attraction for Tallon, but who wouldn't with his all-American blond hair, blue eyes, and a body meant for Greek gods? This could make it ten times worse. Or better.

What if I gave in to this desire? What if I just let something happen between us because I wanted him?

Bad Remington. Bad. Bad. Bad.

Sure, now I knew they didn't avoid me or not call to be dicks, but still, doing anything more than solving the case could be disastrous.

I licked my lips at the thought. Disastrous yet also lots of fun. And when was the last time I did that? The few dates I went on were terrible. The one that went decently and we went back to his place ended in disappointment. The two men in front of me set a standard for the way my body should be touched and teased.

"I'd love to know what you're thinking about."

Jameson's voice snapped me out of my head. Movement and deep voices all around the apartment had me leaping from the chair straight into his chest, where he'd been bent over me. His arms wrapped around my middle and tightened, restraining me against him. I struggled to break free as panic rushed through me.

"It's the movers," he said into my ear.

I stilled, taking a second from my freak-out moment to really look around. Several men in matching uniforms moved around with dollies, carting stacks of boxes out the door. Tallon stood beside one shorter man who held a clipboard, though his blue eyes were trained on me, and his lips dipped in a frown.

"Did the memory loss thing just happen again?" Jameson asked quietly.

Did it? Did I just forget that the movers were in the apartment, lose a minute of memory, or was I too lost in my head to have heard it?

"I... I don't know," I admitted. "You can let me go now. I'm good."

His hold immediately loosened, and I stepped away, taking in a lungful of air to calm my racing pulse. Shaking out my hands, I bent forward and grabbed the mug off the floor. Avoiding Jameson's concerned stare, I hurried through the living room to wash the mug and put it in the still-open box on the counter. When I was almost done, the sponge hung midair, the warm water still flowing from the faucet as the sensation of eyes on me froze my muscles.

Forcing myself to remain calm, I peered up through my dark lashes and scanned the room, searching for the cause of the sensation. When nothing caught my eye, the workers all focused and busy doing their jobs, I mentally shrugged off the feeling, chalking it up to my frazzled nerves.

"Do you need a stepstool to see into the sink?"

My face snapped up, finding a mover standing on the other side of the island, an unkind smile stretched across his face. There was an edge to it, and if anyone knew a conniving, manipulative grin, it was me. I'd give Jett that—all those years with him taught me exactly which red flags to catch immediately. And this smile and the degrading comment he was trying to pass off as a joke were two major red flags.

Time to nip his attention in the ass and get the asshole away from me.

"Do you need a pair of tweezers and a magnifying glass to find your dick to piss?" I layered my tone with sarcasm and fake innocence as I batted my lashes.

"Wow, defensive much?" he said, adjusting his grip on the box he was holding. "I was just trying to make conversation."

"No, you weren't," I said, not falling for that shit. Been there, done that, got the fucking scars to prove it.

"Sorry. I found you pretty, despite the way your lips are too thin." One straightforward compliment paired with a backhanded one. *Fuck, do they teach guys this shit in Assholery 101 or something?*

"If you value your life, I suggest you drop that box and get the fuck out of my apartment."

Eyes wide, I twisted to face a furious, and now very

close, Tallon. Arms crossed, face completely void of emotion, he glared at the man who had yet to move.

"Sorry, man, didn't know she was taken." The asshole shrugged and shot me a dismissive glance. "I don't like them so mouthy anyway."

Tallon rounded the island in a second, slamming his hand on the mover's shoulder. His knuckles went white with the tightening grip. The box the jackass held tumbled to the floor as he let out a yelp of pain.

"Get the fuck out. Now. You're fired."

"You can't do that." Apparently, the idiot didn't see the rage simmering behind Tallon's blue eyes. But I sure did. It should have scared me, yet the fact that it was directed at a man I knew was up to no good settled my nerves and hammering heart. Unlike with Jett, Tallon's anger wasn't focused on me—it was in defense of me.

And fucking hell, that was hot.

Sure, I could handle myself, but fuck, it was nice that someone else was stepping in to carry that burden. Now that I'd finally given in and was accepting his and Jameson's protection, I craved more of that feeling.

Of not having my guard up every second, doing every-thing on my own.

"George, you're done." The man Tallon had been speaking to before finally caught on to the seriousness of the situation and moved toward us. "Leave now."

The man—George, apparently—yanked his shoulder out of Tallon's grip. Before leaving, he shot a scathing look over his shoulder in my direction. Tallon shifted, using his body as a shield, blocking the asshole's view. When his back muscles relaxed, arms falling to his side, I knew the jackass was gone.

Jameson slid to my side and draped an arm over my

shoulders. "Tweezers and a magnifying glass, huh?" I shrugged and shot him a half smile, which he returned, but it wasn't as carefree as earlier. "This reminds me of something. I read your statement from the shed. It said you mouthed off to our unsub. Why in the hell would you do that?"

"Why not?" I offered a one-shoulder shrug and went back to rinsing off the mug before setting it on a clean towel.

Not letting me get away with that simple answer, Jameson leaned in close and raised a single brow.

I sighed. "Fine. I swore when I left my ex that I'd never take shit from a man again," I whispered so low that only he could hear me. "So I took self-defense training and grew a backbone. I've been on my own for a long time now. The only one who'll protect me from assholes like that guy is me."

"So no boyfriend?"

I huffed and crossed my arms over my vintage gray Nirvana shirt. "No, no boyfriend." Thank fuck he didn't ask about a husband or I'd have to lie to him, which, oddly enough, I really didn't want to do.

Jameson was kind. The calmer of the two men now stuck to my side until we caught the bastard.

"I want to know about the case," I stated. "I can help."

"I'm not allowed to discuss an active case."

"Just think about it. If we're going to catch this guy before anyone else gets hurt—"

"Too late." Jameson and I both turned our full attention to Tallon, who was staring at the phone tightly clutched in his hand. "They just found another body."

9

TALLON

I'd completely lost my mind.

Spending the last ten years stressed to the max, running on only a few hours of sleep on the daily, teetering on the brink of exhaustion, had finally caught up to me. There was no other reason to explain this odd mental break. Earlier in the apartment, I was close to snapping that fucker's neck, not caring about silly things like manslaughter or jail time, for not only what he said to Remy but for daring to look at her. It took every ounce of restraint to not declare her mine.

Which she wasn't.

And never would be.

The hard plastic chair slid beneath my slacks as I adjusted to find a more comfortable position, if that was even possible. Commercials for various drugs played softly in the background while the dinging of the office phone cut through indistinct murmurs of other patients in the waiting room. Though each scratch of the pen beside me was the loudest.

Every time she marked something on the new patient

paperwork, my eyes automatically slid from the phone screen to see what she'd answered. With a huff, she shifted, angling her back to block me from seeing the paper.

Cute. She thought she could stop me from snooping.

"This is ridiculous," she whispered. The bite in her tone had one corner of my lips twitching. "No, correction, you're ridiculous."

So much fire in the beautiful woman.

Fire that made me want to turn her round ass pink.

"It's necessary," I muttered, turning my attention back to the screen, though I couldn't focus on my email. "You were hurt trying to help my sister." Yep, that was the only reason for this obsessive need to ensure she was okay. "It's the least I can do."

"What about you?" she asked, shifting around until her knee touched mine.

I stared at the point of contact in amazement. "What about me?"

"Per your buddy, you were drugged too. You said you were fine, but there's no way, so what about you? Or do you not have an appointment because there isn't an overbearing ass who thought he had the right to—"

Reaching out, I gripped just above her knee, my hand engulfing her bare thigh through the gaping holes in her jeans. Her next words were cut off with a harsh gasp.

"Do you always push back when someone's trying to help you?" I muttered, eyes flicking around the small waiting room. "Because I'll be honest, I'm at a loss for why you're upset."

Her lips pursed, and green eyes flashed with clear indignation. "Because you didn't give me a choice. You booked this without my approval. I won't be controlled."

"I'm not trying to control you," I said, leaning in closer,

only a few inches between our lips. "I'm just trying to take care of you."

Her eyes narrowed into thin slits. A chuckle built in my chest as I marveled at her fight, completely unintimidated by me.

"Why?" Remy demanded. "And don't give me some bull-shit about it being because of your sister. This is beyond that."

"Is it that bad that someone wants to give you a break from looking out for yourself?"

"Dotson."

Both our heads whipped to the nurse standing with the door open. Remy cut her eyes my way, and a mischievous grin spread across her face.

"That's me," she said, standing. Clipboard in hand, she latched on to my forearm with the other. My brows rose as I glanced between her hand and face, attempting to under-stand what was going on. "Come on. If I have to do this, then so do you."

"I'm fine," I gritted out but didn't dislodge her hold.

Because I didn't want to startle her again. Yeah, that was it. It had nothing to do with the fact that I loved her hands on me, even if it was through my clothes.

"Then so am I." She smirked and turned to the nurse, who looked confused as hell. "Thank you, but this was a mistake." The clipboard smacked against my lap, and she started for the door. "I'll just get an Uber and head home."

Fucking hell, this woman.

I wanted to be pissed at her stubbornness, but I fought a grin instead. She knew she had me by the balls. If I wanted to sate this need to ensure she was okay, then I had to do as she said in return.

Smart, conniving, brilliant woman.

Keeping my movement slow, I grasped her wrist, halting her exit.

"Fine," I said, forcing exasperation into my voice, and jutted out the clipboard for her to take. In reality, I fucking loved it. I hadn't been this challenged by a woman in years. Her defiance of not doing exactly what I told her was sexy as hell. I craved control, but her fighting it? Well, it shouldn't have been as much of a turn-on as it was.

The nurse looked at us. "Are you family—"

"Dr. Richards won't mind," I said with a calm smile, which the nurse returned. "This is a unique visit."

"Okay, uh, yeah, sure," she stammered, not looking away from me. When she didn't move, I raised both brows in question to the delay, which had her cheeks flushing red. "Right, sorry."

Turning, she led us down the long hall, passing doors for the exam rooms and offices on each side. There really wasn't an appointment slot to fit Remy into, but he made room for her after I texted him directly.

The first few years of my life were a living hell until Mom left my father and married Rich. Which was how I even had a doctor's number on speed dial. Dr. Richards was golfing buddies with my stepfather and had been our go-to doctor for years.

Without thinking, I guided Remy into the exam room the nurse directed us toward with a hand hovering against her lower back. She stiffened at first, apparently unused to the contact or just pissed I had once again taken control.

Remy handed the nurse the clipboard with her paperwork and took a seat in the lone chair instead of on the exam table. She crossed her arms with a defiant look, but all I could focus on was how the move shoved her full tits upward, exposing more cleavage in her white V-neck tee.

Fucking hell.

"I'll let Dr. Richards know you're here. It might be a while. Make yourselves comfortable."

The door closed with a soft click, leaving us alone.

With the toe of my tennis shoe, I wheeled the small stool closer and lowered myself to the cushioned seat, unable to keep my groan quiet. Leaning back, I rested my head against the wall and closed my eyes.

If I could think of anything other than fucking those tits, that would be fucking amazing right now.

"Are you sore from sleeping on the couch or muscle fatigue from the ketamine?"

I peeked a single eye open before shutting it again. "Both, maybe. Though it could have something to do with not sleeping since I got back from LA."

"What was in LA?" she questioned.

"This case. For almost two years, I've hunted this unsub. He's left bodies all over the country. Every time we've gotten close, we find out he's already somewhere else doing the same damn thing."

"The one who did this to us?"

At the uncertainty in her tone, I blinked both lids open and sat forward, digging my elbows into the tops of my thighs.

"We didn't know it was partners, two sick bastards. The one who orchestrated it all, the technical one who had an obsession with my sister, is no longer a concern. As a team, they were setting up live video feeds, auctioning off punishments and other depraved shit, ending with the one we're still after killing them on a live stream."

"What the hell?" she whispered, eyes wide. "They were making snuff films?"

I nodded and hung my head, rubbing a palm over my

short blond hair. "They've killed dozens of women over the last several years. But we found out the unsub we're after—" I cut myself off and cracked my knuckles. "Sorry, I forget you're not an agent or familiar with all this lingo. An unsub is—"

"I watch TV," she cut in with a lift to her tone. Peeking up, I found her grinning at the wall. "Crime shows, documentaries, things like that are my favorite. So I might not be a super-cool agent or detective, but I'm sure I can keep up."

I nodded, unable to look away from her. That small smile transformed her face. It was as if all the stresses of her life were gone, making her radiate. Fuck, she was beautiful.

"Then why did you refuse our help?" I asked.

She swallowed and ran her hands down the sides of her jean-clad thighs. "This isn't a TV show."

"Yeah, it's worse. It's real life."

"I just couldn't," she whispered. "Please respect that." Those jade-green eyes met mine, soft for once, not filled with animosity or defiance. "I know it wasn't smart, but I'm here now. At the first hint of me really being in trouble, I knew I couldn't protect myself."

And she came to me. My chest puffed out a little with the swelling pride.

She knew she was safe with me.

Gazes locked, I couldn't look away from the vulnerability pouring off her. It would be easy to agree with her, tell her it was a dumb move for rejecting our help in the first place, and make her feel worse in a moment where she was opening up. But I knew that would be a mistake.

"Was it because of our past?" I asked. Her dark hair swished with the dip of her chin. "Why?" I questioned, a tinge of desperation in my tone. A seed of doubt had grown into throbbing guilt since she'd reentered my life. What if I was the asshole who hurt her, who made her flinch at every sudden move? "Was it something we did? Did we hurt you—"

Her head fell forward. "Nothing like that. I mean, yeah, I was disappointed when you didn't call, and that morphed into heartache at the rejection. But that faded. It was... it is something else."

She wrapped her arms around her waist. With her head still dipped, avoiding my gaze, I rolled the chair forward. Two fingers pressed beneath her chin, I forced her face up until sad eyes met mine.

"I'm sorry it worked out the way it did," I mumbled, inching even closer. "My life imploded the moment I got the call about Tinley being missing. Nothing was the same after. Though...." I bit my lower lip as I debated telling her about my effort to find her. Her gaze flicked down to my lips, the tip of her tongue slipping out to glide along hers. "I tried to find you too."

It was almost comical how wide her eyes went. "What?"

I nodded. "Though it was impossible with just a first name." I chuckled. "Which turned out to not even be your real name."

"Why?"

"You ask that a lot," I commented, smiling like a fool. "Curious little thing, aren't you?" Heat flashed behind her gaze, igniting the ever-present urge to press my lips to hers, to make her mine. "And hell if I know why I tried finding you. That night is ingrained in my memory as the last night of normalcy before everything went to shit. Maybe that's why."

"What about Jameson?" she asked.

Jealousy roared in my gut, even if it was unfounded and

Remy wasn't mine to be jealous over. I ground my teeth, jaw clenched tight. "What about him?"

"Did you try to reach out to him? It sounded like you two hadn't seen each other in a while."

"No, I left that part of my life behind."

A small smile curled the edges of her mouth, and I knew what single word was about to come out of her irresistible lips. "Why?"

"Long story."

That smile grew. "Why?"

"I don't remember you being this inquisitive."

The corners of her eyes crinkled, and her cheeks bunched. "Pretty sure we did little talking to find out much about each other."

Not fighting the pull, I leaned in even closer, our lips almost brushing. "I know what makes you scream." A soft breath escaped her parted lips. "I remember you are much more compliant with the right incentive." Her throat worked with a hard swallow. Putting my lips by her ear, I inhaled deep. "No amount of time could pass for me to forget the memory of you begging for more."

This was dangerous. The line between business and personal was quickly vanishing, just like my restraint.

Never had I muddled in this gray area. Struggled with my control with a woman. Yet she was making me wish I wasn't the agent assigned to the case, that I was just a man who could act on the dirty shit playing out in my fucked-up mind.

But I wasn't.

She needed me to pull back to keep her safe. I couldn't protect her if I was balls deep, her legs wrapped around my neck and my hand around her throat. Squeezing my eyes shut, I shoved against the tile floor, sending me rolling until my back hit the far wall. Peeling my lids open, I focused my blurry vision on her.

With her hands clutching the thin metal arms of the chair, cheeks flushed, eyes glassy, I knew she was affected by my words. Hell, if she looked lower, she'd see the obvious bulge pressing against the zipper of my slacks, proving I was just as turned on as she was.

We were playing with fire.

Though with each second around her, I found myself not caring if I got burned.

Because for the first time in years, I wanted something other than to close a case.

I wanted her.

10

REMINGTON

I bit into the meat lover's pizza that just arrived at Tallon's new apartment, where we'd stay for the night until we figured out a better option. After the appointment, we headed here instead of the crime scene to meet up with Jameson. Tallon said technically he should be there on-site as the lead agent, but didn't want to leave me alone or take me with him. Thankfully with the crime scene being in Jameson's jurisdiction, him going with an agent from Tallon's team was sufficient. He was still there and would probably be till late in the night. And while Tallon was busy unpacking what he called necessities, I sat here on the couch after being ordered to eat and relax. Which gave me time to contemplate the results of the doctor's visit earlier in the day.

Dr. Richards was a sweet older man who instantly put me at ease with his comforting demeanor and easily wrinkled grin. After an hour of talking about symptoms and causes, he said exactly what I knew he would after googling how to resolve my random short-term memory loss.

Time.

Time and no stress.

When he told me that with a straight face, I couldn't hold back a snort.

A deranged psychopath wanted me. Pretty sure nothing in my life would be relaxing until they caught the fucker. Though the doctor said the same thing about Tallon's fatigue and trembles after, I forced the stubborn ass to admit he was suffering aftereffects of the drug too.

Stubborn hot ass.

With a great ass.

This was fucking confusing.

The ghost of his lips against mine, the tremble of his finger beneath my chin as he held me exactly where he wanted me, and the flood of heat that engulfed my lower belly were memories I couldn't shake even now, hours later.

The way his jeans hung off his trim waist and hugged his firm backside and thick thighs should have been illegal. This attraction had nothing to do with what happened between us before. This was sheer desire, lust for a man who I not only found hot as hell but felt taken care of around. It wasn't just about the protection and obsession with my safety; it was him putting my needs first too. What man would've made an appointment for some woman they barely knew?

Tallon Harper, that was who.

I wanted that protection, wanted someone to take care of me, to put me first like I did everyone. And that radiated off Tallon. Mix that with his hard body, come-hither blue eyes, and deep, commanding tone, and it would be a shock if I lasted twenty-four hours without wrapping my legs around his waist and hanging on like a baby sloth.

I shook my head and leaned back against the couch. Rolling my head along the back to follow his loud footsteps,

I studied him as he emerged from the bedroom. There was no doubt he was better-looking than I remembered. The man had aged well and took good care of himself. Most of the men I was surrounded by all strutted their dad bods around the office, which did nothing to draw my attention.

No, thank you.

Nothing wrong with it, but it just wasn't for me. I took great pride in working out, staying fit, and wanted to be with someone who felt the same. With my short stature and naturally wider physique, I had to work hard if I wanted to keep my hourglass figure. The type of workouts I did, kick-boxing and high-level self-defense, killed two birds with one stone—helped my confidence and kept me in shape.

At least some of the tension between us three was diminishing fast as we spent more time together. Even being around Tallon, knowing I was holding a big, life-changing secret from him, felt easier. He admitted he didn't want kids, which hurt to hear at the time, but now after a decent night's sleep, I was settled about his revelation.

Though I still needed to learn more about him—and not just if his cock had aged well too—before revealing my big secret. My protective mama bear instincts kept me from telling him now, not until I knew if he was a good man or not. He could claim he didn't want kids all day long, but that could change the moment he found out about his unknown son. So first, I had to make sure he was worthy of being a part of our amazing son's life.

If he wasn't, then after all this was said and done, I would go back to doing it all on my own with Tallon none the wiser. My heart ached at that thought. Reaching up, I pressed the heel of my hand to my sternum and rubbed tiny circles to dispel the pain.

"What's wrong?" Tallon's hand hovered over the closed

pizza box, his light brows furrowed as he studied me. "What do you need? I unpacked the medicine if you need something."

There was no stopping the small smile creeping up my cheeks. Seriously, how could he go from bossy and dominant to sweet and concerned? Was this the same man who forced me to the doctor earlier? Though I figured all the traits really fed off each other. But where did this need to protect come from?

"Yeah, just thinking."

"About?"

Taking a bite of pizza, I studied him, debating on what to say. I could easily brush his concern off, but I didn't want to. This was the first time since he'd reentered my life that we had a chance to talk without tension simmering between us, which seemed to make me defensive and occasionally horny.

"How despite it all—the ketamine after-effects and, you know, the madman after me—I'm enjoying this break."

His features softened. Nodding, he flipped open the pizza box and pulled four pieces onto his awaiting plate. "It's funny. I was thinking the same thing. I'm always surrounded by other agents. I can never let my guard down since I'm their lead. But with you and Jameson, I can do this."

"I can't tell you if I've ever called in sick to work." Guilt built in my chest remembering the call I made this morning to the office telling them I wouldn't be in—again. I called after I kneed Tallon in the balls. I internally winced in embarrassment remembering his pitiful yelp. "And now I've done it several days in the last few weeks. But I can't say I'm not enjoying my day off. Even my vacation days are spent filled with my son, Crew. On those rare days I have off with him, I cram in way too much, hoping to make up for all the times he's with a sitter or waiting at school."

Blond brows pulled together, a look of confusion pinched his features as he chewed. "Why?"

"Mom guilt, maybe?"

"What's mom guilt?"

Careful to keep the three uneaten pizza crusts on top, I tossed the empty paper plate to the coffee table. After wiping the grease off my fingertips, I lobbed the dirty paper towel on top and shifted to a more comfortable position on the couch. Folding one leg over the other, I sat facing where he was on the opposite end.

"Mom guilt is this all-consuming feeling that you're doing it all wrong, or you're not doing enough. I feel guilty working as much as I do, but I have to for us to survive. That means when I am home, I basically suffocate him, thinking if I can cram as much time together as possible, hopefully I'll be a good enough mom for him. Every decision I make, I wonder if it was the right one."

"That sounds terrible," Tallon grumbled. "And relatable." Not saying anything more, he took a large bite and avoided my gaze.

Ignoring that odd comment, I continued. "The guilt of, well, everything follows me to bed," I admit. "It's why I don't sleep well, even though I'm exhausted. I never feel like I'm enough. I wish I could shut it off, but it's just me, you know? Like now, for instance. I know Crew is safe in Texas, right, but I feel guilty that I had to do it, and honestly, I feel guilty about the fact that I'm enjoying myself."

"The not feeling like you're enough, that guilt I understand, but the feeling like you should feel guilty for enjoying yourself, now *that* I'm confused about. Why would you feel bad about being here when your son is there, safe?" Tallon questioned. The way his features pinched in concentration like he was trying to unravel the complexity of mom guilt made him look years younger—cute, even.

"Don't give yourself a headache trying to figure it out. It's just a mom thing. Maybe it's only a working mom thing, but I don't think it is. We all feel this need to give our kids the best and always feel like we're lacking."

Studying the pizza boxes, he tapped the end of the crust in his hand against the plate. "I think the fact that you're worried about it shows you're not lacking or failing. If you didn't care at all, *that* would be the problem, but you're the opposite. Don't be too hard on yourself." His gaze shifted and turned distant. "My mom never put me and Tinley first. I wonder how things would've turned out if she would've. Seeing you, hearing the way you talk about your son and this mom guilt phenomenon makes me realize just how selfish she was, even before Tinley was born."

"No mom is perfect," I offered, "but I'm trying. Though it gets lonely. I can't even make friends at work because I don't have time to see them on the weekends or even for a midweek happy hour."

"My mom stayed with my father even though...." Dropping his head, he gave it a hard shake.

Unable to stop myself, I twisted along the couch and crawled to where he sat. Not waiting for an invitation and praying he didn't shove me away, I snuggled against his side and gripped his bicep, giving it a comforting squeeze.

Sadness leaked from his eyes when they flicked to me. "Nothing was ever good enough for him. I tried everything to be perfect, to make good grades, be good at all the sports he expected me to excel in, but I always, *always* fell short of those expectations. But because my mother was getting what she wanted, she turned a blind eye, not caring that I broke a little more under his thumb. She only gave two shits about the designer handbags and clothes. It probably would've stayed that way if Tinley hadn't come along."

My heart broke for Tallon. Using my head, I wiggled between his arm and side, forcing him to raise his arm and wrap it around my shoulders. Shock and confusion flashed across his features before settling into a shy smile.

"I'm sorry that happened, Tallon. Your mom sounds terrible."

He tossed his head back with a barked laugh. The sound sent vibrations through my ear, making my stomach flip.

"You're right on that. She was—hell, *is* a terrible person." The muscle along his jaw twitched. "It's why I got Tinley out when I could. After she was born, I thought Mom would finally stop being so damn selfish and get us out of that house, but she didn't."

"What happened?" I whispered, snaking my arm around his waist. How I felt comfortable enough to be this touchy, I had no damn clue. But I knew he needed it. Hell, maybe so did I. The warmth radiating off him soothed some of the jagged edges loneliness sharpened through the years. Hell, I felt like I could breathe easier this close to him, felt free even with the weight of his arm pressing down on me. It wasn't confining like a cage, more like the first breath of fresh air I'd taken in years.

Nothing could hurt me here by his side.

He wouldn't allow it.

"I was twelve when I realized Mom wouldn't do anything to protect us." Tears built in my lower lids, threatening to spill over. "Instead of going to school one day, I told my mother I was sick and needed to stay home. She, of course, still had lunch with her fake friends and a shopping trip to make, so she left, leaving me home alone with Tin." A harsh chuckle shifted my position on his chest. "It took me an hour to figure out how to get that damn baby carrier strapped on."

"I was an adult, and it took me two," I said, offering him a watery smile. "So props to kiddo Tallon."

Something like awe washed over his features as he stared down at me. "I haven't talked about this ever." His gaze flicked over me as if searching my face for something. "What are you doing to me?"

"Nothing you're not doing in return," I admitted. I gently jabbed my shoulder into his side. "You got the crazy contraption on to carry your sister and then what?"

"I jumped on my bike and rode to the police station."

"With a baby?" I exclaimed as I pressed a hand to his stomach, the muscles tensing beneath my palm. "That's impressive."

His smile grew. "I bet we were a sight. The tiny thing kept wiggling and messing with my balance. I remember sweating through my shirt from the nerves of what I was doing and being afraid we were going to crash. But I also remember her laughing. I don't think I'll ever forget the sound of her giggle."

I sighed and relaxed back against him.

"You were just a kid yourself," I mused, "yet you were taking care of your sister."

"I couldn't stand by and let her grow up the way I did. She didn't deserve that."

My hand tightened into a fist, pulling the fabric of his shirt between my fingers. "Neither did you."

"At the station, I talked to a female officer who, thank fuck, believed me. She asked if there were any family members we could call. That afternoon, my mom's parents showed up, piled us in the back of their station wagon, and took us to their trailer. They were good people, not rich by any means, but good, loving people, so I knew we'd be safe. They arrested my father for child abuse, but they dropped the charges for neglect on my mom because she agreed to divorce him. We stayed with my grandparents for about a year before Mom met someone else who could support her lifestyle, and then we moved in with her new husband."

I wasn't sure what to say after that. A part of me wanted to tell him about my childhood too. How there wasn't abuse to me but zero warmth just the same. But that would start a conversation I couldn't finish without jeopardizing everything I'd built over the last eleven years. Maybe if it was just me, I could risk opening up about that part of my past, but I had Crew to worry about too.

"Does Tinley know?" I asked.

Tallon sighed and adjusted along the couch, leaning back and pulling me tighter against him.

And it felt right.

More than right. It felt like home.

My heart thumped in my chest at that realization. This was bad. I'd only been around him twenty-four hours and was already slipping into emotions I hadn't felt in decades. Was it because this was so right or because I'd been lonely so long?

Did this make me desperate the way I was clinging to him now, lingering on his every word as he opened up about his past, relishing his strength? Maybe it did, but I was so damn tired. Tired of wanting someone to hold me, to tell me everything was going to be okay, to just be there.

Damnit. The need for that CAT scan for these swinging emotions was moving up the priority list.

"No, she doesn't remember any of it. I thought I was protecting her, but I recently learned some shit that made me realize I'd just taken her from one dangerous situation to another." The hand on his thigh curled into a fist, his frustration clear.

"You didn't know, and again, you were just a kid yourself. You can't blame yourself for other people's actions."

"I wasn't there for her when she needed me most," he rasped.

"You can't be everywhere at once." Pushing to sit on my knees, I grabbed his shoulders and gave him a small shake. "Does she blame you?" He shook his head. I released a small breath. *Good. I really didn't want to kick her ass.* "So why are you?"

"Why do you have that odd mom guilt?" he questioned.

I shrugged. "Because it just comes with the job, I guess?"

"Can you do anything to make it stop? Can you rationalize it to make moving forward easier?"

"Well, no."

"It's the same for me. I know I can't be everywhere, protect everyone, but I still feel guilty when I can't. It's even worse when it's someone I love. So even if she doesn't blame me, I'll never stop blaming myself for being distracted."

I swallowed and sat back on my heels. I got it. I really did. It made little sense, but why did I feel guilty for working when I knew it was to make a better life for Crew? Guilt didn't have to make sense to be there. You couldn't rationalize it, couldn't move past it even though it made little sense to anyone else. It was deep seated, pushing its roots into your mind and every thought, never letting you forget all the places you were failing.

"It's exhausting," I whispered.

He huffed. "Life?"

I grinned. "Exactly."

Reaching forward, he grabbed another slice of pizza

from the box. "How are you feeling? The doctor said you needed to relax. Not sure if this conversation is helping."

Scooting back down the couch, I rested my head on the opposite arm, the tips of my toes barely grazing his thigh. "Although I don't remember this pizza arriving," I said, wincing when he shot me a hard look, "I'm fine. Like he said, it'll take time, just like your shakes."

"You go get ready for bed. I'll clean up in here."

"It's nine," I exclaimed, acting like he was crazy even though nine was my normal bedtime when I wasn't being chased by a killer and eating pizza with a hottie from my past.

"Go."

I arched a challenging brow and placed my interlaced fingers on my stomach, proving I had zero plans to go anywhere. "I'm not sleepy."

"But you need your rest to get better," he stated. "So it's time for bed."

"No." I laughed. "I'm not a kid you can—" My next words were cut off when he shoved off the couch and shifted to stand over me. "Tallon," I warned.

A cruel grin pulled at his lips. "This can either go the easy way or the hard way."

My breath hitched. I should not want the hard way, but fuck, I so did.

"You can't make me go to bed."

Bending forward, he slipped one of his arms beneath my shoulders and hooked the other beneath my knees. He grunted and I shrieked as I was hauled into the air. My cheeks burned from my wide smile. A giggle I hadn't heard in years erupted from my mouth, tickling me from the inside out.

I was pressed hard against his chest as Tallon carried me

to the single bedroom. Then I was airborne. My arms waved and legs kicked as I sailed toward the already made bed. With an "Oof," I hit the center of the mattress. Shoving my loose hair away from my face, I shot him a playful glare.

Crossing his arms like the badass he was, Tallon stared down from the end of the bed. "Now be a good girl and stay there while I clean up. I'll come in when I'm done, and we can watch something."

My core clenched. I so didn't want to be a good girl.

He made me want to be bad.

And because I was so damn horny, my panties drenched, I wanted to push him.

"And if I don't stay in here? What if I'm not a good girl?" My words were barely audible as I panted beneath his heated stare.

"Bad girls get punished," he stated. I almost thought I was imagining this tension between us, but the growing bulge within his dark jeans told me it wasn't just me. "Hmm." At the sound, I dragged my gaze away from his crotch and back up to those striking blue eyes. "I think you like the idea of that."

My heart dropped when he turned and headed for the living room, leaving me hot, wet, and desperate. Tears from his rejection welled.

Fuck, what is going on with me? I was never this desperate woman, yet here I was, almost on the verge of begging for him.

He paused at the doorway, still facing the living room. "I won't be responsible for someone getting hurt again. I don't trust myself to give in to what I want and still keep you safe."

Heart in my throat, I shook my head. *Damn him.*

"Tallon," I croaked and waited for him to turn, giving me his full attention. "I do."

"It's not that simple," he gritted out.

"It is," I offered. I knew it was his trauma talking, from his childhood and even in the recent years with his sister. It made me sad for him, knowing he held himself back because he was scared. Breaking his glare, I turned on the bed, putting my back to him. "Go do what you need to do. I'm going to take a shower. But just so you know, Tallon, I'm not your sister. I'm not a woman who needs protecting from the world. I know you wouldn't do anything to put me in danger. And if I can trust that after everything I've been through, well, then I think you should cut yourself some slack and trust in yourself too."

11

TALLON

Pacing the length of the living room, I cursed under my breath at the smaller square footage that forced me to turn twice as much as my old place. Every turn somehow seemed to draw me closer to the closed bedroom door.

"I do."

Those two words ran on a loop, stamping my brain like a brand.

She trusted me. Despite her past, she trusted me. I wasn't sure how, but I didn't question it, too afraid she'd realize she shouldn't. Not that I would hurt her on purpose; I just seemed to hurt those close to me unintentionally.

When I took Tin away from our father, I thought I did right by her. Instead, I put her in a home where she was abused, mistreated and ignored by my mother, and, even worse, forced to stay silent. Then I hurt Jameson and Remy when I left them behind to help Tinley and others.

The thought of unintentionally hurting Remy caused my stomach to roll. I wouldn't be able to live with myself if something happened to her because of me, leaving her son alone in the world without his amazing mother.

But I also couldn't keep living like this.

Alone.

Exhausted.

Vacant.

Though—I inhaled deep, relishing the lack of tightness in my chest—sharing my childhood story had shifted something deep inside my soul. Each breath came a little easier than it had yesterday. Maybe Tinley wasn't that off base, suggesting I talk to someone. If just exposing that sliver of my past had me feeling this much better, what would I feel like if I unloaded all the baggage from my life?

Maybe then I could get a full night's sleep.

Sliding my phone from the back pocket of my jeans, I studied the device, debating whether to call my sister for advice, before swiping it open. Hitting Tinley's number, I pressed the phone to my ear and made my way to the couch.

"Hey, Tal," she answered after a few rings. "Everything okay?"

I collapsed onto the stiff leather cushion and rubbed at my eyes, pressing my finger and thumb over the closed lids. "Depends on your version of okay."

"You're not dead or dying, right?" she questioned.

"Correct, not dead or dying. So if that's your litmus test for okay, then yeah, I'm okay, Tin. I just... I need to talk to someone."

"Is this about Remy or FBI stuff? Because if I'm being honest, I've had enough of that shit recently. I'll happily pass the phone over to Bryson if that's the case."

"The first," I said drily. "I don't know what to do about... everything."

"Hmm, okay. We'll let's start with identifying the problem. Then we'll work our way toward a solution from there. Just give me a second to get some clothes on—"

I groaned, my stomach turning. "Do not say that shit to me. I'm your brother."

"And I'm in love with your best friend, who has a monster—"

"I will hang up this phone right the fuck now if you mention his dick, Tinley."

"Fine." She sighed. Bryson's rumbled laugh sounded somewhere in the distance. Knowing he was close eased some of the worry I had for her. Worry I'd always have for my kid sister. "Okay, tell me the problem."

My mouth opened, but nothing came out. How could I describe what I felt, the internal debate constantly warring in my mind?

Clearly sensing my dilemma, her laugh tickled through the phone. "Fine, let's start simple. Do you like her?"

"Well, yeah. That's part of the problem."

"Are you attracted to her?"

"Of course. You saw her."

"Yeah, she's hot. And those tattoos? She might be more woman than you can handle. But I digress. Do you want to fuck her?"

I cringed, pressing back into the cushions like they could swallow me whole to prevent this conversation from going further.

I didn't think this through before calling. Could I really have this kind of conversation with my little sister? She was very open about her sex life, whereas I'd grown used to keeping that side of my life hidden.

"Yes, and that's the problem," I stated.

"Because she realizes you have a stick the size of Texas shoved up your ass and a wall thicker than the one around China to protect you from all those big bad feelings out in the world?"

"What the fuck?" I barked, half laughing, half shocked. "Where the hell do you come up with the shit you say? She wants me, too, I can tell, but I'm afraid... and I don't want to get close. What if I let my guard down and Remy gets hurt? How can I be that selfish to put what I want above her safety? To give in to whatever this is knowing it could get her killed?"

"Oh, Tal," Tinley whispered, the disappointment and pain clear. "Listen, I'm going to tell you something, and it will hurt hearing the truth. You ready?" I sat up straight, spine locked, prepared for the worst. "You're not in control of what happens."

I held a tight breath. It burned in my lungs as I processed Tinley's statement.

"I—"

"I'm not done," she snapped. "You cannot alter the future by trying to control everything and everyone around you. It doesn't work that way, big brother. Where you were, who you were with that night, was not why I was taken. Do you hear me? I know you're still dealing with the trauma from all of that and, like a damn idiot, won't get help. You think if you shift your focus from work, someone close to you will fall victim to something terrible. It doesn't work that way, Tal. You living your life doesn't mean something will happen."

I shook my head and ran a hand over my short hair, tugging the ends. "But she's in danger. This time I know the threat and can prepare—"

"Are your doors locked?"

"Of course," I huffed.

"Gun loaded?"

"Yeah. I *am* an agent."

"Both of them?"

"All three, yes," I said with a grin.

"So what else is there to do, Tal? You plan to stare at the door all night to make sure no one comes in? Do you realize how neurotic that sounds? You're doing everything to keep her and you safe. *Everything*. That's all you can do."

"I don't know how to let go," I mumbled.

"Do you know what I'm afraid of, Tal?" Shoving off the couch, I began pacing again. Instead of going from one side of the apartment to the other, I circled the new glass-top breakfast table and chair set that was delivered earlier, checking it for scratches while she continued. "That even though I was taken, you're the one who won't survive." I paused, brows furrowing. "I'm moving on, Tallon. I've *moved* on. I'm doing everything I can to not dwell on what happened. I'm able to love and be loved. Why can't you? Don't let your past keep you from having a future."

"What if something happens?" I rasped. "What if something happens to her because I gave in to what I wanted?"

"And what happens if she's completely fine and walks away without you two knowing if this attraction between you could've been more than a one-night stand ten years ago?"

Falling against the wall, I rested my head back and closed my eyes.

Was she right?

"You're allowed to have a life, Tal. You can do your job, keep her safe, and explore whatever this is between you two. Though I would suggest to stay away from anything revolving around you being tied up. That would prevent you from jumping to action if something were to happen."

"I really, *really* don't want to know where you come up with this shit," I grumbled.

"Porn."

"Fucking hell."

"Though, knowing you, I'd bet my left kidney that you like to be the one doing the tying, not being tied down."

"I'm hanging up now."

"Not sure why you're embarrassed. I love being hand—"

Before her words could taint any more of my mind, I pulled the phone from my ear and hit the End button. I huffed a laugh, knowing my sister was probably cackling right now. Good. She deserved to laugh, even if it was at my expense.

My hand vibrated with an incoming call from Jameson. Swiping my thumb over the screen, I pressed the warm glass to my ear.

"Harper."

"You sound like shit."

I groaned. "Everyone is a critic these days. What did you find out from the scene?"

"It's gory as hell. The level of torture kicked up with this one. I'm going to the station to wait for the ME report. I probably won't see you two until tomorrow sometime. I'll go to my place to clean up before heading over."

"Keep your eyes open when you're alone. I don't want this bastard grabbing you and using you to get to her."

"You're worse than my mother with all your worrying," Jameson stated.

"It's called being cautious."

"Worrywart. How's Remy?"

I opened my mouth, but no words came out. How did I describe the absolute shit show I made of the night by walking away from her?

"Spit it out, Tallon. What did you do?"

"Nothing. That's the problem." I sighed. "I just can't let go of this feeling that if I give in, if I have her like I want, that something will go wrong. That she'll get hurt, or tomorrow I'll wake up and someone will have gotten hurt because I let my guard down."

"Someone will, Tallon." I sucked in a breath, but he kept going. "Because people are hurt and get hurt all the fucking time, and it has nothing to do with you. You can't control every outcome by denying yourself what you want."

I was so fucked in the head. I knew what Tinley and my friend said was true, yet I couldn't shake the fear coating me in a thin, icy sheen. Maybe I wasn't good enough for anyone, too messed up from life to offer anyone more than a single night. Maybe I was destined to be alone, to be the one who watched out for everyone from the shadows, never being seen or living.

"I'll see you tomorrow," I said.

"Fuck, you're stubborn. Fine, waste your life being scared. Just don't come calling me when you're old and your balls are all fucking saggy, looking for a wingman to help you get laid because you realize you've missed out on living."

"Wow." I chuckled. "That's oddly descriptive. Why are you thinking about my balls?"

"Don't flatter yourself," he said, a lightness in his tone that wasn't there just moments ago. "Just remember, nothing bad will happen if you let yourself go. That's PTSD or some shit talking, not reality. See you tomorrow."

After ending the call, I slipped the phone back into my pocket, gaze locked on the bedroom door.

Were they right? Could I be myself, let go, and someone not be hurt in the aftermath? Was this fear that someone I loved would get hurt if I actually lived my life a form of PTSD from ten years ago? Hell, maybe it went further back than that. Maybe it went back to my childhood.

Tinley was safe with Bryson, Jameson was at the station, Mom was... well, I didn't really give a fuck about her. She was the one who fucked my head up, who made me ashamed of how I lived.

If all the people I cared about were safe, could I dare to let go?

Did I even remember how to?

How to let go, not how to fuck. It wasn't as if I'd been celibate since that night. One or two times a year wasn't anything to brag about, of course, but I sure as hell remembered how to do it.

The vision of Remy defying me, pushing back on my control, resulting in delivering punishment that mixed pleasure and pain had a groan catching in my throat. Hopefully she'd be as challenging beneath me as she was fully clothed.

But could I do it?

"Tallon!"

My name shouted from the other room sent panic and adrenaline racing through my veins. Rushing to the door, I flung it open, the knob banging into the opposite wall.

Remy jolted on the bed beneath the covers, wide eyes jumping from my face to the gun tightly clasped between my hands.

Sweeping the room, I scanned the shadows for the cause of her calling out. "What's wrong?"

"What?" she shrieked, tone almost angry, though the shake in her voice gave away her nerves.

After holstering my gun, I stalked to the side of the bed and cupped her face between both hands. "Are you hurt?" My right hand slipped lower, wrapping around the side of her throat, searching for injuries.

"Huh?" The shock and fear drained from her features, leaving confusion. "You're the one who stormed in here guns blazing like there was a drenched gremlin hot on your heels."

My mind blanked.

Did she just say "drenched gremlin"?

Fucking hell, this woman.

Both eyes squeezed shut, I tipped my face to the ceiling. "You yelled my name. How else was I supposed to react?"

"That didn't mean you needed to run in here armed. Fuck, you could've shot me."

I narrowed my eyes, nostrils flaring with each ragged breath. "I wouldn't have shot you. You think I'm some rookie cop?"

"No, but fuck, you scared me to death. And I yelled because the bedroom door was closed. I wanted to get your attention, not because I was being diced up by a serial killer."

"Not funny," I growled.

The hold I had on her neck shifted until it covered the front of her throat. Shock, then something red hot pulsed behind her green eyes when I squeezed, applying the slightest amount of pressure.

Fucking hell.

My demanding cock pressed against the zipper of my jeans, throbbing almost painfully beneath the stiff material.

"You're acting insane," Remy rasped. She swallowed, the movement making her throat work beneath my palm. She swiped the tip of her pink tongue along her lower lip, trans-fixing me with the sensual movement.

I was a fool. A fool to think I could resist this, whatever the hell this was between us. It would be like denying myself oxygen, thinking I'd be fine.

Forgetting about my past, the threat after her, and my role as an agent, I lunged forward, slamming my lips to hers.

There was nothing gentle as I devoured her mouth, forcing those lush lips open with my tongue, demanding she take everything I was giving.

An almost pain-filled moan left her lips, followed by both her hands gripping the back of my neck, forcing us closer. My hold tightened around her neck in a small warning.

"Hands back on the bed, Kitten. There is no topping from the bottom with me. Understood?" There was nothing soft about my smile as I drew back, searching her face for any signs of hesitation, that maybe this was more than she bargained for.

And thank fuck I found none.

"Controlling much?" she sassed, eyebrows raised. Though the glassy sheen over her eyes, the red staining her cheeks, and the rapid pulse hammering beneath my palm signaled she liked my bossy ass despite her tone.

With a tsk, I nipped her bottom lip hard. Her surprised yelp rang in my ears, turning into a moaned curse when I sucked it between my own lips, soothing the hurt away.

"You have no fucking idea just how bossy I can be, Kitten," I rumbled into her ear.

"Oh, I remember," she said. Her quick breaths fanned along my sweat-slick neck. Thumb beneath her chin, I forced her head back, the long column of her neck arching. "I remember everything."

I couldn't hold myself back any longer.

This was happening.

We were inevitable.

Fuck the case, my job, and all my fucking baggage.

I craved this beautiful woman, and clearly she wanted me too. That was all that mattered.

Releasing her throat, I shoved both hands beneath her

arms and lifted her as I stood to full height. Instantly, her muscular legs wrapped around my waist, squeezing so tight I couldn't take a full breath. Heels digging into my ass, she sealed her panty-covered pussy over my hard cock and ground down, rubbing herself against my jeans.

"Fuck," I rasped along her lips. The loud smack from the spank I inflicted on her ass sounded through the bedroom, followed by her gasp. "I'm in control. Don't forget that."

Turning on my bare heels, I strode to the wall of windows, not stopping until her back hit the tinted pane. Grinding my lower half against hers, I swiveled my hips. A sharp hiss escaped through her clenched teeth. I licked my lips, studying the way the extra-large T-shirt she wore bunched around her waist, exposing the thin pink material of her sheer panties. Heat poured from her wet pussy as she continued to grind against me, desperate for friction.

My lips slid along her neck as I sucked and kissed, lingering longer on the spots that had her cursing in my ear. Her movements turned frantic as she chased her release. Restraint thinning, I ripped my lips away from her and pressed my forehead against the window, cooling my over-heated skin as I poured all my focus on not coming in my fucking jeans like a two-pump chump—which I most certainly was not.

A desperate whimper cut through our labored breaths.

"Tallon," she moaned, her body trembling as she let go. "Fuck yes."

With her eyes squeezed shut and face tipped to the ceiling, I smirked, knowing I put that look of pure bliss on her face. Releasing my bruising grip on her ass cheeks, I snaked a hand over the swell of her hip and dipped between her thighs.

Those squeezed lids popped open, lips parted on a half

gasp, half moan as I brushed along her inner thighs. Hooded green eyes locked with my blue ones as I shoved her soaked underwear aside and sank three fingers into her slick cunt. Euphoria washed over her features as she lost the battle of keeping her lids open.

"Eyes on me, Kitten," I rasped as I plunged my fingers in and out, curling the tips to scrape along her sensitive walls. My harsh tsk sounded more like a curse when she refused to obey. I yanked my fingers free, and her eyes immediately popped open in response. "I don't repeat myself," I gritted out.

Despite her whimpers, I lifted three slick digits between us and slipped them past my lips. Swirling my tongue along each, I sucked off her delicious taste.

"Tallon," she breathed, hips flexing but finding zero friction with the small space between us. "Please."

"Will you be a good kitten?" I wiped my slick fingers along her cheekbone, tracing a line to her parted lips. With zero warning, I shoved them into her mouth. "Taste how delicious you are."

The feel of her lips around my fingers, the gentle suck as her tongue swirled, made my own hips jerk, desperate to sink balls deep into her eager pussy. Fuck, I loved this. The push and pull, forgetting about everything but the moment. Controlling every aspect of her pleasure and my own.

This was me letting go, my complete focus on her and egging her on until she pleaded for my dick.

And she would. Memories of her doing just that years ago, on her knees begging for me to fuck her mouth, flashed through my mind. With a hiss, I jerked my fingers free and squeezed my eyes shut to keep from blowing my load.

Fucking hell, I missed this.

Maybe even missed just her.

Gripping my cock over my jeans, I gave it a white-knuckled squeeze to quell the urge to rip off the restraining material and fuck her until she would remember exactly where I'd been with each step tomorrow.

"Eyes open," I growled at the same time I sank the same fingers deep inside her slick heat.

"Yes," she cried. Her small hands wrapped around my shoulders, blunt nails digging into my skin, no doubt leaving marks even through the T-shirt. Lifting up and down, she worked herself on my fingers, muttering various versions of my name, calling out when I curled my fingers just right.

"That's right, Kitten. I own you," I rasped as I studied her face. "This cunt is mine until I say otherwise, you hear me? It's mine to eat." Her whimpered curse had a smirk curling at the corners of my lips. "Mine to fuck and mine to deny."

I wrenched my fingers from her again. The responding cry of anguish that followed shouldn't have caused me as much pleasure as it did.

"Tallon." Tears collected in her lower lids. "I can't... I need... fuck me."

"You want me?" I mused, loving this game. Fuck, why had I held myself back for all these years? All we were missing was Jameson. A grunt caught in my throat at the image of him behind her now, also obeying my every command. "Tell me you want my cock."

"Yes," she begged. "I want your cock. Fuck, yes, please. I need it so bad."

Gripping her jaw in one hand, I held it in place as I lowered my lips to hers.

"Soon."

Prying her legs from around my waist, I gave her a moment of holding her own weight before flipping her around and pressing her chest and face to the glass. Beyond us, the downtown buildings glittered, and the red brake lights of the crowded streets dotted the ground.

Fingers gripping the thin fabric, I gave her panties a hard yank, ripping the scrap of material from her body. Chest sealed to her back, I brushed a hand over her ass before dipping low and plunging deep between her thighs. With my free hand, I popped the top button of my jeans and released the zipper. Her gasp filled the small bedroom when my hard cock slapped against her ass.

Dragging her arousal back, I slicked between her cheeks over and over. Her back shuddered beneath my chest with each of her ragged breaths, maybe from desire or curiosity about what I was about to do, yet she didn't whisper a word.

"Good girl," I praised. "Good girl, trusting me."

Situating my dick between her slippery cheeks, I groaned and bit down on the soft flesh between her shoulder and neck.

Thrusting forward, I slid against her skin. It wasn't her wet cunt, but I wasn't ready for that, and neither was she, even though she begged for it. This would have to do for tonight.

Only for tonight.

Tomorrow we'd really play when Jameson was around to participate.

Plunging my fingers in and out of her pussy, I flicked the tip of my thumb against her swollen nub with every thrust against her ass. Her silky strands slipped between my fingers as I gathered her hair at the base of her neck and yanked, forcing her neck and back to arch.

I stared at her reflection in the window, watching as her face contorted, giving away how close she was to the edge again. Increasing my pace, I chased my release, sealing my eyes shut and focusing on every place our skin touched.

With a yelled curse, her walls clamped around my fingers, pulling them even deeper as she came. Movements jerky, I ground against her ass, hissing her name as I came as well, cum shooting onto her back and splattering her shirt.

Sagging forward, I braced both forearms on either side of her head to keep from smashing her to the glass any more than she already was.

Holy fuck, that was amazing.

And we were just getting started.

12

REMINGTON

A painfully full bladder pulled me from a deep sleep, demanding I get up and take care of the situation. Blinking to get my vision to focus, I scooted along the bed, the sheets and comforter tugging against me like cotton hands, refusing to let me go.

"You okay?"

Tallon's rough voice had me glancing over my shoulder. The bright lights of downtown streamed through the windows, highlighting where he lay sprawled out on the bed, only wearing a pair of snug boxer briefs. I couldn't help but give his hard body a slow, appreciative once-over. *Yummy.*

"Remy?"

"Hmm?"

"What's wrong?" Leaning to his side, he propped his head up with an elbow pressed onto the bed.

"Bathroom." I hooked a thumb in that direction and stood. "No boogeyman in the shadows."

"Not funny when there *is* a sicker fuck than that with his focus on you."

I rolled my eyes at his dramatics. "Go back to sleep, crazy man. Everything is fine."

After using the restroom, I washed my hands while studying my reflection. I didn't look any different, but I sure as hell felt better than I had in years. Even the toys I spent way too much purchasing couldn't replicate the mind-blowing orgasms from earlier. Biting my lip to stop the smile creeping up my cheeks, I wiped my hands on the perfectly arranged hand towel and tiptoed back to the bedroom.

A soft sigh escaped me as I sank onto the comfortable bed and pulled the covers up to my chin. There was a chill to the air, yet Tallon was sleeping basically naked and without even the thin sheet draped over him.

"You'd tell me, right?" he said.

I startled, having expected him to have fallen back asleep.

Turning to lie on my side, I pressed both hands together and slid them beneath my cheek. Now, with my eyes adjusted to the dim light, I found his open ones in the dark.

"Tell you what?"

"If what I am, how I control, triggers you. I don't want.... I couldn't stand the thought of you being afraid of me because of your past."

Oh, sweet man.

How in the hell was he constantly considering me, my well-being, over what he wanted? It was his nature to control, that was clear, but it didn't mean he wanted to control my life, or do it to hurt me. It was the opposite. Tallon wanted to control the situation, any situation, so I was taken care of and safe.

"You being you triggers nothing. If you did it for selfish reasons or just because you could, then yeah, it would be a problem, but you don't. Your need for control is honestly an enormous relief. I've had to be on guard and aware of absolutely everything around me for so long, doing all this on my own, that I'm kind of relishing in the comfort that your need for control offers. You're doing all this for me, not the opposite."

"Why? Why did you stay with him for that long if it was that bad?"

I shifted my gaze to stare past him as I debated my answer.

"My parents loved him," I finally replied. "He came from an equally good family and had the same... ideals."

"Why do I feel like I'm about to get fucking pissed?" he grumbled and rolled to his back, tossing a thick forearm over his eyes.

I snorted a laugh. "Because you're an excellent agent."

"Explain the ideals piece."

"You sure?"

"Yes."

I eyed him for a minute before blowing out a loud breath. "Okay, so... a vacant shell with a beautiful outside. That was the highest aspiration my parents had for me. Becoming a Stepford wife, the perfect woman—all put together, always seen but never heard. My ex had the same ideals on how women should behave. Though his became more twisted the longer we were together. I was basically a chew toy for his anger and resentment rather than just a silent, dutiful girl on his arm."

"Remy," he said, voice strained. "If I ever see him, I will make him pay for not only what he did to you but for how he views women. No piece of shit should breathe the same air as those of us who think women are anything else than beautiful, equal partners and, in most cases, stronger than us."

Well, fuck me.

He had to stop doing this. Stop being so damn perfect or else I'd lose my heart to him faster than I already was. Only the reminder of my secret kept me from sinking too deep into the feelings that kept bubbling in my heart. I couldn't get too close. He'd leave, be pissed when he found out. And the longer I waited to tell him, the worse it would be, but I couldn't do it.

I couldn't tell him. Not yet.

Soon. Just not now. I wanted this comfort, this unblemished time with him now that he'd ripped down his walls keeping us from sinking into this pull between us.

"I get the first shot," I said, forcing a grin so he wouldn't see the heaviness now clouding my thoughts. "I haven't trained this long just for someone else to stand up to him for me. Imagining the look on his face when I break his nose with a single punch has gotten me through a lot of low times."

"Is he close?"

"Is this really a three in the morning conversation?"

"Yes, because you're in my bed and not running when the conversation gets personal."

I scrunched my nose. "I don't run." His huff told me he didn't agree. "Fine, maybe with you guys, but that's just because it's easy with you guys."

"To run?"

"To open up. What if I tell you something that risks everything I've worked to put behind me?"

"You should know by now that I'd never intentionally risk you."

Seconds ticked by without another word between us. My lids drooped, only to snap back open when his rumbled voice cut through the dark once again.

"What's the sleeping thing? You said he'd wait until you were unaware. What did that mean?"

I swallowed hard and rolled onto my back. "Just that. He waited until I was comfortable, asleep or reading a book, and bam, my world would turn upside down with him screaming and demanding whatever he could think of that was wrong with me or the house. Looking back, I think he enjoyed keeping me on edge, constantly walking on eggshells every second of my life. Toward the end, I was never at ease. My anxiety was through the roof because I was constantly worried about what would set him off next or when it would happen."

I licked my dry lips, debating telling him my final straw. The night I decided I couldn't live like that any longer.

"One night," I rasped, "I startled awake when the blankets were ripped off me and water was poured over me." I sucked in a breath and squeezed my eyes shut. If I told him the details, would it change his opinion of me? Would he see me as weak that I'd stayed for so damn long; or strong, like I now saw myself, for getting out? But talking about this for the first time felt cleansing, as if the words spilling from my mouth cleaned the shame and disgust for myself from my heart. "Except it wasn't water," I whispered. "He'd pissed all over me and the bed. Then he screamed in my face that the bathroom was too disgusting for him to use, so he'd just used me instead."

The bed shifted, making the tears building behind my closed lids slip free. A heavy arm draped around my shoulders and tugged me against a bare, hard chest. He said nothing, just held me so tight that taking a full breath was impossible.

Stealing from his strength, I pushed forward.

"He pulled me from the bed, his grip so hard that I

thought he'd snap my arm in half, and dragged me into the bathroom. My head hit the edge of the vanity, splitting the corner of my eye and knocking me unconscious. When I came to, he was still ranting, pacing the bathroom about how terrible of a—" I choked on the word. No, he didn't need to know I was dumb enough to marry that bastard. "How terrible I was that I didn't deserve him. Reminding me I was too pathetic, unable to do anything right. Before he stormed out, he threw my toothbrush at me, told me the bathroom had better be spotless by morning, and locked me in there. That was my breaking point. I didn't cry as I stared at my toothbrush lying on the gray tile, clothes still wet from his piss and fucking cold because he'd turned the AC on full blast. Instead of just giving in like I'd done so many times before, I got mad. Mad at the world, at my parents for knowing things were bad but telling me to get over it for pretense's sake. That was the night I formed a plan while I scrubbed the floor, a plan to leave him and everyone I'd ever known to find a better life. A life I knew was out there, and I deserved."

Only the slight tremble of his body told me he was still awake and heard every word. Breathing hard, I fought against the urge to push him away, to hide from the pity I knew he now felt for me. Who wouldn't? I was a pathetic person for staying with him as long as I did. Sure, I got out, but—

"I look forward to meeting that bastard," Tallon said, tone cold, "and treating him with the same care he treated you."

My cheek slid along his skin, now damp from my tears, as I shifted to peer up at him. Shock and awe pulsed through me, chasing away my own doubts at the rage, not pity, clearly written across his face.

"Yeah, sure, you can have a turn. After mine. Though I've taken precautions to make sure I'll never see him again. I left and never looked back."

"Has he tried to find you?"

I swallowed, hating that I was about to lie to his face. "No. I ran far enough that he couldn't find me."

"What about your parents?"

"I'm sure they were just glad to be rid of their embarrassment of a daughter who dared to not fit into their mold. I was an adult, so there was nothing they could do."

He didn't need to know how, to them, I literally vanished. How Remington Sawyer ceased to exist the day I stepped out of that house. My new background was solid, thanks to Charlie. They were none the wiser that I was only two states away living a life I wanted.

Free.

Free to wear what I wanted, to work, and speak my mind.

Though it sucked, I had to be careful to not give anyone hints that the life I now lived was a lie. Well, the information was a lie. I wasn't. I was me, the real me now. And it was glorious.

"You amaze me, Remington Dotson. I know you could kick that fucker's ass. However, I still have this urge to fuck you senseless until you give me his name so I can hunt him down and enact justice by ripping off his dick and making him choke on it."

That should not have been a turn-on, but I sucked in a sharp breath as my lower belly twisted with warm desire. Tallon's need for violence should have terrified me, but it did the exact opposite.

It was liberating.

"Tal—"

That was all I got out before a blinding white light pulsed and a warning siren screeched through the room.

Faster than humanly possible, Tallon leapt off the bed, dragging me along with him. Having grabbed the gun off the nightstand, he pulled me toward the corner of the room and spun me around, pressing my spine to where the walls met.

Bile surged up my throat as my heart threatened to beat right out of my chest.

The calm, then sudden surge of adrenaline was all too familiar, forcing memories I'd long forgotten back to the forefront of my mind. I swallowed a pitiful sob, trying to hold my shit together as Tallon darted around the room.

"What's going on?" I screamed over the ear-piercing siren. Sealing both sweaty palms over my ears, I pressed hard to protect my hearing.

"Fire alarm." His shouted words were barely audible over the alarm and through my hands.

My body trembled from the adrenaline thrumming through my veins. I tracked Tallon's every move as he flung open drawers and boxes. The flashing light made the harsh lines of his scowl appear menacing.

The ground beneath my feet shook as he stormed back to the corner where I hadn't dared move an inch. He dropped to a low squat in front of my feet.

"Left foot first, Remy," he shouted as he tapped my bare foot.

A bit confused about what the hell was going on, I complied. Soft cotton slipped over my skin as he tugged a pair of too-large sweatpants over my shin before repeating the process on the other leg. Securing the tie as tight as possible, he rolled the waist down a few times, but I still had to hold on to the cotton to keep the pants from slipping off.

Thankfully, I'd fallen asleep in one of his T-shirts, so my top half was already covered.

Standing quickly, Tallon pulled on the other pair of sweats, shifting the gun from one hand to the other as he yanked them up his thighs.

"You won't like this," he shouted, "but I don't care right now."

"Like what?"

When he reached for me, I tried to back away but had nowhere to go. The siren swallowed my scream as he lifted me off my feet.

"Either wrap your arms and legs around me or you're going over my shoulder. Your call."

"You're insane," I yelled in his face.

"Choose or I choose for you."

Grumbling under my breath about annoying dominant men and being able to walk on my own, I wrapped my arms and legs around him, sealing myself against his chest.

"Good girl," he muttered into my ear.

And damnit if his praise didn't make me smile.

"You okay?" he asked, caution behind those blue eyes as they flicked my way before darting back out the windshield.

I finished my text to Charlie checking in on Crew and gave myself a second, not sure how to respond.

Was I okay?

After he'd hauled me down the nineteen flights of stairs, basically threatening to shoot anyone who got near us in the head, we'd waited over an hour just for the fire department to announce there was no fire.

Someone had triggered the alarm on a lower floor, but they didn't know who.

That unknown sent Agent Paranoid into overprotective mode. Of course, he assumed the unsub had attempted to use the diversion to get me out into the open. And I agreed with him. The timing was awfully suspicious. Now after changing and packing our bags we were speeding down the highway in his FBI-issued black SUV on the way to my house. At six in the fucking morning.

I'd now been awake since three, manhandled—okay, that actually wasn't so bad—and to make everything worse, the coffee in my hand that I couldn't wait to drink was still too hot unless I wanted third-degree burns on the roof of my mouth.

Not even last night's soul-liquefying orgasms could ward off my ultra-cranky mood.

So, thinking back to his question, I wasn't really okay, but even cranky Remy knew not to tell him that. Who knew how he'd react? Hell, he'd probably force me back to the doctor even though it was a Saturday.

I wasn't hurt, in pain, or scared. I was safe with Tallon, so maybe I was okay.

"Yeah," I said with a sigh. "Just tired and coming down from the adrenaline rush, I guess."

He nodded as he switched hands on the steering wheel. "The exact opposite of what the doctor wanted." His fingers tightened around the wheel. "If this is getting to be too much, you can go to Texas too. Jameson and I will handle the case—"

"Hell no," I exclaimed. "You do not get to ship me off and cut me out of the case."

There was nothing nice about his all-teeth grin. "Actually, I do. Lead agent, remember?"

Groaning, I rubbed two fingers in tight circles along my temples. Then a thought had me snapping my eyes his way. If he was so determined to keep me safe and stress-free, then I could use that against him.

"Knowing details about what's happening around me, helping in any way I can... hell, just listening to you two talk will keep me less stressed than not knowing." Tallon's lips pursed as he considered my statement. Turning, I stared out the window, the reflection mirroring my smirk. "So if you want me to actually follow the doctor's orders, then I need to be kept in the loop."

"It's against protocol to release details of an active case," he grumbled after a minute. "But you have a point. It's not like we'll be able to keep you from hearing the details anyway, since we're all bunking at your place for a while."

Heat flashed beneath my skin at the reminder.

All three of us.

Would it piss Jameson off that something happened between Tallon and me last night?

Would he want to join if it happened again?

"What do we know about this guy?" I asked to derail my lusty thoughts. You'd think two orgasms within the last twelve hours would calm my lust-filled thoughts, but it did the opposite.

I wanted more.

I wanted it all.

Shifting along the seat, he leaned his head back. The muscles along his jaw twitched as he worked it back and forth. "Who he is? Not much. The only thing we have to go off of is what my sister said about him when he showed up at her work, which isn't a lot. Just that he was handsome and a little taller than her."

"That's something," I offered. "Have you ever watched documentaries on famous serial killers?"

"I see enough of that demented shit in my day-to-day life, so no."

"Not mine. My job is boring as hell. Just hours of coding only broken up by pop-ins from my asshole project manager." I lifted a shoulder in a half shrug. "Well, maybe you should. It's super informative and interesting. How they hunt and capture their victims, the why behind it, is fascinating." He arched a brow and glanced my way. "I have a point."

"Feel free to share it. I'm not inclined to agree with your assessment of fascinating. Not when you're the one who has to interview the families after. See their devastation and how, because of one person, it changed their entire future."

I swallowed hard. He had a point. What I watched as a diversion, the evil in the world, was his reality.

"A lot are good-looking. It's how they attract their victims. I'm sure there's some science behind how someone assumes a person who's good-looking is more trustworthy or lowers their guard. Either way, they have an ability to make their victims trust them. So maybe they're con artists, able to adapt to achieve their end goal."

Tallon thumped his thumb on top of the steering wheel. Those bright blue eyes focused out the windshield to the traffic.

"That would make sense considering this guy showed up at Tinley's bar and then again at your son's school. He must be charming for him to not raise any suspicions." He tilted his head to the side. "What we know about him from before was that his victims seemed like victims of opportunity rather than being targeted and stalked."

"Like me," I whispered. "How did he even find out where

to find me or my son?"

"We don't know," Tallon said, sounding defeated. "If our assumptions are correct and the technical one, the Vincent guy, is dead, then how did this unsub get your information?"

I chewed on my lip, staring at the black dash, thinking through all the possibilities. "If he can't hack into databases, which would be extremely difficult, then he got it from someone. But he'd have to know where to start looking to ask around."

"Well," Tallon said as he flipped the blinker on to turn right, following the directions mapped out on the navigation screen, "he knew one place to find you initially."

My brows narrowed before my jaw dropped. "Your place."

"That would make sense. He was waiting for the opportunity to follow the ambulance, so he knew where I lived. Maybe not the exact apartment but the building for sure, which is why he pulled the fire alarm last night instead of coming to my door. What if he was waiting somewhere close to see if you came back by?"

"That night, the Sunday when I first saw you and Jameson."

"And ran," Tallon grumbled.

"Fast walked," I retorted with a grin.

"Did you feel anyone following you home?"

I shook my head and shrugged at the same time. "I honestly don't remember the drive home."

"That's comforting."

I flipped him the bird, making him chuckle. "You heard the doctor yesterday. It's not like I'm blacking out. It's just that the memory is a black hole."

"Either way, you're not driving until you're feeling better."

"You signing up to be my chauffeur?" I joked.

"Yes."

My barked laugh caught in my throat, making me cough. "Seriously?"

"Don't sound surprised."

"Have you always been this—" I waved a hand as I tried to come up with the right word. "—obsessive over keeping people safe?"

Tallon shot a grin in my direction. I sucked in a breath at the way his eyes appeared to twinkle. He seemed... happy. Well, maybe not happy right now, but lighter, at least.

"Ever since Tinley's initial abduction, it's been worse. With every victim, I see them as someone I couldn't save, that I didn't work hard enough to catch the bastard before they were hurt or killed."

"Tallon," I whispered. "That's not your fault."

"Yes and no. But with you, in this instance, I can make sure you stay unharmed. So yeah, I might take this overboard, but...." His Adam's apple shifted with his hard swallow. "Just know where it's coming from. It's my job."

It felt like my heart deflated, sinking right into my stomach. I guess I thought that, after last night, maybe he saw me as more. Different to him than the others he'd dedicated himself to protect. My stomach soured at the thought of him carrying another woman like he did me to rush her from a threat.

Anger quickly replaced the growing sadness.

"Okay," I said flippantly. If he didn't care, then I didn't care.

I stared out the window, contemplating how to keep my hurt feelings from showing, as the hospital close to my house came into view. My gaze locked on it, and a case-breaking idea tickled on the outskirts of my thoughts.

"Oh shit!" I shouted as the theory solidified.

What if the hospital was where he followed me from or how he got my information?

"What?" Tallon yelled and slammed on the brakes. Tires screeched, and horns blared all around us as the back end of the SUV fishtailed. My seat belt snapped taut as I jerked forward. Both hands whipped out, slamming onto the dash.

Chest heaving with erratic pants, I turned wide eyes to the driver seat. An emotionless mask had slipped over his face as attentive blue eyes scanned the surrounding area. It was the gun clutched in his hand that had me shuffling back until my spine hit the passenger door.

"What did you see?"

A shiver went down my spine at his cold tone.

Holy fuck. Was I scared or turned on?

Both?

Damnit, what did that say about me?

I always knew I was a little more Hot Topic and less Abercrombie with my kinks, but this was a darker level than ball gags and threesomes.

"Remington," he barked. "Tell me."

I licked my lips. "The hospital."

His blazing eyes locked on me. A horn honked behind us, but he didn't flinch.

"The hospital," he repeated. "What about the hospital? Do you need to go? Are you feeling worse?" As he spoke, the calm facade crumbled, turning his tone urgent.

Shit, why did I mention the hospital? The thought was right there but then vanished in the chaos.

"Erm, don't be pissed, but I forgot what I was going to say," I grumbled.

Dropping the gun to his thigh, he scrubbed a hand over his face. "I'm confused." Inhaling deep like he needed all the patience in the world to handle me, he twisted in the seat, mirroring the way I used the door as support. "Are you hurt?" I shook my head. "Do you need to go to the hospital?" Again, the tip of my ponytail swung with my response. "Did you see something that made you think I should pull over to investigate right now?"

"No. It was just a thought," I said with a wince.

Okay, so he was one of those guys who got all rattled just because the passenger shouted or made a loud noise. Got it. I would hold in all gasps and exclamations while he was driving in the future.

Reaching down, he secured the gun back in his ankle holster, then wrapped both hands around the steering wheel like a damn lifeline. Every single knuckle bled white with his tightening grip.

"Next time," he said through gritted teeth, "don't shout like that unless we are in danger."

"Well, you kind of overreacted," I remarked.

Based on his responding death glare, that was the wrong thing to say.

"Because there is a serial killer after you," he said, voice eerily calm.

"Fine," I said like a pouting teenager, hoping that would shatter the tension in the SUV. "Though I can't make a blanket promise, because if we see a PF Chang's, I will shout for that place all day, every day to make you pull over."

His hands slipped off the wheel, plopping to his lap as he turned to face me, a look of sheer confusion on his face.

"What?" I shrugged. "They have the best soup and lettuce wraps."

"Okay," he said slowly and scrubbed a hand over his face. Then came a few mumbled words that I couldn't make out—all positive, I was sure. "Unless we are in urgent danger or you see a PF Chang's, please refrain from shouting while I'm driving. I'm a little—"

"Tense?"

He froze like any sudden movement might send him over the edge of sanity. "Reactive."

"That was my next guess." Turning all the way around in the leather seat, I stared out the back window. "I'm shocked we didn't get in a wreck. Traffic is awful around here."

Before I spun back around, the SUV moved, only speeding up when I was safely in my seat. My stomach dropped when, between blinks, we went from several blocks from my home to pulling up along the curb.

Shit. Maybe there was something to say about the surge of stress making the memory loss worse. I would keep the confirmation of the doctor's prognosis to myself.

He cut the engine as I stared at the house, wondering how in the hell I'd make this work. There were way too many pictures of Crew around the house. If Tallon got a good look at any of them, there would be no more putting off telling him he was the father.

The dull click of Tallon's seat belt disengaging had me whipping a hand across the center console and grabbing his seat belt.

"I want to go in first."

An amused look passed over his face. "Not even a sliver of a chance, Remy."

I ground my teeth. "Please. I need to pick up a few things before you guys come inside."

And put away all pictures of Crew so he didn't see the uncanny resemblance his son had to him. You know, minor details that needed to be tidied up.

"We need to clear the house before you go in. Serial killer, remember?"

Fucking hell with this man and him being so ultra-agent. I sure as hell hoped his boss knew how protective Tallon was in the field. He really deserved a gold star for all-around safety.

And orgasms.

Five stars, highly recommend.

"Fine." I hitched a chin to where Jameson stood waiting on my porch. "He goes in first, makes sure it's all good, and then you both wait on the porch until I tell you to come in."

"Five minutes. That's as long as you'll have before we come in, with or without your approval."

"You're an asshole, you know that?"

That sharp grin had me releasing his seat belt and retreating. "The same asshole who's doing everything he can to keep you alive."

He was right, but so was I. He didn't have to be so damn rude and overbearing about it all. It felt like there was more going on than he let on. My heart raced at the hope that maybe, just maybe, he was an overprotective asshole because I was special to him. I wanted that protection because of who I was to the person, something I'd never had, yet these last two days, Tallon had shown me a sliver of how amazing it could feel.

I'd been controlled, yes, but protected like a precious treasure? Never.

It was a fine line between the two, but somehow, Tallon never even toed that line. Okay, maybe forcing me to go to the doctor was controlling, but it was for me, to keep me healthy. So it wasn't about him but me, which made all the difference.

Inhaling deep, I gripped the door handle and pushed it open.

Time for this shit show to really start.

13

———

TALLON

What the hell was that *about?*

I studied my friend as I stormed toward the concrete front porch where Jameson and Remy stood talking. As I approached, I took in the smaller cottage-style home, which was typical for the historical area of Franklin, Tennessee. The house itself was a pale blue with white trim and a decent-sized front porch where a single wooden swing currently shifted with the January wind.

Turning my focus upward, I studied the gray billowy clouds that hung low in the sky. This overcast day was typical January weather for Nashville, with the heavy air making the cold seep through your clothes faster than other places in the country.

Jameson's chin hitch in my general direction drew my focus back to the two of them. He said something I couldn't hear to Remy before turning for the front door.

Seriously, what the hell is going on? It made little sense why she was so adamant about me not going in first, unless she was hiding something.

But even if she was, why the hell did I care? We had a fun night, which ended with us back in fucking danger.

Though the unsettled twist in my gut when I thought about what she was hiding or me never touching her smooth skin again was annoying and equally concerning. If her secrets didn't pertain to the case, what did it matter what she wanted to keep from us? Even before last night, when we took it a step over the line between agent and witness, I felt this need to know everything about her. Almost as if my heart had already decided this wasn't just a fling of opportunity.

But it had to be.

She was a victim. A witness who I, unfortunately, was insanely attracted to in *too* many ways.

In all the ways that mattered.

But it shouldn't. When this was all done and the bastard who'd killed all those women was caught, we would all go our separate ways. There was nothing tying me to Remy, nothing keeping me from going back to the lonely existence of working nonstop I'd lived before she barreled back into my life.

Right?

"I'll just take a few minutes to secure the place," Jameson said over his shoulder, gun already clasped between his hands as he stepped over the threshold. The screen door slammed shut behind him, though he left the heavy wooden door open wide.

Remy fidgeted, shifting on her feet and tugging at the thick loose sweater that hung down to her knees. Her choice of clothes this morning had me shaking my head in amusement.

Hot pink sugar skulls decorated thick black leggings that disappeared into a pair of matte black Doc Martens. The oversized black sweater added coverage and warmth over the loose white tank she wore beneath.

"Your style," I said, continuing my slow perusal. "It's unique."

Her green eyes flicked to me. "After being told what I could and couldn't or shouldn't wear all my life, I'm kind of all over the board on what I choose to buy and wear. It's like I can't make up my mind on a certain style, so I just roll with them all."

"It fits you," I said, offering a reassuring smile. "Better than that all-business outfit you wore when we came to your office."

"You mean ambushed me at my office," she grumbled. "Yeah, I have to wear stuff like that to fit in at work. They don't value individuality like I do. It makes you more of a target for issues. Plus with the tattoos," she mused, holding up her arms and pushing back the sleeves of her sweater. Black ink decorated one arm, covering every inch of skin from the wrist up, while the other arm was all color, depicting various flowers. "It's easier to keep them hidden so I don't have to answer all the dumb questions people ask."

I nodded and opened my mouth to ask more, but the screen door swung open. Jameson stepped out with an odd look on his face as he studied Remy.

"Did you find something?" I questioned, my hand already sliding toward my gun even though his was put away.

He shook his head and gestured for Remy to go ahead.

"Five minutes," I called, earning me a delicate middle finger shoved high in the air just before she slipped into the house. I didn't hide my chuckle as I moved to the other end of the porch, eying the swing. Metal squeaked and the wood creaked as I carefully sat down and then rocked back and forth with the heels of my shoes.

"You're acting strange," I commented offhandedly to Jameson, studying his features for a hint of reaction.

He pursed his lips and chanced a glance inside the house before stepping closer. I paused my movements and leaned forward.

"Did you read the report that came over earlier?" he asked. "It's her background that you asked for."

"No, haven't had a chance yet. We've been busy."

A small smirk tugged at his lips. "Hopefully the good kind."

Before he could dodge, I punched him in the thigh, holding myself back to not really hurt him. "That was last night," I said, twisting to survey the quiet residential street for threats.

He barked a laugh. "Thank fuck."

"What's that supposed to mean?"

"It means the sexual tension between you two is fucking intense, and I'm glad you did something about it. Finally."

"Fucking hell." I pinched the bridge of my nose. "It can't happen again. He's getting too close for us to be distracted."

"Sure. We're all staying in a tiny two-bedroom house with tensions high. You're an idiot if you think what you two did last night was a one-and-done thing."

"Hoping to join in?" I said in jest.

"If you don't snap my neck for touching her, yeah," he retorted with a wry smile as he also studied the quiet street.

I groaned and shifted on the swing. I could not think about the three of us. That would not and could not happen. Even if my semihard cock had other ideas. Though it was crazy how the idea of another man even looking at Remy made me want to throat-punch them, it was the opposite with Jameson. Maybe it had to do with our background or the fact that we'd shared her before, but I *wanted* him to touch her.

With me directing their every move, of course.

"The background," I bit out like a curse to change the subject. Based on his growing smile, he knew exactly what I was doing. "Why the fuck did you bring it up?"

"It's boring."

"Boring?"

"Yeah. School here, undergrad. Had a few jobs over the last few years. It just felt odd considering what she told us about her past, you know? She said her ex was controlling, yet she went to college? Plus the timeframe she admitted to being with him, and she also said that's how she ended up in Nashville."

Furrowing my brow, I studied the cracks along the smooth concrete porch. She was secretive about the house, I'd already thought she was hiding something, and now this escalated the suspicions.

"She told me she got far enough away from her family and the ex that they didn't look for her."

"Which contradicts the background that states she's from here," he said. I dipped my chin in a clipped nod. "It doesn't pertain to our investigation, but I'm curious."

"Same. She's hiding something," I muttered. Hanging my head, I ran a hand over my short hair as I processed this new information. "You're right. It doesn't matter about the case, but it's still something we need to investigate." Because I wanted to know everything about this woman who'd infected my every thought. "Did they lift any of her prints from the crime scene?"

A line formed between Jameson's brows. "I'm sure they did, but I don't know if they're processed or not. Since they didn't find any on the torture tools, they pushed the prints to the back burner and focused on the DNA."

"Get them on it." A screech ripped through the air as the screen door swung open. I stood and stretched both arms high over my head. "You had thirty seconds left before I came in after you."

A dark head of hair and an annoyed face poked out of the house. She shot me a scowl, but there was a hint of humor she failed to hide. "I'm surprised you actually waited."

"I'm nothing if I'm not a man of my word," I stated.

She gave me a funny look before shaking her head, the smooth dark hair swishing with the movement, then nodded toward the house. "Come on in. It's freaking cold out there." Jameson and I shared a look. It was actually kind of warm for January. I shrugged and started for the door. "Now, no snooping." For emphasis, she pointed a tiny finger at Jameson before swinging it my way. "Promise."

Sliding my hands into the pockets of my jeans, I cocked an eyebrow while smirking down at her. "Can't do that, Kitten."

"Oh, are we at the pet name stage?" Jameson chuckled as he shouldered past me and stepped into the house. "Guessing that happened last night when you two had all the fun without me."

I rolled my eyes, feeling lighter than I had in years with the comfortable banter.

Remy's hand pressed to the center of my chest, stopping me in my tracks as I tried to pass where she stood just inside the doorway.

"I meant to ask last night but was, uh, distracted. What's this 'Kitten' business?" she questioned. "That better not be derogatory, or I'll lay your ass out right here, embarrassing you in front of your friend."

Her fingers curled, gathering the fabric of my gray long-sleeve tee as I closed the slight distance between us.

"Is that right?" Confidence shone in her green eyes, making me question what I actually knew about this woman. I'd been around so many women who needed my protection, and at the time, I loved it. Thrived on their need for me to be the strong FBI agent. Yet here was Remington, strong, fierce in her own right, not needing or desperate for my strength.

No, she had her own in spades.

Was that from what she survived under a controlling ex or being a single mother? I wasn't sure.

Whatever it was, it was sexy as hell.

I still craved to be that rock for her, to be the one to chase away the monsters, but something tight in my chest unwound knowing I didn't have to do it on my own for her. Equals in our courage, strength, and ability—if the moves I'd already seen were anything to go by.

"What do you mean, derogatory?" I asked.

"Kitten, cat, pussy...." Her words pushed breaths into my face that urged me closer. A soft blush dusted her cheeks.

"Hmm, no, not derogatory. You know I would never. You're a tiny thing with claws. A kitten. Unassuming until you claw someone's eyes out." The look of frustration on her features fell, turning more contemplative. "Don't overthink it."

Knowing I was in danger of crowding her until her back hit the door so I could capture those parted lips with my own, I cleared my throat and sidestepped around her. With her cheeks flushed, chest rising in quick succession, a smug sense of satisfaction thrummed through me knowing I wasn't the only one affected by our proximity.

Jameson was right. I was a fool to think what happened last night was a one-time thing.

There was no way I could resist her pull.

"If you two plan to fuck, I suggest you do it *after* you close the door, or I'll have to arrest you both for indecent exposure."

I whipped my head to Jameson, who sat on the pink velvet love seat along the far wall, smirking like an interfering asshole. Exactly what he was. Most likely so he could join in on the action sooner than later.

"Fuck off," I grunted and fully entered the house.

Standing in the middle of the room, I took in the space. Like most of the older homes in this area, the original coal-burning fireplace with green glazed tiles surrounding it and the few feet in front on the floor was the focal point of the living room. Original hardwoods looked well-worn yet in good shape. Straight ahead through a narrow doorway, I caught sight of a small round table, and just past that was another doorway, which probably led to the kitchen.

The living room furniture was mismatched, yet it coordinated in color and style somehow. Once again showing her uniqueness in odd ways that fit her perfectly. In front of the light pink love seat was a trunk that looked to function as a coffee table. Two chairs sat on either end of the trunk that appeared strong enough to hold the weight of a toddler.

"I've always loved the personality of homes like this," Jameson said, arms now stretched out along the back of the small couch. "How long have you lived here?"

After shutting the front door and locking it, which seemed to be almost habit, she fell into the seashell-shaped, deep purple chair, laying her arms on top of the smooth fabric.

"A few years, and same. It's why I wanted to live in this area. Sure, the houses are on the smaller side, but we don't need that much space. It gets cold in the winter, though." She ran her hands along the chair. "I need to replace the windows, but that's way down the need list. Plus, the chill gives me a reason to keep buying and hoarding soft blankets."

She flicked her wrist toward a tall woven basket beside the couch that was in fact overflowing with blankets of various colors and fabrics.

"What's at the top of this need list?" I asked absentmindedly. Staring at the chair that matched the one Remy sat in, I wondered if it would support my weight. The furniture—hell, even the house itself—was clearly not purchased with the thought of grown men in the home. Which should not have made me as happy as it did.

"Braces," Remy complained. "They do all this stuff now when the kids are younger, and then they have to have them again later. I'm almost positive it's just a racket to make more money, but what can I do? I'm not an orthodontist, no matter how much I research on Google, and I want to give him everything he needs no matter the cost or stress."

If it was possible, that simple statement made her ten times more attractive, or maybe it was more admiration. The way she smiled when she spoke about him, along with mentions of her putting her son's needs above her own, was proof of how amazing a mother she was, doing what she could to give him the best. That was the type of woman I would want as a mother for my kids. Selfless and loving, so unlike my own.

My mother was a manipulative bitch from the start. No

one understood, not like me and Tinley, the extent of what she'd do to get what she wanted. My stomach twisted as memories desperately tried to overtake me.

"Let's talk about the case," I said, clearing my throat, hoping that would get my thoughts back on track. I held up a hand when Jameson started to speak. "Yeah, I know it's against protocol, but I think it's best if she knows exactly what she's up against. I'll take the heat if someone finds out. But, Remy, know that anything discussed here between us three is confidential. This is an active investigation."

She nodded. "Understood, and thank you."

"Fine. Okay, so, Remy, you already know the depravity of this guy since you were locked in a shed with him. Then belittled our killer despite him wielding torture tools and being restrained."

My fingers curled into tight fists at the reminder. I didn't have to imagine what happened in that shed. The bastard had caught it all on film. Those images were burned into my brain and haunted me more than any other crime scene photos.

"I wanted him to underestimate me," she said with a single-shoulder shrug, like what she did wasn't that big a deal. The urge to bend her over the couch and turn her ass red so she never did something so reckless again was almost too strong to deny. "That's why I kept mouthing off. I knew my only chance to get out was for him to release me, thinking he had the upper hand. But," she said with a frown, "I think it had the opposite effect."

"So we saw," Jameson bit out. Her head snapped to him as he nodded. "He was recording. Though in his hasty escape, he forgot to take it with him."

"Burn it," she pleaded, desperation leaking into her soft tone. "Please don't let anyone...." Her shoulders shook.

Fuck, she didn't know. In two steps, I stood beside the chair, resting a comforting hand on her rounded shoulder.

"We can't burn it. It's evidence," I mumbled. "But we can keep it locked up. Though if this goes to trial—"

"Let's just take it one step at a time," Jameson cut in. Widening his eyes to draw my attention, he tilted his head toward Remy's trembling form, face buried in her hands. "But he's right. We can lock it up so no one else sees it." He leaned forward, pressing his forearms on top of his thighs. "Does that help?"

"But you two saw it," she whispered. Peeking through her fingers, her green eyes searched mine. Then it hit me why she was so upset. Her most vulnerable moment was caught on camera. I tightened my grip, remembering the few seconds he ground himself against her.

"We did," I said, being honest with her. "Disturbing as it all was, I was also amazed by your strength in such a terrifying moment, and after being drugged." Forcing a smile, I slipped my hand around to engulf the back of her neck, brushing my thumb along her smooth skin in slow, comforting strokes. "I know men who would've pissed themselves, yet you fought back."

"Let's talk about the connected cases. We told you about his recent involvement in the online bidding and snuff films, right?" Jameson questioned, effectively shifting us off the topic. I gave him an appreciative nod.

"Yes, you mentioned he was a part of a team and had murdered a lot of women."

Jameson twisted one knuckle at a time, popping the digits absentmindedly. "With the DNA discovered in that shed, we linked him to murders that dated before he ever met his partner." He leaned back stiffly, not nearly as relaxed as earlier. "Back then, he was labeled by the media as the Bad Samaritan."

"Oh, that's all kinds of disturbing," Remy remarked. Some of her natural spirit returned now that we were off the video topic.

Thank fuck. I never wanted to see her so desolate again.

"Over five years, he tortured, raped, and murdered sixteen women. All the bodies were discarded in various dumpsters around the greater Chicago area. The name was derived from the way he abducted his victims. All the victims' cars were found on the side of the road with either engine trouble or a flat tire. The investigators at the time assumed it was a crime of opportunity, but I'm—"

I cleared my throat.

"Right." Jameson gestured between us. "*We* don't think it was that simple."

"Why is that?" Remy asked, leaning forward, clearly caught up in the conversation.

With her trembling subsided for now, I slipped my hand from her soft skin and moved to lean against the wall. A single nail poking out from the plaster near my shoulder had me frowning as I examined it. That was odd. A random nail. Maybe a picture once hung there, but where was it now? Mentally dismissing the oddness, I shifted my full attention back to the conversation.

"Because the odds of that happening to women of a similar age, alone, late at night, in areas where no one noticed them being abducted were almost nonexistent," I clarified. "It would make more sense if he identified his victims, targeted their car, and then waited until they were stranded to make his move. With someone like this, Jameson doesn't think he'd leave anything to chance, and I agree."

Jameson hummed in agreement. "He's been able to avoid identification despite them having his DNA."

"How did they have it? Seems sloppy." Remy's face was downturned, eyes flicking back and forth. I could almost hear her curious brain working overtime to piece together the clues.

"They found it on the tenth victim. The case notes suggested the condom he used broke without him knowing." Remy's eyes snapped up to Jameson's as he continued. "It happens more often than you think. Especially with the level of violence he—"

"Enough," I snapped, noticing the color drain from her face.

A line formed between her dark brows. "So you don't think he stalked them? More met them at a bar or something, tampered with their cars, then grabbed them when they were vulnerable?"

"In summary, yes," Jameson agreed.

"But he's after me, stalking and fixated on me. Why? Shouldn't he be bored or frustrated and move on to a less protected victim? Why not run back to Chicago or another city where the cops and the FBI aren't looking for him?"

I shared a quick look with Jameson, a silent conversation passing between us. We'd deliberated why Remy was special.

"And," she said before either of us could respond, "why didn't they tie him to the other murders that he did while working with his partner?"

"There was no DNA on the bodies," I explained. "They washed those victims clean, and significant time had passed between when they were dumped and found. This is the first time we've found the location where he took his victims. And the way he murdered them changed with the partner involved, his signature. Which we now assume was to maximize the drama for their viewers."

"Disgusting," Jameson grumbled.

"Evil," I corrected.

"How did it change?" she asked.

It was Jameson who spoke up this time. "The murders during the partnership, those done on film, the victims all had their throats slashed with a jagged instrument." Remy winced. "Before, well, it was a little more brutal."

"How so?" she asked.

Damn her curiosity. How am I supposed to keep her calm like the doctor directed if she's this damn inquisitive?

"I'm not sure you want to be curious about this one, K itten," I cautioned.

"Tell me." Her voice was hard and demanding. "This involves me. The more I know, the better prepared I am, which could mean life or death if he gets what he wants."

My entire body tensed at her words. She was right, but fucking hell, the mention of her in that fucker's hands again made me want to shoot something.

At Jameson's questioning glance, I dipped my chin in confirmation. If she wanted to know, we'd tell her. No secrets, since it seemed she had enough for all of us. Plus, I didn't need to coddle her like others. She was stronger from what she'd already survived.

"He cut out their reproductive organs." Remy's shocked gasp vibrated through the room, her fingers now hovering over her gaping mouth. "The coroner's report stated there were signs of them being alive when he—"

She held up her other hand, stopping Jameson before he could get another graphic word in.

"Enough. I.... Fuck." She squeezed her eyes shut, her chest rising and falling with three deep breaths. When she raised her lids, that fire that seemed to hypnotize me once again flickered in her green eyes. "So now what?"

"Now," I said, shoving off the wall and pacing, though I only made it three steps before I had to spin around, "we work together and catch the fucker. Jameson, tell us everything you learned from the crime scene yesterday."

14

———

REMINGTON

Cold seeped into my palms from the glass of tap water I was holding as I stared unseeing out the window over the sink. That was a lot to take in. I'd wanted to know, but fuck. I was well aware the bastard who abducted me was vile and disturbed, but after hearing the details of what he did... no, what he enjoyed doing to women, I felt physically sick. Now I understood Charlie's initial urgency for me to get somewhere safe. He'd known what was after me but couldn't go into detail.

"So I have a question."

The glass slipped, almost dropping to the sink as I startled at Jameson's voice behind me.

Spinning around, I leaned against the counter, the rounded edge pressing into my lower spine. He stood in the doorway that led to the dining room. Alone. I flicked my gaze over his shoulder, searching for Tallon.

"He's talking to the officer stationed out front about our stay and plan."

"Okay, what's your question?"

He tracked my shaking hand as I set the glass on top of

the tile counter. Gripping the edges of my bulky sweater, I hugged it tighter around me.

With a glance over his shoulder, he stepped into the small kitchen, not stopping until the toes of his boots were touching the rounded edges of my Doc Martens. I swallowed down the mounting nerves before tipping my face up to his. I wasn't intimidated or wary of Jameson, even with his tall stature. What shocked me was that the overwhelming need to touch him wasn't there as strongly as it was with Tallon. Yes, desire swirled within me at our closeness, but this was more of a gentle wave than a tsunami like Tallon's presence invoked.

"I noticed after your five minutes alone in the house to 'clean' that there seem to be a few things missing." I stopped breathing. *Fuck.* Of course, he was observant; he was a damn detective, after all. "Several pictures, to be exact."

"I don't know what you're talking about," I whispered. My pulse raced, turning my breath ragged as I fought to keep my panic hidden.

"See, watching that reaction"—he gestured to my face—"I think you do. I'm a detective, remember? I know how to tell when someone is lying to me." A strong waft of his woodsy cologne surrounded me as he leaned closer until his lips brushed against the shell of my ear. "So tell me, Remy, why in the hell would you take down all the pictures of your son?"

I couldn't breathe, couldn't even blink, holding his demanding stare. Tears gathered on my lower lids.

"A son who looks awfully familiar. Though the person he reminds me of hasn't smiled like that in a long while, but I remember it all the same."

"Please," I begged, not sure what I was even asking of him.

"I tried to convince myself after reading your background report that you having a nine-year-old was just a coincidence. But then I walked into your house, and the first picture I saw was my friend's blue eyes staring right back at me, but it wasn't him."

"Jameson," I rasped. "You don't understand."

"Enlighten me," he demanded. Placing a hand on either side of my lax arms, gripping the counter's edge, he leaned in even closer. "Tell me how and why."

"You know the how," I snapped, anger now replacing the fear. "And why what?"

"Why didn't you tell him?"

Reaching up, I shoved at his chest, but he was prepared for the move and didn't budge an inch. Fuck both these men and their strong, sexy bodies.

"Don't you think I tried?" I whisper-yelled. "That's why I went back to that bar night after night after night. Until the waitstaff looked at me with pity in their eyes when I kept asking if they'd seen you two around. I didn't have your full names. Hell, I thought you'd given me a last name. Who the hell names their kid Jameson?"

"Erm, my mom," he said, a little taken back.

"And who the hell spells Tallon with two *L*'s? I spent hours looking for a Talon, one *L*."

"I'm sorry?"

"Fuck, I digress," I snapped, and waved both hands in agitation. Fuck him for thinking I kept it from Tallon on purpose. He had no idea how embarrassing it was to try to find two men who, I assumed, wanted nothing to do with me. "Anyway, I tried to find you after I found out, but you both just vanished."

The hands gripping the counter slipped around me and pulled me into a hug. I stilled, unsure of his motive for the embrace, before relaxing against him. Inhaling deep, I soaked up the comfort of his gentle hold, allowing his scent to soothe my panic from the inside out.

"You're right. Fuck, I'm sorry. I assumed the worst. I was just surprised. Though none of what you just said explains why you haven't told him now. Why does he still not know, Remy?"

"I don't know him," I mumbled against his chest, hoping he'd understand my reasoning. "I don't want him to take Crew away from me or try to be a part of his life and it inadvertently hurt Crew. I couldn't handle knowing something happened because I didn't do my due diligence. Just because Tallon is his biological father doesn't mean he's a good man or good enough to know his son." Pulling back, I allowed the gathered tears to leak from the corners of my eyes, tracking thin streaks down my cheeks. "Crew is my life, and I will do whatever I have to do to keep him safe."

Jameson's honey-brown eyes searched my face. "Okay, but for what it's worth, I know him—well, I used to—and I think you should give him the benefit of the doubt about this. He deserves to know, and he's a good guy, Remy. Hell, he's ruined his own life to protect and potentially save others. He might be a tad overbearing—" I snorted, making the corners of his lips twitch upward, "—but he means well. That's what you should focus on and... he doesn't do surprises well. At all. Him acting like a controlling asshole is him trying to protect himself from being surprised again."

"I'll tell him," I pleaded. "I know. I need to tell him. Especially after...." I stopped. Shit, what if he was pissed that something happened between Tallon and me last night without him?

Jameson's lips pressed in a tight line. "I hate saying this, because if he finds out I knew and didn't tell him it could be the end of our friendship forever, but maybe wait until after the case is closed. We need his full focus on catching this bastard, and you telling him now could derail that. Whatever is going on between you two is enough distraction for now."

I blanched. "Are you jealous?"

"No," he said firmly enough that I relaxed a fraction, believing him. "I told Tallon I was good with whatever happened between you two, or the three of us, if you're down for that again."

They'd talked about it on their own. Interesting. "How does that work, the sharing part without jealousy?"

Jameson considered me for a second before sighing and looking out the window over my shoulder. "The Tallon before and the Tallon now are different people. Before, there was no jealousy because it was just fun. The women we met all knew it wasn't a long-term thing, just like he and I knew. Neither of us wanted a relationship together with a woman. It was just fun. But despite how much Tallon is trying to deny it, there's something different with you."

My heart leapt into my throat with hope, but I shoved it back down. I couldn't be hopeful, not when I kept an enormous secret from him. A secret that would make him run for the hills or hate me, or possibly both.

I licked my lips. "Do you think... do you think he'd be too 'different with me' to let us three...?" I let the thought hang in the air, hoping he'd pick up on what I was asking, hoping for, instead of making me say it out loud.

Jameson shrugged. "I think that's up to you, Remy. If us three is what you want to dabble in again, well, that will be your choice. Based on what I've witnessed, I'm not sure there's much you could ask for that he wouldn't give you."

"So," I said slowly, needing to dispense the heaviness of

the conversation, "what you're saying is back then, you two were one-hit wonders, never going back to the same woman twice?"

Head back, Jameson released a loud, easy laugh. When he tipped his face back down to meet mine, a new heat lingered behind his gaze. "I'm certain you remember from that night that there is nothing 'one-hit' with me or Tallon."

Heat crept up my neck and flooded my cheeks.

"Do you still share women?" I asked, suddenly curious about his life.

Huh, maybe Tallon wasn't that far off with his kitten assessment.

"Nope, but I'm still a one-and-done type of guy," he said with a salacious wink that sent my heart fluttering. "Though, like you, I'd be down for more with you and Tallon if the opportunity arises."

"Everything okay in here?"

I dropped my hold around Jameson's waist where my hands had migrated and shifted to see around him. Standing in the doorway, Tallon studied Jameson and me, a mix of intrigue and heat flashing over his features.

"Yeah, just catching up," Jameson said, twisting around. "Everything good with the uniform outside?"

Tallon dipped his chin in a clipped nod. "I want to go back over the timeline of when the latest victim went missing and was found. I feel like we're missing something."

Suddenly parched, I downed what remained in the glass before following them back into the living room, which felt significantly smaller with the two men standing around. Choosing the small love seat, I shifted along the cushions.

Across the room, Jameson eyed the small chair, clearly apprehensive. "Will that thing hold me?"

I shrugged. "Not sure. It holds me or Crew, who weighs seventy pounds."

Bypassing the chair, he folded himself down onto the floor, using the wall as back support. "They found the recent victim's Corolla on a backcountry road, tire flat. A family member filed a missing person's report when they didn't hear from her. Ten days later, a sous chef found her body in the restaurant's dumpster in downtown Franklin."

Both men turned my way.

"I'm guessing that was supposed to be a warning that he's close," I mused darkly.

Tallon half sat on the rounded arm of the love seat, one foot planted on the floor while the other hovered in the air. "We should watch for suspicious activity when we go out."

"Great." I sighed and leaned back.

"He probably knows about the unmarked car out front," Jameson muttered almost to himself. "He's watching. Did you ever find out how he found your location?"

I shook my head. "No clue. Tallon thinks he might have followed me home that night from his apartment."

"Oh, when you ran from us?" Jameson laughed at my middle finger. "Sorry, fast walked."

I pointed at him and stared at Tallon. "See? Fast walked. I didn't run."

"What did she do?" was his only response, eyes trained on the floor. "The victim's occupation?"

Jameson whipped out his phone and studied the bright screen. "Says she was an RN."

A memory tickled in the back of my mind. *What was I thinking earlier that revolved around something medical?*

Reaching over, Tallon pressed a thumb between my pinched brows until they softened. "Do you have something to add, Remy?"

I blinked up at him, taken aback by his gentle gesture. "That reminds me of the idea I had, you know when I freaked you out and you completely overreacted?"

His light brown brow arched. "You mean when you yelled, making me think I was about to run over a kid?"

"It wasn't that bad," I said, and slapped his thigh, trying to dislodge him from his perch. It didn't work. "The hospital and now this victim being an RN, what if this guy got my information from the hospital? Whether by acting like a cop or detective like he did at Crew's school or charming the information out of someone. Does it say which hospital she worked for?"

Jameson brushed his thumb over the screen, clearly scrolling through the report. "It looks like she was a traveling nurse but based out of Nashville. I can call the hospital and see if she was working where you were. Though at this point, yes, it would be great to identify why this woman was targeted if it was for information about you, but we already have enough to tie these cases together so it's a moot point."

"Have there been other women reported missing with their cars found abandoned?" Tallon asked, the small smile vanishing when he turned to Jameson.

"I asked, and the guys at the station are working on finding out."

My stomach chose that moment to grumble loudly.

Tallon frowned. "I didn't feed you this morning."

"I'm not a farm animal," I joked, and waved off his concern. "I normally don't eat breakfast. Plus, I wasn't hungry after all the drama this morning."

"Let's see what you have in that kitchen of yours, and I'll make us something," Tallon stated, pushing to stand. Before he made a move in that direction, he reached a hand down and waited. "You coming?"

My grin widened. He clasped my hand in his, and a squeal of surprise escaped when he tugged hard, lifting me in the air. My chest smacked against his, the soft material of his shirt shifting beneath my chin as I angled my face up to his, ready to smart off.

Except my retort dried up before I could even open my mouth. The soft smile pulling at his full lips sent my heart stuttering with the sudden swell of emotion.

Oh shit. Shitty shit.

This was bad. Really, really bad.

This was a dangerous line I teetered along with these two.

It wouldn't last.

But did it need to? What if we were all on the same page of expectations after this case closed, everyone going their own way? My heart ached at that thought. I was already in too deep to not be affected if they vanished again.

Reluctantly pulling my hand out of his, I retreated a step, putting much-needed distance between us. "I wasn't expecting anyone, so I assume you'll find Lunchables, organic milk, and grape jelly in the fridge, and the pantry probably isn't much better."

I trailed behind Tallon to the kitchen and stood to the side as he inspected the contents of my refrigerator.

"Your assessment was accurate minus the almost empty jar of pickles and half a sip of orange juice left in the jug." With a pensive look, he shut the door and pulled his phone from his front pocket. "I'll Instacart some groceries that should get us through the next couple days. But until then...." His fingers paused as he peered through his blond lashes, smiling. "How about I have PF Chang's delivered for lunch?"

My stomach growled even louder than earlier at the mention of my favorite restaurant.

A smile so wide my cheeks hurt stretched across my face. "Yes, please."

"You go lie down for a bit," he said before turning back to his phone. "I'll order our lunch, groceries, and come get you when the food is here."

"But I'm not tired," I said just as a wave of exhaustion hit me. I twisted around to hide my wide yawn from him.

"What did I say last night, Kitten?" Setting the phone on the counter, he closed the distance between us as I held my ground. Wrapping a hand around the back of my neck, he gave it a tight squeeze.

Heart pounding, I stared up, completely lost in his touch.

"I don't repeat myself," he stated, answering his question for me. Thank fuck. I'd forgotten he'd even asked something. "Though after this morning, I'll offer a little grace and say it again without punishment." My lips parted as I sucked down tiny gulps of air. "Go. Lie. Down."

But what if I wanted the punishment?

That sounded delightful.

What if I wanted it to help me forget about the shit show that was going on around me?

Fuck what the doctor said. Who knew how long I'd have with him, with them, and I didn't want to waste a single opportunity to have his hands on me. Not when weeks from now I'd be back to doing all this alone. I needed something to get me through the crushing weight of day-to-day life.

And what better way to forget than the memory of a few mind-blowing orgasms?

"No," I stated, and attempted to retreat a step. Though that grip on my neck kept me exactly where he wanted me.

"No?" he parroted.

"I'm not tired." My words were barely audible over the blood rushing in my ears. "And you can't make me."

But please, by all means, try.

And ask for help from Jameson. This feels like it could be a two-person job.

Tallon tipped forward, soft lips brushing my own. Desire-fueled heat seared through every cell, my lower belly flipping while my core clenched around nothing. Arousal soaked my panties, no doubt leaving a wet spot on my leggings.

"I know what you're doing." He slipped his hand forward to grasp my throat. I swallowed down a moan, shivering at the feel of my throat working beneath his palm. Holy fuck, that was hot.

Between blinks, the heat left his blazing blue eyes, something like resignation making him pull back. Immediately, I knew he was pulling away, ready to deny us both out of an abundance of caution.

Without second-guessing myself, pushing aside the worry of rejection, I ran both hands up his inner thighs. I swallowed down a moan at the feel of his thick muscles beneath my fingers. I watched his lids flutter, a hiss escaping his clenched teeth when my searching fingers wrapped around the bulge tenting the front of his jeans.

My mouth watered, ready to feel him inside me, to watch him fall apart from my lips wrapped around his thick dick.

"Fucking hell," he gritted out. "You don't play fair, Kitten." I tightened my grip, rubbing the heel of my palm up and down his length, emphasizing his point. Fire flashed behind his eyes. "Neither do I."

Releasing his hold around my throat, he dipped both

hands beneath the band of my leggings. Hot palms engulfed my ass cheeks, fingers digging in with a bruising grip. Using that hold, he dragged me up his body until my legs wrapped around his waist.

Determination clear on his tight features, he held my gaze as he strode from the kitchen. The scrape of wooden legs along the hardwood floor had me breaking our stare to the dining chair he pulled from beneath the table before he dropped into the wooden seat.

Every inch of skin tingled, my nerves flaring in anticipation of what was to come.

I wanted it. Needed the promised pain, the pleasure I knew would follow.

Breath coming in short pants, I returned my focus to his bright blue eyes, anxiously waiting for whatever he had planned. An answering cocky smirk was all the warning I got before his grip disappeared around my ass and the world spun. Manhandled in the best way possible, he flipped and arranged my body until my stomach pressed against his spread thighs, a tight hold around my hair at the base of my neck.

Completely at his mercy.

A desperate groan vibrated in my throat as I arched along his lap.

"Oh fuck," I muttered, loving every second. The way he knew what I wanted, encouraged this need to be dominated, to release all control and love, it was amazing. I'd been in control of everything from the second those two pink lines showed up on that damn stick, yet now I was eager to give him all of it. Was it because I trusted him or because he demanded it? Both. I gave it to him because I knew he wouldn't hurt me, would only push me as far as I was comfortable.

Desire flooded my core. The sensation of it dripping made me even hotter.

"This looks promising." I started at Jameson's close voice. The painful grip on my hair held firm as I pulled, my hair tugging at the scalp, to find Jameson staring at us, a cocky smirk on his lips. "What's going on?"

"I told her to go lie down, and you know what she said?" Tallon said, his grip on my hair tightening as he smoothed his hand down the globes of my ass. "She said no, even after the threat of punishment."

Jameson's chuckle sent a shiver racing down my spine. "Can I watch?"

I sucked in a gasp as his words sent another rush of wetness to soak my panties.

Can he watch?

Can he watch?

Fuck yes, he can watch. Or participate.

Preferably the latter.

I wanted Tallon, yet I craved the three of us too.

"What will it be, Kitten?" Tallon asked as he slipped a hand beneath the band of my leggings and explored until his fingers swiped through my drenched slit. "Do you want Jameson to watch while I spank your fine ass for disobeying a direct order?"

"Yes," I whispered. "Fuck yes."

"Good girl."

15

TALLON

For the second time in less than twenty-four hours, I was seconds from blowing my motherfucking load. What was it about this woman that made me lose control, made me so desperate I couldn't think straight?

Holy fuck, she was everything I could ever want and more.

Responsive, smart mouth, beautiful, defiant.

Keeping my hold on her hair with one hand, I worked the snug leggings down both legs until that round bare ass was exposed to the room. Unable to look away, I reverently brushed a palm along her soft creamy skin, eager to see it turn all shades of red.

I flicked my gaze to Jameson, who still stood in the doorway between the two rooms, his hand slowly working up and down the front of his slacks. Jealousy flared for a second before I shut it down. Remy wanted this, wanted him to watch, and I enjoyed the extra tease for her too, but something felt different with this interaction than any of the others when we'd shared in the past.

Call it jealousy or possessiveness, whatever it was, I had to keep that shit locked down since she wasn't mine.

"Watch Jameson," I ordered as I used my hold on her hair to angle her face, forcing her to watch him stroke himself. "Is this what you want, Kitten?"

"Yes," she whimpered.

Sneaking my hand between her thighs once again, I pushed two fingers into her tight pussy, barely holding back a growl at the way she tightened around me.

Fucking hell, this might be more torture for me than her.

She shoved her hips back, making my fingers sink deeper into her soaked core. With a tsk, I pressed a forearm down between her shoulders, restricting her movement.

"I don't think so. This is a punishment, remember?"

"Please, Tallon," she begged. I closed my eyes and sucked in a breath to keep from twisting her around and impaling her on my steel-hard cock. I wanted her so fucking bad, but not yet. "I want you. I want you both."

"You should've thought about that before you disobeyed me."

Yanking my fingers from her cunt, I smacked the wet digits against her ass. Her scream of pleasure and frustration had my hips reflexively shifting off the chair, digging my restrained cock into her stomach. Hand raised a second time, I smacked a full palm to one ass cheek before quickly shifting focus to the other. This time her cries were more of shock and pain, but the arch of her back and panting that followed her cries urged me to keep going.

Five hard smacks to each ass cheek turned her creamy skin bright red. With her quiet cries filling the room, I caressed the abused flesh, savoring the warmth now radiating from the pink skin, holding myself back from more.

The clink of a belt had me glancing Jameson's way, who'd undone his pants enough to shove his hand down the front.

If she weren't stretched across my lap, I no doubt would do the same. The musky scent of her arousal, his groan as he wrapped a bare hand around his dick, and the vision of her completely at my mercy made the need to come almost as desperate as my need to breathe.

"Watch him," I said against the shell of Remy's ear. Releasing her hair, I slipped that hand around to the front of her throat, the grip just tight enough to direct her movements but not hurt. "Watch him fuck his hand at the sight of your pink ass, desperate to feel you."

Her pitiful, desperate whimper shot a bolt of lust straight through me.

"Please," she begged, the word making her throat work beneath my palm. Slamming my lids shut, it took everything to not envision how amazing she'd feel when I got the chance to fuck that perfect mouth of hers.

Jameson's hooded, lust-filled gaze met mine, his hand stilling as he arched a brow in a silent question. Movement stiff, I hitched my chin toward the closest chair. There was zero hesitation before he closed his hand around the wooden back and drew it even closer until it sat right in front of her flushed face. Remy shifted, tracking his every movement as he sat, pants still undone.

"Are you sure, Kitten?" I questioned while smoothing a hand up and down her ass, each pass dipping farther between her clenched thighs. She wiggled, shifting to draw my fingers closer to where she wanted them, causing her torso to rub against my cock. A harsh breath hissed through my clenched teeth, and my palm met her already red ass in response. "Words, Remy. Yes or no to Jameson participating."

"Yes," she whimpered, clearly lost in desire at this point. "Him, you, I want it all."

"Hmm, that's a good girl," I praised as I slipped a finger between her slick lips and flicked her swollen clit, her cry of pleasure hiking up my own. "Let's see you take all of him into that snarky mouth of yours."

I barely got the words out, my desire to see her deep-throat my friend making the words raspy, yet the urge to yank her away and keep this moment for just me was just as strong.

She ran her small hands up his thighs, fingers clumsily working his zipper farther down before tugging the band of his boxer briefs low enough to free the full length of his cock.

Sealing my lids shut, I recited the FBI motto on repeat to keep from exploding in my pants.

How the hell did I leave this part of my life behind?

Flexing my fingers, I massaged along the column of her throat as her jaw hinged open, taking the swollen head of his dick between her wet lips.

Jameson's garbled groan echoed in the room as his head fell back, jaw clenched.

Her head bobbed as she took him deeper, her throat working beneath my palm, a blissful torture that I fucking loved. Denial, edging, complete control was exactly what I enjoyed about having a partner. There was something fucked-up that I craved, the added intensity three brought to the moment instead of just two.

"Fuck, fuck, fuck," Jameson grunted, his hips jerking off the chair, thrusting himself deeper until her nose almost hit his abs.

"Swallow," I rasped, fully engrossed in watching her obey my single command.

Did she remember this from ten years ago like I did? How we'd push her boundaries just to see how gloriously we could all let go together? Though not all of us would find release. Maybe it made me a sick bastard to deny myself, but the next time I came, I wanted to be deep inside her tight cunt. Last night took the edge off for only a few hours, my need for her roaring back tenfold today.

Wrapping her lips around his cock, she pushed down, taking all of him before sliding back up. Jameson's hands tightened into fists where they lay trembling on top of his thighs. His restraint allowed my hold on her throat to dictate the cadence so I remained in complete control.

Helping her bob up and down his cock, I slipped a hand between her spread thighs, groaning at the dripping wetness coating her hot pussy.

"Fuck, you're soaked for us," I grunted, shoving three fingers into her tight channel.

She moaned, sending Jameson over the edge. His mix of curses and praises for her dirty mouth filled the room as she swallowed everything he gave. I continued to fingerfuck her, the sound driving my desire to nuclear levels. Her hips jerked back, keeping pace with my quick, plunging thrusts.

Just as her walls tightened around my fingers, her body trembling, I yanked them free and tugged her lips off Jameson. Her outcry of frustration and desperation vibrated beneath my palm and around the room.

Sliding my hand up to cup her jaw, I tilted her face toward mine. "Bad girls don't get to come," I said with a sharp, reprimanding grin.

Furious, tear-lined green eyes glared up at me. My smile grew only to fall when her clear sexual-frustration-fueled anger morphed into a sassy smile. I held a breath, waiting for her move. If she reached for my cock—hell, even looked at it—my restraint might snap.

Instead, the brilliant, clever woman of mine said the only thing that would break my resolve on denying her a release as punishment.

"I'm not very relaxed in this state," she said, biting her lower lip. "Doesn't that go against the doctor's orders?"

Oh, she's good.

Fucking smart as hell and beautiful.

Instead of anger rushing through me at her defiance, a shiver of excitement thrummed through my veins. She was absolutely perfect. Giving and pushing me in exactly the right moments that gave us both some semblance of control.

Scooping her off my lap, I carefully laid her slight frame on top of the round dining table so her ass hung precariously over the side. With a hard pull, her leggings were down her lean legs and tossed aside. With a firm grip on her quivering thighs to keep her balanced, I spread them wide and sat in the chair I'd just vacated as I positioned her right where I wanted her.

The musky scent of her arousal filled my nose as I pressed it against her soaked panties and inhaled deep. Whimpers and whispered begging flooded the background noise as I tugged the scrap of lace to the side and sealed my lips around her swollen nub. Sucking it between my lips, I scraped my teeth along the sensitive flesh. My name poured like a curse from her lips, and I smiled against her pussy, flicking my tongue back and forth teasingly. With my sweat-soaked shirt adhered to my back, my restraint to not fuck her senseless was nearly at its breaking point.

But not yet.

Muscles straining, I lifted her hips, positioning her so I could plunge my tongue into her weeping center. Tongue flat, I licked up to suck her clit and shifted my hold on her ass to push both thumbs into her. Instantly her pleasure-filled cry echoed around the room as she came, her muscular thighs sealing around my ears, muffling the sound of the outside world.

Like a starving man, I didn't let up, continuing to suck and nip, devouring her center until she came again, flooding my mouth with her release. Only when she slumped against the table, her screams of passion now barely whimpers, her legs falling open, did I pull back.

Face slick with her arousal, I smirked between her thighs.

"Holy shit," she half sobbed, half cried. Flinging an arm over her eyes, she laughed. "That was beyond amazing. There are zero toys to mimic that." Lifting her arm, she peeked one eye open, considering me. "Um, but what about you?"

She shifted on the table, making to climb off, but I pushed her back so she didn't fall off the edge and stood. I slapped my hands on the smooth wooden surface on either side of her head. Muscles trembling, I leaned closer until we were nose to nose.

"Only good girls get my cock, Kitten." Swiping a slick thumb along her lower lip, I growled low when she lapped it clean with her tongue.

Shoving off the table, I lifted her into my arms and turned. Striding back through the living room, I laughed, finding Jameson lying half on the couch, half hanging off with his eyes closed. Careful to not hit her head along the hall wall, I made my way toward the master bedroom and kicked the door open.

She squealed in surprise as she sailed through the air, cutting herself off when she landed in the middle of the bed.

I pointed at her as I backed away, too afraid to get closer, too on edge from denying myself. "Sleep," I ordered.

Her mouth opened, but I grabbed my cock and thrust into my hand, reminding her what I would again deny if she disobeyed.

"Fine," she grumbled and gripped the hem of her T-shirt, pulling it over her head. Reaching behind her back, she unclasped her bra and shrugged out of the straps. Her full breasts jiggled as she lay back along the stack of pillows, drawing my attention. "You sure?" she questioned, no doubt seeing the last strands of my restraint fraying at the sight of her naked body.

"I will fuck those one day," I said slowly, drawing my gaze up to her face. "And you. Now sleep. I'll wake you up when the food gets here."

Stomping out of the room, I slammed the door shut behind me harder than I wanted. Slumping against the solid wood, I scrubbed a hand down my face only to groan at the lingering scent of her on my hands.

Soon.

Soon I would have all of her.

DESPITE THE CRAZY start to the day and full afternoon and evening I couldn't fall sleep. So here I was laying in the same bed with Remy at almost three in the morning watching her sleep. Which was creepy as hell but I couldn't stop. Not with my girl so close, just an arm's length away.

Hold the fuck up.

My girl?

My short hair rasped along the pillow as I turned my head to stare at the ceiling as if it would help me sleep somehow. What the hell was I even thinking? I couldn't see her that way, couldn't claim her as mine. For one, she wasn't.

My jaw clenched at that statement.

And it, we, couldn't happen. She had a kid, for fuck's sake. Not that I cared, it just added another level of complication considering I was only here in Nashville a few days, a week at best, every month.

Actually, the idea of being a dad, having that connection and relationship, wasn't as bad as I'd made it sound when I answered Remy's question at the apartment. The opposite, actually. After seeing her, the way she lit up when she talked about her son, Crew, well, I wanted that. Wanted that light.

It didn't help that I knew I was running out of time with zero prospects. Hell, my relationships these days only lasted an hour or so. The last time I'd spent all night with a woman was ten years ago, with the beauty currently softly snoring beside me.

Maybe if I found the right woman, I'd take a step back. Put my life before the job for a while. But it would take someone special.

Someone like Remy, maybe.

Smart, stunning, original, curious, stubborn, and unique.

Giving up on sleep, I climbed out of the king-sized bed, careful to not disturb her. Though tonight it seemed she was at peace while sleeping, not burrowed down deep in the covers like they could protect her from the monster in her memories.

With the back of my hand, I swiped at a bead of sweat that slicked down my forehead. *Holy hell, she keeps her house hot.* My lungs, nose, and throat were to the point of cracking like the desert landscape, and it hadn't even been a day. It seemed my kitten was beyond cold natured.

I frowned and glanced over my shoulder at her sleeping form. I should've had her ask the doctor about that too. Maybe it wasn't normal to be this obsessive over her well-being, but I wanted to take care of her. Not because she couldn't do it herself, but because I didn't want her to have to.

When the tables flipped at the doctor's office and she was concerned about my health, even if it was just blackmail, I relished the feeling of her concern. Fuck, it had been a while since anyone gave a shit enough to be concerned for me. Tinley did her best, but she was my little sister; it was my job to take care of her, not the other way around.

Not that I'd done a great job of that over the last few years. In my need for control and zero surprises, I expected her to repeat the addiction cycle instead of hoping for the best. She was very clear last month when we hashed shit out over coffee and a therapy session on how she felt about *that*.

Smiling at the memory, I padded down the short hall, my bare feet hardly making a sound along the hardwood floor. As I neared the living room, a noise froze me in my tracks.

Studying what I could see from this point of view, I saw a shadow pass along the far wall from the single lamp Remy wanted to leave on. I stretched my hand back, reaching for my gun, then mouthed a string of silent curses as bare skin met my hand where my gun should've been. Of course, I didn't have my sidearm. It was three in the damn morning, and I was only in boxer briefs.

Calming my quick breaths, I listened for any other sign of the intruder to gauge how many I was up against.

A frustrated voice carried down the hall.

Prepared for the fight of my life to protect Remy and Jameson, who slept in the only other bedroom, I crept closer, easing along the hall wall. With three quick breaths, I ducked around the corner, muscles tense and fists raised, quickly sweeping the living room for the assumed threat.

"What the hell?" I whisper-shouted.

16

TALLON

"**F**uck," Jameson exclaimed, his voice carrying. I wouldn't be surprised if the neighbors heard his curse. "You scared the shit out of me."

"What are you doing?" I asked, not admitting that I'd felt the same when I prepared myself to fight a damn serial killer with my bare hands. I tossed both hands in the air, my nerves switching from anticipation to annoyance.

"Working," he grumbled, falling back onto the love seat.

"At three in the morning?" I questioned. Though I couldn't judge him, since I did the same when on the road. Nothing else to do.

"Yeah, I'm trying to create a more complex profile. I'll be doing it soon enough full time. Might as well use this as practice."

Eyeing the dainty chair with caution, I sidestepped it and lowered to the floor. My spine cracked, muscles stretching as I lay back on the hard flooring. Needing a pillow, I yanked one of the million throw blankets she had lying around and tucked it behind my head.

"Comfy?" Jameson joked.

"Far from it. Tell me what you have so far on the profile."

Papers shuffled along the coffee table. "Caucasian male, midthirties—"

"That young?" I tallied the math in my head. "That means he was late teens, early twenties when he was killing in Chicago."

"Exactly. The rage he exhibited in his first kills displayed a lack of control you'd find in a younger man. With age, killers learn to take their time, are more precise in their torture to prolong the pain, which is their primary goal. This unsub had no preference for torture devices. The beating he inflicted on the original victims showed immaturity in a way. No plan, no control, just rage."

Damn. "Well, hell, that makes sense when you describe it like that."

"Thank you." Pride filled his tone. "He has a preference in age, which makes me think he specifically targeted the prior victims, that they weren't victims of opportunity like the cold case reports suggested. If he didn't target these women, there would be a broader range of ages in his specific victims. They were all early to midtwenties. Well, until this new victim."

I thought on that as I watched the ceiling fan blades circle the hot air. If it weren't for the breach in security, I'd open a window for a quick reprieve.

"What's your theory about the new age difference in his victims? We assumed the partner chose the victims before since he was the voyeur, so we're leaving those out of the equation, correct?" The blanket shifted beneath my head as I turned to Jameson.

Staring out the front bay window, he appeared lost in his

own thoughts for a few moments before he finally spoke. "Correct on the victims from them as a partnership being excluded, since we're profiling him as an individual now. I have two theories in the new age bracket for his victims. First, he's older now, so he would choose victims that would match his age difference, or the age gap represents the age difference between him and the motivator of his rage. The catalyst, if you will."

"I'll allow it," I remarked with a smirk.

"Second theory isn't one you'll like."

"I don't *like* any of this."

"He's using these older women as his version of a poor man's Remy. Assuming her older age or maybe the fact that she had a son that made her fight. He thrives on breaking women, and he saw—*sees*—Remy as the ultimate challenge, so he's trying to find that again in a new victim until he can get his hands on Remy herself."

In one fluid motion, I sat up and twisted to face him. Knees bent, I rested a forearm on both, hands clasped. "Fuck." I studied the lines of the geometric rug. He was right. I didn't like that theory at all. It meant Remy would never be safe. "What's with cutting out their reproductive organs?"

Taking the pen from off the table, he spun it between his fingers. "That we won't know until we catch him, but it has something to do with rage toward a certain female figure in his current life or past. That much I'm almost positive on. Based on how young he was when all this started, I'm thinking a young mother. Maybe she didn't protect him or was his abuser. Again, we won't know what his trigger is exactly until we talk to him, but it's clear the bastard won't stop until he's caught."

"And he has a sick obsession with Remy," I gritted out, jaw clenched so tight the muscles burned.

"Speaking of Remy," he said, gaining my full attention. The couch shifted as he flopped back, still spinning the pen as he smiled at the wall. "Earlier was fucking hot as hell. Though I'm shocked you held out."

I blinked at Jameson, face blank to not give him a hint of what I was thinking. Where in the hell was he going with this conversation?

"It's almost like you're not rushing because you know she's different," he stated casually, like we were talking about the damn weather. "Which I'm inclined to agree. You act different around her, and you sure as hell haven't denied yourself in the past when we shared."

"Maybe this is different," I murmured, more to myself. "There's more of a connection than I've ever felt with a woman, that's for damn sure. But that means nothing. She's fun to be around and hot as hell, that's it."

When did I get so good at lying to myself?

His brows dipped, a deep line forming between them. He shook his head and leaned forward, going back to work on the profile. "Idiot," he muttered under his breath.

Palms to the floor, I shoved upward, standing with an aching groan as my back protested from daring to sit on the floor at my age. Getting old sucked, hard. "I'm going to see what she has to drink. Something stiff."

Jameson snorted, a small smile tugging at his lips even though his eyes didn't leave the paper. "I'm sure you're stiff enough after earlier."

Huffing a laugh, I shot him the bird and started for the kitchen. "You want something?"

"Only if it's coffee. The sooner we solve this, the better, so I should keep working on the profile."

"You're no fun," I grumbled.

"Considering what we did earlier, I'm pretty sure your statement is invalid." His gaze snapped to me, pausing my retreat to the kitchen. "And you know, if you want me to step away... if us three is too much because of how you're feeling about her, just tell me and I will."

I scrubbed a hand along my jaw, the scruff scraping along my calloused palm. "It's what she wants, though I'm not saying it's not a struggle to keep her to myself. There might come a time when sharing isn't something we can keep doing without me strangling you." Jameson barked a laugh, then grimaced when he saw I was serious. "But we're not there yet."

"Just make sure you tell me before the strangling happens. I'd hate for you to lose your career as the FBI's golden child because you're in jail for murder."

Chuckling to myself, I moved through the dining room, pausing a second to stare at the table where I ate her delicious pussy earlier before continuing to the kitchen in search of alcohol. Not bothering with the light switch, I pulled the fridge door open, a soft yellow glow immediately clicking on. For several seconds, I stared at the now-stocked shelves after my grocery delivery earlier, wishing the six-pack of beer I didn't end up ordering would magically appear.

Giving up on my booze hunt, I snagged a glass from the strainer, one I'd cleaned after dinner, and held it under the faucet. I shut off the tap when the water nearly flowed over and then raised the glass to my lips. Hopefully five or six glasses would help me not look like a dehydrated piece of meat in the morning.

As I guzzled down half the contents, my gaze shifted to staring out the window into the dark night.

A face—not my reflection—stared right back at me.

Without a second thought, I dropped the glass. The immediate shattering boomed in the quiet. The worn linoleum squeaked beneath my bare feet as I spun for the back door. I wrapped my hand around the antique door-knob and twisted hard, eager to get outside and tackle the son of a bitch.

Only the knob snapped clean off.

"Son of a bitch," I roared at the useless chunk of metal in my hand. Throwing it to the floor, I searched along the counter, hand smacking around in the dark. Dark glee swept through me when it hit the knife block. Taking one in each hand, I palmed the hilts and raced through the dining room, focused on the front door.

"Grab your gun and get to her room," I snapped to Jameson, who stood, glancing between me and my knives in utter confusion. "Someone is outside."

That confusion vanished. Without another word, he darted down the hall.

Not thinking about anything other than catching the stalking motherfucker, I flung the front door open, then shoved the screen door out of the way. I didn't have time to relish the glorious feeling of the bitter frosty night air against my sizzling skin, though it was a welcomed relief.

My sweaty palms molded around the knives' smooth plastic hilts as I adjusted my grip. Fighting with knives was more of a "learned it by watching action movies" skill instead of practical knowledge, but without my gun, they would have to do. Back against the brick, I crept along the porch, moving in the direction of the kitchen window. Each thundering thump of my heart felt like it wanted to beat right out of my chest. Only a few times in my career had I taken down an unsub on my own, though the times it happened, I fucking loved every single second of it.

Pausing at the corner of the house, I held a full breath and waited, listening for any signs of the unsub. Dead leaves rustled along the ground, swirling with the wind. Somewhere close, the muffled words of a television filtered through the night.

Ready to end the standoff, I turned and leapt off the concrete porch, knives at the ready. Mulch and dead leaves poked and jabbed into the soles of my bare feet, but I pushed off the bite of pain as I crept along the side of the house, eyes swiveling, taking in every inch of the somewhat overgrown side yard to avoid a surprise attack.

A male shout from inside followed by a loud thump that seemed to rattle the whole house sent a bolt of icy dread through my veins. Turning on the balls of my feet, I sped back to the front door. Adrenaline pumping, I yanked the screen door harder than I wanted, sending it slamming against the brick at the same time I kicked the main door in. A sharp crack sounded at my back, but I continued inside, not caring about the now broken door.

Eyes wild, I quickly scanned the living room, looking for the source of the earlier sound, but Remy's pleading words from down the hall stole my focus, sending me hurtling in her direction. Bits of debris still clung to my feet, embedding into the tender skin as I turned to race down the hall and save—

I skidded to a halt. Chest heaving with my ragged breaths, I blinked, trying to understand what in the hell I was looking at.

Jameson rocked in the fetal position on the floor right outside her bedroom door, his pain-filled groans echoing in the hall. Remy, still in the sweatpants and sweatshirt she went to sleep in, was on her knees hovering over him, gently patting him while apologizing over and over.

My arms went limp, the adrenaline leaving in a rush. Utter exhaustion engulfed me in its wake.

Remy glanced up, doing a double take when she found me silently piecing together the scene.

"I didn't mean to?" she said a little hysterically, pitch so high I winced. "He was coming into my room. I'd heard a noise—"

"Are you okay?" I asked, cutting off her rambling. She blinked, wide green eyes holding mine. "Remy, are you hurt?"

"No," she said with a frantic giggle. "But he is." She gestured to the still-groaning Jameson with a...

I moved a single step closer to get a better look at what she held in her right hand.

"Is that... is that a Taser?"

"Don't you dare judge me," she said, wearing a manic smile.

Fuck, she's on the edge of losing it. This was the opposite of what the doctor wanted. Or me. Based on Jameson's current situation, I did not want to get hit with that thing in her hand.

"I don't want a gun in the house with Crew, and this is the next best thing," she explained.

"Fuck," Jameson groaned. I slid my gaze to him, wincing at his sweaty, red face. "My balls are still twitching. If this is your kink, Rem, I'm out."

Falling against the wall, I went to scrub at my face but almost jabbed the end of the knife into my eye. "Fuck is right," I huffed.

"What is going on?" Remy asked, still running her free hand over Jameson like that would help. Hell, maybe it would. Pretty sure those hands exploring my body would cure just about any ailment.

I bit my lip and turned my head to look toward the living room.

If I told her what I saw, who I assumed was lurking around the house, she'd be even more worried than she already was, but it would also solidify the seriousness of what was going on.

"I was getting a glass of water when I saw someone outside the kitchen window." Turning back, I grimaced at the lack of color in her now-blank face. "I asked Jameson to grab his gun and come protect you, but he was apparently attacked by an armed kitten in the process."

Her dark lashes fanned down with slow blinks before her shock wore off and her eyes narrowed. "I'll show you a kitten," she hissed.

Keeping my smile restrained, I nodded. "Anytime, anywhere, Kitten."

And just like that, with a few instigating words, the color was slowly coming back to her cheeks, and that feisty glint flickered behind those green eyes.

Good. Mission accomplished.

"I need to go check the perimeter and make sure he's gone." Which he would be by now. I had a feeling he wasn't expecting to see me in the house tonight. "But I can't until Jameson can hold a gun without his finger twitching and pulling the trigger."

"Fuck off, man," he said, pushing himself up to a seated position and leaning against the wall for support, his head falling back with a thump. "Is that thing military grade?"

"Maybe. I bought it off an Instagram ad."

"What in the hell are you searching for that an ad like that would pop up in your feed?" I asked.

"Self-defense, home security, how to protect your kid from being bullied at school—"

I shoved off the wall. "He's being bullied?"

"That's what you heard?" Her tiny nose scrunched. "Yeah, but I think we have more urgent issues. I'll take his gun—"

"No," Jameson and I shouted at the same time.

She rolled her eyes and grabbed the 9mm anyway. "I might not own one, but I know how to shoot it. Point, pull trigger, down goes the bad guy. Go run your checks, and I'll protect the invalid."

"I want to be mad, but I'm more impressed," Jameson said before coughing and groaning. "Okay, and slightly mad."

"You barged into my room with a gun, and it was dark," Remy said with a huff. "This is after I heard glass breaking. I've now taken down you *and* Tallon—"

"Just because you surprised me," I grumbled.

"You two should totally be impressed and realize I can take care of myself."

I studied Remy. "We're not saying you can't. We're just here to help so you don't have to do it alone."

With her free hand, she pushed off the hardwood floor. Rolling her shoulders back, she leveled a look my way and hitched her chin toward the living room. "Go. We're fine." She glanced down at Jameson, who was looking a little green, and winced. "Well, I'm fine. He will be. Eventually."

I stalked forward, and her eyes widened as I closed the distance between us. Standing her ground, she refused to retreat a single inch. Only when we were toe to toe did I stop. Inches separated us, the heat from earlier flaring back to life despite the danger surrounding us.

The tip of her tongue poked out and slid along her lower lip. I swallowed down a groan.

She would be the death of me, I was certain.

"Can I help you?" she whispered, a hint of lust in her tone.

Smiling despite the circumstances, I leaned closer. Silky dark strands brushed against my lips as I pressed them to the shell of her ear. A thrum of pride swelled when she shook with a full-body shiver.

"Remy," I breathed.

"Yes?" she responded shakily.

"You're blocking the bedroom." Pulling back, I inclined my head to the side. I could physically move her, but that wasn't smart with the knives still clutched in my hands.

"Huh?"

Careful with the blade, I nudged her to the side with one hand so I could slip past. "If I'm going out there, I need my gun." Her dark lashes fanned up and down with long blinks. "The knives were my only option earlier, but now I want my gun since it's just there." The tip of the blade glinted in the hallway light as I pointed to the three nine-millimeter handguns lying on top of the dresser.

"Oh," she rasped. "Right. Let me just…." She slid a trembling hand along her chest and then wrapped it around her thin neck. I tracked the movement like a fucking predator stalked prey, my mind flooding with images of my hand wrapping around her throat while taking everything she was willing to give.

Shaking my head to focus on the problem, I set the knives down and grabbed one gun, not giving her a second look as I marched out of the bedroom and back out into the night. If I saw the same want in her gaze, her need for me,

I'd bend her over that damn bed and fuck her until she was hoarse from screaming my name.

Later.

Not now with the killer eager to turn my kitten into his next victim lurking outside our door.

First, I'd find the bastard, ensure he could never hurt another woman again, and then I'd fuck the voice out of Remy.

Sounded like a great fucking plan to me.

17

———

REMINGTON

Coffee now cold from the air and the length of time I'd held the mug, I fixed my unfocused gaze on the dark liquid to keep from watching the various agents scattered around my property in search of evidence. At least the sun was peeking over the horizon, offering the promise of light and warmth soon. My slow breaths fogged in front of me. With every blink, it was like scraping sandpaper over my tired, dry eyes, yet I couldn't sleep. I'd been awake now since a little before four. After accidentally tasing Jameson and knowing the crazy fucker was so close, there was no way I could go back to bed.

How long could I physically go on like this?

After last night, almost being attacked in my home, and also startled awake by a fire alarm, which triggered too many terrible memories—I wasn't sure if I'd ever sleep again. At least not until we caught the bastard.

And who knew when that would be?

My pulse raced as I considered all the aspects of my life that were unsettled because the sick bastard wanted me. Who knew when Crew could come home and return to school? Then there was my job. I was already in hot water from being out for two days with no warning a few weeks ago and then calling in sick last week.

"You okay?" Tallon asked. The porch swing shifted backward, the chain squeaking under his heavier weight as he sat beside me.

Stare locked on my coffee mug, I shook my head. "I don't think I am, honestly. This won't stop," I stated, my tone void of emotion, too exhausted to be upset or panicked. Emptiness and feeling lost held me in this static state of awareness, yet emotionless. It was the same state I would slip into when Jett would berate me. In this dark void, nothing mattered. "And I don't know where to start in getting my life back together. Should I just move?" That wasn't ideal, but it was an option. "That would mean ripping Crew out of school halfway through the year and me finding a new job, selling the house...."

The enormity of it all had tears building in my lower lids, though that emptiness still gripped me tight, refusing to let me feel the swelling panic and sadness.

When I twisted to face where Tallon sat, he blanched, no doubt seeing the tears and blank face. "I'm overwhelmed, exhausted, and lost," I admitted, my voice shaky.

He simply nodded and wrapped an arm around my shoulders, drawing me closer to his side. With the heavy weight of his arm, his comforting presence, and blazing body heat, my body relaxed, allowing me to mold against him. With him, the void ebbed away, allowing the full force of my emotions to barrel through me.

"I don't know what to do, Tallon," I whispered. "What am I supposed to do?"

"I'm here, Remy," he said. A smile spread across my face

when he rested his head on top of mine. "I'm not going anywhere until you're safe."

Wiping at a rogue tear, I snuggled deeper into his embrace, wallowing in the overwhelming sensation of practically dry drowning in problems with no good solutions. The need to see Crew, to squish his sweet face, hear his laugh, and see his warm smile hit me square in the chest, knocking the breath from my lungs.

I needed to see him. To witness with my own eyes that he was safe and happy.

That would make some of this better, ease the edge of desperation that was slowly creeping over me.

Sure, being a single mother was exhausting and hard, but he made it all worth it. I wasn't exaggerating when I told Jameson that Crew was my life. Every morning I woke up excited to see him and went to bed fretting over all the ways I failed, the mistakes I made that day, and planning how to be better the next. Was that the mom-guilt phenomenon? Maybe, but really, I just wanted to do everything I could to give him a better childhood than I had.

"I miss him so much," I admitted out loud.

He tensed, the firm muscles along my side hardening. "Who?"

"Crew. We've been this two-person team for so long, and it's difficult being away from him. I know he's safe, but I just miss the hell out of that kid. Miss his jokes that make little sense, his insistent questions, and his smile."

Tallon's soft T-shirt bunched beneath my cheek as I shifted to see his reaction to all this. My lips parted, a soft gasp releasing when I found him already looking down at me, a gentle expression on his normally firm features.

"He's lucky to have you," he said as his lips tugged into a hesitant smile. "And he sounds like a great kid."

My stomach flipped as my heart leapt. If he thought that, maybe there was a chance he'd want Crew.

Want *us*.

"He is," I rasped, emotions squeezing my throat. "And thanks. We've come a long way together. What's amazing is he knows I try, so he doesn't give me shit about it. Sometimes I whip into school on two wheels, rushing to get him for the last pickup, and he's the only one there waiting. I, of course, feel like shit, a terrible mother for it all, but he doesn't make me feel bad about it. I'm lucky to have him."

"I'd say it says a lot about you as a mother. Can I ask about his father and why he isn't in the picture?"

I swallowed hard, forcing down my nerves. "He's a good guy," I murmured. "But it just didn't work out between us."

"He's not that great of a guy if he let someone like you get away and left you doing all this on your own."

I stilled at the anger in his tone. *Holy hell, is he... is he defending me?*

"You have no clue. I could be a royal bitch to be with long-term."

His chuckle vibrated against me, easing another layer of my jumbled emotions. "I highly doubt that."

"Plus, we're doing okay on our own. I've worked hard to not need anyone else."

"So this bullying thing you mentioned," he started as he shoved the heels of his dress shoes against the concrete. The swing rocked back and forth, as if this were any lazy Sunday with zero problems or worries. "Want to talk about it?"

I choked back a sob. *Holy fuck, is this what it's like to have another parental figure? To have someone to talk through the everyday issues, a sounding board to make sure you're doing it right and not fucking up your kids for life?*

I wanted that, this, so badly my heart hurt.

"It's not really bullying. It's just… well, he's different from the other kids. We're not rich. I work hard to afford that tuition. I buy his uniforms in the secondhand shop since he grows out of them so fast, and that doesn't go unnoticed by the other kids. It's a bunch of little things, but Crew doesn't let it get him down. It's more me hating it for him because I feel responsible for it. If I just work harder, do more—"

"You're giving him what's most important. Money means nothing to a kid, but you being there for him is everything. He sees you fighting and working your ass off. That's more important than having a trust fund and parents who are gone more than they're home. Half of the kids I went to school with never saw their parents, and that showed. They were shitheads doing whatever they could for attention—good or bad."

"Which were you?" I asked. Leaning forward, I set the mug on the concrete before snuggling back against his side.

Fuck, I never want to leave this little cocoon blocking me from reality.

"Guess."

"I take you as a rule follower, not wanting to get in trouble. Probably a little reserved. I don't see you putting up with kid-type bullshit."

His brows rose. "That's pretty accurate. Maybe you should be a profiler."

My cheeks bunched with a growing grin. "Nah, I'll stick to programming."

"How did you get into it? It's a pretty male-dominated field, right?"

"It is." I chewed on my lip and stared at the thick blond-and-brown scruff covering his jaw. "My dad is a big computer guy. From an early age, I was fascinated with computers and read different things he'd bring home from work." I stopped, knowing I was already telling him too much. He couldn't know more about the family who didn't know how to find me. "So I guess you could say it's in my blood."

My stomach sank when I looked up and found his brows furrowed. "I thought you said you didn't have any family to help you. If your parents are still around, why not ask them for help?"

I swallowed and slowly peeled myself away from his side. He monitored my every movement as I slid to the opposite end of the porch swing, though the small space between us didn't feel like enough.

"It's complicated."

"Interesting," he mused, though his tone had a hard edge to it. "Tell me where you went to school again."

My stomach dropped. Heart thundering, I stood on shaky legs. Shit, this was becoming messy, all because of me and my secrets, my past. "I think I need to go lie down for a bit."

"What are you hiding, Remy?" Tallon asked, suddenly right in front of me.

I studied the center of his chest, refusing to meet his demanding stare. "Nothing." Though that was an outright lie. I was hiding everything—everything from them. This wasn't just about Crew. This was about me, my past, what I ran from.

Who I was still running from.

Warm fingers wrapped around my chin, forcing me to look up. His blue eyes searched mine. "Are you in trouble?"

"Not anymore," I answered honestly. "I did what I had to do. Just... please don't ask. I can't."

"Why?"

"Because," I nearly cried. The worry and concern radiating off him made it impossible to ignore. "I can't go back, Tallon. I won't let him find me. Telling you more would jeopardize that. Don't you get it?"

"Remington," a male voice shouted.

Quickly yanking from Tallon's hold, I stepped around him and forced a fake smile on my face. I raised my hand, waving at my neighbor as he jogged across the brown front lawn.

"Hey," he wheezed, hunching over to grip his knees. "Dang, I'm out of shape."

"Hey, Brett."

When he stood up, breathing under control, he zeroed in on Tallon. I was sure it looked odd, considering I was still in my sweats and Tallon was ready to tackle the day in his slacks and dress shirt.

"Do you know what's going on? Who are all these people?" he asked, shifting to taking in the long line of black SUVs lining the curb.

"Attempted burglary." Keeping the surprise from my face, I twisted around to Tallon. "Did you see anything unusual last night?" he asked Brett, ignoring me.

Brett's brows pushed together. "Not that I can think of. Are you a cop?"

"In a way." Tallon stepped to my side and wrapped an arm around me. With a firm tug, I was crushed against him, and his hand tightened around my waist. I sent Tallon a death glare, knowing exactly what he was doing, though not hating it—the opposite, if the swelling in my heart meant anything.

"Oh, okay." Brett's curious gaze volleyed between us.

"Hey, Remy, do you have any more towels?" Tallon's arm fell away as I turned toward the open front door. Jameson stood on the other side of the broken screen in just a pair of light gray sweatpants. My cheeks blazed as I took in his ripped chest and abs. Fuck, this did not look good. All displayed in front of the neighborhood's biggest gossip. "I was about to take a shower, but Tallon used them all."

And that made this awkward moment even more tantalizing.

"Um, I should go," my neighbor said cheerfully, clearly elated at this juicy tidbit. I sighed and fought the urge to pull the hoodie over my head and tighten the string to block out this whole encounter. "Good luck with all that."

By the time I turned back around, Brett was across the lawn, already on his cell phone.

"Fuck," I complained into my hands as I hid my hot face. "Seriously, you two? What the actual hell was that all about?"

"What?" they both questioned in unison.

"This." I jabbed a finger in Jameson's direction. "You being half naked talking about a shower, and you"—I poked at Tallon's hard chest—"with the whole territory marking."

"The what?" he asked, crossing his arms over his chest. Oh, he knew what I was referring to. That damn cocky-ass smirk said it all.

Bastard.

I fucking loved it.

But bastard all the same.

"The arm over my shoulder stunt. That was a blinking neon sign stating 'my property.' Now Brett is taking this new sizzling gossip to... well, everyone. Then the entire neighborhood will think I'm sleeping with two men. Fucking hell, can my life become any more of a damn soap opera?"

I shoved Tallon, which didn't even move him an inch, which pissed me off even more. With a low growl, I stepped around him only for a firm grip on my wrist to yank me back against him. A shudder raced down my spine when he pressed his lips against the shell of my ear.

"I told you, Kitten. You're mine, and I will make sure every fucker who comes around trying to take what's mine knows exactly whose you are."

That should not have been hot. It should frighten me.

But it didn't. Instead, I had to swallow down a whimper and lean against him so I wouldn't turn into a puddle on the damn porch.

Jameson shoved open the screen door. It groaned, shifting awkwardly as it hung off the hinges on an odd angle.

I gaped at the broken door. How in the hell did I miss that earlier? "What the hell happened to my door?"

Jameson grimaced and pointed at Tallon. "He did it."

Whirling around, I pressed both hands to my hips. "Fix it."

"I was planning on it. Hey, I think you need to"—his hands moved up and down in a placating motion—"calm down a little. Doctor's orders."

My teeth ground together as I clenched my jaw. "My life is blowing up around me, and you're telling me to calm down?" I took a menacing step toward him, ready to knock that damn grin off his face. My arms trembled with restless energy. If I didn't get out of here, I'd kill one of them. "Actually, I have a better idea."

"This doesn't sound promising," Jameson voiced behind me. "She's scary when she's mad. Shit, where's my gun?"

"What's your plan, Kitten?" Tallon asked.

"How about a little stress relief?"

"I lied," Jameson cut in. "This sounds promising."

Behind my back, I shot Jameson a double middle finger. "I haven't worked out in a few days."

"You're not going anywhere alone," Tallon stated, as if his word was law.

I rolled my eyes. "Figured as much. Come on, let's get changed. This will be fun. Promise."

"For who?" Jameson laughed.

I grinned over my shoulder. "Me."

"HOLY SHIT," Jameson gasped. Sprawled on the mat like a starfish, he blinked up at the ceiling. "I was actually trying that time."

The coarse cotton towel dragged along my forehead as I wiped away the sweat before it could drip into my eyes. I beamed down at his prone form, about to taunt him into going another round, when a loud shout pulled my attention to the other side of the gym. Set up in a large warehouse, it housed various areas with workout equipment and also kickboxing sections ranging from floor mats, where Jameson and I were sparring, to actual roped-off rings, which was where my attention was now, observing the fight between Tallon and the gym owner.

With a quick throw, Tallon tossed the owner to the ground. Ripping off a single glove, Tallon hovered over the cursing man and reached down, offering to help him from the floor. Both men had lost their shirts at some point, and they both were cut. I couldn't pull my eyes from Tallon's chest, skin glistening with sweat.

I swallowed hard, my parched throat having nothing to do with the last hour sparring with Jameson. Tallon drew both arms high over his head, stretching his thick back muscles.

Holy hell, he's cut like a fucking god.

He wasn't perfect. I knew none of us were, but there was more to him, now that I broke down his tough exterior, than just a sexy body and talented tongue. Tallon was kind, thoughtful, overly protective in an endearing way.

Just thinking about how this morning, on the way here, he wouldn't stop driving until I told him what I wanted for breakfast and finished at least half the taquito, made me smile, made me fucking happy.

For the first time in a long time, I felt good about myself. He was there to counter every negative thought I had, help me see I was enough, doing enough. And if that wasn't just another thing that made him insanely attractive.

"You have a little drool." Jameson chuckled as he popped off the mat. A single finger swiped along my lower lip, his honey-brown eyes twinkling with mischief. "See something you like there, Remy?"

"No," I denied way too quickly to be true. Jameson's grin widened, making the corners of his eyes wrinkle. "Fine, yes. I mean, you both are...." Not sure how to put it to words, I just fanned myself for a moment. "Better than I remember," I finally finished.

"Same, sweetheart," he remarked. "Though I think we should give him a little extra push toward this."

I frowned, not understanding. "This?"

"You and him. Isn't that obvious?"

"No? He says I'm just a witness." Jameson barked a laugh and shook his head. I narrowed my eyes. "What? That's what he said. Sure, we've had some fun—hot fun—but it means nothing to him."

Not like it did me.

"Him saying that is just him deflecting because you're so much more than all that." He studied me for a second, that playfulness vanishing. "I think you need to tell him about Crew sooner than later."

"I thought you said to wait?" I hissed.

"I know what I said, but whatever is brewing between you two, it's explosive. When that secret comes out, it might break whatever you've built. He'll see it as you either lying to him this whole time or you not trusting him with the truth."

"Which is half true. Well, was true." I sucked my lower lip between my teeth as I studied the red mat beneath my feet. "I don't know how to bring it up, you know."

"No, I don't know." I shot him a scowl, but he just shrugged. "Okay, back to pushing Tallon closer to the edge of breaking his dumb resolve to not fuck you."

"The what—" But my words stuttered when he gripped the hem of his sweat-soaked shirt and ripped it over his head. Unable to not stare, I licked my lips as I took in every inch of his sculpted chest and toned stomach. He was seriously hot. Ripped, lean, and all smooth, tan skin. He didn't make my heart pound like Tallon, but he sure as hell made me want to get closer.

"You have a sports bra under that, right?" Before I could answer, his fingers gripped my loose workout tank, tips brushing against my skin, making me involuntarily shiver, and yanked it upward. Following the motion, my arms automatically went up, allowing the tank to come off easily. He tossed it on top of his and nodded, seeming happy with whatever he was trying to achieve. "Perfect. Now let's see how long it takes."

"What takes?" I asked, resituating the band that held my hair back from my face.

"After yesterday's showdown of him trying to prove to himself he could give you what you need while denying himself because he's a damn masochist." That last part was more of a grumble. "And after the situation last night, he's tense as fuck. Which is why he's on to yet another sparring partner over there and has been going at it nonstop for over an hour." Shaking out his arms, he planted both bare feet and raised his hands in the ready position. "You both need that push to really fall into whatever this is. Now come at me."

I mimicked his stance, and we shifted in a circle, both waiting for the other to make the first move. "I'm confused. Wouldn't that make you jealous?" I paused for a second as I thought that through. Jameson took my distraction and lunged. I skirted around him, his fingers barely brushing my bare side.

"Jealous?"

"Yeah, me and Tallon, just us?" He'd said it was fine before, but was it really?

Sweat flung from his hair with the sharp shake. "Nope. Remember what I said? We always did it for fun." He shot me a wink. "I've been with plenty of women on my own." He waggled his brows suggestively. "And I'm good at what I do. I can read that there's more than just physical attraction between you two. And it clearly has nothing to do with the fact that he's your baby daddy since he doesn't know. It's all you."

"Huh." My hands dropped to my side at that revelation. Like the sneaky bastard he was, Jameson lunged, wrapping his arms around my middle. The air exploded from my lungs as my back slammed to the mat. Heart racing, I closed my eyes and focused on calming my breathing. "Cheater," I croaked.

"That's for tasing my balls." With a groan, he rolled off me and collapsed onto the mat. "Now we're even."

"What the hell are you two doing?"

My chin hit my chest, following the sound of Tallon's voice. He stood just off to the side, arms crossed over his naked pecs, which made his corded arm muscles flex. Damn. I wasn't positive which version of Tallon I enjoyed ogling best: the hot suits, ass-sculpting jeans, or bare chest. "Where is your fucking shirt, Remy?"

"Less than two minutes," Jameson said under his breath, just for me to hear. "Three minutes faster than I expected."

"You're incorrigible." I laughed and smacked the back of my hand against his chest.

"I've been called worse."

My smile dropped at his suddenly serious tone. I met his now-distant gaze. "Whoever said that, they were wrong. You're all kinds of fantastic, Jameson."

"Except for the whole first name being a last name thing."

My lips quirked. "Well, yeah, except that. Everything else is exceptional."

An undistinguishable look pasted across his sweaty face. "Thank you."

"Up, you two," Tallon ordered, now standing beside me, hand hovering midair to help me up. I smacked my smaller one into his. A squeal erupted as I basically flew upward. Grabbing my waist, he held me against him, hands encircling my middle until I was steady on my feet. "Again, where is your damn shirt?"

I hooked a thumb toward Jameson. "He took it."

Tallon rubbed at his scruff-covered jaw. "He did, did he? What are you playing at, Jameson?"

The man in question lifted a single shoulder. "Nothing. She looked too warm. Though now it seems we've drawn attention."

I glanced around, and sure enough, several regulars who

normally didn't pay me any attention—well, not that I ever noticed—were eyeing us.

No. Not us. Me.

Tallon cursed. With one arm wrapped around my back, he hauled me an inch in the air and stormed over to his discarded clothes. With a few quick movements, his still-damp shirt was tugged over my head and my arms pulled through the gaping sleeves.

I glanced down and pursed my lips before glaring up at him.

"I look ridiculous," I snapped. I was swimming in his shirt. "You can't see that I'm wearing shorts." Though I didn't hate it as much as I let on. It smelled like him, after all.

"You look covered." Interlacing our fingers, he tugged me along, headed for the front door. "Come on. Time to go home and let me feed you."

My steps faltered at the word.

Home.

That sounded absolutely fantastic coming from his lips.

18

TALLON

"Have you heard from your boss?" I called over my shoulder.

The edges of the sourdough bread crunched beneath the sharp blade as I sliced the sandwich I'd constructed for Remy in half. Sliding the knife beneath both halves, I carefully placed them on the white plate. Moving to mine and Jameson's, I did the same, placing his on the blue plate with small white flowers and mine on a plastic one that said "Happy Birthday."

I grinned like a damn fool at the mismatched plates. It was the same with the cups, silverware, and, well, basically everything in the house. It was unique to Remy, and for some reason, it made sense for her home. She made it all fit together, even though it could look cluttered and disorganized.

"This looks delicious," she said as I set the plate in front of where she sat around the small dining table. "Thank you." The smile she shot me was genuine, full, and bright. "And yeah, but I don't think you'll like his response."

After grabbing the other two plates, I handed Jameson

his before taking the chair to Remy's right. The same chair I sat in yesterday while I ate her pussy from this very table. I choked on a groan and shifted uncomfortably in the seat.

"If he said you still have to come into the office, despite the threat to yourself and others in the office, then yeah, you'd be correct about me not liking his dumbass response," I said before taking a giant bite of my ham, turkey, and bacon sandwich. You'd think being on the road so much, I would love fast food or eating out, but I was over it at this point.

Maybe over it *all*. The time away from home, the crappy food, little sleep, and never-ending cycles of work.

"He said we're too close to the deadline on this project, and he needs me there since I was out a few days last week. I'm the fastest programmer they have, so they need me on-site to ensure we implement on time."

"Can't you do your job from anywhere?" Jameson remarked. "I thought that was a perk of being in IT."

Her thick cream sweater slipped off her shoulder with a nonchalant shrug. Sandwich in one hand, I reached over with the other and tugged it back in place.

With a wry grin, she stared at her now-covered shoulder. "Technically, yeah, I can, but this is a big corporation. They aren't as flexible as other smaller ones or start-ups. And those are outstanding work environments, but they don't offer the stability or pay like I have now. Plus, there's the fact that my project manager is a complete asshole." Picking up her sandwich, she studied all sides before flicking a look my way. "How in the hell will this fit in my mouth?"

Sandwich hovering in front of my open mouth, I barked a laugh, Jameson doing the same except choking on the bite he was chewing.

Remy's eyes widened, realizing what she'd just said. "Oh, fuck off, you two. It's so big—"

"You should stop," I said with a smile. Fuck, when had I smiled this much?

"There's just so much meat—"

"Now you're just fucking with us," I said, roaring with laughter. She huffed, but clearly wasn't upset at us laughing at her, and rolled her eyes. "Just open wide and shove it in." I shot her a wink before doing just as I instructed to my sandwich.

"It's your small hands," Jameson said, having finally regained some of his composure. "It makes it look bigger than what it is."

"Is that what you tell yourself?" she volleyed back. Shaking her head, she went to take a bite but paused. "Stop staring. You're making me nervous."

"You're the one who started it," I offered.

"Bottom line, I'm going to work tomorrow," she said, changing the subject. "He told me I have to be there, so I'll be there. I know you have reservations—"

"They aren't reservations, Remy. It's not safe for you or your coworkers. Just don't go. Fuck what he says."

"I can't do that." She groaned. "I'm a single working mother, guys. The benefits are amazing, and the pay is almost twice my last job. Yes, I have to deal with the asshole who I swear likes to make me feel as small as possible just because he's a guy and I'm, well...."

"A woman?" I offered, confused why she didn't readily know that answer.

"Small. Guys who are bigger than me, which is most, sometimes use their size to intimidate me."

Jameson and I shared a look.

He thrust his thumb my way before swinging back to his chest. "Do we do that?"

She hid her grin with a small bite, her dark hair swishing with the shake of her head.

I released a gradual breath. *Thank fuck.* I wasn't consciously trying to intimidate her, but I could see how it would be easy to do considering our size difference.

"Good," I grunted. "Want me to talk to your boss?"

Remy stared at the table as she chewed. "Let me think about that. Maybe if it came from you as an FBI agent, he'd understand the seriousness of the situation. And you're bigger than him. Can I have your pickle?"

This woman would be the death of me. I knew she was talking about the single pickle spears I'd placed on each of our plates, but my mind went straight to the gutter, envisioning her asking for my cock with the same hopeful look in her eye.

"You can have mine," Jameson said after a few beats of silence.

Her cheeks bunched with a wide smile, and little lines burst from the corners of her green eyes.

Fuck, she was gorgeous.

Careful to keep my movements subtle, I adjusted in the chair to ease the stiffness happening in my jeans. Grabbing the last bite of my sandwich, I pushed my plate toward her, offering the actual pickle she'd asked for.

"It's settled, then," I said. "We'll go to your office tomorrow morning and sort this shit out."

"Without me getting fired," she demanded, pointing the half-eaten pickle spear my way.

"Without getting you fired... on purpose," I said. Who knew what would happen once I met the bastard? If he'd been intimidating Remy on purpose, well, reciprocating, that was well within reason.

"I have some work I need to get done this afternoon," Jameson said, dusting his hands over his empty plate.

"Same. I need to update the task force on the recent victim. And my boss," I said with a groan. "Fuck, he'll want a step-by-step plan of action on how we plan to catch this fucker, and I'm at a loss."

"We have little to go on," Jameson agreed. "The profile is solid but doesn't give us a theory on how to catch him before he gets what he wants."

The look I shot his way would kill a lesser man. Jameson cringed and sent an apologetic glance toward Remy. "Sorry, Remy."

She opened her mouth, but I shut her down. "Don't even say what I think you're thinking."

Those perfectly fuckable lips pressed into a thin line. "And what was I thinking?"

"That we use you as bait to get to this fucker. It's not happening, so don't even suggest it. Hell, don't even think it," I nearly growled as I leaned closer, invading her space.

"That's the dumbest idea I've ever heard," she stated, face blank.

"This coming from the woman who mouthed off to him once already."

"That wasn't dumb. It was strategy."

"Right." Reaching over, I swiped the edge of my thumb along her lip, brushing a crumb from the corner of her mouth. "Okay, Kitten. If you weren't going to offer yourself up as bait, then what were you about to say?"

Those damn green eyes sparkled. "I was going to ask, if you're both working this afternoon, what should we do tonight? I figured you'd be against going out to do something fun."

"Like Putt-Putt?"

Remy and I slowly turned our heads toward Jameson, who looked way too excited about the idea.

"I was thinking a movie," Remy corrected, losing the battle on not laughing. "You're the cutest, Jameson."

Her words made me pause, but the lack of heat, the more playfulness in her features as she studied Jameson, put me at ease. They were friends. Friends and a little more. Knowing Jameson would leave for Texas when this was all done made the sharing idea easier for now.

"How about a movie here?" I suggested. "We can order in, or I can cook."

"Sounds great," Remy agreed. The chair legs scraped across the hardwood floor as she pushed back. When she reached for my plate, I tugged it just beyond her grasp. "You made lunch. I'll clean up. Pretty sure I get the better end of the bargain, considering I'm just tossing these in the dishwasher." I reluctantly released my hold. "Oh, and fix the doors at some point today, okay? I'm still not sure how you ripped the knob off the back one. They built this house in the thirties. It's survived that long, yet in less than twenty-four hours, you broke a doorknob and a screen door."

"And almost elbowed a hole in the shower wall. It's cramped as hell."

She scoffed. "It's fine for me and Crew."

"Well, yeah, because you're no taller than five foot two—"

"Five foot three, to be exact."

"Yeah, with those boots you wear," Jameson chimed in.

"And your son is...." I paused. "How old is he again?"

She and Jameson shared a look I couldn't read. My

hackles rose as I watched them, instincts telling me they were hiding something from me.

"He's nine," Remy stated before hurrying to the kitchen.

Something tingled in my mind, indicating I was missing something. But then the phone in my pocket vibrated against my leg, chasing away that line of thought. Leaning back, I pulled out the small device and groaned, reading the name flashing on the screen.

"It's my boss. I need to take this."

Jameson studied me for a second before nodding. "Yeah, you do that. I'll go work with Agent Riggs to see if we can get a suspect pool going based on the profile I've been working on."

Before answering the call, I stood, my focus on the doorway that led to the kitchen. Remy was hunched over, elbows pressed against the counter with her head cradled in her hands.

Something was definitely going on, and I was determined to find out.

"Yeah, sounds good," Jameson remarked into the phone pressed between his cheek and shoulder as he quickly jotted down notes. "Let me know what he comes up with. A narrowed-down list, no matter how long, is better than what we have right now. Thanks, Rhyan." His hand paused, the pen hovering over the notepad. "Yeah, I'm excited to join the team too. Let me know when Charlie finds something."

The phone clattered to the trunk in front of the couch. Heels of both hands pressed to his closed eyes, Jameson leaned back until his head thumped against the wall.

"Charlie will run a search for any male midtwenties to

late thirties, Caucasian, no listed employment here in middle Tennessee who also lived in the greater Chicago area over ten years ago and now lives here."

"Nice," I commented as I finished the email with an extensive to-do list for my task force. They weren't happy that I was smack in the middle of the danger, one of the female agents in particular the most vocal about the arrangement, and they needed a reminder of who was in charge. What better way to do that than give them a shit ton of work to do? "That's a great idea."

"Thanks, that's what Rhyan said too. I'm hoping it can give us a list of suspects to look into. Anything is better than waiting for this unsub to form a new plan to grab Remy."

The thought of that bastard getting his hands on her spiked my pulse. "That will not happen."

He sighed. "We can't stay here forever, Tallon. We have to solve this, or we'll both be reassigned when the case goes cold, leaving her helpless."

I huffed an incredulous laugh. "Pretty sure that's one word I'd *never* use to describe that woman." After hitting Send, I tossed my phone beside his and stretched my long legs out along the floor. "What?" I asked, seeing his smirk out of the corner of my eye.

"Nothing," he said, that grin growing into a wide smile.

"Fuck off." I groaned, the zero sleep from the night before finally catching up with me. With a quick check of my watch, I grabbed a small pillow from the couch and tucked it under my head. "Wake me up in an hour and I'll start dinner."

"Sure." The single word was muffled and slightly slurred, signaling he was on the edge of sleep too.

Folding both hands over my stomach, I inhaled deep and released it slowly, allowing my muscles and mind to relax. It did nothing for the worry gnawing in my gut that Jameson's comment about us having to leave created.

I didn't want to admit it, but he was spot-on. Neither of our bosses would approve the resources needed to stick around if the case went cold.

That was if he quit killing until he had Remy. Which was highly unlikely. No, this psychopath wouldn't stop. Even if he got his hands on Remy, that would only entertain him for a short while. Evil like this wouldn't stop until we forced him to.

If hunting and killing this bastard kept Remy out of his grasp, then that was exactly what I'd do. No matter how long it took, I'd end his reign of terror before he could lay a hand on her.

Dead or dead.

With that resolution firmly branded in my mind, I drifted off to sleep, dreams of soft hands caressing and calming my soul, muscular legs wrapped around my waist keeping us close, and bright green eyes locked with mine with pure unadulterated happiness shining through.

19

REMINGTON

The fleece blanket caressed my fingertips as I released the edge, draping its warmth over Tallon's lower half. Turning for the blanket basket, I snagged another ultrasoft throw and laid it over Jameson. Soft snores vibrated through the room as the two dozed peacefully.

I watched them for a minute or two, unable to stop the small smile that slid up my cheeks or the swell of emotion building in my chest. It was strange feeling this way when they were invading my space, yet I loved it. I'd been lonely for so long, desperate for the ease of friendship and touch of another.

Most didn't see the hollowness that sometimes developed too heavy to handle. I never let Crew or anyone else see me break under the weight of doing all this on my own, not even a single family member to help carry the load. I learned how to keep my sobs quiet, muffled by a pillow against my face that absorbed my tears and cries.

Then these two entered my life for a second time. This time was longer than a few hours of fun. We were building something, a friendship—trust. Though at some point, it would all end. They'd go back to work, and I'd go back to that lonely life, only existing for Crew.

Heel of my hand pressed to my sternum, I rubbed at the growing ache.

Don't go there. I couldn't think about being alone now that I knew what it was like to have friends. I almost burst into tears this afternoon when Tallon made me lunch.

Made *me* lunch.

When was the last time someone did such a simple gesture to take care of me? Hell, last year when I had strep and could barely stay conscious from waiting too long to see a doctor, I had to call an Uber. I had no one to depend on.

Except now, maybe them.

"Come here."

I startled, snapping my gaze to the couch. Jameson's lids opened a sliver. Snaking a hand out from under the blanket, he gestured in invitation. With a quick look to the floor where Tallon lay, still fast asleep, I crawled under the blanket, careful to not make a sound. Draping an arm across my shoulders, he tucked me closer. "Sleep. We've got you."

Tears collected in my lower lids, but I refused to let a single one fall. Damn this man and his kind words that speared straight through me. They both needed to stop, or I wouldn't be able to let them go.

Knowing I was safe, I shifted to find a more comfortable position, pressing my cheek to his chest. Sooner than I expected, my lids grew heavy. The slow cadence of Jameson's chest rising and falling with each breath, the steady beat of his heart thumping beneath my ear, chased away all my worries and fears, dragging me into a deep, dreamless sleep.

I NUZZLED into the hard pillow, soft murmurs and the smell of something delicious urging me awake. Blinking through the haze from the too-long nap, I stayed still as my mind slowly cleared. Across from the couch, a game show I'd never seen before played on the TV, the volume so low I couldn't make out any of the words.

Hand to Jameson's shoulder, I pressed up, wiping my free hand at the corners of my mouth, checking for dried drool. Fingers trailed through my hair, and my eyes automatically fluttered shut at the blissful sensation.

"Nice nap?" His voice was rough, as if he'd just woken up too.

"Yeah," I rasped, stretching my arms up high. A small squeak slipped out as my stiff muscles protested. "How long was I out?"

"It's almost seven," he commented, like it wasn't a big deal.

"I slept for three hours?" My shock radiated in my voice. No wonder my head throbbed and I couldn't tell you what year it was. "Holy hell."

His brown eyes surveyed my face. "Does that not happen much?"

I snorted. "No. There's always too much to do. Naps only happen by accident, and never this long."

"I'm taking that as a compliment, then. Must have been your sleeping buddy," he joked, puffing his chest out. "You can sleep on me anytime." He shot a wink my way before turning his attention back to the TV.

"What smells so good?"

"Chicken tortilla soup."

The fabric of the couch twisted beneath me as I turned to face Tallon, who stood in the doorway between the living room and dining room.

"Really?" I questioned. "I don't remember you buying any soup cans."

It was then that I took in what he was wearing. Over a pair of black sweatpants and a gray T-shirt was... my flamingo-print apron. The apron that only saw the light of day once a year when I attempted to cook Thanksgiving lunch.

"I didn't," he stated like I'd offended him. "It's from scratch. I found a recipe I wanted to try a while back, and now I get to. I ordered all the ingredients yesterday when you and Jameson were bickering about which type of M&M's to put in the cart."

"Plain or nothing," I exclaimed.

"Peanut or bust," Jameson grumbled at the same time.

"You two are ridiculous." Tallon huffed, but the quirk of his lips told me he loved it. "Should be ready in a few." Turning around, he disappeared into the kitchen.

Lifting the blanket, I scrambled off the couch, hurrying after him. Chafing both hands up and down my arms to chase away the chill, I leaned against the wide doorframe and studied Tallon's back. The muscles along his arms flexed as he stirred the large pot.

"It smells amazing," I offered. My stomach growled, agreeing with my assessment.

He didn't startle, just glanced over his shoulder with a shy smile. "I love to cook. Though there aren't many chances these days. When I'm on the road for a case, I try to book an extended-stay place that has a small kitchen in the room, but that doesn't always happen. The fast food and stale donuts get old fast."

Comfortable silence settled between us, with just the bubbling of the soup meeting my ears. Shifting to the cutting board, Tallon chopped fresh cilantro, the amazing smell overtaking the other scents, with a skill I never managed despite all my time in the kitchen when I was younger. Gaze focused on his movements, the urge to tell him something about me, just because I knew I could trust him, pressed against me.

"I hate cooking," I stated. "I was raised super old-school. From an early age, I was in the kitchen learning how to cook for my future husband." His smooth movements faltered. "I was never great at it, much to my mother's dismay. She just knew that meant I'd never find a good husband." I huffed and rested my head against the dark wood doorframe. "Which I guess that was true. I never fit their mold. It didn't bother me, but they never let me forget I was a disappointment because I wouldn't conform."

"You're fucking with me, right?" Tallon had turned, leaning his ass against the edge of the counter. The tight fit of his T-shirt showed off every defined muscle, making the pink apron barely covering his wide chest even more comical.

"I wish I was, but nope. My parents didn't know what to do when they caught me studying my dad's programming and network books instead of reading *Good Housekeeping*." I snorted at the memory. "They grounded me for a week, which I loved despite them intending it as a punishment."

"Why?"

"It meant they didn't force me to go out with my so-called friends. My parents were popular, well known in the community, so they forced me to hang out with their friends' kids to be a part of the 'in' crowd. I went to every dance, after-school event, hell, I was even a cheerleader." I pointed at myself. "Can you imagine me as a cheerleader?"

Those bright blue eyes dipped, giving me a slow once-over that felt like an intimate caress.

"I can imagine you in the outfit, yes, but the actual cheering part, not so much."

My cheeks heated. That grin grew, brightening his entire face at my obvious embarrassment.

"Anyway, I hate cooking because"—I waved a hand in the air—"of all that."

His chin dipped in a slow nod. "Well, you don't have to worry about cooking for me. Ever. Zero expectations on what you should or shouldn't be doing while we're here."

While they're here.

Fuck, the reminder of them eventually having to leave made me want to cry. Sucking in a breath, I forced a smile and turned, ready to retreat to the living room before I could get emotional. But an arm snaked around my waist and hauled me backward against a hard chest. The tips of my toes scraped the worn linoleum floor as he held me against him.

"What about what I just said made you upset?"

Damn him and his observation skills.

I swallowed down the unshed tears. "You didn't."

His arm tightened around me. "Don't lie to me, Kitten."

Heat engulfed me from the inside out. My breathing grew short as my heart raced.

"It reminded me that you'll have to leave."

"And you don't want that?"

Twisting until I was fully turned around in his arms, I pressed my forehead to his chest. "It's just been nice."

"What?"

Tipping my face up, I stared into his concerned gaze. "Not being alone." Hands against his chest, I forced him to break his tight hold. "But you will. Leave, that is."

"You make it sound like it's a fact. That there are no other options."

"It is."

"And why's that?"

"Because as soon as you find out my secrets, you'll leave."

His brows dipped. "What are you hiding?"

A single tear escaped from the corner of my eye. "Everything." I wiped at my cheek and huffed at myself for being so damn weak around this man. "It's fine. We all know this is just for now, right? Catch a killer, and maybe the three of us have some fun too." Faking confidence, I arched a single challenging brow. "I'm just a witness, a victim you're protecting. Right?"

His jaw clenched tight. I swear I heard his teeth grinding. "Right."

Turning to the stove, he went back to making dinner, though his movements were sharper and jerkier than earlier. I frowned as I watched him. A part of me wanted to comfort him, tell him all my darkest secrets so they could be out in the open, and maybe, hopefully, he would stay despite the lies.

But he wouldn't.

Not when he found out about Crew.

Or uncovered that my current life was one big lie.

The biggest being the tiny fact that I was technically still married to Jett.

Disgusted with myself, sad at the turn of events, and just all around depressed, I shuffled back to the living room. With a loud, dramatic sigh, I plopped on the couch beside Jameson.

Shifting his gaze from the laptop screen, he shot me a side-eyed glance. "What's wrong with you?"

"I can't tell him." I sighed. "It will ruin everything, and

I'm not... I'm not ready for that. I want this, what we have right now, a little longer."

"You don't know that. It will change things, but you have no clue how until you tell him."

I shrugged, my eyes on *The Office* rerun now playing on the TV though I wasn't really watching. "I'd just like to soak this in for a few more days. To not have that complication between us. Is it so bad for me to just want to be free from it all for a little while?"

"Remy, I'm not sure what that says about your daily life if you see being confined to the house because a serial killer is after you as you being free."

I inclined my head his way. "True, but you're not a single parent. It sounds terrible, but it's even more restricting. I wouldn't want it any other way, but—" I turned on the couch to face him, leaning against the tufted back, "—for the first time since I found out I was pregnant, I'm doing something for me. Am I allowed to be selfish for a few more days? There's no stress of having to find a place for Crew to spend the night, not having to work around his school schedule, not carting him to and from practices and games and school. Thinking about dinner as I'm making lunch—"

Jameson reached out and grabbed my hand. "Yeah, you're allowed that. Plus, I'm thinking you'll have more time than you think to tell him."

"What does that mean?"

"It means I see it in him, the change with you. I don't think this is a fling. He seems happy."

"You think he'll stay?" I whispered, almost too afraid to voice those hopeful thoughts.

"Only way to find out is to lay it all out on the table and ask him to."

"And you?" I asked, feeling a little guilty that we were

talking so much about Tallon and me and not even considering his feelings.

"As soon as we wrap this case up, I'm leaving."

"Leaving?"

He nodded, clearly excited. "I've accepted a job in Texas. It's a great opportunity."

"Doing what?"

"A profiler with the FBI. I'll be heading to Quantico for training, then to Texas to join the team Special Agent Rhyan Riggs is putting together."

"Charlie's Rhyan?" He nodded. I blew out a loud raspberry. "Well, if you're going anywhere, I'm glad it's with them. Charlie is amazing, and I have to assume Rhyan is too, even though I haven't met her yet."

"How do you two know each other?"

I chewed on the corner of my lip and shot a look over my shoulder to make sure Tallon wasn't lingering close by. "He helped me out of a situation a long time ago, and we've been friends ever since. He knows Crew's dad isn't a part of his life, but he isn't aware that it's Tallon. I owe a lot to Charlie, and not just because of his friendship that's gotten me through a lot of dark days over the years."

"Well, I'm glad you had him."

"Me too." Running a hand through my hair, I shook my head to dispel all the memories that always crept forward when thinking about how Charlie and I met. I hitched my chin to the now-dark laptop. "What are you working on?"

Slipping his hand from mine, Jameson tugged the laptop closer and activated the screen. "I asked Charlie to run some names of people who matched the basic profile, but the list is long. Too long to even narrow down." He released a deflated sigh and slammed the laptop closed. "We're no closer than before, and it's fucking driving me insane."

"You have his DNA, right?" He nodded. "Why not run that against all those who have been incarcerated on that list?"

Seemed all those hours watching crime documentaries was paying off.

"We've run it through CODIS multiple times, but no hits. Though I love how you're thinking. Keep going."

I preened a little at his words. Yep, I totally had a praise kink. Who knew?

"Okay, how about his prints?" I offered as all the possibilities began flooding through my head. "Take the prints you got from the shed and run them through the list too. You only get DNA swabbed if you're incarcerated, but they'll have fingerprints on file for anyone who's been arrested for a basic DUI or other misdemeanors."

Jameson's encouraging smile fell into a frown. "We don't have them." His brows pulled together. "They only found your fingerprints on the chair."

My heart stuttered in my chest.

Fuck. Fuck. Fuck. Fuck.

"Which made no sense to me," Jameson said as I silently freaked out, "but now that you bring up that point, I bet it's because his fingerprints *are* on file. He knows we could tie him to the cases based on fingerprints but not on DNA."

"What does that mean?" I croaked.

"That he *was* probably arrested in the past." With renewed excitement, he pushed the laptop open and began typing. "I'll see who has fingerprints on file on this list."

"Jameson," I whispered, so quiet it was barely audible over the sound of the keys clacking. "Jameson," I said again, this time stronger.

"Hmm?" he questioned, not looking away from the screen.

"How do you know they were my prints?" Maybe it was the tremble in my voice, or the fact that I had latched on to his forearm with a death grip, but his brown eyes met mine. "How, Jameson?"

"Well, I'm assuming they're yours considering where they were found on the chair's arms."

"Have you run them through the system?" I could barely get the words out around the terror growing in my chest. Hell, it was hard to breathe beneath the swelling feeling as I waited for his answer.

"Yeah, but we haven't gotten the results back yet." My grip slipped from his forearm. He stared at my now-limp hand that rested on the couch between us. "Remy, what's wrong?"

Too stunned to answer, I slowly rose off the couch, ignoring him calling my name as I zombie-walked through the living room and down the hall toward my bedroom.

The door clicked softly closed behind me. Making my way to the bed, I sat on the edge, my back to the door, facing the window. Outside, bright rays of sun glittered, making everything seem cheery.

But it wasn't.

They had no idea what they'd just triggered by running my prints.

Inside I was frozen, the panic unable to break through the numbness.

Because this was bad. There was no coming back from their innocent inquiry.

There was no hiding now.

20

TALLON

The ingredients bubbled, swirling in the pot, holding my gaze as I categorized all the hints Remy offered the last few days regarding her past. Clearly whatever she hid, tied to that fucking abusive asshole ex of hers. But how, I wasn't positive. It made little sense. She said she ran and was far enough away, so why did she still feel the need to hide things from me?

I could help her.

I wanted to help her.

Did she assume I would bolt once I found out? I wouldn't, because somehow she'd dug those tiny claws into me, fastening her to my heart and soul. If she ever walked away, there would always be the scars of our time together imprinted on me for as long as I lived, or if she stayed to tell me what she was hiding, then those claws could sink deeper, keeping her in my life forever.

But how did I say that when I couldn't offer her anything more than words?

Words that she'd already flung back in my face.

Why I ever suggested she was just another witness or

victim was asinine. From the moment I saw her in my old apartment when she came to say bye to Tinley, I knew she was more than that. It was like a kick to the heart, jump-starting it after years of disuse. I woke up that night, the fog of work and duty cleared, allowing me to see what was important.

Living.

And fucking hell, I wanted to do that with her.

But not if she didn't trust me enough with her past, with her fears and worries. How could I ever be the man she needed in her life, who her son needed? If she didn't trust me with her past, then how in the hell would she ever fully trust me with her future?

"Tallon."

The sharp tone of Jameson's voice snapped my spine straight. Whirling around, I took a step toward him, hands curled into tight fists, ready to jump into action.

"What's wrong?" Instinctively, I glanced over his shoulder, looking for the tiny wonder of a woman who'd ensnared every cell in my mind and body.

"It's Remy," he said.

Not waiting for more, I stormed past him. He cursed, sealing himself against the wall so I didn't knock him over. I paused in the living room, searching every corner and shadow for her.

"Where is she?" My heart raced, adrenaline spiking as I continued to search but came up empty.

"I said something." Ice filled my veins as I turned to face him, my jaw working as I fought the urge to snap at him. "We were talking about the case, and we mentioned fingerprints. She asked if we ran hers, and when I said yes, she just...." He cursed under his breath and scrubbed a hand over his face. "She shut down, Tallon. I mean completely void of emotion. Then she went to her bedroom."

I swallowed down my panic as relief soaked through me. She was safe. Not fine, but safe. Okay, I could deal with that.

"Theory?" I asked, amazed I could get that single word out around my clenched jaw. I hated knowing she was back there alone for several reasons, but mostly because she was hurting with no one to lean on, no one to comfort her. Fucking hell, I wanted to be that guy, wanted to be back there with her.

"Well," he mused, eyeing me like one would a crazy man with a gun. Hell, maybe that description wasn't too far off since my hand kept instinctively inching toward my back where I normally kept my sidearm. "With the inconsistencies of her background, and now this, it makes me wonder what's really true with Remington Dotson. What do we know? Besides the fact she's in danger and has a son. Everything else seems... shallow."

I nodded, completely agreeing with him. "I'll go... talk to her?" I said, way less confident in that response than I'd been in years.

"Sounds like a solid plan to me," Jameson said with a smirk. "From what I can tell about Remy from my professional, almost a profiler, opinion?" I nodded when he paused, giving him the floor, so to speak. "Whatever she's hiding, it's because she scared. There isn't a manipulative bone in that woman's body. Anything and everything she does is to keep herself or her son safe. So go into this knowing that whatever she tells you, it wasn't to dupe us or you. It's self-preservation in its finest."

"She said she wouldn't ever go back," I muttered.

"And that's probably been a fear of hers since she left that bastard. We don't understand that constant fear of being dragged back into a hell you escaped out of sheer willpower. That would drive anyone to desperate measures so they don't land back in that hellish prison again."

I stared at the worn hardwood floors, contemplating Jameson's assessment. "What does that mean?"

"It means listen. Don't cast judgment. Let her tell you. Don't interrogate." I pursed my lips into a tight line, and chuckled. "Come on, that's not too far out-of-bounds for you. You care about her and want answers. Just be careful the way you go about getting those answers. Let her come to you."

"Got it." Halfway across the room, I turned back to my friend. "Thank you. For... this."

He nodded in return. "I told you. You two have something, and just because I was there for the start doesn't mean I'm expecting to be a part of it in the future. I'm happy for you, Tallon. Beyond fucking happy. Just don't fuck it up, whatever she tells you now or in the future. Understand that beneath that hard, tatted exterior, she's just a scared single mother doing everything she can to survive day to day in a lonely ass world."

My heart clenched at the idea of her being alone.

I didn't want that for her.

Fuck, I didn't want that for me anymore.

In that moment, none of it mattered except getting to her.

On silent feet, I moved down the short hall, eyes locked on the closed bedroom door. I stared at the dark stained wood, debating the protocol here. A single knuckle raised, I tapped against the wood, so softly it barely met my ears. The silence that resonated from the other side sent my heart thundering. Shit, what if something terrible had happened to her in the last five minutes?

Ignoring any sense of privacy, my need to see her safe and unharmed overriding every other thought, I twisted the doorknob, conscious this time of the delicate metal, and shoved the door open. My breath whooshed in a relieved breath finding her perched on the bed, back to the door, head drooped forward.

"Remy?" I said as I quietly closed the door and leaned against it to keep from rushing over and enveloping her in my arms.

No response.

Swallowing down my nerves, I shoved off the wood and strode to her side. Her face was downturned, sleek, dark hair acting like a shield, preventing me from seeing her face and reading her emotions that were always so clearly written there. Desperate to see her, to know what the hell was going on, I slipped a hand through her hair. Wetness met my calloused fingers as I cupped her cheek, urging that gorgeous face up to mine.

My heart shattered, fracturing in my chest at the utter desolation clearly written across her sullen features.

Wet tracks streamed down her cheeks, proof tears had flowed.

Tears from whatever we set in motion by running her fingerprints.

Not saying a word, I sat beside her, her body angling toward mine with the dip of the mattress. Wrapping an arm around her waist, I curled her tiny frame to my side in what felt like the most natural move I'd made in a while.

I needed her close, desperately wanted to absorb her sadness. If I had to shoulder her worries and pain so she didn't, that was a burden I'd take every second of the day.

She was all that mattered.

"Don't leave me," Remy whispered.

I didn't even think, just lifted her off the bed and settled her on top of my lap. She leaned her head against my shoulder, a soft, choked cry escaping her lips. Running my fingers through her hair, strumming comforting strokes down her spine, I simply held her as those tears started anew.

This felt right. Her in my arms, comforting her.

"Whatever it is, Remy, I'm not leaving." Wrapping my arms around her frame, I squeezed her even closer, wishing I could forever seal her body to mine. "But to protect you from whatever you're scared of...." I stopped, not wanting to push her like Jameson suggested. But I wanted answers so I could come up with a solution.

"I met Jett when I was fifteen."

I pressed my lips together to keep from interrupting, allowing her to explain at her own pace. But fucking hell, that was a test of my patience. I wanted to demand more about this fucking Jett character. It would be nice to know all the details about the man I would go to prison for murdering. Well, go to prison if I got caught.

"It was fine at first," she continued. "I mean, we were kids, right? We couldn't even drive. His parents' driver carted us around for dates." *Driver? What the fuck? Who is this guy?* "He was cute, but it was always more our parents pushing us together than my physical attraction to him.

"I knew from the start it wasn't what I wanted. Just like I knew I was too different for their world. I was electric pink when everyone else was blush, you know?" I didn't even know what blush fucking was, but sure. "Dating turned into more, and then suddenly we were the 'it couple' in our town. Even then I knew someone else was dictating my life, but I didn't know any differently or how to even stop it from happening. Understand, my father was—hell, probably still is—a dictator over my mother. She was there to look pretty, and that's it. I saw the sadness in her eyes. Sometimes she'd cry with zero emotion on her face. Just tears streaming down her cheeks while she stared at me with this blank look. It was fucking disturbing, and I knew it wasn't right."

"Smart, even from an early age," I whispered into her hair.

"We were engaged before I even realized I should stop the snowball that was happening in my life. I was seventeen, and my dad said yes when Jett asked him. Hell, I think my dad orchestrated the whole thing."

"Kitten," I whispered, almost too afraid where this conversation was headed to want to know more. Not because of how I'd feel about her but how I'd react. Would burning down the world in her honor be justifiable in court? It was in my mind, so possibly.

"I wouldn't say I was unwilling the first time. It was more of a done decision, if that makes sense. I mean, we were engaged, so of course there should be a physical relationship too. I had zero feelings, no emotional attachment the entire time. And what I remember is that he didn't care. I didn't realize how attuned a man should be to his partner, even if just for a night, much less the woman you're going to marry, until I met you and Jameson. And that night, you two cared. You just fucking read me. Read me the entire time as we did what we did, and you always checked in. Jett couldn't do that when it was even just us, and then there you were controlling three people, and it was just easy. Everything was an uphill battle with Jett, even the sex since it was so one-sided. I just felt nothing, and he had no clue. Or maybe he did and didn't care." Her chest expanded as she released a huffed laugh. "It's disgusting how long I allowed it to happen. How weak was I that—"

"No," I demanded. "Don't you even think that shit. You

were strong for surviving that. There isn't a weak bone in your body."

Her body shivered against my own. "I was weak when I didn't fight back. I didn't even like him, yet I walked down that aisle. All because I didn't see a way out. I was seventeen, Tallon. Seventeen. What was I supposed to do?"

"Nothing," I hissed. "You expected your parents to do the best for you, but apparently it was the opposite." I choked down the other words I wanted to bellow, defending the sweet, terrified girl she was.

"They didn't even let me finish high school," she whispered so softly I almost missed it. "They decided a high school education wasn't important for someone like me. Honestly, I think my parents loved the idea that if I didn't have a high school diploma, I couldn't go to college. Jett was a sophomore in college at that point, studying computer engineering, so even though he wasn't able to support us, our parents paid for everything, knowing we were following their footsteps. It was a sick cycle. How every male thought they had superiority over their wives. But what could I do?"

"Nothing. You were underage. Kitten, I want to rip out your parents' throats with my bare hands." Despite the jail time, I wanted to do that for her. Wanted a bloody form of justice for what they put her through. I needed their blood on my hands more than my next meal. Vengeance was now my source of sustenance, and until I got that for her, I would forever be starved.

"You can't. He's the CEO of QRT, the largest software company in the south."

Well, fuck me.

"My father, not Jett. Though Jett probably still rose through the ranks despite my vanishing. I never looked back when I walked away, so I have no idea what happened after I left. I was always too afraid of them somehow figuring out how to trace my search history and find me. Though I don't think they would've put that much work into chasing me down."

"You've told me what happened at its worst. How did you get out?"

"I told you about that night, the night I finally realized if I didn't get out, I'd die in that house. And I knew it was true, that even if they didn't find a body, I'd be a shell. A fraction of who I was meant to be. Do you know what that's like? To live every day knowing you were meant for so much more? It's smothering. Like every day, you breathe less than the previous. I was dying, suffocating in that house. Until that day when I got out."

Her green eyes met mine, and I held her stare, hoping she felt the support and strength I poured from myself over to her. Not that she needed it. The woman had strength in spades.

"Do you hate me yet?" she whispered.

"Not even close."

"I married him."

"I'm pretty sure that was under coercion."

Those thick black lashes fanned down her cheeks. "How are you so sure?"

"Because I'm sure about you, Remy."

A single tear trickled down her cheek. "Thank you."

"For what?"

"For giving me the benefit of the doubt."

"You're a lot of things, Remy, but deceptive is not one of them. I've met people in the past who sold a lie, all to alter your idea of them for the better. You're not one of those people. You're the one who alters perception for survival."

"I'm still technically married to him."

"Okay."

"Does that not bother you?"

"No." I meant the single word with all my heart. "Does it bother you that I did shit in my past, not meaning it? How many girls Jameson and I shared? Yet none of that meant anything until I met you."

"Well, it bothers me. I left. I ran; I drained what was liquid in our savings account, which was about sixty thousand dollars, and ran. I'm from Georgia, a small town outside Augusta, and ran to Nashville. I'd heard my parents and husband talk about the influx of people swarming to the city and thought maybe, just maybe, I'd be able to hide here. My funds were dwindling, and I knew I needed to work, but how could I with my parents and ex no doubt monitoring my social security number for activity?"

It hit me like a train to the chest. "Charlie."

She half smirked. "Charlie. He caught me hacking into the social security database. I was good, but fucking hell, he was better. He caught me, sought me out at the coffee shop I was using for their free WiFi, and... well, he asked me why. He asked me why I was looking to change my social security number. I told him. Actually, I broke down and told him everything. Not all that Jett did, but that I was running from someone bad. He's a good guy. He helped me reconstruct my entire identity. My whole identity except for—"

"Your fingerprints."

She nodded. "It's impossible to alter those once someone has the original set. Which my dad has. Odd, I know. He was super intense during a short span, thinking we would be taken and held for ransom, so he fingerprinted me, my mom, hell, even all the staff."

"Is your name Remington?" I hated asking, but it fit her.

I couldn't imagine another name for such a unique individual.

"Yes," she said with a pushed laugh. "It's the one thing I couldn't let go of. It always felt like a part of me, you know?"

"It fits you."

"I agree," she said, finally smiling up at me. Fucking hell, I'd crush the world to resurrect that smile again and again. "It's why I couldn't let it go. The last name, his last name, was easy to ditch. Remington Castle Sawyer. That's my actual name, though now it feels so removed I'm not sure what's real. It feels like Remington Blair Dotson is who I am, who I was meant to be."

A beat of silence settled between us.

"Castle," I whispered. The name sounded familiar. "That was your maiden name?"

"Yep. Like a good Southern girl, I changed my middle name to my maiden name when I got married. Sounds familiar, right?"

Definitely. And it wasn't just familiar because he was a millionaire; it was something else that rang a bell. From my time in the white-collar crimes division of the FBI. Her father was shady as fuck. Seemed he was the same at home and in the boardroom.

Either way, this wasn't good. Not only did her father have the means to track her down if he wanted to, but he no doubt would. Men like him didn't take being hoodwinked by someone they saw as beneath them without repercussions.

Now knowing who her father was, maybe I could come about my vengeance for her a different way. Less bloody and more... blackmail.

"I can't believe you're still sitting here," she whispered.

"There's nowhere else I want to be, Remy. But we need to make a plan on what to do if they come looking for you."

She tipped her face up to mine, a wicked smile stretching across it. "Punching my husband and dad in the dick is step one. I've envisioned that for years, but from there, I'm open to suggestions."

Reaching up, I tucked a smooth lock of hair behind her ear. "Dick punching is a great place to start. We'll figure something out, Remy. I won't let them hurt you again."

"There's more," she whispered. "More I need to tell you." A loud growl rumbled from her stomach, stopping her. She dipped her face, cheeks already tinted pink.

Like she weighed nothing, I lifted her off my lap and helped her stand, my hands not leaving her hips until she was steady on her feet.

"How about you tell me the rest later? Let's go get you fed and then watch that movie. Everything else can wait till tomorrow."

Or the next day.

Or the following.

Because I wasn't going anywhere.

21

REMINGTON

"Thanks," I said with a genuine smile as I accepted the metal bowl filled with freshly popped popcorn. "I'm not sure how much more I can eat, though."

Even now, my leggings were a little too snug around my full belly. The soup was phenomenal. So much so that I went back for another bowl, even though I was stuffed after the first. Tallon smiled and shrugged before falling down onto the couch beside me, his arm automatically lifting up and over my shoulders, tugging me to his side.

The dull burn in my cheeks signaled the smile I'd worn the last hour was still firmly planted on my face.

He knew my past and was still here. Jameson too.

During dinner, I filled Jameson in on what I'd disclosed to Tallon, so he knew exactly why I became so despondent earlier. And like Tallon, Jameson didn't miss a beat, simply listened, growing angrier on my behalf with each word. Afterward, the two discussed what we could do if my parents or Jett showed up at my door while devouring their own dinner.

Jameson sat on the floor by my feet, laptop open on his lap. "What are we watching?"

Flicking over to Netflix, I absentmindedly scrolled through the options. "What are we in the mood for? With everything that happened today, I prefer one I've seen before so I can zone out, you know?"

Jameson shifted on the floor, elbow pressed into the couch by my knee. "Why?"

I lifted a single shoulder in a half shrug. "Just a lot in a short amount of time. Having an hour or two to just veg out would be nice."

His light brown eyes flicked to Tallon. "You're stressed?"

"Overwhelmed might be a better word. I can't seem to shut my mind off."

"Hmm," Tallon hummed beside me. Two fingers began caressing up and down my neck. Goose bumps erupted in their wake. "That's not good. We're supposed to do everything we can to keep you calm. How can we fix that, Kitten?"

His low tone and the insinuation had me sucking in a hasty breath. I opened my mouth but nothing came out, too afraid to voice what I really wanted.

Them.

Even though we'd fooled around yesterday and there was obvious interest, heat even, in both their intent gazes, a part of me didn't want to voice it out loud and be rejected.

"Do you need help relaxing, Remy?" Jameson offered.

A slight shiver raced down my spine at his seductive, low tone.

I swallowed, mouth and throat dry. Just thinking about having their hands on me again, more this time, sent my pulse racing. Heat spread through my core, lower belly tensing and relaxing.

"Yes," I rasped.

"That's a good girl," Tallon whispered against the shell of my ear. "Tell us what you want."

"Everything," I said. There was no shame at the slight begging in my tone. "I want you both."

Lifting me carefully, Tallon situated me on his lap facing Jameson, hooking my legs over his thighs and spreading them wide. "Are you on birth control?" he asked into my hair, fingers now trailing up and down the insides of my spread thighs.

"Yes, I have an IUD."

"Good, because I want nothing between us, Kitten. If this ever gets to be too much, just say the word and we'll stop. This is to help you relax, not make the stress worse."

The tips of his fingers swept along the heated skin of my waist as he gripped the hem of my vintage Green Day shirt and slowly lifted the soft cotton over my head. Except he didn't pull it all the way free. As soon as my mouth and nose were visible, Tallon dropped the bulk of the fabric, leaving my eyes covered.

Bits of light still filtered through the thin material, but the effect of having my vision hampered was like a match to gasoline to my need for them.

"Tallon," I whimpered, not sure what I was asking or wanted.

"Shh, Kitten. Let us take care of you. Just relax against me and feel us. Give us a chance to worship this beautiful body like it's meant to be." As he spoke, he trailed the tips of his fingers along my bare stomach, swirling around my belly button and caressing each rib. "All you have to say is stop and we will. Understood?"

I nodded.

A firm grip on my chin stopped the sluggish movements. "Words, Remy. I need to know without a doubt that you'll stop us if this becomes too much." Another set of hands began massaging my calves, kneading the stress from the tight muscles. "Because we won't stop until you can't take any more. Until you're limp in my arms and all the stress from the last few days is not even a fleeting thought."

"Yes, okay," I muttered, head lolling along his shoulder. The sensation of two sets of hands was overwhelming and not enough all in the same breath. My core throbbed, anticipating their next move, and I desperately wanted them to hurry to where I needed them most.

Higher and higher, Tallon's fingers caressed along my stomach. My heart hammered against my chest, breath hitching as he skimmed over the cups of my demi bra, zeroing in on my pebbled nipples beneath the lace. A pitiful whimper crept up my throat, back arching off Tallon's firm chest, when those deft fingers dipped beneath the cups and tugged the material down until the cool air hit my exposed nipples.

Jameson's hands continued working the tension from my legs, hands now massaging my upper thighs. Fingers hooked beneath the waistband of my yoga pants. The waft of cool air was a welcomed relief against my overheated skin as the fabric slowly peeled away, down over my hips, my needy center now completely exposed. Still blind, I felt more than saw him work my feet free of my pants and panties. Hooking one knee over Tallon's, the other side followed, completely exposing me to where I sensed him kneeling between my spread thighs.

"She's fucking perfect, isn't she?" Tallon said to Jameson as soft, wet lips brushed along the column of my neck. I shifted, giving him more access, wanting his lips and teeth all over me. "Lick that perfect pussy clean."

My head rolled side to side as soft lips trailed along one

inner thigh, stopping just shy of my slick center before moving to the other leg and repeating the process. The hand that teased at my nipples trailed up my sternum to wrap around my throat.

I sucked in a breath. Wiggling, I ground down on Tallon's erection that pressed against my ass, rewarding me with a sharp hiss. The hold on my throat tightened only a fraction in warning.

"Stay still, Kitten. Take everything we're giving you. You're ours for now."

A moan crept up my throat that turned into a gasped curse when he pinched and twisted a single nipple at the same moment Jameson sealed his lips around my swollen clit.

"Fuck yes," I rasped, my throat working beneath Tallon's palm. "Tallon. I need you, please."

"You need me?" he whispered into my ear.

"Yes, please." I sank my upper teeth into my lower lip to quiet a scream as Jameson sucked hard, teeth scraping against the sensitive nub.

"On your knees, then, Kitten."

Tallon must have given Jameson a tap, because he pulled away, though the fingers he had slid inside me stayed firmly in place, stuffing me full.

With some help, I blindly maneuvered around the arm between my legs and dropped to the floor, facing the couch, the worn rug pressing against my bare knees. Through the fabric, I could see Tallon's jean-clad thighs, his hand wrapped around his restrained cock.

"Spread those thighs, Remy."

Slick lips slipped along my spine, trailing lower and lower as those three fingers pumped in and out in a torturously slow rhythm. A yelp rang through the room when

Jameson bit one ass cheek, then sucked the abused flesh between his lips.

Large hands engulfed my trembling ones, guiding them up Tallon's legs.

"If you want me, then you have to work for it, Kitten." His deep voice sent a shiver through me.

Feeling my way toward the top button of his jeans, I clumsily popped it open and worked the zipper down. Just as I wrapped my hand around his thick cock, a warm breath blew along my wet slit.

Hips flexing, I ground my center against Jameson's face, his responding chuckle making my thighs tremble. Desperate for friction, I tried to move again, but a tight hold on my hip kept me in place as he leisurely licked and sucked at my center.

"Focus, Kitten," Tallon commanded.

Blindly, I worked his jeans lower, freeing his long, thick cock. Wrapping both hands around him, I leaned forward, careful to not pull my core away from Jameson's tongue and thrusting fingers.

The first swipe of my tongue along his swollen head had us both groaning. The salty flavor of him inched up my arousal, making a new rush of wetness leak around Jameson's fingers. Taking Tallon deeper, I widened my jaw to take all of him, hollowing out my cheeks as I bobbed up and down his cock.

Higher and higher, Jameson's tongue and fingers drove me closer to the edge of bliss, my entire body firing with sparks of pleasure as I worked to take Tallon as deep as possible.

"That's it, Kitten. Such a good girl, that dirty fucking mouth taking all of my cock." I groaned at his words. In response, his hips hitched off the couch, driving himself deeper into my throat. "Fucking hell. Swallow for me, baby. Work that throat around... fuck, yes."

Too soon, a body-trembling orgasm raced through me. Pulling my lips free, I pressed my forehead to Tallon's thigh as I gasped, trying to catch my breath.

Strong hands gripped beneath my arms and jerked me higher like I weighed nothing at all. The T-shirt was pulled from my eyes. Blinking, I found Tallon's hooded blue eyes locked on mine. Gripping my hips, he slowly worked me over his cock, still slick from my mouth, the swollen head hitting my sensitive clit with each pass.

Tossing my head back, I groaned at the sensation.

"Please," I begged over and over, desperately needing more than just their fingers. It had been so long since I was stretched and filled with something that wasn't a toy.

Again like I weighed nothing, I was twisted, the room spinning with the quick movement until I faced where Jameson kneeled, a cocky smile on his lips. Confusion flickered for just a second before my thighs were pushed wider and Tallon's cock nudged against my entrance, pushing inside an inch before retreating.

My eyes slammed shut, tuning all my focus on where he teased me, barely plunging in and out. Desperate whimpers filled the room, pleading for more as I shifted desperately to impale myself on his dick, but the bruising hold on my hips kept me from taking control.

My lids flung open at the feel of smooth skin pressing hard against my lips, forcing them to part. Jameson stared down, dick in his hand as he fed it into my willing mouth.

"That's right, Kitten. You get us both just like you wanted. Now open wide so he can fuck that dirty mouth of yours while I take this delicious cunt and make it mine."

Yes, please.

Jameson's fingers combed through my hair before fisting a section, holding me in place as he thrust, nearly shoving all of him down in one push. But I didn't care, not when Tallon was slowly easing me down onto his hard dick, my body stretching wide to accommodate him.

With a heaved sigh, I conceded control as the two men worked in sync with each other. Each time I bottomed out on Tallon's dick, Jameson surged forward, tapping the back of my throat.

Lost in the sensation of being gloriously taken by the two men, I startled when one of them flicked my bundle of nerves. My lids flew open as a pleasure-filled scream vibrated in my throat. I tried to retreat, but Jameson held me firm.

"Fuck," he grunted above me. "I can't last much longer. Not with her doing that while she sucks down my cock."

Tallon didn't respond, only increased his pace, adding in a flick to my clit every time my hips slammed down to meet his. Tingles erupted all along my skin, my muscles flexing and relaxing as another body-trembling orgasm rushed through me. Jameson quickly followed, shoving himself down my throat and holding there as he came with a string of barked curses and praises for my dirty mouth.

Still, Tallon railed into me, slamming so hard I knew I'd have bruises from his fingers and along my thighs where his hip bones pressed into the soft flesh.

Jameson staggered back, finding his footing before he fell to the floor.

"Play with her tits," Tallon barked. "I want to fucking feel that again, feel her strangle my cock with her tight pussy."

I moaned, loving his dirty words.

Jameson shot me a wicked grin as he tucked himself

back into his jeans, leaving the front open. I wondered for half a second if he did that on purpose, hoping for another round before the night was over. Sinking to his knees in front of me, he cupped my face and pulled me close.

Before our lips touched, Jameson flicked a questioning glance over my shoulder. Finding whatever acceptance or answer he needed, he closed the short distance, devouring my lips like he could suck the taste of himself off my tongue.

I gasped as his fingers found my pebbled nipples and pinched. Tugging the stiff peak, he pulled until a whimper of pain passed from my lips to his. Tallon's thumb continued to stroke my clit, sending tiny shock waves of smaller orgasms to flutter through my lower belly.

Releasing my mouth, Jameson took a single nipple between his lips and sucked hard, nipping at the tip with enough bite to be painful before quickly morphing into a rush of pleasure.

Up and down, I slid along Tallon's cock. With Jameson's mouth on my breast and Tallon's thumb flicking my clit, another orgasm built. Whimpering, I tossed my head back, knowing this one would hurt, the pleasure too intense after having already come so many times.

Tallon pushed me all the way down and pinched my clit, shooting me over the edge with a hoarse scream. With a grunt, he followed, movements jerky as he came. A chorus of our harsh breaths filled the living room as we all came down from the high.

Falling back against Tallon's chest, I didn't halt the slow, very satisfied smile that crept up my cheeks.

"Still stressed, Kitten?" Tallon's breaths brushed past my ear. I shook my head, unable to open my eyes. "Good." He pulled me off his lap, and I sighed in disappointment when his semihard cock slipped out, leaving me feeling empty without him. "Let's get you in the shower and then in bed."

"But I'm not tired," I said, already feeling almost halfway asleep.

"We can watch the movie in bed. But first, you have my cum dripping down your thighs." I sucked in a breath, his dirty-ass words igniting another flame of want inside my lower belly. "We need to get you cleaned up before we can. Then we sleep. Together."

I wondered briefly if he meant all three of us, then let the thought float away as he scooped me up in his arms and carried me to the small bathroom. The cold countertop against my heated skin jarred me awake, eyes flicking open as Tallon set me on the edge, keeping me steady with one hand while the other grabbed a washcloth from the floating shelf above the toilet.

A small smile played at his lips as he waited for the water to warm before sticking the white cotton beneath the faucet, ensuring it soaked all the way through before swiping it between my thighs. A cross between a moan and hiss escaped as he slowly caressed my abused center until he was satisfied I was clean.

Reaching behind me, he unhooked my bra, dragging the thin straps down my arms before tossing it into the hamper in the corner. His blue eyes skimmed over my naked body before rising to scan my face.

"Beautiful," he muttered. "Absolutely fucking beautiful."

I wanted to shy away from him because I didn't fully believe the sentiment. Yes, I worked out, but I was still a mom. This compact frame had carried a baby, leaving behind stretch marks and a slight bump of fat that never seemed to go away no matter what I did or cut out of my diet.

As if he could sense where my mind had gone, he leaned forward, sealing our foreheads together.

"Now that I've had you, Remington Dotson, I might never let you go."

I sucked in a breath, though not because I was scared.

Because yes, I wanted that—desperately.

22

TALLON

The mismatched clothes fit her personality better than the stiff charcoal pencil skirt and long-sleeve button-up shirt that hid her armful of tattoos. But they did accentuate other features. Her round ass held my attention as I followed her down the hall toward her company's lobby.

Except if I saw how great her ass looked, then so did every other male she passed.

Maybe she would agree to only wearing baggy sweats from now on when she went out. Though even that wouldn't distract other bastards from noticing the firm curves hiding underneath.

"You look ready to take a suspect down." I shot Jameson an annoyed look at his comment. "With a knife to the throat, ensuring he never gets back up. What the hell is going on with you?"

"I don't enjoy being this exposed," I grumbled. Though that was a half-truth. Ever since I took Remy last night, this possessiveness had grown a thousand times worse. Hell, I didn't even want Jameson anywhere close to her, which was a big motherfucking problem considering he was my friend and helping me keep her safe.

Plus, Remy wanted the three of us.

I frowned.

Would I alone ever be enough to keep her happy?

"Just remember, the goal is to gain permission to work from home, not lose my job." Unaware of the way my thoughts had drifted, Remy shot a smirk over her shoulder before reaching for the glass door.

Her fingers had just brushed the chrome metal handle when I gripped it and pulled the door open for her. My own smirk played at my lips as I gestured for her to enter first, remembering when we'd done something similar just a few weeks ago.

Things had changed a bit since then.

Such as me now knowing how delicious she tasted, how her tight pussy choked the life out of my cock when she came. Now I knew she was a mother, a good one, and a woman on the run from someone who would die by my hand if he breathed the same air as her ever again.

"They need to check in," the reception called after us when Remy marched past the front desk.

"It's fine. Carl is expecting us. We're his first meeting."

The older woman grumbled under her breath, clearly frustrated by the break in protocol. When her tired eyes met mine, I shot her a warm grin. "We won't be long."

Which we wouldn't. I fully intended to make this quick and painless. Either he agreed to Remy working from home or he'd die.

Okay, I wouldn't take it that far, but I wouldn't allow this prick to put her or others in jeopardy because he wanted to assert his control.

I snorted under my breath. How ironic that I, a controlling bastard, didn't want someone controlling what I wanted to control.

Pausing outside a glass office door, Remy smoothed her skirt over her full hips in an unusual display of nerves.

"It will be fine, Remy," I muttered under my breath and brushed a knuckle down her spine. "We'll get it worked out."

Her returning smile was forced, but I'd take it for now. She knew I wouldn't do anything to hurt her on purpose. I just had to prove that taking care of this was also a way of me protecting her.

What could I say? My need to protect her in every way was becoming a full-time hobby.

Hobby/obsession.

"Come in" came a whiny voice from inside the office.

Remy looked as if she suppressed an eye roll as she tugged the office door open and stepped inside.

Degrees and other certifications lined the back wall behind the man's desk, all displaying what he no doubt viewed as his significant accomplishments proving his worth and intelligence. He didn't even stand from where he sat behind the simple metal desk as we piled into the room. His eyes lingered on Remy a second longer than what I deemed appropriate before sliding over to me, then Jameson.

"Bringing your boyfriend in to help talk me into letting you work from home?" The man curled his lip in disgust, showing us exactly what he thought of that. "You're needed here more than you're needed on your back, Remington."

"Excuse me?" I said. Thankfully my voice was devoid of the rage coursing through my body.

He huffed and crossed his arms over his chest, leaning

back in his chair like he owned the place. "The answer is no. We need her here with us—"

"Here's the thing, Kale," I stated, mimicking his posture and crossing both arms over my chest, which opened my suit jacket enough for him to see the gun on my hip. A fraction of the confidence he postured faded.

"It's Carl."

"Doesn't matter. What does matter is that this is no longer a decision you get to make because of that egotistical stick up your ass, which I'm assuming stems from the fact that Ms. Dotson here is not only better at her job than you could ever hope to be but also faster."

"Get the—"

Reaching inside my suit jacket, I pulled out my FBI credentials and took a step closer to the edge of the desk, thrusting them in his face. "This is now an FBI matter. Ms. Dotson is a protected witness who is kind enough to offer to work from home instead of not assisting her team in completing the project you're working on. Insisting she stay here is not only putting you at risk of my anger but of the man—who's killed dozens of women—coming into this office and murdering everyone who stands in his way of getting to Ms. Dotson."

I should not find such enjoyment in the way the blood drained from his face and his arms flopped uselessly at his side.

But I did.

A lot of enjoyment, actually. I'd keep this memory for bad days when I needed a pick-me-up.

"So you will either grant her the ability to work from home, or you will give her leave to ensure the safety of herself and your staff. Which will it be, Curt?"

"It's Carl."

I smirked. "Again, doesn't matter."

He swallowed, the large Adam's apple on his thin neck working as he thought over the two options.

"Fine," he said, voice shaking. "One week. Then she's back here." His beady eyes shifted to Remy, narrowing. "I want progress reports delivered every hour. And you logged on each morning by seven. With you not being here, I'll need double the amount of work since you won't waste time commuting."

I tilted my head. "Eight, normal workload, and two-hour lunch breaks."

"That's—"

"Did you forget that there is a serial killer sniffing around?" Jameson added, his tone as harsh and annoyed as mine. "The longer you continue to barter, the closer he'll circle around this office and come looking for anyone who can help him find the only witness who's survived him."

"Detective Bend, please escort Ms. Dotson to gather the things she'll need from her desk. Cole and I will complete the details while you're gone."

I kept my gaze locked on the now-trembling, weak-ass man as Jameson ushered Remy out of the office, only moving when the door shut behind them, leaving me alone with the dipshit. Fanning out my jacket, I sat in one of the chairs facing the douchebag's desk and smoothed out the light gray fabric of my slacks before resting my left ankle on top of my right knee.

"Here is what's going to happen going forward, Cunt."

The man's lip curled into a snarl. "It's Carl."

I didn't stop the cocky-ass smirk that played at my lips. "I know. I just don't give a fuck."

"She's fired," he hissed. "You can't come in here demanding all this shit just because you're FBI."

I tilted my head as I listened to his pathetic rambling.

"Here's the thing. I can, and I am. You will also stop being a fucking dick to her when she returns to a normal work week, which will be after we've caught this bastard. If you don't, I'll make sure every conversation you've ever had with a female employee in this job or others is recorded and submitted to a class action suit against you filing sexual harassment."

The greenish tint that washed over his face told me I'd hit a nerve.

Motherfucker. I couldn't stand men who used their position of power to make those who reported to them feel weak —male or female. Maybe I'd ask Charlie to keep a digital eye on him even if Carl obeyed my rules. Though I'd known a lot of men like him, and I knew he wouldn't. Hell, he would probably start making Remy's life more difficult starting the minute I walked out of this office just because he could.

"If I find out you've given her any backlash or grief over what we've discussed today, then I will stick you in the federal pen until you're just a forgotten name, a number that no one will miss. Do you understand me?"

Carl's lips pursed into a thin line. I wanted him to backtalk so fucking badly. Hell, it would be even better if he strapped on some actual balls and took a swing at me, because then I could retaliate. I would take a swing now, but the bureau hated it when I started a fight instead of ending it.

Slapping both palms to the tops of my thighs, I stood and buttoned my suit jacket like I had all the time in the world. "I'll be watching. Don't forget that."

Putting my back to him was easy, knowing the weak fucker wouldn't do a damn thing to me. Hell, even if he came at me, what was he going to do? Sure, he had height, but I not only outweighed him but also had training to take him down.

Unsure of where Remy's desk was located, I strolled back toward the lobby to wait for her and Jameson. The memory of that morning when we—okay, more me—demanded she be put into protective custody flashed in my mind, making me smile despite the anger still rolling through me.

"I hope she's not in some kind of trouble."

Realizing the older woman behind the desk was talking to me, I spun on my heels and shot her a comforting smile. "She's not."

"The other detective said she was in danger," she said, gaze snapping all around the lobby as if she were afraid of who would overhear the conversation. "I don't want her to bring that around here."

Well, there goes the genuine concern for Remy. Clearly this woman only cared about what might happen to her.

"We're taking care of it. It's why we're here making sure she can get her things and work from home until this is resolved. We'll continue to monitor her until it's safe." *Keep an eye on, sleep beside—same thing.*

The woman's penciled-on brows dipped. "If you're monitoring her, why didn't you know she wasn't here Friday?"

My full attention snapped to the woman. I stepped closer to the desk. "What do you mean?"

She huffed, bristling at my tone. "A detective came here, said he needed to talk to Ms. Dotson, but was shocked when she wasn't here. Do you people not communicate?" She eyed me suspiciously. "Seems like a waste of taxpayer money, if you ask me."

Ignoring her, I searched the lobby, looking for cameras. "Do you have any surveillance cameras here?"

"No, but I think the building does down in the main lobby."

"Would you remember this man if you saw him again?"

"Probably not." She tapped her right eye. "I don't see that well out of this one. He was wearing a hat, too, so I couldn't even tell you his hair color."

"Everything okay?"

I spun on my heels toward Remy's voice. Her brows were pulled together as she looked between me and the woman behind the desk.

Not answering, I motioned for both her and Jameson to hurry. Pressing a hand to Remy's lower back, I guided her through the lobby, out the doors, and toward the elevator. Both their gazes kept flicking to where my hand rested on top of my gun.

"What happened?" Jameson shuffled the laptop and notebooks in his arms to hit the down arrow.

"The receptionist said another detective stopped by Friday looking to talk to Remy."

"Fuck," she whispered.

"Shit," Jameson cursed at the same time. "He was looking for her at work, and when he didn't find her, he went to your apartment. And then her house. This fucker isn't...." Gaze unfocused, he stared at the wall just over my shoulder. "He's used that routine several times before, the detective act."

"Yeah?" I stated. The elevator arrived, the three of us climbing inside, thankfully finding it empty of other occupants.

"It would mean he's comfortable with that ruse," Remy added. The elevator jolted beneath our feet as it descended.

"What would make him comfortable impersonating a detective over and over?"

"Either he's watched too many TV shows, or—" I cut myself off with a low curse. "Or because he was one."

"Or an officer who watched detectives and knew how they worked." Jameson leaned against the far wall, using it as leverage to keep the stack of things in his arms from falling over as he extracted his phone from his pocket.

"The fingerprints," Remy exclaimed, clapping her hands together.

Jameson and I stilled, eyes glued on her.

"What about them?" I prodded.

"It's why he's so careful about his fingerprints. Aren't all officers of the law fingerprinted in case something happens in the line of duty?" I nodded. "That's why, even when he didn't think anyone would find his torture shed." I couldn't stop a growl from building in my chest at the mention of that shit shed where he held her. She shot me a look, which immediately quieted me down. "He was careful with his prints because he knows they could tie him to the crimes."

The elevator leveled off, and the chime of its arrival echoed in the silence that settled as we all absorbed what we'd just pieced together.

"Run that list Charlie sent you," I said to Jameson as we stepped out into the lobby, "searching for anyone who has any ties to law enforcement."

"That's how he got the women out of the car, I bet," Remy mused beside me. "Any woman would trust a squad car or police officer if they were in trouble on the side of the road."

"I hate this motherfucker even more," Jameson seethed. "Using his position of power against the people who looked to him for safety."

I clapped him on the shoulder and gave it a hard squeeze. "I fucking know. Stay with Remy. I'm going to the security office to see if I can get the feed from Friday sent over to my task team. They'll review the hours of footage for us while we keep working the case from this angle."

I looked at Remy, who just smirked. "Yeah, I know. Don't leave his side. Don't do anything stupid. And don't, under any circumstances, follow a strange officer into a van, even if he promises me PF Chang's."

Despite it all, a laugh rumbled in my chest. Lightly grabbing her elbow, I pulled her close until she had to tip her head back to look up at me. "Exactly. Be good."

"Aren't I always?"

I winked. "Only with the right incentive."

She shifted her gaze like she was thinking about my response. "And what incentive is that today?"

Leaning down, I pressed my lips to the shell of her ear, nipping at the lobe. "A repeat of last night."

Her heavy exhale brushed against me. "Yes, please."

Despite the light banter between us, doubt crept in again, wondering if I would ever be enough, just me. After a quick scan of the area, ensuring we were alone, I smacked her tempting ass and started toward the security office. "Stay with him."

As I walked away, I couldn't help but feel the tug to stick close to her side, but I pushed through the urge, knowing I had a fucking job to do. The sooner we solved this case, the sooner I'd have the answers plaguing me that revolved around a potential future with the tiny spitfire of a woman.

23

REMINGTON

"I'm hoping soon, buddy," I said, the guilt of not having a timeframe for Crew eating me alive inside. Leaning my forehead against the passenger side window, I closed my eyes, listening to the pounding rain pelt the windshield. "Are you having fun with Uncle Charlie?"

"Yeah, he bought me a Nintendo since I left mine at home."

I rolled my eyes. "Please tell me you're doing something other than playing those shooting games all day and night."

"Okay, I won't tell you," Crew said, voice light with humor.

"Funny kid," I muttered. "I miss you." My heart swelled as I said the words out loud.

"Sounds good, Mom." I rolled my eyes behind my closed lids. *Boys.* "I gotta go. Uncle Charlie and I are planning a *Super Smash Bros* marathon."

"Delightful," I said sarcastically. "Can you put him on the phone, please?"

"Sure. Bye, Mom." Muffled words passed in the background as Crew no doubt tossed Charlie the phone.

"Hey, I swear I'm not damaging his brain cells with this. It's educational," Charlie proclaimed.

"How is it educational?" I groaned but couldn't help but smile. Sometimes my friend could be more of a kid than my nine-year-old.

"Strategy, of course. So what's this? You texted me about those idiots running your prints."

Knowing Tallon and Jameson could hear every word I said, I ran through the CliffsNotes version of yesterday and also the revelations we'd made today about the unsub.

"I saw Jameson's request earlier. I'll get on that as soon as we get off the phone. You okay?"

I shrugged, even though he couldn't see the movement. "Yes and no. Things are complicated."

"Hmm," he mused. "Complicated sounds juicy."

Shooting a side-eyed glance at Tallon in the driver seat to make sure I didn't have his full attention, I said, "Yep."

"Are they in the car with you?"

"Yep."

"Fine, text me later if you need to talk. What are you going to do about the fingerprint situation?"

"Nothing. What can I do? It's done. If my parents or Jett have an alert with a private detective or one of their officer friends, then they'll know how to find me. It will be easy to follow the trail from there."

"You could always run. I'll help you create a new identity for you and Crew—"

"No, I'm not running again." Tallon shot a look my way, his hands tightening on the steering wheel. "I'm not doing that to Crew or me. Plus, I'm stronger now. If they come at me, I'll face it head-on. Maybe I'll even grow a set and demand a divorce."

"Or we could kill him."

I barked a laugh. "Charlie, we are not killing him."

"I agree with Charlie," Tallon said, too calmly for my liking.

"You guys are the worst. I think there's enough death around us to not add another body to the mix. Give Crew a hug and kiss for me. I asked the school to send me all the work he's missing while he's out. Hopefully they'll email me that packet today, and I can get it to you ASAP so Crew doesn't fall behind."

After a quick goodbye and a promise to keep him updated on any new developments, I hit the End Call button and tossed the phone into my purse.

"You all right?" Tallon asked.

In the back seat, the clack of keys as Jameson worked on his laptop barely sounded over the pounding rain and occasional roll of thunder. I twisted in the seat, brows furrowed with worry. Apparently, this case wasn't top priority to captivate all of Jameson's attention. His boss gave him another case involving a string of petty theft crimes in a prominent area of Nashville.

"Sure. I just miss him." I turned back around and fiddled with the hem of my skirt. "Plus, there's just so much going on right now. I'm not sure what else I can put on my plate. It would be nice to have a few hours without a major life-altering issue popping up, you know?"

As if those words triggered something in the universe, we rounded the last turn onto my street.

"You expecting someone?" Tallon asked, pointing at the white Range Rover parked along the curb right outside my house. Through quick swipes of the wiper blades, displacing the sheets of rain, I studied the small-framed woman who stood talking to a man in a suit on my front porch.

"No," I stated softly.

"I assume the guy is the plain-clothes officer stationed out front of your house this shift." The SUV slowed, coming to a stop directly behind the Range Rover. "Let me—"

"Oh," I exclaimed, now that I could see the woman's features better. "It's the principal at Crew's school." I frowned. "What is she doing here?"

Shoving open the door, I dashed into the downpour, Tallon's and Jameson's shouts for me to stop cut off when I slammed the door shut. Hands over my head, like it would do anything to protect me, I dodged the deeper puddles and hurried up the front walk toward the house.

"Hi," I breathed, smiling at the older woman. "Sorry, I wasn't expecting you to stop by." Digging my keys out of my purse, I swung open the newly mended screen door and unlocked the solid wood one, shoving it open with a shoulder to the center. "Come in. Man, this weather is crazy."

"Remington." I shivered at the deep commanding voice following me into the house. "You need to wait for me."

Flinging my purse into the chair, I turned with a wide fake smile to the principal, though it faltered when I found her staring up at Tallon. My heart stilled. *There's no way she'd be that observant, right?* Except the way her narrowed eyes widened before swinging to me told me she just might be.

My entire body went stiff.

"Right, well, you asked for Crew's assignments while he's out, so I thought I'd bring them by instead of asking you to come to the school and pick them up."

I pointed at the thick file folder clutched to her chest. "All that for two weeks?"

With a half-smile, she handed the papers over to me.

"Yes. And I'm not sure what's going on with Crew, but I need to remind you we only allow ten days of unexcused absences each year. Any more and I won't be able to pass him on to fourth grade."

My jaw dropped. "But he's making straight A's," I sputtered.

"Rules are rules, Ms. Dotson. I understand you're going through some family issues." She cast a knowing look at Tallon. "But I can't make exceptions. I'm sorry." She tracked Tallon as he moved to stand by my side. "I am happy to see you have some help from family. The resemblance is uncanny. Crew could be his son."

I stopped breathing when Tallon stilled. Jameson let out a quiet curse before stepping forward and showing the principal to the door. The sound of the rain intensified as the front door swung open, followed by Jameson asking the officer still on the porch to help the woman to her car.

I couldn't move, my wide-eyed stare focused on the rug beneath my feet, too scared to look over at Tallon. *What is he thinking? Is he putting two and two together, or is he just blowing off what the woman said as odd ramblings?*

The tension in the air magnified. The cold drops of rain lingering on my skin made goose bumps erupt along my arms.

Fuck, this is bad.

I wanted to scream at myself for not telling him before now and cry in loss of whatever was building between us. No doubt it was shattered now. For a couple days, I had normalcy. Even though Tallon had yet to say anything, I knew everything had just changed.

"Tal—"

"Show me," he snapped.

He didn't need to say more than that.

Sighing in defeat, shoulders slumped, I reached into my purse and dug out my phone. Swiping it open, I clicked the pictures icon and began scrolling to find the clearest picture. I paused on one I'd snapped just three weeks ago of us grinning like fools in front of the Christmas tree we'd finished decorating.

Swallowing down my fears, I thrust the phone out to him, releasing it the second he snatched it from my fingers. Shifting, I moved to stand beside Jameson, who placed a comforting hand on my shoulder. Finding courage, I dared a glance at Tallon, who studied my phone, the screen just a few inches from his face.

A rumble of thunder shook the house, making me jump. Rubbing my hands up and down my arms, I bit my tongue to keep from talking. He deserved this minute to arrange all the pieces together, all the little clues I'd given over the last few days.

When those blue eyes finally met mine, a pitiful whimper passed my trembling lips at the array of emotions warring behind them. When they shifted to the hand on my shoulder, his brows furrowed before realization flared.

"You knew." There was no question, just a harsh statement to Jameson, who nodded.

"I figured it out that first day we came here." How he sounded so sure of himself, so calm, I didn't know. But I guess not much was riding on the outcome of this mess for him like it did for me.

I wanted Tallon, and not just until the case was over. I also wanted him to want Crew, but based on the angry look he shot the picture on my phone, I was fairly certain that wasn't the case now, or hell, maybe ever.

"Why?" he gritted out, knuckles turning white as he gripped my phone tighter in his large hand.

"I tried to find you. Both of you," I whispered. Feeling drained, I slumped down into one of the small chairs. "But I never did. You never came back to that bar, and I just moved on."

"That doesn't explain why you didn't tell me now, Remington."

Tears gathered in my lower lids, hearing my full name fall from his lips. "I wanted to, but that first night in your apartment, you said you didn't want kids—"

"Bullshit," he yelled. Pointing at me, he took a menacing step closer. "That's bullshit, and you know it. Yes, I said those words, but you were looking for an excuse to not tell me. Fuck, would you have ever told me I had a son? A fucking nine-year-old son." Something like regret and pain flashed over his features before he sealed himself off once again.

"I didn't know you," I shouted. Finding my strength and backbone, I rose from the chair and moved closer to him. "I didn't know a single damn thing about you, Tallon. What if you were like my ex, huh? What if you found out and tried to take Crew away from me, or if me telling you put Crew in a bad situation—"

"Again," he hissed, "I'm calling bullshit. I told you. Everything about my past." His nostrils flared. "You knew I wouldn't hurt him. What was the endgame in all this, Remington?"

"I didn't have one. I was going to tell you after the case—"

"Were you?" Fucking hell, the devastation in his low tone cut me deeper than him yelling. "Or were you hoping for the easy way out? For me to never know, and you could go on without me in his life?" He sucked in a breath, something like surprise flashing over his features. "You were never going to tell me because this meant nothing to you."

A sob shook my shoulders. "And it did to you?" I cried. "I'm just a witness, right?"

Everything I felt in that moment—fear, regret, soul-crushing sadness—seemed to war inside him as we stared each other down. Without another word, he strode through the living room, ripped open the front door, and disappeared, not bothering to close the door behind him.

Overwhelmed by the conflicting emotions, I gave in to the need to fall apart. Sinking to the floor, I curled my knees to my chest and sealed my forehead to my thighs, allowing the hot tears to freely flow.

I couldn't be mad at his reaction. He was right. I should've told him from the beginning. I'd looked for an excuse to not tell him. To not disrupt Crew's life, even if that meant the two of them would never know each other. Was that so wrong of me to be overprotective of the little life Crew and I had built together?

It wasn't wrong, per se, but I knew better.

I knew deep in my gut that the longer I waited to tell Tallon, the worse it would be.

Well, it couldn't get any worse than him walking away looking like someone just ripped his heart clean out of his chest.

And that was all on me.

24

―――――――

TALLON

Lightning flashed in the dark sky, and thunder immediately rolled, shaking the SUV while sheets of rain pelted the windshield, preventing me from seeing anything but the waterfall of water. All around me the vicious thunderstorm raged, but it had *nothing* on the one warring in my heart. Freezing drops of rain dripped along my chilled skin as I stared at Remy's cell phone clutched tightly in my hand, the bright picture the only light. The screen faded. Quickly, I tapped it for what felt like the thousandth time in the last few minutes to continue studying Crew's picture.

Knowing it was wrong but doing it anyway, I swiped across the screen to see what other photos would pop up. Picture after picture appeared as I kept snooping through her album. Every single one was of them two or some of just him playing various sports. Remy was clearly a devoted mom, her whole life dedicated to ensuring Crew had a good childhood and was set up for success.

My stomach flipped for the hundredth time in the last fifteen minutes.

I had a son.

A mini me, if the pictures were any indication. Same bright blue eyes, blond hair, and that smile. It was my smile, the one that had disappeared until Remy reentered my life.

Anger and regret clashed as I continued to flick through the pictures. The more I flipped, the younger he appeared. Nine years. I'd missed it all. His birth, first steps, first day of school.... For years I'd lived my life unaware that I was missing out on so damn much.

My swiping stilled when the Play symbol appeared on the screen. A glutton for punishment, I pressed the little sideways triangle, heart lodged in my throat. Soft childlike giggles filled the SUV's cab over the rain hammering on the roof. Remy's voice came over the speaker, the video shifting as if she were running. No, chasing Crew. Blue eyes—my blue eyes—glanced over his shoulder, my smile on his face before he turned and took off as fast as his chubby legs could take him.

Laughter.

Smiles.

Love.

Everything I didn't have as a child, she gave him, yet still... I was angry at how much I missed. Maybe not angry, because I didn't feel angry toward Remy, more desolate. So much time had passed. What had she even told him about me? Did my son think I was a deadbeat who wanted nothing to do with him?

I cleared my throat of the tears that thought invoked.

Remy's distraught face, the tears that my reaction to this crazy, amazing revelation caused streaming down her cheeks flashed in my mind, making me grimace. I wasn't angry with her exactly, more about the situation and how unprepared I was for the realization that I had a son.

But now... not only did I have this amazing son but also a tether to Remy. One that could keep us connected for longer than the case. If she wanted me in Crew's life, which was a big *if,* considering how I said she was just a witness, nothing special.

Fucking moron.

I was a fool to say that, nothing more than someone I needed to protect out of duty. Now she was in there crushed, thinking... thinking I didn't want her or Crew. Which I did. Desperately. Now that I knew he was mine, I wanted them both. Wanted a life with them and only them. To wake up every day knowing I had two people counting on me, wanting me.

Setting the phone on the dash, I leaned back in the seat and thumped my head against the back, eyes closed. Surprises were not my strong suit, and I reacted badly. I didn't mean to storm out like I was pissed at the news. I just needed a second. A moment alone to fucking take a breath and realize my entire life had just shifted. I did everything I could, controlling every second, to not let something like this happen. To not be caught unaware ever again, yet here I was reeling.

But unlike when Tinley was abducted, which left me hurting and feeling inadequate to even take care of my baby sister, this revelation made me feel....

A smile tugged at my lips.

Happy.

Fulfilled and scared and desperate.

So yes, she should've told me the second she saw me, but what would I have done if the roles were reversed? If I gave everything to my child, and one day someone showed up threatening to upend that slice of chaotic perfection we'd carved out in this crazy world?

Pride grew in my chest the more I thought about it.

What a fucking amazing woman.

Doing all she did on her own. Running from an abusive asshole only to turn up pregnant from a one-night stand and make it fucking work. Not just work but build this.

I slid to gaze out the driver side window, taking in the small cottage-style house with new appreciation. She did everything for our son. Was lonely and exhausted all to be an excellent mother for him.

And when she saw me, all she thought about was how it would affect Crew, not how she could use me to make her life slightly more comfortable. She could've seen me, slapped a paternity suit in my face, and demanded nine years of back child support. Instead... instead, that amazing woman kept her mouth shut until she knew if I was good enough for our son.

Was I?

Hell, I wasn't sure I was good enough for her, much less our son.

But I knew for fucking certain that from this moment forward, I would do everything in my power to be good enough for her.

For them.

Not giving it a second thought, I grabbed the phone, shoved the SUV door open, and stepped out. Sheets of rain immediately drenched every inch of me, but I didn't care. Not now, not when she needed to know.

Jogging up the front walk, I leapt up the steps and stormed through the door with as much passion as I had when I left.

Chest heaving with my heavy breaths, I scanned the living room, pausing when I found her on the couch, face buried in her hands with Jameson beside her. I glared at that comforting arm tossed over her shoulders, that possessive feeling I'd felt for her now a thousand times worse.

Whatever crossed over my face had Jameson's eyes widening as he dragged his arm away.

My shoes squeaked against the hardwood as I approached. Those delicate hands dropped to her lap, red-rimmed eyes wide as she blinked up at me.

"I'll be... fuck, anywhere but here," Jameson grumbled as he darted off.

Smart man.

I had no plans to make my apology quiet as I begged for her to have me.

Not just for now. Not just until the case was over and she was safe.

But forever.

And I'd use every fucking piece of me, every bit of knowledge I had, to convince her to let me be a part of their lives. To make hers a little easier. To allow me the opportunity to know our amazing son. To spend every day for the rest of my life showing her she made the right decision to let me into their lives.

She weighed nothing as I lifted her off the couch. Those muscular legs wrapped around my waist, settling some nerves racing through my veins.

"I'm sorry," she whispered, green eyes searching mine. "I should—"

"You were always more than just the job," I said, cutting her off. Pressing her back to the hallway wall for support, I cupped her face, holding her still. "You're everything, Remy."

Not waiting for a response, I slammed my mouth to hers.

Driving my tongue between her lips, I pushed the overwhelming emotions I couldn't articulate into the kiss, hoping she'd understand. Her fingers wrapped around my neck, blunt nails digging into the bare skin, urging me to take more.

Her skirt bunched around her hips as I pressed against her, grinding my hard cock to her hot center. Not releasing her lips, I ripped open her blouse. Buttons flew in various directions, scattering to the floor. My dick pulsed as I took handfuls of her lush breasts in each hand and squeezed. She gasped in surprise at my brutal treatment. I grinned against her lips.

Kissing along the soft skin of her throat, I worked my way down to her chest. Through the silky lace of her bra, I nipped at her pebbled nipple, holding it between my teeth until Remy's harsh gasp filled the hall. Her back bowed off the wall, shoving more of her full tit into my salivating mouth.

With only my teeth, I pulled the lace cup down, exposing her hard tip to my eager teeth and tongue. Clamping the tight bud between my teeth, I drew back until she hissed from the pain. I flicked the tip of my tongue back and forth like I would soon do to her needy center, drawing pleas and curses from her lips.

"Tallon," she begged.

"I want you," I said, moving to her other breast. "I want you both. Now. Forever. A family."

"What?" she whimpered.

Pulling back, I stared into her glazed green eyes. "This isn't a fling. It's not just until the case is over. I want you to be mine. For you and Crew to know I'm yours." Leaning in, I peppered her jaw with soft kisses as I worked my way to her ear. "And, Remy, you're all mine. Only mine. No more sharing. Just us."

I pulled back, searching her face for any signs of disappointment.

The corners of her lips pulled up in a lust-drunk grin. "You're mine?"

"All yours."

"And I'm yours?" she questioned.

"Mine," I said, grinding my steel-hard cock against her.

"Then show me," she breathed.

A wide grin stretched across my face as I stared down at her.

Mine. This amazing woman was all mine and wanted me to prove it.

"You want a reminder of every place I touched?" I snaked a hand between us. Gripping her soaked panties, I gave them a hard tug and ripped them away. Heel of my hand pressed to her clit, I rubbed as I thrust three fingers into her tight center. "You want me to brand you from the inside out as mine?"

"Fuck. Yes."

"Gladly, Remy. Fucking gladly."

Working my belt loose, I shoved my pants and boxer briefs down just enough to free my cock. One hand wrapped around my dick, the other full of her plump ass, I guided myself to her weeping entrance. Our combined groans filled the silent hall as the tip pushed inside.

Teeth clenched, I studied her with rapt attention as I slowly pushed forward, watching my cock disappear inside her.

"Fucking hell, you're amazing," I said through gritted teeth. Forearms pressed to the wall on either side of her head, I thrust hard, sinking every inch into her delicious cunt. My breaths stuttered, my quick pants matching her own. "Mine."

Pulling back, I shoved forward again and again, brutally marking her as mine just like she wanted. My name on her lips echoed in the hall, followed by desperate pleas for more. Keeping the quick, demanding pace, I wedged a hand between us and pinched her clit, shooting her over the edge.

Her entire body convulsed beneath me as I continued to pound into her pussy, working her through the aftershocks of her orgasm.

Slicking a finger with her release, I moved around to her other tight hole, pressing against the tight ring of muscles.

She stilled, eyes wide as she searched my hooded gaze.

"Has anyone had you here?" I murmured as I pushed the tip of my finger inside. She wiggled, drawing a low, guttural groan from my chest as she shook her head back and forth. Excitement had my dick twitching inside her, making her gasp. "Good. I'll be the first and only." I chuckled as her eyes widened further. "Don't worry. Not today, Kitten. We need to prep you first so you'll enjoy every second as I fuck that amazing ass."

Her core clamped down around me. Lids slammed shut, a groan rumbled up my throat as I fought against the need to come.

"Play with your tits," I commanded. Instantly, her tiny fingers caressed over the swell of her breasts, pinching the tips between two fingers until she whimpered. "That's it, just like I would. A little pain for a lot of pleasure. Pinch and twist until it burns."

Picking up my pace, I watched, teeth clamped on my lower lip to keep from cursing. I moved the single finger in and out, matching the rhythm as I pounded into her pussy.

"Fuck," I growled as I felt her quiver around me, close to another soul-shuddering orgasm. "Give it to me, Kitten," I snapped, slamming into her once, twice, until she screamed her release as I shouted my own.

Over my harsh breaths, her little whimpers reached my ears. Leaning back, I studied her smiling face.

"I think you orgasmed me to death. Not complaining, but fucking hell, I might walk funny tomorrow."

Lips to her neck, I chuckled. "Good. Everyone will know it was me who gave you a good fucking. Now, are you ready for more, Kitten?"

"More?"

"More."

"I don't know if I can—"

Pulling back, I nipped at her lower lip. "You can and you will."

"Yes, sir."

With a low growl, I stepped back, wrapping both arms around her back to keep her sealed to me as I started for the bedroom. "Keep up with the 'sir' shit and you might not walk at all tomorrow."

A wicked smile curved up her lips. "Understood. Sir."

The bed shifted as I laid her on top, both hands pressed beside her head as I studied her beautiful face, taking in every glorious inch of the woman who was now mine.

Mine.

"Don't say I didn't warn you. Now, on your knees. I'm going to spank your ass before fucking you from behind until your legs give out."

And I did.

Again and again, shooting her and me over the edge to pure bliss. Showing her with my body that she was mine, and I was hers.

Hours later, we both collapsed to the disheveled bed, completely spent.

Brushing a damp lock of hair from her forehead, I relished the sleepy smile she offered in return.

"I promise I'll be the man you both deserve," I murmured as I continued to take in every inch of her face.

"Tallon," she whispered. Those bright green eyes misted over, and for half a second, I wondered if her next words would be cruel. "Don't you see it?" Her small hand cupped my face, thumb brushing along my cheek. "You already are."

And just like that, my past life was over and a whole new one began.

25

REMINGTON

"Holy shit."

I peeked over the rim of my laptop, fingers hovering over the keys at Jameson's excited tone. "Care to share with the class?" I questioned when he didn't elaborate past the outburst, just continued gaping at the laptop perched on his lap.

"Out of that long-ass list, the original profile curated only one name that meets all the new parameters we discussed yesterday."

A jolt of excitement raced through my veins, sending my pulse spiking. Forgetting about work, I set my laptop aside and shifted to peer at his screen.

"That's great, right? One name means we have our guy."

"Tallon," Jameson yelled. I flinched as the word rang in my ear. "Get your ass in here."

"Fucking hell, you're bossy," Tallon grumbled as he appeared around the corner, a tiny white towel wrapped around his waist.

"Pot meet kettle." I pointed between them. "Though if

we're having a bossy contest, Tallon wins hands down every time."

A smirk tugged at his lips as he prowled closer, stopping just in front of where I sat on the couch. With a firm grip on my chin, he forced my gaze upward. "You like me bossy."

"I do," I rasped.

"Can you two fucking focus?" Jameson grumbled, but there was a hint of humor in his tone instead of frustration. "We have a solid lead."

"Tell me," Tallon commanded, making me arch an eyebrow at his tone. His grip loosened to slip a palm over my cheek and dip his fingers into my hair. My eyes fluttered closed as he gently massaged my scalp.

Fucking hell, I might start purring.

"Andrew Sam Carting." I shivered at the name, an ominous feeling slithering down my spine. Tallon shot a concerned look at me before turning his attention back to the excited Jameson. "Spent a few years as a deputy sheriff for a small town outside Chicago. Applied to the police academy as soon as he graduated high school. Worked there until he left ten years ago." His light brown eyes lifted to shift between me and Tallon. "Which is when the murders around Chicago stopped and the first instance of the snuff films hit the dark web."

"It has to be him," I said, heart hammering, literally pounding with excitement. "Can we arrest him?"

"No, but we can consider him a strong suspect. What does it list as his occupation now?" Tallon asked.

"Nothing. I don't see a current employer listed. In fact, the last time he actually held a job was in Chicago. I would wonder where he earned money to afford life, but I'm pretty sure I know."

Tallon's hand slipped from my neck, where he'd been

massaging the tight muscles with his expert fingers. He paced the room, and I watched as his thick thigh muscles flexed with each step, the rise and fall of his solid bare chest with each deep breath. My fingers itched to reach out and snag the towel to see all of him.

"You look ready to pounce, Kitten."

Slowly dragging my eyes up to his face, I shrugged at his smile. "Sorry, not sorry."

He huffed a laugh, but the humor quickly vanished. "We should bring him in for questioning," Tallon remarked. "We have enough circumstantial evidence that we can request a meeting. Maybe we could pull a trick to get his DNA and compare it to the samples we have from recent cases and the cold cases."

"On it," Jameson stated as he grabbed his phone from the coffee table. "Hopefully we can get something set up today."

My heart leapt with hope. How amazing would it be for all this to be over? Before, I somewhat dreaded the case wrapping up, knowing that meant Tallon would disappear from my life a second time. Of course, I'd wanted the bastard caught so no one else got hurt, but there was always that tinge of disappointment that came along with it.

Now though, he'd promised to stay, to be here for me and Crew.

"I'll finish getting ready," Tallon said. "Let me know if you can get something scheduled."

Jameson nodded, already absorbed in locating and contacting this Andrew guy.

Shoving off the couch, I followed Tallon's bare back as he marched down the hall toward the master bedroom.

"You think it's him?" I asked as I quietly shut the door behind us. Moving to the bed, I perched on the edge and blew out a slow breath. "I almost don't want to get my hopes up, you know?"

"It sounds promising." I watched with rapt attention as he bent over, digging around in his duffel bag. "We'll know soon enough. If he's the guy, we'll know immediately, even if we don't have any concrete evidence."

"How is that?"

Tallon turned, clutching a white undershirt. "As many women as he's killed, the amount of rage that's needed to do what he does to his victims, you can't hide that. Or if he tries to hide it, we'll see through that too. A suspect can't cover that kind of evil when you know what to look for."

I shivered at the thought. I was almost one of those victims, another number. A dead body he and Jameson would've viewed while talking to the coroner about the cause of death. But we were here now, together and moving forward with a solid lead that could put this evil behind bars.

"Hey." Tallon tossed the shirt to the bed and moved to stand in front of me. "You're safe. I won't let anything happen to you."

"I know. I was just thinking about what could've happened. How I could've been another statistic you studied. You would've never known...." I sighed. "It just snuck up on me, the reality of it all."

Hot palms sealed around my neck, the tips of both thumbs pressed beneath my chin, forcing my face up to his. "But it didn't because you were fucking brilliant and gave the tactical team time to get to you." His blue eyes searched mine. "How are you feeling? Any gaps in memory?"

I nibbled on the corner of my lip as I considered the question. There were small gaps but nothing that stood out as more than me losing time lost in thought. "Nope. Sex is a miracle worker, apparently."

A soft chuckle rumbled in his chest, drawing my gaze to his defined muscles. I trailed my fingertips along the still-damp skin, moving lower and lower until I traced along the top of the towel still tightly secured around his waist.

The fear of what could've happened, the urge to live life to its fullest in every moment we were given, ignited the always smoldering need for him. The cotton slid over my fingers as I tugged until it loosened and dropped to the floor.

My stomach flipped, core throbbing as I reached for him.

"Kitten," Tallon rasped.

Pitching forward, I looked up, locking my gaze with his, then licked up his hard cock from base to tip. It twitched, almost as if it was reaching out for more. *Fucking gladly.* Clutching handfuls of his ass, I urged him closer, which he did without hesitation.

We groaned simultaneously as I wrapped my lips around his silky head, lapping at the bead of precum. My lids fluttered closed, heat now thrumming through my veins as I slipped him deeper into my mouth, shivering at his soft curse. Drawing back, I blinked slowly, holding his smoldering gaze as I swirled my tongue around the head before taking him all the way down my throat.

Fighting past my gag reflex, I swallowed, working my throat to massage his dick. Tears slipped from the corners of both eyes as I slowly pulled back. A hand pressed to the back of my head, keeping me exactly where he wanted me.

A moan of desire had his hips flexing, thrusting himself deeper. Fucking hell, I loved his control. Though I loved the gentle yet uber-possessive and safety-conscious sides too.

If I loved the various faces of Tallon, did that mean…

I loved him?

For a while I'd loved the idea of him, but this, the real him, was better than I ever dreamed.

"Fucking hell, Kitten," he grunted. With a curse, he tangled his fingers into my hair, holding me in place as he stepped back. His cock popped from between my lips, now bobbing just out of reach. "On your back."

Pressing the back of my hand against my lips, I wiped the saliva from the corners. The mattress shifted as I flopped back, grinning in excited anticipation.

A hard jerk around the elastic band lowered the too-large black sweats until they drooped around my knees. Heart racing, I licked my lips, high on the excitement of what he planned. Lifting both of my legs, he placed one foot on each of his shoulders, the sweats hugging the back of his neck, and moved between my thighs.

With no prep, he shoved himself inside in one hard thrust. My back arched off the bed, eyes slammed shut at the sudden, glorious intrusion. The angle and pressure from my slightly closed thighs, the feel of him sliding in and out, stretching me to the max, was ten times more intense than usual.

Weight against my legs had my knees bending until they tucked against my chest. At the new angle, the pressure of his weight pressing me into the bed had my eyes rolling back with each plunge.

"Fuck," I whimpered. Gripping handfuls of the comforter, I held on tight to keep from sliding back with each demanding thrust.

"Is this what you needed, Kitten? My cock pounding into you to help you relax?"

"Yes," I cried out, almost choking on the word.

"Tell me you craved my dick," he demanded.

I sealed my lips shut, not because I didn't believe the words he wanted to hear, but for the punishment I knew would come. From the slight smirk that tugged at his lips, he knew.

And gave me exactly what I needed.

The loud crack as his hand connected with my ass sounded through the room. The pain shot me over the edge. Body shuddering, I whimpered his name as I came, lifting to meet his hard thrusts as he found his own release with a curse.

Sweat slicked my forehead, chest heaving with each gasp as I tried to catch my breath. I winced as he slowly withdrew, lowering my legs before stepping back.

"Stay there," he ordered. Legs tingling as the blood rushed to my toes, I grinned at the ceiling, waiting for him to return. Seconds later he was back, a damp, warm cloth in hand.

I hissed as he pressed it against my center, slowly cleaning me with a reverent touch.

"I'm sorry." His brows dipped in concentration as he focused between my legs.

My hair slid along the comforter as I shook my head. "I love it," I offered. "Nothing to be sorry for."

"I don't want to hurt you. Ever."

"Well, I like the pain, and my opinion wins."

He arched a single brow. "Does it now?" Tossing the cloth into the hamper, he helped me stand and tugged my sweats back up. Still crouched, he pursed his lips, seeming to be lost in thought.

"What?" I asked hesitantly. *Fuck, what is he thinking?*

"Once Crew comes back, we might need to keep you quiet. How do you feel about a ball gag?"

"A what?" I squeaked in surprise. *Shit, was that an excited high-pitched tone or a scared one?*

He nodded as if he didn't hear me, too lost in his own thoughts. Shoving off the floor, he slowly took in the bedroom. "Or we could soundproof the room. Think he's old enough to pick up on something like that?"

I gaped. *He's serious. Should I be mortified or elated?* If it meant more of what we'd done together in the last twenty-four hours....

Elated.

I settled on elated.

A loud pounding shook the door. I jumped in surprise, slamming into his chest.

"Wrap it up, you two," Jameson called from the other side. "I reached the suspect, and he's meeting us at the station in two hours."

Tallon ran a calculating eye over me before opening the door, using his wide frame to block Jameson's view into the room. Possessive bastard.

"Listen, yeah, I've seen your dick plenty of times, but put some clothes on, for fuck's sake."

"How did he sound?" Tallon asked.

"Your dick? Pretty sure—"

Tallon muttered a string of curses. "The suspect, you fucker."

"Right, good. Because that would've been damn awkward—"

"Get to the point, Bend," Tallon groaned in obvious exasperation.

"If I didn't know any better, I'd think the fucker was waiting on my call. He didn't sound shocked that a detective reached out requesting he come to the station. Get dressed. I want to get there with plenty of time to prep for the interrogation. We might only have one shot at this bastard."

Tallon glanced over his shoulder, a frown tugging at his lips.

I swiped a hand through the air, cutting off his line of thought. "Absolutely not."

"What?" he said, feigning innocence.

"I'm going. You are not leaving me here." I stomped my foot when his lips pressed into a thin line. "What if it's not him?" I reasoned. "Do you really want to leave me here, alone, with just one officer outside?"

He grumbled something about me being too smart for my own good, making me preen a little. "Give us fifteen and we'll be ready to go."

With a wide grin, I shifted toward my closet and pulled the door open.

Tapping a finger against my lips, I stared at the hangers of clothes nearly busting out of the small space. "What does one wear when interviewing a potential serial killer?"

Strong arms wrapped around my waist, and soft lips sealed to the side of my neck.

"Layers," he whispered into my ear. "Lots of fucking layers."

With a sharp slap to my backside, he retreated to the other side of the room to get ready. I didn't even need to turn to know exactly what he'd wear: black suit, starched dress shirt, and armed to the teeth.

Comfortable silence settled between us as we hurried to get ready. My heart swelled. This right here was everything I imagined sharing my space with someone would be. Easy and comforting.

"What?" he asked while situating the cuff of his jacket.

I smothered my cheerful smile and shrugged. "Nothing. Just happy, I guess."

The shy, sweet smile he shot back turned my insides to mushy goo. "Same, Remy. Now let's go get this bastard so we can put this all behind us."

And now that I knew Tallon would be in my future, I couldn't wait.

26

TALLON

The stench of burnt coffee and stale smoke engulfed the small viewing area. The two-way mirror along the wall exposed the interrogation room on the other side. Two empty chairs and a long metal table between them were the only three things in the room. For now. Soon this Andrew fucker would sit in one chair, me in the other while I attempted to extract a confession or make him slip up, revealing something that could help us close the cases.

If I could get him to slip up just once, that was all I needed to get a warrant for his DNA.

I slid my gaze from the empty room to my side. Remy's wide, excited smile hadn't dimmed since we walked into the station. Either she loved all this because she was a self-proclaimed crime show junkie or thought today could mark the end of this fucker's reign of terror.

A wash of nerves made heat build beneath my skin. Sweat slicked down my spine despite the cool AC blowing. What if I failed? If I couldn't get a confession out of him, this fucker would be back on the street hunting women—hunting what was mine.

Mine.

My chest swelled with pride just thinking about last night and all we'd shared. The sex was fucking fantastic, and this morning too, but we connected on a deeper level than I'd ever felt with anyone before. Last night confirmed that she was mine just as much as I was hers.

This needed to be done. Close this case so I could figure out what the fuck to do next. I knew for certain there was no going back to three-hundred-plus nights on the road. There was no way in hell I wanted to be away from her that much. Plus, I wanted all those extra hours here to make up for time lost with Crew.

What that would look like, I wasn't sure. But no matter what happened, I wasn't going anywhere. Not now. Not ever.

"This reminds me so much of that show *Castle*'s set," Remy whispered more to herself as she touched the two-way mirror. "This is so fucking cool."

Grinning ear to ear, I shook my head and tugged her closer, not liking the small distance between us. "I'm glad you approve. Though the one at the FBI office smells better."

"This one smells authentic," she mused, her small nose scrunching as she took in all the scents. "How much longer do we have to wait—"

The door to the interrogation room swung open, attracting both our attention. Even though I knew the fucker couldn't see us, I sidestepped, putting myself between Remy and the evil incarnate striding into the room.

Dressed in a blue Italian suit and white dress shirt, the smug asshole looked ready for a press interview, not an interrogation. The wide smile he directed to the mirror had the hairs on the back of my neck standing on end.

"I'm totally getting Ted Bundy vibes," Remy whispered

conspiratorially. "He's attractive." I snarled at her words, not taking my eyes off the jackass. She snorted. "Don't get your boxers in a twist. I said attractive, not hot like you."

"He doesn't look that big," I mused. "I thought your reports said he was bigger?"

"Tallon. Look at me. Everyone is bigger, especially when they're standing and I'm tied to a damn chair."

I winced. "Sorry."

"And don't get caught up on size. It doesn't take much to overtake a panicked, untrained woman. Plus, that probably benefited him."

"How so?"

"Less intimidating. Let's say your agent buddy Bryson approached me on the side of a road at night. I'd be less agreeable to talking to him than, say, Jameson. The sheer size of some men just reminds us how vulnerable we are. Which you know I like"—she hit her hip against my thigh—"in certain instances, but not when you don't know the person. No groundwork of trust."

Humming in understanding, I watched the fucker unbutton his jacket and fold into the metal chair. The damn cocky-ass smirk that hadn't faded irked the hell out of me. It was like he knew something we didn't.

Rolling my neck to ease some of the building tension, I turned for the door just as Jameson walked in.

"He's a fucking prick," he muttered as he slapped a file folder to my chest. "Good luck breaking him. The asshole refused counsel, said he doesn't need representation." I nodded and started for the door, but he grabbed my bicep, making me pause. "I already offered him a drink, hoping we could swab the can for DNA later. The fucker laughed. He's smart and knows our playbook."

With a clipped nod, I stepped out of the room and shut

the door behind me. The sounds of the busy police station filled my ears as I took a deep breath to clear my head. Now wasn't the time to worry about Remy or our future. She needed me to be the hard-ass FBI agent who got shit done. The asshole who'd closed more cases in a decade than any other agent on the East Coast.

Slipping on my tried-and-true emotionless mask, I strode to the other door and pushed it open. Though the arctic air was meant to put the suspect on edge, it was a welcome relief. I slapped the file folder against the table. With a smirk, Andrew Carting stared at it before leaning back in the chair, locking nearly black eyes on mine.

"They made me aware that you declined counsel," I said, so there was no mistaking that he walked in here without a lawyer.

"Considering I do not know why the Davidson County police have asked me to come down today, I don't see why I would need legal counsel."

I arched a brow.

He matched it.

Holy fuck, I might accidentally strangle this bastard. Is that plausible in court? "Your Honor, I tripped over the table, and my hands wrapped around his neck as I tried to catch myself. The muscles cramped, forcing them to choke him to death."

"I'm Special Agent Harper with the FBI. You're here today, Mr. Carting, because you came up in a suspect search."

Hands folded on top of his knee, he looked completely at ease. "Search for what? A good-looking, single man in this great town of Nashville, Tennessee?" His smile grew. "Guilty on all counts, Special Agent Harper." His eyes flicked over my shoulder, staring at the two-way mirror. "I'm sure others will agree."

Yanking out the chair, I sat and leaned forward, resting my clasped hands on top of the file folder.

"Why did you move to Nashville?" I asked, ignoring his taunting.

"The crime rate in Chicago skyrocketed. Hadn't you heard?" I swear that smile of his turned more snakelike. "After leaving my job as deputy sheriff, I found a more peaceful town."

Fighting the urge to punch that cocky-ass look off his fucking face, I yanked open the file, scanning the contents. "Where were you living between the time you left Chicago and moving to Nashville?"

He shrugged and dusted an imaginary piece of lint off his pants. "Here and there, trying to find the right fit. It's so difficult to find a place that can keep someone like me entertained."

"How did you afford that? Moving around when you didn't have a job?"

I knew how he afforded it. Through the money made from the fucking auction site and snuff films he and that bastard Vincent created. But I highly doubted he'd come out and say that.

"I invested wisely through the years."

"And what are you doing now for work?"

"Hunting."

A low snarl built in my chest, which made that smile stretch even wider, his excitement clear.

"But I guess you could call that a hobby, not a job. There are so many great hunting grounds in the area, I'm not sure I'll ever grow bored with this city." His eyes sparkled with evil intent. "Though a few weeks ago, I missed one, a delectable and feisty prey. I'm hoping to ensnare that missed opportunity soon, though there are—" He tilted his head side to side like he was weighing his words. "—obstacles I have to overcome first."

"Obstacles," I gritted out, hating that I needed to play his motherfucking games to keep him talking. We both knew who he was talking about. I wanted to rip his head from his fucking shoulders for his words, but I couldn't. Yet.

"Yes, though the best things in life don't come easy. Where would the fun be in that?" Breaking off my stare, he flicked his wrist and glanced at his watch. "I have early dinner plans, so if we could wrap this up."

"Are you not going to ask why you came up on a list of names?"

"I figured a special agent like yourself would get around to that eventually."

Forget ripping off his head. I would rip out his tongue and shove it up his ass.

"We are investigating a string of violent crimes here in Nashville, and your background fits the suspect we're looking for."

"Does it now?" he said, completely unfazed. "So, you have a picture of this man?" He arched a brow. "Or matched my DNA and fingerprints tying me to these crimes? Or is this just a good old-fashioned witch hunt because you're so fucking terrible at your job that you don't know who you're looking for?"

I gritted my teeth so hard the muscles of my jaw ached. "Where were you three nights ago?"

He tilted his head back and released a low chuckle. "I see. So you're trying to pin these crimes on me? That's why I need an alibi?"

"Just answer the question." If I could place him near Remy's house, maybe, just maybe, I could convince a judge to sign a warrant for his DNA. Then it would be an open-and-shut case.

"I'd have to look at my calendar, but three nights ago?" he mused. "That could've been the night I had those two women in my bed." He paused and leveled a knowing look across the metal table. My stomach soured knowing exactly where he was going with that statement. "You'd know about that, wouldn't you? Except I don't share pussy."

Hiding my hands beneath the table, which the asshat noted with a smirk, I tightened them into white-knuckled fists.

"I don't know what you're getting at, Mr. Carting."

Both forearms pressed to the metal edge, he shifted, leaning toward the middle of the table. "I'm insinuating that you also enjoy a roll on the dark side. So what's the difference between you and me? Hmm?"

The taste of copper coated my tongue from where I bit down hard to keep from lashing out.

"The difference?" I somehow got out of my clenched jaw. I forced a cocky smirk just to piss him off. "All the women we're with want to be with us. Now, Mr. Carting, can you say the same?"

A flash of fire burned behind his dark eyes before he smothered the small reaction.

"None of them have ever complained."

"Because they were satisfied or dead?" Again, he laughed, but this time it was strained, as if I'd hit a nerve. "Our profile says the man responsible for these crimes does it because he has a dick so small he'll be forever angry. Pouting like a toddler that no one wants to play with the small equipment he's packing."

I smiled at the flare of his nostrils, the earlier unblemished skin along his neck now red and splotchy. Doubling down, I shifted in my seat to lean back, propping one ankle over the opposite knee.

"There's also the other thing," I baited.

"This should be entertaining," he muttered, gesturing for me to continue. "Please enlighten me on all the ways I'm not like the man you're after. If you need proof, well, I'm not afraid of an old-fashioned measuring contest if you're not. I have nothing to be ashamed of."

"Nah," I said, waving him off. He smiled triumphantly. "I only pick on men my size. No need to hurt your ego over something you can't control."

That deep anger-fueled flush now seeped across his cheeks.

"The other thing?" he snapped.

"Oh, right, that? Well, besides the small pecker part"—I grinned and shot a look at his crotch—"it's the whole mommy issue. We figured the mother doted on him too much, made his life absolutely perfect. So when his victims refuse him, he throws a tantrum of sorts, killing them for rejecting him."

This was the complete opposite of the profile, which was why I took this chance to get under his skin. Rhyan and Jameson assumed the unsub grew up with an abusive female figure, most likely his mother. That was why he enjoyed the torture, and cut out their reproductive organs.

His right eye twitched.

Excitement raced through my veins, knowing I'd pushed him, hopefully to the point of an outburst.

"Well, that is certainly a great story, Harper—"

"Agent Harper," I clarified.

There was nothing nice about the sharp smile he shot across the table toward me. "Right. Now, since you're not charging me with anything, I will be on my way." Standing, he buttoned his jacket like the gentleman he wasn't and held out his hand.

I slapped mine into his and gave it a death-grip squeeze. After releasing him, I dug in my back pocket and handed him my card.

He took it with a grin. "What is this for?"

"A reminder that we will catch you."

He canted his head to the side. "Catch me doing what, Agent Harper? Living my life? I've done nothing wrong, and you will remember that or I'll file a harassment claim against you and the FBI."

At the door, he paused and glanced over his shoulder. "Oh, and enjoy your trip."

I felt my brows pull inward.

Trip?

What fucking trip?

Before I could ask, he was gone.

Storming to the viewing room door, I yanked it open and stepped inside.

Standing in front of the mirror, Remy and Jameson shared a look. The latter grimaced and pushed at Remy's back, urging her toward me. "Calm him down."

She shot a glare over her shoulder. "I'm not his security blanket," she hissed.

"No," I grumbled and pulled her against my chest. The tension drained the moment my arms wrapped around her in a crushing hug. "You're better."

"That shit about a trip sounded ominous," Jameson mused, turning back to the empty interrogation room. "I'm putting a tail on him."

"Make it a team," I said over Remy's head, still not having the strength to let her go. After being in the room with the fucktard, I needed the reassurance that she was there with me. "He's smart, and there's safety in numbers."

Jameson nodded and headed out without a backward glance.

"I'm sorry," I muttered, the heavy weight of guilt sitting on my chest making it hard to breathe.

"What the hell are you apologizing for?" Remy wedged her hands between us and pushed. Reluctantly, I released her and shoved both hands into the side pockets of my slacks. "Tallon?"

"I didn't get a confession out of him, didn't get a shred of evidence to help the case. That fucker is back on the street because of me."

"Tallon," she whispered, eyes going soft. "You can't take on the world. It's not possible. You did your best, and that's all anyone can ask for."

I shook my head. "No. If I would've been more prepared, maybe I would've gotten to him."

"Who says you didn't? He might go out there and make a mistake because you rattled him in there." She hitched a thumb toward the empty room on the other side of the glass. "Tallon, you can't save everyone, and those people he hurts, all those women, that's on him, not you."

"Then why does it feel like it is?" I muttered, hating showing this vulnerability. But I was drowning in the guilt. How could I expect her to trust me if I couldn't even do my job well enough to get the evil shit after her?

Closing the distance, she smiled sweetly before drawing her arm back and sailing a fist right to the center of my stomach. All the air in my lungs expelled past my parted lips as I hunched over from the unexpected blow.

"What the hell was that for?"

"Are you blaming yourself for my actions?"

I shot her a glare, already knowing where this was going. "No."

"Do you feel bad, feel guilty because you didn't stop it?"

"Remy—"

"Do you think if you were prepared enough, you could've stopped me from wanting to punch you, from figuring out a way around your defenses and sneaking a sucker punch in when you least expected it?"

"It's not the same," I hissed.

"It is, Tallon. Just because you feel the echoing pain of someone else's actions does not mean you were the source or reason for it happening. You're carrying this weight that no single person should bear."

"I don't like you very much right now," I grumbled, not meaning a single word. "You and all your woman logic."

"I can totally mansplain the various types and levels of guilt and self-deprecating thoughts all day, every day, if you need me to. I went through an array with Jett." She turned her face from me, hiding her own vulnerable moment. "If you don't let it go, the weight will bury you alive, and, Tallon...."

I eyed her warily as she approached, only relaxing when her hands gently caressed down my chest.

"I like your dick way too much to let that happen."

And that was it.

Tossing my head back, I laughed harder than I had in a long, long time.

The bubble of guilt shattered, the oppressive weight lifted all because of her.

And I knew it at that moment.

There wasn't a life I wanted to live without her in it.

27

REMINGTON

R idiculous.

With all the technology in that damn school, they sent paper sheets for Crew's makeup work, which I now had to mail to him.

My white Doc Martens stomped against the sidewalk as I weaved between those going too slow. Like the two men trailing me. Knowing they were keeping up, I forged ahead, juggling the stack of paperwork so I didn't lose a single page to the bursts of chilly wind.

Grappling with the metal door handle, I'd just gotten my fingers around the edge when another hand reached around and pulled it open for me.

"You're fast for someone so tiny," Tallon said, smirking down at me.

"Are you trying for another punch to the gut like yesterday, or are you hoping for the nuts this time?"

He chuckled, following me into the FedEx store. He leaned in close, still smiling. "You like my cock too much, remember? If you need a reminder, I think Jameson heard you screaming for more last—"

I cut him off with an elbow to the ribs and hurried over to the counter, where a teenager who looked like he'd rather be anywhere else than at work stood.

"Hi," I greeted and dropped the stack of papers onto the counter in front of him. "I need to mail these to Texas because my son's school is apparently too cheap to go all digital, yet they charge me—"

"Do you have a box?" he droned.

I pursed my lips. This morning started off bad with my fuckhead of a project manager insisting we video-chat for me to update him on where I was with my work. The funny thing about his constant hounding was, if he pulled his head out of his ass, he'd realize that I actually completed a full day's worth of work before lunch. Why didn't I bring that to his attention? Because I knew for a fact that they wouldn't pay more for the extra workload just because I was faster than everyone else.

In fact, I was almost certain I was the least paid developer they employed.

"She has a box, just not the one you're looking for," Jameson said somewhere behind me. I rolled my eyes. "You might want to grab her one."

The teenager grumbled something under his breath, probably because I dared to make him work today, and shuffled off toward the back room.

"How much does his school cost?" Tallon asked, leaning a hip against the counter, arms crossed.

"More than I want to spend, but worth every penny." I grinned up at him. "I'm just in a shit mood. The paperwork is fine. No one needs the rain forests anyway."

Tallon chuckled and leaned closer but paused, eyes locked on something behind me.

Figuring it was Jameson doing something childish, I spun around, mouth open to chastise him for acting like a kid, but the words dried up in my mouth.

"Hello, Remington."

Tallon's muscles flexed as he shoved me behind his back, blocking me from Andrew Carting's view.

"What in the hell are you doing here?" Tallon ground out.

I strained to hear Carting's response through the background noise of the other customers in the store. *Shit, he wouldn't try something with so many people around, would he?* I swallowed. I knew the answer to that. This sicko would do whatever it took to get what he wanted.

I shivered and fisted the back of Tallon's snug long-sleeve T-shirt.

"Contemplating a paper purchase. Why else would someone come here? Am I not allowed to run my errands while your men follow me about town?"

I cursed in my head. This wasn't good. If he saw them, did that mean he could easily evade the officers following him?

"How did you know my name?" I asked before I could stop myself. Determined not to cower, to stay true to that promise I made myself after leaving Jett, I stepped around Tallon and met the devil's eyes straight on.

He raised a single shoulder. "A lucky guess, maybe." He winked, telling me everything I already knew.

Fear licked up my spine and dread pooled in my gut as I scanned the five other customers' faces. We had to get out of here. Now.

Grabbing the stack of papers, I began pushing Tallon toward the door.

"And where were you mailing all that schoolwork to?" I froze. Turning on the heels of my boots, I narrowed my eyes. "Did I hear you mention Texas—"

So apparently the scene I was afraid this man or Tallon would make in the store would be made by me, not them. Because hearing that subtle threat, him even mentioning knowing where Crew was, sent me over the edge of fury.

"Stay the fuck away from him," I yelled as I lunged. Papers fluttered to the floor as I reached out, ready to strangle the life out of his pathetic body. Only my fingers never wrapped around flesh, because a muscular arm hooked my middle and hauled me back just out of murdering reach.

The air knocked from my lungs when my back slammed against Tallon's chest.

"Stop," he hissed. "It's what he wants."

Breaths coming in sharp pants, I glared at the bastard, letting him see my full intent to rip out his heart if he dared to say one more thing about Crew.

"I love a woman with spunk," Carting stated with a Cheshire cat grin. "See you around, Remington." Whistling a cheery tune, he exited the store and disappeared from view.

I jerked in Tallon's hold, trying to break free.

"Let me go," I seethed, hating that Carting was just walking out the door like he wasn't evil incarnate.

"No. You go after him and it makes us pinning all these cases on him that much harder. He wanted you to react, Remy. Think about why."

Now that some of the anger haze had begun to clear, I considered what Tallon said and cursed. He was right. In that damn shed, he liked my sass, my fight, which was exactly what he got just now by egging me on.

I played right into his hands.

"I won't cower to him," I said instead of apologizing for overreacting.

Tallon's hold slowly eased, allowing me to step away. "And I don't expect you to. But we have to be smart about this. Clearly, he's following us. Hell, maybe he hired someone to follow us and update him on our every move. We stick together and work the case—"

The shrill of a phone ringing cut him off. Jamming his hand into the front pocket of his jeans, he pulled out his phone and glanced at the screen.

"Harper," he barked the second he pressed it to his ear. Monitoring him, I bent to the floor and began gathering the scattered papers. An ever-deeper line formed between his brows. "Yes, this is Special Agent Harper. Who is this?"

Still listening, Tallon hitched his chin toward Jameson, then the front doors. It was almost hilarious how hands-off Jameson was as he approached me and then gestured for us to leave, hovering a hand over the small of my back as we walked. I mean, I had the guy's dick down my throat just a few days ago, so not sure why he acted all shy now. Though I guess he was going overboard to respect his friend's claim that I was his.

Outside, the cold damp air settled over every inch of exposed skin, making me shiver. Or maybe it was the lingering sense of pure evil left in the wake of that horrible bastard. Jameson lingered in the doorway listening to Tallon's conversation before hurrying to catch up.

"That doesn't sound good," Jameson muttered under his breath as he scanned the streets.

Pausing, I waited until Tallon caught up with us so I could eavesdrop on his conversation.

"Right, that is odd. Have the bodies already been sent to the ME?"

I winced. "Yeah, the mention of bodies, as in plural, is never a good thing. Who is he talking to?"

"No clue."

"What bodies?"

"Not sure," Jameson said with a smirk. His light brown eyes found mine before going back to surveying the busy sidewalk. "You're living up to that nickname more than ever. So curious."

I curled my fingers like I had actual claws and hissed at him. Laughing, he stepped closer to me to allow someone to easily pass.

"I really am happy for you two. Seeing him like this...." He grimaced when he saw Tallon's face. "Well, not like this right now, but when he's not discussing dead bodies, is great. And you too."

"What about me?"

"You look happier, not as stressed as that first day or two. Maybe that's because all your secrets are out or because you know you don't have to do it all alone. Either way, it's a good look for you."

I bit my lip to stop my growing smile.

He was right. I was happier in so many ways, which was completely at odds with the amount of danger we were all in.

"Could be all the sex," he added as he looked away to hide his mischievous grin.

"But what about you?" I commented. "Sure, me and Tallon are"—I waved a hand—"what we are...."

"Soul mates." Jameson snorted, clearly having amused himself.

"Figuring things out," I corrected, elbowing him in the side. "But seriously, I want you to be this happy."

His head bobbed slightly as he nodded. "I'm not *not* happy. And just because we started together doesn't mean I expected all three of us to find a relationship together. I, for one, couldn't deal with that controlling bastard."

"Hmm, that's an aspect I like. Usually."

"But don't worry about me, Remy. I'm golden. Maybe someday I'll find what you two have going on, but until then, I'm very happy with just flings and no-commitment sex to fill the few nights I actually have free. Mostly the job keeps me too busy to even contemplate a relationship, hence why Tallon and I did what we did all those years ago. Easier for everyone."

At the SUV, Jameson pulled the back passenger door open and helped me inside. I frowned at the stack of papers I didn't get a chance to mail. But there was no way I was going back to that store. Maybe I could schedule a pickup or something, order an envelope large enough to hold it all.

Tallon climbed into the SUV and tossed the phone into the cupholder as Jameson snapped the seat belt across his lap in the passenger seat.

"What was that about?" Jameson asked offhandedly. Silence from the driver side had him turning his full attention that direction. "Tallon?"

"Enjoy your trip," Tallon muttered under his breath, almost too quiet to hear. With a curse, he slammed both curled fists against the top of the steering wheel. "That motherfucker. I'm going to kill him myself. Fuck the justice system."

As he reached for the door handle, I lunged forward and gripped his bicep. If he really wanted to get out of the car, he could easily drag me with him, but he stilled.

"What's going on?" I asked.

"Call the officers tailing Carting," Tallon said instead of responding to me. "Ask what he did last night. Where he went. If he had any company. I want to know where the motherfucker was every second since he left the police station yesterday."

Jameson's features pinched. "What did he do?"

I swallowed. Considering there was a mention of bodies and now this reaction, things just went from bad to worse.

"Three female bodies were found in different dumpsters around the downtown Chattanooga area." I gasped, fingers trembling as they covered my open mouth. "They were beaten so badly they'll either have to wait for a DNA match or dental records to identify the victims." He took a deep breath, his chest puffing out before deflating as he slowly released it through pursed lips. "Their reproductive organs were removed. Based on the coroner on-site, at least one showed signs that he did the mutilation premortem."

Blazing heat washed over me followed by ice freezing my veins as Tallon's words sank deep. Three women. Three more victims. My lungs stopped working, only quick, wheezing breaths able to pull in and out. Death grip on the back of Jameson's seat, my nails dug into the leather. I focused on pulling in gulps of air. Darkness encroached on the corners of my vision, the entire world spinning as I clung to the seat like a lifeline, keeping me from being swept away by the river of terror attempting to drown me.

Shouts sounded close by, but I couldn't respond. Not when I was this close to blacking out. Squeezing both eyes closed, I shut out the world.

"Remington." Tallon's voice cracked above me, snapping me out of the panic-induced haze. I blinked and met his pleading gaze. "I promise."

My forehead wrinkled, brows dipped as I studied his stricken expression. "Promise what?" I shifted along the seat to sit up.

No, not the seat.

Tallon's lap.

Searching the SUV, I startled, finding myself now in Tallon's lap with Jameson outside the open back door, eyes wide.

"That I'll keep you safe. That we will keep you safe."

Oh fuck.

I sealed my eyes shut so Tallon wouldn't see the truth.

How much time did I lose? The urge to ask was strong, but I couldn't risk it. If Tallon knew I'd just lost a few minutes of memory, he wouldn't tell me any more details of the case to keep me from stress overload.

"I know," I rasped, throat dry. "I know you will, Tallon. It was just... hearing those details after just being face-to-face with that monster. Before, when we talked about the victims, he was a phantom, a dark shadow who I escaped from. But today, he was so close... too close. And to hear what he did to those three—"

"Stop," Jameson ordered. "We'll figure this out, Remy." He paused when his own cell rang. Looking at the screen, he held up a single finger, telling us to give him a second. "Yes, sir, I'm here," I heard him say before he turned and stepped away from the SUV.

"What's going on?" I asked.

"I'm not following," Tallon responded as he brushed a finger across my forehead, dislodging a few strands of hair.

"The Carting guy showing up here, the new bodies in another city, and I don't know why, maybe I'm reading too much into it, but the call Jameson is on now with who I'm assuming is his boss, it all feels ominous, like a buildup to something big."

"Like what?"

I pursed my lips, afraid to voice my theory to the world.

"The influx of vandalism has jumped." Scrambling off Tallon's lap, I shifted around to face Jameson. He gripped the roof of the SUV, his chest and head slightly bowed inside, his expression unreadable. "My captain is shifting my focus to those cases since the one revolving around the woman murdered last week hasn't produced any solid leads."

"But the guy, Andrew—" I started.

"We have nothing to tie him to the case. In fact, I would almost say this shift in priorities is a direct result of us bringing him in yesterday. He has unlimited funds, and if he put pressure on my captain because he felt targeted... well, that could shift case focus real quick."

I chewed on my lower lip, eyes flicking back and forth as I processed the new information.

"So what you're telling me is this," I stated as emotional numbness seeped through me. "Three new murders with the same signature popped up a city over two hours away from here, which means Tallon, as the task force leader for this case, will more than likely have to go examine the bodies and scenes in person."

"I don't—"

I held up a hand. "And now there's a spike in crime here, in Nashville, that's pulling Jameson away from focusing on this case." Silence greeted me when I paused. "Does this seem suspicious to anyone else?"

A heavy weight pressed on the top of my shoulders and tugged me to Tallon's side. "Kitten, we won't let anything happen to you. I promise."

I forced a smile and nodded.

I wanted to believe him.

But the promise was one I knew deep in my gut wasn't likely to be kept.

An evil storm brewed around us.

With me smack in the eye with a demented serial killer willing to ensure I was his next victim.

28

TALLON

"Sir," I grated out through my clenched teeth. "My task force can handle the murders in Chattanooga—"

"You are their lead, Special Agent Harper, and I expect the leader of the team to be on-site to verify if the recent cases are connected to the others associated with this unsub." He paused, which had me cursing. We'd worked together long enough that he knew me trying to get out of traveling to a scene was very unlike me. "Is there something going on that I should know?"

I swallowed down my response of *"Yes, I have a son and a fucking brilliant and sexy-as-hell girlfriend who I intend to make my wife one day soon."* If he knew all that, then he'd pull me off the case entirely to ensure there were no emotions mixed in with my decision-making. Which was also why I wouldn't tell him how I'd plotted seven different ways to murder this fucker Carting.

Pretty sure there was a rule somewhere in our manual that stated murdering a suspect because he looked at your girl was not allowed. Though since I couldn't quote the exact page or rule number, maybe not.

"Harper," my boss barked.

"You're right, sir." I cleared my throat. "I'll get to Chattanooga as soon as possible and report what I find."

Tossing the phone onto the wooden swing, I sealed my eyes shut, tipped my head back, and groaned. This couldn't be worse, which was exactly what Carting planned all along. Remy saw it first, and as soon as she laid out the pieces of the puzzle, I saw it too.

He was separating us, making us vulnerable.

We knew he'd use Jameson or me against Remy if he got his hands on us. So now not only did I need to worry about keeping Remy safe while I was gone, but also Jameson and myself too.

I could take Remy with me, but leaving her alone in the hotel room while I visited crime scenes, talked to witnesses, and visited the morgue was worse than leaving her here with the officers stationed out front.

A screech cut through the early evening quiet as the screen door slowly opened.

"Hey," Remy said as she stepped onto the porch.

I couldn't help but smile at how adorable she looked all bundled up. With the setting sun, the temperature steadily dropped into the high thirties, making it chilly without a coat, but the thick quilted blanket wrapped around Remy's shoulders seemed like overkill to me.

"Hey, yourself." The smooth wood pressed against my palm as I patted the spot next to me. "Done with work?"

The bright twinkle in her green eyes as she sat down told me she found that last statement funny. Not sure why.

"Yeah. How did the call go with your boss?"

My heavy exhale fogged in front of my face.

"That good?" she joked. Curling the edges of the blanket

tighter, she leaned her head against my shoulder. "He wants you in Chattanooga, doesn't he?"

"He does."

"I'll be fine," she whispered.

"I'm wondering—" I started but cut myself off.

I'm wondering if I can stand to be away from you for a single night now or in the future.

That was what I wanted to say. Was it too soon?

Fuck, I'm terrible at relationships.

"Crew has to come back," she said, snapping me out of my thoughts. "But it's not safe, so I'm not sure what to do."

Her silky hair shifted beneath my lips as I planted a kiss on her crown before pressing my cheek on top. "One day at a time. That's all we can do. Take this one day at a time."

"When do you leave?"

"I pushed it to tomorrow. That gives the detectives there time to gather evidence and get reports together for me to review. I'll only be gone two nights at most." A thought hit me. "Why don't you go stay at my apartment? I can have an officer stationed outside the door at all times."

I swiveled my head to the street as a car slowed, my tension dropping when I noticed the two young girls on bikes it had slowed for. Taking a deep breath, I took in the various houses on the street. It was a quaint neighborhood, perfect for families.

We hadn't discussed living arrangements after the case closed and life went back to normal.

A new normal.

"I'll think about it," she said, answering my earlier question. "How do you think he did it?"

I shook my head. Over dinner, we discussed how the officers tailing Carting stated his car never left the driveway of his Green Hills home. So according to them, he never left, but he'd obviously figured out a way to sneak past them, considering there were three bodies as proof.

"Didn't you say your sister saw this guy? He went to her job?" she asked. "Or the security footage from my work? Did anything come from that?"

"The security footage from the lobby of your building was shit, so no that was a dead end. But yeah, Tinley saw him but with the low lights, she said she wouldn't be able to positively ID him, and even if she could, technically he did nothing wrong that night. Nothing we could charge him for, anyway. He wasn't using a fake badge when he pretended to be a detective, even though he lied and stated that he was one, so we wouldn't be able to charge him for impersonating an officer."

"Would it bother you if I asked Jameson to stay in the apartment with me and had the officer stationed outside?"

I huffed, making her twist to look up at my face. "No, Kitten. Just because I'm a possessive asshole with you doesn't mean I'd ever put that over your safety and security. I'd prefer if he was in there with you."

It didn't even cross my mind to be jealous. Sure, they were together recently and before, but something had settled between the three of us after the Crew revelation. I felt secure in my growing feelings for Remy, and I knew Jameson supported that, wanted that for me.

"Then that's what I'll do. Even with one exit, I think I'd sleep better knowing there was a single point of entry."

My grin widened at her thought process.

"Smart, funny, and sexy as hell," I mused. "How the hell did I get so lucky?"

"Wait till you meet our son. You'll no doubt be saying that as much as I do."

Our son.

I couldn't fucking wait.

I had to close this case, get that Carting bastard behind bars so I could finally meet Crew without a looming dark cloud.

"What did you tell him? About his father? About me?"

"You know what's crazy is I had no idea what your profession was, but any time Crew asked me about his father, I said he was out fighting the bad guys."

My heart swelled and thundered in my chest.

"So I'm a good guy in his eyes?" I asked hesitantly. A part of me worried she'd bad-mouthed me considering how he was conceived and then I vanished. Though I knew better. Remy wasn't that type of woman.

"Yes, but honestly, I think he knew how much it bothered me when he asked about his father, so he stopped a while back. I know it's dumb, but when he would ask, it made me feel inadequate. I mean, I was doing everything I could to be a father and a mother, so when he asked, it made me think he saw all the areas I was lacking."

"He was just curious, Remy. It had nothing to do with you."

She sighed. "Mom guilt, remember? It's a heady influencer over all my thoughts."

"All your thoughts?" A dirty plan formed in my mind. "What about now, Kitten?"

Something in my low tone must have signaled where my mind had wandered, because her green eyes flicked upward.

"Yes."

"Well, we can't have that when you've already had a stressful day," I admonished. Scanning the streets, I eyed the unmarked police car two houses down, knowing their attention was on us. "Tug the blanket around to cover your lap."

I wanted to leave tomorrow with no doubt in her mind exactly who she belonged to.

Within minutes of my fingers finding her wet center beneath the blanket, Remy's cry, muffled by the hand pressed against her lips, filled my ears as she squeezed the life out of them. Pulling them free, I slipped all three into my mouth and sucked her sweetness from the slick digits.

This wasn't enough.

If I was leaving for potentially two nights away from this amazing woman, I wanted more.

Thank fuck I'd already packed.

***

MIDDLE OF THE LIVING ROOM, hands on my hips, I rotated, taking in the apartment. For the last hour, the three of us unpacked essentials for Remy and Jameson's potential two-day stay, shoving the remaining boxes into the corner to deal with after I returned from Chattanooga.

"I agree it is essential," Jameson remarked to Remy, whose head was buried in a box labeled "kitchen utensils."

Yes, I detailed the contents of the boxes in alphabetical order.

I was anal pre-Remy, though she shattered my sad existence in the best way possible.

"Found it," she exclaimed, and held up the ice cream scoop high in the air. "Good thing we have all these very specific labels." She tapped a single finger on the side of the box with a smirk.

Yes, I owned and frequently used a label maker.

"I like—or liked—order," I grumbled. "Makes life easier when you know exactly where to find everything. Aren't you glad they're there?" I arched a brow and pointed to the stack of unopened boxes. "So you didn't waste time going through all those to find what you needed?"

"It's cute. Don't take offense." Remy scoffed. Tossing the ice cream scoop to Jameson, she went back to digging through the box. "Though if you didn't notice, my life is a little less... organized."

"When we move in together, we'll find a compromise."

Whatever was in her hand clattered to the bottom of the box. Wide eyes met mine.

Fuck. Is that panic?

"Move in together," she repeated.

"Well, yeah." I shrugged. *Shit, did I read this all wrong?* "If you want to, that is."

She blinked, her dark lashes fanning down her now somewhat pink cheeks. "It hasn't even been a week since we reconnected."

"I know what I want, Remy. But I won't pressure you. I can wait for you to realize I'm not going anywhere."

"When are you heading out?" Jameson asked, breaking the somewhat awkward silence that followed my statement.

I checked my watch and cursed. "Now. I want to get on the road before rush hour. The drive shouldn't take me too long."

"Any new details?" Remington asked. Hands full of forks, knives, and spoons, she dumped them on the island and began sorting them.

"Not a lot. Time of death between the three was only a few hours, which doesn't have the same feel of Carting. With past victims, he tortured them for an extended period, but the removal of their reproductive organs rings true to his signature."

"Well, he didn't have time to do what he normally likes," Jameson said, helping Remy put the silverware away into a drawer. "That takes time and a remote location where his victims can't be heard. Plus, like we've discussed, those women meant nothing to him. They were a means to an end."

"Enjoy your trip."

That fucker planned this. We still didn't know how Carting evaded the surveillance team, but there was no doubt in my mind that this was all part of his plan. And we were playing right into it, but we didn't have a choice.

Remy agreeing to stay here with Jameson and a uniform stationed outside the door eased some of my worry, but not much. I hated the idea of just the one exit, but I had to choose the lesser of the two evils, and my apartment won. Now to get to Chattanooga, do my job, and get my ass back here as soon as possible.

Hopefully Carting left some kind of evidence behind so we could issue a warrant for the evil fucker's arrest.

But to do that, I had to leave.

Though my feet refused to budge.

I didn't want to say goodbye. This amazing thing between us just started. It was too soon to leave, especially with the surrounding danger.

"Go, Tallon." Remy laughed. Moving around the island, she walked toward me, arms outstretched. Some of the tension drained from my tight muscles when she engulfed my waist in a tight hug. "We'll be fine for a couple days."

"And you'll wear the tracker if you leave the apartment." I glanced between the two of them. Yeah, I even gave one to Jameson with the same strict instructions. Not because I didn't think he could handle himself, more because he could be used as leverage against Remy in a worst-case scenario.

"Yes, Dad," Remy huffed.

My dick twitched in my boxer briefs. Gripping her chin, I tilted her face up to meet mine. "Hmm, I think I like the sound of you calling me daddy."

"Well, hurry back and we can see how that plays out." She winked and stepped out of my arms, fingers brushing along my sides as if she were just as reluctant to put space between us.

With a groan, I picked up my duffel and gave her a pointed look.

"No opening the door unless you're armed with the gun I left you. If someone says it's me or Jameson, they need to say the code word to enter, which is...?"

Jameson raised his hand. "I know!"

I shot him a glare before turning my full attention back to Remy, who was completely flushed.

"Remy has the sweetest pussy I've ever eaten," she muttered.

A wide smile grew, making my cheeks bunch. "Only Jameson and I know it."

"Thank fuck," she grumbled.

"The code word for the officer is coconut. He'll announce the code word when asked, and then you're free to open the door, with the gun, safety off and one in the chamber." Yes, I was going 100 percent overboard on all this, but I didn't give a fuck. It made it easier to leave, knowing she was as safe as she could be.

"I'm thinking you've forgotten I can handle myself." She crossed her arms over her chest and widened her stance.

I shook my head. "I haven't forgotten, Remy. I'm just doing everything I can to protect the woman I love."

Shit.

I said it out loud.

Maybe I've hung around Tinley too long, and her terrible timing has rubbed off on me.

Remy's lips parted.

Not allowing her to say a word, I stepped forward, wrapped my free hand around her waist, and tugged her close, sealing our lips together.

Pulling back, I said, "I'll be back soon. Be safe. And yeah, Kitten, I do love you. Every tiny bit."

After a quick peck to her forehead, I turned and marched out the door. The officer stationed outside stood from his seat and offered me a clipped nod.

Pausing, I stared at the closed door before sliding my gaze to him.

"That's my life in there," I gritted out, hating how damn emotional I sounded. "Do not let anything happen to her. Understood?"

"Yes, Agent Harper. Detective Bend gave me a picture of the man I should be on the lookout for. I'll pass it on to the officer who takes the next shift."

With a deep breath, I started toward the elevator, more than ready to get this trip over with so I could be back home with Remy.

They'd be fine.

She had to be.

REMINGTON

This was the funny thing about being a mom that confused the hell out of me. While I was busy working, helping with schoolwork, driving Crew around to sporting events and practices, all I wanted was a few minutes alone to do nothing, but now that I had the time to do absolutely nothing, I felt bad for doing just that.

Mom guilt was such a bitch sometimes.

Snapping my laptop screen shut, I turned to glance over the back of the couch into the kitchen. Jameson sat on one stool working the recent cases he was assigned, a half-full beer sitting on the island beside him. Maybe a little alcohol would help settle my nerves, make me not feel like I was crawling out of my skin with the need of something to do.

Setting the computer on the cushion next to me, I stood, stretching my arms high over my head as I released a loud groan, followed by Jameson's responding chuckle. Turning on my thick sock-covered feet, I padded to the kitchen and opened the fridge.

Empty.

Well, not completely empty. Five glass bottles of beer sat

inside. With a sigh, I grabbed one, twisted off the cap, and turned to Jameson. The cool metal of the fridge immediately soaked through my loose gray sweater, making me shiver, the cold bottle in my hand not helping my sudden chill.

"Do you think he's made it there yet?" I asked.

Jameson tapped his phone screen, checking the time. "Probably. He left about four hours ago, right?"

I nodded and took a sip, the chilled liquid soothing my nerves a fraction. "What do you want for dinner? There's nothing in the fridge, and I really don't want to go to the grocery store. Maybe tomorrow, but not tonight."

Jameson peered over the top of his laptop screen. "What do you feel like? I would've picked up more than beer on the way here, but I just assumed Tallon ordered in groceries like he did at your place." He snorted. "Shows you how thrown off he was if he forgot to obsess over feeding you."

"It's cute," I admitted.

"It's primal."

I rolled my eyes and took another drink. "So, dinner? It's almost eight."

His lips pressed into a thin line. "I don't like the idea of someone bringing food here or the idea of going out."

"I have to eat. You do not want to be locked in an apartment with me when I'm hungry. It gets ugly."

"We have beer," he offered, holding up his own bottle before taking a long pull.

"That's not food, and even if it were, we only have four left. Let's order food, and the officer outside can take it from the delivery kid. Oh, in fact, we should see what he wants to eat too."

Jameson's smile softened. "I'm sure he'd love that. Okay, what sounds good?"

"PF Changs?"

He tossed his head back and laughed. "What is it with you and that place?"

"It has the best food ever," I stated, acting offended by his question.

"Well, I'm feeling less Asian and more Italian. How does that sound?"

"Fine." Setting the beer down, I pulled out my phone and began searching for local Italian places. Clicking on the one with the best reviews, I scanned the menu. "I could do pizza from this place."

I slid my phone across the bar, and Jameson picked it up and scanned the menu. "Same. Pepperoni with extra pepperoni, and some garlic knots. Want their warm brownies?"

"Is that even a question?" I joked, taking the phone back. "I'll go ask the guy guarding the castle."

"Don't forget the gun." I shot him an incredulous look. "What? I do not want Tallon's wrath focused on me, and you shouldn't either. You wouldn't be able to sit for a week."

My cheeks instantly flamed. Face to the floor, I hurried to the bedroom, where I left the gun. After securing the holster to my hip, I stepped into the living room and gestured to the gun with both middle fingers.

Jameson's rumbling laugh followed me to the door. Fingers hovering over the chrome handle, I twisted around and shot him a small smile. "I'll miss you. I'm excited for you. It's an amazing opportunity, but still, I've liked this." I gestured between us. "The friendship. It's easy, you know, and I haven't had that with anyone in a long time besides Charlie."

"Ditto, Remy. But considering you're friends with Charlie and me being on his girlfriend's team, I know we'll continue to be in constant communication. You're not losing this."

My heart swelled, loving that response. I didn't want to lose my new friend.

Feeling lighter than I had in days, almost forgetting about the evil cloud hovering over us, I twisted the handle, then released it with a quick shake of my head. Totally forgot about the safety protocols Tallon put in place.

A gentle knock sounded as I rapped my knuckle against the door, expecting an immediate response.

But one didn't come.

Frowning at the dark fake wood door, I knocked again, this time a little louder.

"We're ordering food," I called out hesitantly into the seam between the door and frame. "Do you want something?"

Again, nothing.

My hair flared out around me as I twisted, lips parted to ask Jameson what I should do, only to find his attention already on me.

"Maybe he went on a walk?" I mused, the tremble in my voice relaying my rising nerves.

"Maybe," Jameson muttered. Shoving the stool back, he strode to my side. Hand closed into a tight fist, he beat it against the door, making it rattle on its hinges. "Hey, man, are you good out there?"

Heart in my throat, I leaned closer, ears straining to hear anything coming from the other side.

"Hey, man," Jameson yelled, hitting the door again. "Answer me."

"Do you have his number?" I asked, sweat slicking along my brow as my nerves pumped heat through my veins.

"No, but I can call the station. It's fine, Remy." Though his pinched features and tight voice said otherwise.

Just as he pulled out his phone, ready to make the call, a deep voice came from the other side of the door. "Did you guys need something? Sorry, I was handling a situation. A guy was loitering in the hall."

My shoulders slumped as relief washed through me.

"Everything good?" Jameson asked. Some of the worry had faded, but his brows were still pinched together, a deep line forming between them.

"Yeah, some fucker messing with his ex. It's handled. What did you guys need?"

"We're ordering food. You want some?" I called out, pushing up to my tip toes like that could help my voice carry more through the door.

"Yeah, sure, thanks. Where are you ordering from?"

"It's fucking ridiculous to keep yelling," I muttered to Jameson. "Just open the damn door."

He glared at the door. "What's the code word?"

My heart skipped when a single beat of silence followed. "Coconut."

My shoulders slumped, the calm smile from earlier returning. I gestured to the door. "See? We're golden. Now come on, let's get his order so we can call it all in. I'm starving."

With a grumbled response, Jameson undid the first deadbolt, then the other before shoving the lever down and pulling the door open wide.

Obvious confusion flared over his features. When I stepped to see around the door, the same confusion pulsed through me.

The space just outside the door was empty.

Had we imagined those responses?

"Hey," Jameson said, already in motion to check down the hall when it happened.

When our peaceful night switched to the start of a horror film.

It took a second for me to catalog everything, delaying my fight-or-flight response.

First, it was the look of sheer terror on the young officer's pale face.

Then the gun, the thick round barrel of the silencer pressed to his temple.

I followed the hand holding the gun, down the arm to a shoulder, and made my way up to a very familiar face.

Jameson cursed, his hand jutting back toward his sidearm.

It all happened too fast, and all I could do was stand numbly staring as the gun shifted from the officer's temple and whipped in my direction.

"Touch that, and I put a bullet between her eyes, then yours." There was no anger in Andrew Carting's voice. He almost sounded bored. "Make wise choices here, Detective Bend."

Muscles stiff, movement jerky, Jameson pulled his hand away from the gun on his hip and held both up in surrender.

"Smart man."

With a hard shove to his shoulder, the officer stumbled into the apartment, Carting keeping close with that gun still pointed at my face. The door slammed shut of its own accord. I stood numbly watching it all unfold, unable to do anything but continue sucking in enough air to stay conscious.

"Thank you for your help," Carting said, "but your usefulness is over."

The young officer grunted, features pulled tight as if in extreme pain.

The following squelching sound of the knife pulling free had me gagging. The officer immediately crumpled to the floor of the apartment, a pool of deep crimson collecting beneath him.

No.

Tears welled as I watched the young man squirm in pain, soft cries of anguish filling the apartment.

Slowly, I lifted my watery gaze to Carting's. His cold, dark stare made my shoulders shudder and a pitiful whimper develop in my throat, but I swallowed it down. I wasn't weak. I had survived him once, and for too long with Jett.

Sure, this bastard was worse than Jett. Jett was a narcissist with anger issues; Carting was a psychopath with a gun and knife. But what I learned the last decade, the training and conditioning I not only put my body through but my mind to know how to be prepared, was to treat all dangerous situations like these the same.

Wait for the right moment.

Strike when he least expects it.

Show no mercy.

Swallowing down the urge to lunge over the officer's limp body to attack the evil fucker, I forced my gaze to drop.

He clicked his tongue, clearly not liking my show of submission.

"I don't think so, Remington. You forget I know you." Unable to stop it, my lip tugged up into a snarl. "Ah, there's that fight. But don't worry, you'll give it to me one way or another. Now, you both." Peering up through my lashes, I studied him as he addressed Jameson, then slid the barrel of the gun my way. "It's time to say goodbye to those guns."

He drew closer on silent feet, an evil grin tugging at his lips as he flicked his gaze between me and Jameson, ensuring neither of us made a move he didn't authorize. A pitiful whimper I had no hope of stopping made its way up my throat as his fingers brushed down my side.

"Get your fucking hands off her," Jameson shouted, voice wavering.

"Hmm." His voice vibrated in my ear as he pressed closer.

Holding a breath to keep from screaming, I swayed as his hand moved to the center of my stomach.

I wasn't sure *what* I expected. I assumed the deranged asshole would move his hand lower to assault me in a way I might never recover from.

But that didn't happen.

All the air exploded from my lungs as he pulled back and slammed his fist into my gut, knuckles brushing my ribs. Doubling over, I wheezed, desperate to suck down air, but my lungs failed.

Too focused on trying to breathe, I wasn't prepared for the next hit. Only Jameson's warning shout echoed through the apartment before pain exploded in my head and I crumpled to the floor. The darkness was a welcome relief as I submitted, slumping unconscious in a puddle of a dead man's blood.

30

———————

TALLON

"You're positive the same person killed all three women within a few hours of each other?" I asked the ME as she draped a white sheet over the third victim's body.

"I am. Not only are the injuries too similar to be done by different assailants, but the cut marks when he removed the reproductive organs are the same. Not only the same tool but the sequence of cuts on the body. He always starts with the right side. That's where I saw the most blood flow on each victim."

Studying the now-covered body, I said a silent apology to the three women lying on individual autopsy tables. Though the guilt didn't ride me as hard or deep as it had in the past. I knew that was Remy's doing. She got through to me with that little punch to the stomach exercise.

My fingers itched to grab my phone and check in, but I couldn't afford the distraction. I'd sped into town, immediately meeting up with the detectives and now the ME since it was her only availability until tomorrow. I hadn't even told Remy or Jameson I made it safely to Chattanooga.

"You know what I found odd?" I shifted my focus from the autopsy table to the older woman. With her extensive experience, I was hesitant to ask what she could find odd. "He discarded the three sets of organs in the same dumpster. Not the one with the last victim, but in the same alley."

My brows flew up my forehead. "That's new. That's some serious police work to search the surrounding dumpsters for evidence."

"That's another reason I know they were all done by the same person. Hell, I can tell you which one was killed first because the level of insect activity was higher with the first—"

I held up a hand. There were some things important to the case that I needed to know. Details of insect activity on a victim we already knew the TOD for wasn't one of them. Though the fact that he tossed the organs was interesting. We'd just assumed he took them, but maybe he tossed them in a different dumpster with the previous victims and the local officers just never found them.

"Is there anything, any evidence at all, that can link the potential suspect we have to these murders?"

The corners of her lips tugged down as she surveyed the covered body between us. "The last victim of the night. We found a single hair embedded in one wound. Probably came off during the assault to the face."

Disappointment rushed through me. We already had DNA associated with the unsub for the cases in Chicago. This could tie them all together, sure, but not tie that fucker Carting to the murders until a judge signed off on a warrant for his DNA.

"Great, let's get it processed as top priority. I'll call the lab and tell them to expect the sample and to compare the DNA recovered in earlier murders."

"He's been at this a long time." I nodded, even though it sounded like more of a statement than a question. She sighed, a look of defeat crossing her weathered face. "I'll keep looking for other bits of evidence. You have a strong suspect?"

"We do. But we can't get his DNA without a warrant. The fucker is smart."

She studied me. "Does he have any living relatives?"

"What?" Even as I said the word, I was already piecing together what she was insinuating. "But they would've found a match in CODIS."

"Not if they haven't committed a crime. Just because the monster who did this is evil incarnate doesn't mean his extended family are."

I gaped at the woman before reaching out over the body, grabbing her shoulders. She startled but didn't pull away. Fucking hell, this would be huge. If we found a relative of Carting's to compare the DNA on the body to and got a familial match when he was supposedly still in Nashville, there was no doubt a judge would sign off on a warrant for his DNA.

"You're fucking brilliant," I said, the excitement coursing through me making me shout. "Fucking brilliant."

She blushed and dramatically fluttered her lids. "Well, thank you, Agent Harper."

Releasing her, I hurried for the swinging metal door that would lead me toward the precinct. "Thank you," I called over my shoulder.

As I jogged, phone in hand, I flicked my gaze from the screen to the empty hallway.

I wanted to call Remy, check in and make sure she and Jameson were good, but that would take time I didn't have right now despite the pressure in my chest urging me to reach out. Instead of clicking her name, I scrolled down to Agent Charlie Bekham's number and tapped the contact.

"This better be about—"

I rolled my eyes as I shoved the metal lever, disengaging the lock and pushing the door open. The crisp evening air soothed the heat from our newest revelation.

"I need you to run a relative search for Carting," I stated, not bothering with pleasantries. The keys to the SUV swung around my finger as I kept up my fast pace to the vehicle. "We have some DNA evidence on the body here, and the ME had a brilliant idea. If his matching DNA isn't in CODIS, then we find a relative match. We just need to know who to ask for a sample from."

There was a pause on the other end as I hauled myself into the SUV, but I knew it wasn't him being rude, more processing the sliver of information I'd presented. That pressure in my chest grew to check in, but I pushed past it. This was the longest we'd been apart since we reconnected. That had to cause this almost panicked feeling.

"I could go back to the birth certificate," he mused. Fucking hell, he was smart. And a good man if he helped Remy create a whole new identity without knowing her. "Look at the mother and father listed and go from there. Give me the ME's name, and I'll send her a fruit basket or some shit. That's fucking brilliant."

"Agreed. I have copies of the detective's notes and just left the ME's office. A quick rainstorm last night washed away any evidence from the crime scenes. There's nothing else I can do here, so I'm heading back to Nashville."

"To Remington, you mean."

I rolled my eyes at his instigating tone. "Yes." Flicking the blinker, I turned at a light and sped up to merge onto the highway. "How's Crew doing?"

This time the pause felt heavy, as if he was weighing his words.

"Did Remy tell you?" I asked, my anticipation mounting. Not sure why it was a big deal if she told Charlie I was Crew's biological father, but it felt like it was since they were so close.

"She did, and he's good." There was a shuffle in the background. "He really is a good kid, and she's an amazing woman. If I ever hear that you hurt either of them, I will kill you and make sure no one ever finds your body."

I wanted to laugh, but I felt fucking grateful.

Grateful Remy had this friend in her life while I wasn't around.

"Understood. Let me know what you find in that search, and we'll go from there. And thank you, man. Thank you for —" emotions clogged in my throat, "—for taking care of her, of them when I couldn't."

Pressing on the gas, I pushed the SUV faster, hauling down the interstate. At eight o'clock on a Thursday night, it was almost deserted. Good. I'd be back in Nashville sooner than later. I could've stayed till tomorrow to follow up on a few more things, but that could be handled over the phone.

"No problem," Charlie responded. "Have you talked to her tonight?"

My heart slammed against my chest. "No?" Odd question. "I haven't stopped since I arrived. Why?"

"Crew and I tried calling earlier, but it went to voicemail about an hour ago, and she hasn't called me back."

That could mean anything. "Was she expecting your call?"

"Yeah, that's what I'm finding odd."

Not odd.

Wrong.

"I'm in the car. Add her to the call and let's see if it happens again."

The panic in my tone must have conveyed the sense of urgency, because he didn't give me any lip about ordering him around. Quiet, and then the ring of another line filtered through the SUV. It rang and rang before Remy's voicemail picked up, sending a wash of dread to chill me to the bone.

"Told you," Charlie stated, voice tight.

"Can you make the call coming from my phone?" I urged. It was a wild hunch, but I needed to hear her voice, to know she was okay.

Without response, the line rang again.

Three long rings, and then a click cut them off as the line connected.

Heart slamming against my chest, I stared out the windshield, waiting for her to say something. Waited for her to laugh at my overreactive ass and tell me everything was okay.

"Hello."

Dread sank in my stomach like a hundred-pound weight. The exhaustion and tremble in her tone told me all I needed to know.

Everything was not okay.

"Hey, Remington," I said, forcing a lightness to my voice as I pressed the gas pedal to the floorboard. "Just calling to check in."

A pause.

A long fucking pause that spoke volumes.

"Hey," she croaked. "Did you make it to Chattanooga okay?"

"Yep, I'm here now. It's proving to be worthless so far, so I'm staying at least another night. We have zero fucking leads to tie our suspect to the murders."

Another long pause.

Fucking hell. Flicking the switch to activate my emergency lights but not the siren, I yanked the wheel to haul ass along the shoulder, bypassing the sudden heavy construction traffic.

"Oh yeah, that's terrible."

"Everything okay there?"

"Here? Oh yeah, everything is fine."

"Where is Jameson?"

"He's a little tied up—" A whimper cut off her next words.

"Remy, everything okay? Do I need to come home?"

"No," she rasped, clearly fighting back tears. "All good. He's just busy."

This was dangerous. I wasn't sure how long she could play the part or how long I could hold back from shouting all the ways I would murder the fuckhead. But first, I had to be smart about this.

She needed me to be Agent Harper.

"Okay. Hey, you know we have a code word. I need to hear it to make sure you're okay."

This was it, the final straw.

If she answered wrong, my next call would send the full force of the FBI and local police to my apartment.

"Coconut."

Tight fist pressed to my mouth, I clamped down on a single white knuckle to keep from yelling.

"Yep," I responded, voice strained. "Did you guys end up leaving to get food?"

Simple question, but it would tell me if they left the apartment or not. If they did, hopefully they slipped the trackers into their pockets like I demanded, but I couldn't pull up the signal to double-check while weaving through traffic at ninety miles an hour.

"Nope, stayed here."

"That's good. Well, I'll be here at least until tomorrow. I'll call you then?"

"Tallon," she cried, her soft sob making my own eyes water. "I loved you too."

Everything went silent when the connection ended.

I swallowed down the swelling emotions threatening to cloud my thoughts.

"Coconut wasn't the code word, was it?" Charlie demanded. "I'm triangulating her cell now and Jameson's. Fuck."

"No, it wasn't. That was the one for the officer at the door, not the one for me and Jameson."

"Jameson's is off. The last time it pinged a cell tower, it was in the same place as Remington's, and hers hasn't moved since this afternoon."

That fit the timeline of when we got there.

I left at three. It was a little after eight now.

Fuck, how long—

No. I gave my head a violent shake and tightened the grip on the steering wheel. I couldn't think that way.

"I'm at least two hours out, maybe less if I can sustain this speed." With a curse, I jerked the wheel to avoid slamming into the back of a semi. "Okay, we need a fucking plan. I won't get there in time, and we need to... before he can—"

"We will. Don't fucking think like that. She's survived him once. She'll do it again."

Clearing my throat, I focused on the road while running through our options.

"You're right. Okay, here's what we're going to do..."

31

REMINGTON

Hot, angry tears slipped along my cheeks as I watched Andrew Carting tap the screen, ending the call with Tallon. His damn cocky smirk fueled my rising fury, shoving all fear and terror aside. With little care, he tossed my phone to the couch and reached forward, resituating the gag, forcing the dishrag tied around my head between my lips, the corners already cut and raw.

A steady throb continued to thump against my skull from what I assumed was a hit to the head, which was how I ended up unconscious, though my stomach ached too. I fought against the restraints securing both wrists behind the metal chair.

The same chair Jameson was tied to, though that was where our current similarities stopped. I was hurting, yes, but Jameson... he was in terrible shape.

Time sluggish, I wasn't sure how long it had been since I woke up, head throbbing and bound to this chair, forced to watch Carting beat the shit out of Jameson. I couldn't remember much of what happened to put me in this position either, but hazy memories of Carting forcing his way into the apartment flickered in the back of my mind.

Standing between where he had Jameson and me tied up, a few feet separating us, Carting's smile grew. His leather-gloved hand palmed the hilt of a knife as he stalked toward Jameson. Tallon calling interrupted Carting using Jameson as his personal punching bag, but from the maniacal look on his face, he wasn't done, despite Jameson barely hanging on to consciousness.

And he hadn't even gotten to the good stuff yet, per the evil bastard. He enjoyed tormenting us, making me watch him beat Jameson up. A flash of pure pleasure would flash over his features when I begged him to stop hurting my friend. Which was why I'd stopped responding, simply stared ahead with a blank expression, much to Carting's disappointment.

"Now, where were we?" He moved behind Jameson's chair, that black-gloved hand hovering above Jameson's head before snatching a handful of brown hair. With a sharp tug, Carting yanked Jameson's head backward. He cried out, words gurgled as if he were choking on his own blood.

I sealed my lips closed, refusing to give Carting any reaction. Though my eyes widened when the living room light glinted off a metal blade as it slowly rose and pressed to Jameson's fully exposed throat.

Jameson sealed his lids shut as if accepting his fate. Turning away as much as I could, I swallowed down my soul-shaking sobs.

"Do you not want to watch, Remington?" Words fought their way up my throat, but I shoved them down. "You're the reason he's about to die. How does that make you feel?"

Turning back to the heartbreaking scene, I fought

against the restraints. "Don't," I pleaded around the gag, my dry tongue sticking to the cloth. "Please."

He tipped his head back, hands remaining steady, and groaned in pure pleasure. "Oh, I love when you beg. Though it does nothing for Detective Bend. Whether he lives or dies is entirely up to him." The sharp edge of the knife scraped against too pale skin. Bright red blood bubbled up, dripping down Jameson's throat and disappearing beneath his shirt. "All he has to do is tell me where it is, and all this can be over. For him."

It being the tracker Jameson "accidentally" let slip that we had somewhere on our bodies after Carting announced he'd selected a special place for me. A place they would never find me, where he could play with me until I lost the fight he loved so much.

It was clear what Jameson had accomplished by revealing we wore trackers that would allow the FBI to know our exact locations if activated. Because of the deliberate slip, we were still here in Tallon's apartment and not in some torture shed deep in the woods somewhere.

Jameson knew that slip was our only hope of me ever being found—dead or alive.

And so far, the lie benefited us. Well, me. While Carting attempted to beat the information out of Jameson, I could only watch.

Carting roughly yanked Jameson's gag down, the razor-sharp tip of the knife pressed behind his ear in a silent warning to not call out. Though, just like a few times before, Jameson only used the minor break from the gag as a chance to pull in gulps of air. From what I could tell, his nose was broken, the bridge at an odd angle, though the blood stopped pouring a bit ago. Not sure if that was a good or bad sign.

Fuck, how long have we been tied up? If I could just remember what time it was when I woke up, that would be an enormous help. Except there were spots missing from my memory, some longer timeframes, others just little blips. Maybe it was a blessing in disguise, because I didn't want to remember every second of Jameson being beaten by this evil asshole.

Without warning, Carting tsked. Leaning forward, he drew the knife back, an evil glint in his eye as he swung it forward. Terror erupted, jolting me in the seat. My panicked, crackled scream scratched up my throat, the gag muffling the sound.

The blade sank into Jameson's thigh, the dull thud signaling the tip of the long thin blade hit the chair, slicing all the way through the thick muscle. Jameson's cry of anguish pierced through the pounding in my ears only for Carting's hand to seal over his wide-open mouth.

"Not a sound, remember, or I'll do this all to her, forcing you to watch. I'm giving you this small mercy."

"You're doing it to torture us both," I screamed around the gag.

Carting shrugged and ripped the blade out of Jameson's leg. Another muffled anguished shout filled the apartment. The stench of copper mixed with the gory sight sent my stomach rolling. I gagged, abdominal muscles flexing as my stomach fought to expel the few sips of beer from earlier.

"Now, unless you want me to repeat the process on the other leg, you'll tell me where the tracker is."

He'd already patted me down and removed all my clothing, leaving me in just my sports bra and boy shorts. Thank fuck I didn't remember that part, the only blessing of the short-term memory loss. Another bout of nausea rose up my throat, wondering where all he'd poked and prodded trying to find the nonexistent device. And the man believed what he saw on TV, thank fuck. He thought since he couldn't find a physical tracker, we'd used a military-grade invisible one that adhered to my skin.

Where he got that notion, I had zero clue, but there wasn't much I wanted to understand about the way his mind worked.

While Carting grilled Jameson on the tracker's location, I struggled against the binding securing my wrists together. I couldn't see what he used, but it was tight. Not hard like plastic zip ties or metal like handcuffs. Whatever it was, it crinkled.

I tracked the river of blood flowing from Jameson's leg wound to where it puddled on the floor by his feet.

His bound feet.

The clear plastic wrap that looped around his ankles shimmered each time Jameson shifted. Careful to not make any sudden movements, I tested my ankles for similar restraints. My breath stuttered when my feet moved freely.

Hope swelled in my chest, making fresh tears collect in my lower lids.

The cocky, narcissistic asshole forgot to bind my feet.

Still grilling Jameson, Carting glanced my way. I stilled, barely even breathing to not give away the plan now forming as I weighed my options. There weren't many good ones to get us out of this, which meant the dumb, reckless plan was the only way to go.

I had to do something, hold Carting off from killing Jameson and taking me. Help would come soon. Tallon knew we were in trouble the moment I recited the incorrect code. Knowing him, he'd called the president himself asking for military support.

Help was on the way. I just had to ensure Jameson and I both survived until they arrived.

"Fuck."

My attention snapped up. Carting tossed Jameson's limp head forward. It lolled to the side, the tension in his body gone as he slumped, only the restraints keeping him in the chair.

"No," I cried, resuming my struggle against the restraints around my wrists. Warm liquid slid down my fingers, dripping from the tips.

Two gloved fingers to Jameson's throat, Carting stared at him with a frown. My held breath burned in my lungs as I watched with rapt attention. Then it whooshed out around the gag at the sinister smile that crawled across Carting's face.

Jameson was alive. There was no way he'd be that happy about him dying before the fucker intended.

That surge of relief vanished when black eyes met mine.

"You will tell me where it is." Clutching the knife, he stomped over and yanked my gag down. "Where is it?"

"I don't know," I rasped, throat and mouth dry. "I have memory loss, like I said before, from the drugs your partner gave me."

"Dead partner," he said with a knowing smile. Reaching out, he traced a single gloved finger along my jawline. "Well, then, I guess we'll have to figure out something to do until he wakes up."

Jaw clenched, I gritted my teeth to keep from lashing out. My fire and fight were what he wanted from me. If I kept my boiling anger suppressed, maybe, just maybe, I could survive a second encounter with this evil bastard.

He traced a single finger down the column of my neck, pressing so hard I knew a bruise would be left in its wake.

"Tell me why," I said, my throat working, making his finger dig even harder into the delicate flesh.

"Why?" He continued lower until that damn finger pressed right over my heart. "Why am I looking forward to breaking your mind and spirit, then slicing you open while watching the life fade from your eyes?"

Well, fuck, I didn't need him to be that *descriptive.*

Damn psychopath.

"You're all the same," he muttered, almost as if he were talking to himself. "Selfish." He pressed his finger harder into my flesh. "Condescending." I restrained a pitiful whimper as he pressed harder, as if he wanted to punch through my heart with his finger. "Horrible creatures."

"So your mom was a bad one," I rasped, the words barely audible, but I kept pushing forward. "Why blame every woman?"

"Bad?" He snorted in the most humanlike act I'd seen him do since he walked in the door. "Bad is whipping a child for misbehaving. I prayed for a simple beating," he snarled in my face, eyes wild. "Instead of what she made me do to her, to her friends for their sick entertainment. Forcing me to take care of them, over and over, using me like their personal sex pet."

Bile surged, forcing its way up my throat. Without the gag, I gave in to the urge, lurching to the side. My measly stomach contents splattered everywhere, some ricocheting off the floor, spotting the toe of his black boots. Instead of wiping off the trace evidence, he stood as still as a statue, zoned out, lost in the memories my questioning stirred up.

"They laughed." His wild, unfocused gaze jerked down to me. With a hate-filled sneer, he withdrew the hand not holding the knife.

I didn't look away from him, gaze locked on his as that

hand flew toward my face. Knuckles slammed against my cheek, snapping my head to the side, pain blooming every place the back of his hand connected.

"They laughed at me when I couldn't…. They dared to point, claiming I was broken. Broken by them," he roared in my face, spit flying from his parted lips, spraying across my throbbing face. He clutched my jaw in one powerful hand, pressing until my cry of pain became too much to hold back. Tears leaked down my hot cheeks as I panted through the agony. "But I got the last laugh."

He stared at me, his eyes filled with manic glee. "You want to know why? Because I fucking could. I finally had control, could do what I wanted to do to those whores, my filthy-ass mother. Cut out the part of them that made them vile, that made them disposable. And that's when I found my cure." His hold relaxed as he stepped back. His free hand wrapped around his hard cock as if presenting me with evidence of whatever the hell he was rambling about. "It's the fear, seeing it in someone else's eyes instead of my own. Then comes the blood." His lids slid shut as he pumped his hand over his jeans. "The screams, the pain of fucking them—"

"Stop," I shouted. "Stop, you fucking—"

"Stop?" He chuckled. "You asked why. Don't be shy now. Though you will get firsthand experience soon. You'll scream and beg for it all to stop, but I won't until you're nothing more than a broken body. No one will come for you. No one will save you this time. Then when you're broken, all that fight I look forward to bleeding from you gone, I'll cut you open and pull you apart piece by piece."

True terror spiked in my veins as my stomach lurched, but this time all I did was dry heave as he explained my depressing fate. Tears cascaded down my face.

Thoughts of Crew and Tallon ran on a loop. They'd never find me, never know what happened. Which could be for the better, except then they'd be denied closure to help them move forward past this dark spot in their lives.

My heart ached at the idea of never seeing either of them again. I didn't want to leave them. The complicated, beautiful dream of a future of us all together, a family, had finally become a future reality.

But now this monster promised to take it away.

A sharp curse snapped my attention out of my spiraling thoughts to Carting, who glared at the watch on his wrist. Time was running out before shift change happened for the officer at the door, who was dead just a few feet away. Palming the hilt of the knife, he paced, shooting an angry glare Jameson's way every few steps.

"I think he's lying." He jabbed the tip of the knife in Jameson's direction. "About the tracker. We leave now. No more waiting."

My heart kicked into high gear, hammering against my chest so fast I couldn't catch my breath.

No. No, he couldn't take me. I was as good as tortured, then dead if he got me out of the apartment.

A low groan stopped his approach. Turning on his heels, Carting swiveled to face Jameson. A blubbered sob rattled my chest when Jameson's head swayed, bobbing as he slowly came to.

Alive.

Jameson was alive.

For now.

"Time to end this part of the evening," Carting muttered under his breath as he tugged the gag back between my lips despite my fight. He smacked his soft leather glove against my cheek in an aggressive, condescending gesture. "Then on to the rest of your brief life, Remington."

I screamed. The sound crackled from my raw voice as he twisted, adjusting his grip on the knife. Each menacing step toward Jameson was like a death knell sounding, inching up my panic.

My erratic thoughts whirled, breaths stuttering as I sucked down gulps of air around the gag.

I couldn't let this happen.

But what could I do bound to a fucking chair too far away to—

It hit me like a punch to the stomach.

My hands were bound, yes, but my feet were not.

In the time it took Carting to close the distance to stand in front of Jameson, his back to me, I formed a stupid, utterly dangerous plan.

If I lived through this, Tallon would ensure I didn't sit for a week.

"I'm taking her," Carting goaded, swinging a clenched fist at Jameson's face. I winced at the sound of skin hitting skin, of Jameson's responding grunt of pain. "And there's nothing you or that fucker Harper can do about it."

I watched, waiting for the right moment. The hand holding the knife rose, the blood-covered steel flashing. This was my chance, the only opportunity to save Jameson's life and my own. Him from the knife about to slice across his throat, and me from being tortured, murdered, and buried in an unmarked grave.

But I couldn't move, the fear and panic riding too high to unlock my muscles despite my effort.

Then I thought of them. Of the utter sorrow and grief that would fill both hearts, one a boy grieving his mother, the other a man devastated over a future that would never happen. Thinking of them, not myself, forced my body to respond.

I wouldn't let that happen. Wouldn't let them suffer. If I died, it would be here, in this apartment, where they would know I fought to stay with them, for a future that was slipping through my fingers like tiny grains of sand.

This was for Crew.

For Jameson.

For Tallon.

For all the victims this bastard hurt and ripped away futures from.

For me.

Muscles straining, burning from exhaustion, I pushed to stand. I faltered. The odd angle of walking while strapped to the chair made each step painful and awkward. I gathered all my strength and courage.

Teeth clenched around the gag to further silence the battle cry rising in my chest, I glared with all the hate and loathing I could muster at the evil bastard's back.

And I charged.

32

TALLON

I wouldn't make it in time.

The weight was like thirty pounds dropped in my stomach. I weaved through the traffic, sirens blasting and lights flashing, but I wasn't close enough.

"You still there?" I asked the empty SUV.

"I'm here," Charlie said, tone as somber as I felt. "How far out are you?"

I flicked my gaze from the road to the map on my phone screen. "An hour. We have to send SWAT in without me." I swallowed hard, hating those words. But Remy's life was worth more than my pride. I'd crawl on my knees and beg if that meant the bastard holding her and Jameson would spare their lives.

"Understood. They're at the apartment building now and ready for the order. I have the live feed from their mics if you want to listen as they infiltrate the apartment—"

"Do it."

Hearing the takedown happen in real time was better than nothing. The desperate need to know she was okay, alive, was like a vise grip around my lungs. My hands tightened around the steering wheel, knuckles draining of color as I stared out the windshield, waiting. A static-like crackle poured through the speakers followed by several deep male voices and the click of clips slammed into various weapons.

"We're going in through the rear entrance."

I nodded, not that anyone could see me. Breaching the building through that entrance was my suggestion when we called the SWAT team into action. My particular apartment windows faced the front, so if Carting was watching the street for police activity, he'd see the SWAT van and cruisers if they came through the lobby.

"A stairwell is fifteen paces from point of entry through a metal, unlocked door on our right," the team leader continued. "Rodriguez and Mitchell will wait at the bottom of the stairs to watch the elevator and ensure the suspect and hostages do not leave."

I swallowed down my growing ball of rage.

Not being there to help save my kitten was like pouring salt on the thousand cuts on my soul. We'd played right into this motherfucker's hand. Charlie tried to calm my guilt-riddled ramblings earlier, but it didn't calm the devastation knowing I failed her.

I'd promised to keep her safe, and I failed.

"The rest of the team will ascend to the nineteenth floor to apartment 1904. There we wait until visual confirmation from the snake camera verifying locations of the suspect and two hostages. Once that is established and a clear take-down plan is in place, we storm the apartment. The two hostages are one female and one male, our own Detective Bend. I stationed EMTs in a holding pattern around the block and will immediately deploy once I give the all clear. Understood?"

A round of deep "Yes, sirs" sounded before the line went silent.

My pulse skipped as I tapped the phone screen, checking the connection.

"At the entry point. Going in."

I swallowed hard, fighting back the worry threatening to make me vomit.

They'd get her out. Everything would be fine.

I just prayed they weren't too late to save them both.

33

REMINGTON

Two steps away, Carting turned, utter shock filling his dark eyes.

The metal back of the chair clipped his shoulder before the momentum slammed my body into his. Unprepared for the attack, he stumbled backward, narrowly missing Jameson. Following Carting, I fell with him right into the round glass tabletop.

With no way to catch myself, I squeezed my lids shut and braced for impact. Carting's bellow rang in my ears as glass shattered around us.

I jolted, head snapping to the side as I crashed to the floor. Searing pain shot through my arm and a loud snap seemed to echo in my ears as it vibrated up my arm. Teeth sawing against the gag, a gargled scream tore up my throat. My head lolled to the side, each breath feeling like the broken glass around me in my lungs as I sobbed.

I couldn't see, couldn't think past the pain. Blood pounded in my ears, drowning out every other sound. For several minutes, all I could do was focus on my breathing, desperately attempting to stay conscious.

Until Carting groaned, shifting along the floor.

Despite the mind-numbing agony, I forced myself to focus. This was my chance.

Just as that thought solidified, something hard slammed into my stomach. My muffled scream was covered up by the scraping of the chair skidding across the floor. Shards of glass sliced into my bare skin, leaving a trail of blood in my wake.

Carting's wild black eyes locked on me, and he snarled. The blood dripping from the various cuts on his face made him even more terrifying.

Desperate to get away, I shoved against the floor, inch by inch, putting more space between us until a firm grip wrapped around my ankle and hauled me back toward him.

A scream lodged in my raw throat, only a broken cry escaping around the gag.

"You fucking cunt." With a hard shove, he flipped the chair, my weight grinding both hands into the bits of glass littering the floor. "You want to play? We'll play that way. This ends now for you both." Sliding closer, he waved the knife in front of my face. "This will hurt." He flicked his gaze to the gag and smiled. Tugging it free, he placed a hand over my mouth, sealing his palm against my lips. "I want to feel you scream, beg for my mercy. But I won't give it to you. You're nothing. I'll keep cutting until the light fades from your eyes and then throw you out like the trash you are."

My vision wavered as blood and tears mixed, coating my eyes. But I didn't need to see his movements as the tip of the knife sliced along my lower belly. Sobbing from the pain and panic, I twisted, moving as far as I could away from the blade. Remembering my legs were free, I kicked wildly, hoping to connect with some part of him.

I didn't want to die.

A strong arm sealed around my legs, squeezing them to the chair, but he couldn't stop me from shifting back and forth with his other hand still sealed over my mouth. My hands and wrists screamed in agony, grinding against the floor with each shift of my weight, but I pushed past it all.

If I didn't keep moving, this was how I'd die.

Painfully.

Apparently done trying to keep me still, the pressure on my legs vanished, and fiery pain bloomed along my stomach. Deep and deeper, the knife sliced through my belly, the pain all-consuming. Warm liquid trailed down my sides, creating little hot rivers along my skin. Squeezing both eyes shut, I dug deep for my last bit of strength and then snapped forward, taking a chunk of glove and thick flesh between my teeth, and bit—hard.

His hand jerked. A roar of anger and pain rattled in my ear, but I ground my teeth together until they touched as I bit through his flesh. With another jerk, his hand came free, and I tilted to the side, spitting out the blood that had soaked through his glove.

Before he could recover, I did the only option my failing body and mind had left.

I screamed for my life.

First it came out broken just like my body, but built in strength as I forced all the air from my lungs.

A now bare, blood-coated hand slapped over my face, blocking my mouth and nose.

"I fucking love your fight." My lids snapped open, not expecting those to be the words to come from his mouth. He leaned over me, his demented smile hovering too close. "This will be a first, hopefully not the last."

Not understanding, I followed the movement of his

hand, knife discarded, down to the button of his jeans as he flicked it open.

Awareness dawned on me as he slowly lowered his zipper.

No.

Whipping my head side to side, I managed a bit of air and yelled for help, though it was cut off by his palm smacking across my face. My vision tunneled, and everything around me shifted, even though I wasn't moving.

"I've been dreaming of this," he said as he gripped my boy shorts and tugged one side lower.

That was as far as he got.

The crack of wood splintering followed by stomping feet and shouts filled my ears. My head lolled to the side, though even with the new angle, I couldn't see around Carting, who still hovered over me.

"Andrew Carting," a male voice I didn't recognize bellowed through the room. "Release her and step away from the hostage."

Numbness crept along my body, slowly dulling the pain. Hope flared for half a second before being smothered by acceptance when Carting's dark eyes met mine.

This was the end of the line for him.

And if he was going down...

Then so was I.

Movements slow and deliberate, he ignored the shouts for him to move away from me or they'd shoot. He knew as well as I did that they wouldn't dare shoot because of his position over me. There wasn't a clear shot. Which was why he reached for the discarded knife, gripping it in his blood-soaked palm.

Without a word, he thrust the blade deep into my belly, my responding scream ringing through the apartment as I felt it slice through me. Shouts erupted all around us. Through the pain, the darkness bordering my vision, I knew this wasn't the end for him unless I did something.

If he intended to kill me, then I should return the favor.

Legs no longer pinned, I threw all my remaining energy into flinging them to the side. The momentum rocked the chair. For half a second, I teetered before falling to the side, out from under Carting.

The knife was still buried in my gut, twisting with the movement. A flash of blinding pain made my vision go dark, the earlier numbness quickly engulfing my entire body as I slumped to the floor.

Holding on to the last bit of consciousness, I didn't flinch as gunfire erupted, the boom of each shot rattling my teeth and echoing in my ears.

It was done.

I might not have won, but neither did he.

As I slipped into the beckoning darkness, all I could think about were my boys.

I wanted to see them one more time.

To tell them I loved them.

And that I'd always be with them.

Even when I was gone.

34

TALLON

"Andrew Carting." I zoned out as the SWAT lead's voice boomed through the SUV. "Release her and step away from the hostage."

My stomach dropped, and all breath lodged in my lungs, refusing to release until I heard her voice. Fear like I'd never known coursed through my veins, making me tremble, yet sweat slicked my skin. I blinked at the phone, waiting for more.

"Stop."

Fuck this.

I slammed on the brakes, jerking the wheel to skid to a stop on the side of the interstate.

"Put the fucking knife down, Carting."

My hands shook as I peeled them off the steering wheel.

"Fucking hell, get him off her."

A scream ripped through the line, shooting a chill down my spine.

Remy.

They didn't need to confirm. I knew that was my kitten.

Lungs burning, I leaned closer to the phone, as if that would make this any easier.

Ear-piercing booms rattled through the SUV's speakers as guns fired on the other end of the line. Cars zoomed by, their lights filling the dark inside the SUV as I stared unblinking, waiting.

"Get that fucking medic," another man shouted a little farther away from the lead.

"Put pressure on the damn wound. Fucking hell, what did he do to Bend?"

My world slowed as if hung in midair. Nothing else mattered but these next few breaths where I'd learn my fate. Guilt and grief wrapped around me like a well-worn blanket.

A single tear escaped, rolling down my cheek as the chaos ensued on the other end of the line with shouts and the shuffle of bodies in my tiny apartment.

Swallowing down my emotions, I cleared my throat.

"Is she okay?" I croaked. No response. "I asked if she's okay," I repeated, louder this time with command in my tone.

"Agent Harper, it doesn't look good."

I sucked in a breath and held it to keep from mentally breaking on the side of the fucking interstate.

"And the detective? Jameson?"

"He's... he's lost a lot of blood. We're doing what we can for both until the EMTs— Fucking finally! Where the fuck were you?" he roared, clearly talking to the medics who just walked in. "Get them stabilized."

"Call Vanderbilt," a female voice shouted somewhere close to the SWAT lead's mic. "We need two operating rooms booked now."

"You hear that?" the SWAT lead's deep voice rumbled.

"Yes."

"You en route?"

I couldn't speak, too afraid my weakness would be clear in my voice.

No, not weakness—brokenness. Because that was exactly how I felt.

Utterly broken without the hope of her in my life.

How was this fucking fair? I just got her back, just realized what I'd missed out on the past decade, and now it was gone?

No.

I wouldn't allow it.

This wasn't over.

We weren't over. Not now, not ever.

"Yes, I'm en fucking route. I'll be there in twenty."

"10-4."

The line went quiet for a second before a low sniffle sounded.

"She'll make it, Charlie," I said, believing every word. "Don't give up on her. She's a fighter. You know that."

"I don't want to be the one to tell him," he murmured. "She has to make it."

My stomach tensed at the raw emotion in his voice. He had time for that. He was in Texas, not close enough to get to the hospital before they got her into surgery. No, I had to be the rock for us both. For all of us.

"I'm going to the hospital now and will tell her I won't let her die on me. She doesn't get to waltz into my life, uprooting everything and showing me how fucking miserable I've been in the last decade, and then leave me. No, it doesn't work that way. She's mine, now and forever. We're going to grow fucking old together and fight about stupid shit. I'll still be a controlling ass, and she'll still be a curious, brilliant, beautiful—" My voice broke. "She will make it, Charlie. I won't accept anything else."

SIRENS WAILED THROUGH THE NIGHT, covering the clip of my shoes along the concrete outside the ambulance bay. Two nurses and one security officer had already tried to remove me from the area. Too bad for them, I pulled the FBI card and told them it was a federal matter.

Abuse of power? Sure. Not that I gave a fuck.

Red lights flashed as an ambulance turned and sped closer. Sucking in a breath, I stood off to the side as it screeched to a halt. Immediately, the back doors flung open and a chorus of voices erupted from inside, a team rushing out of the hospital ready to receive the incoming patient.

I shifted to see the person on the stretcher as it was hauled out of the ambulance, my heart stopping at the sight of Jameson's slack face.

"Facial fractures, contusions along abdomen, and deep puncture wound in right thigh..."

The EMT continued talking about blood pressure and other stats, but all that faded to the background as I lurched forward. Everyone kept moving around me as I gripped Jameson's limp hand.

"You will fucking make it through this," I stated, though the words were lost in the chaos around us as another ambulance entered the bay. "You hear me, Bend?"

His hand was yanked from mine as they wheeled him down the long white hall. Taking a deep breath, I turned just as the back doors of the recently arrived ambulance opened. A woman in an EMT uniform sat on top of the stretcher, her hands pressing on the person's stomach.

"Small lacerations along the skin, compound fracture of the left arm, knife embedded in abdomen. Object still in, reducing potential bleed-out..."

I stared at the hilt of the knife protruding from the middle of Remy's body as they slowly lowered her and the female EMT from the ambulance. Rushing forward, I reached for her, brushing back the wet clumps of hair from her clammy forehead.

"Sir, we need you to move."

I ignored the man yelling at me and moved alongside the stretcher as they wheeled it toward the sliding glass doors. Leaning forward, I put my lips against her ear as I jogged, heels clipping along the linoleum floor.

"Kitten." My voice broke on the word. "Please don't leave me. Fight for me, for Crew. Fight for our future as a family. I'll do anything you want, give you everything I have if you'll just... don't go."

"Sir." Firm hands on my shoulders stopped me as the stretcher continued through metal swinging doors. "You have to stay here."

I blinked, barely seeing the woman in scrubs.

"Please," I begged. "Please."

It was all I could say. Nothing else seemed worthy of the moment.

"We'll do everything we can for your wife, sir." I didn't correct her before she turned and disappeared through the same doors they took Remy.

Swaying on my feet, I stumbled backward. The wall caught me, my back slamming into the drywall and knocking what little breath I had in my lungs free. Completely lost and emotionally drained, I slowly slid down the wall until my ass hit the floor.

Knees bent, forearms resting on top, I zoned out,

ignoring the noises around me as I stared at the opposite wall.

There was nothing I could do. Remy's and Jameson's lives were in the surgeons' and nurses' hands. With nothing to control, no Remy to distract my dark thoughts, the guilt I'd pushed off since I spoke to her hours earlier washed over me like a fucking tsunami, smothering the flicker of hope I'd fought to keep alive.

Even if she survived, how could she ever forgive me for allowing this to happen?

Why would she? I left her knowing it was a terrible decision, all for my fucking job. When she woke up, she'd hate me, resent me for doing this to her. And she should. Fuck, I hated myself, and I wasn't the one on the operating table fighting for my life.

I wouldn't hold her to those four words she said on the phone.

"I loved you too."

Because who could love the disappointing, worthless man who broke his promise?

THREE HOURS.

Phone dead, I focused on the clock on the far wall, studying the second hand as it continued to go round and round, ticking off the minutes and hours she was in surgery.

Jameson's surgeon came out an hour ago stating he'd lost a lot of blood but would make a full recovery. I'd asked for a status update on Remy, but he'd huffed, saying he was a little busy saving my friend's life to ask the other operating room how it was going.

Asshole.

But I deserved the response.

Now all I could do was wait.

"Tal!" I shot off the uncomfortable waiting room chair and turned to the sliding glass doors leading outside. Tinley raced forward, Bryson hot on her heels, and didn't stop until she slammed into my chest, wrapping her arms around my neck. "Oh, Tal."

"What are you doing here, Tin?" I pulled back and searched her face. Features pinched, face pale, she looked absolutely terrified. "What's going on?"

"She's fine," Bryson said, pulling her away before immediately engulfing me in a hard hug with a firm slap to my back. "We're here for you."

"How...?" It clicked who told them the moment I said the word. "Charlie."

"Yep. Charlie." Tucking Tinley against his side, Bryson's eyes swept the waiting room. "Any news?"

"Jameson is out of surgery and is expected to make a full recovery."

"Oh thank fuck," Tinley whispered and slouched against my best friend.

A part of me cracked at that sight. Seeing her put all her trust in him to protect her, to be her rock. Would Remy ever feel that way toward me again? Surely, I'd lost her trust forever.

I swallowed hard.

"Remy is still in surgery," I finished, looking away from the happy couple.

"You're a fucking moron." I snapped my gaze to Bryson, who'd switched from looking relieved to see me to fucking pissed. We'd been friends since college. He no doubt knew where my thoughts went. With a dramatic roll of his eyes, he turned to face Tinley. "Did you blame your brother when that fuckhead Vincent got his hands on you?"

Her eyes went wide in surprise. "What? No! Of course not. That's fucking dumb."

Bryson waved a hand at Tinley as if proving his point.

"That's different. I left her and Jameson—"

"Oh, so you left the front door open, unlocked, without a guard out front and them completely unarmed inside."

I pursed my lips. "You don't understand."

"Oh," Tinley said, catching on to what we were vaguely referencing. "Tal, you can't blame yourself for this. For any of it. I thought we already covered this? You can't control everything, and just because someone did something bad doesn't mean you have to wear that guilt like a damn hazmat suit."

The corner of my lips twitched. "Hazmat suit, huh?"

"Yeah, keeps you safe but isolated. Alone."

I ran a hand through my hair. "How could she trust me ever again? I failed her."

Tinley's features tightened in a frustrated look I was well acquainted with being her brother. "You only fail her if you give up or if you take the choice away from her to choose you. I doubt she'll blame you for anything that happened, but don't you dare make that decision for her. If you're this torn up about it, then you care for her—*really* care for her. Don't give up just because you're scared."

"I'm not scared," I grumbled.

Tinley shot Bryson a smirk. "Just give her a chance to tell you how she feels, not how you're expecting her to. I think you'll be pleasantly surprised—"

"She has a son," I blurted. Tinley's eyes widened. "A nine-year-old."

"Okay..." she drawled. "That doesn't mean—"

"Her son, he's mine. I'm the father."

If I weren't wallowing in guilt and worry, I'd find their gaping shocked looks hilarious.

"What. The. Actual. Fuck?" Tinley finally managed.

Smiling, I shook my head and turned to look at the swinging doors, willing them to open and reveal a doctor with good news.

"Congratulations." Bryson reached out and clasped my shoulder, his smile wide. "If you don't step up as a dad, I'll murder you."

"The hell?"

He shrugged like he didn't just threaten me.

"What's my nephew's name?" Tinley said, clapping her hands and bouncing on her feet. Seeing the worry and exhaustion fade from my sister was worth the awkwardly timed announcement.

"Crew, and apparently he's amazing."

"Well, of course he is. Great genes." She smirked. "From his mother's side."

I barked a laugh. Fuck, I needed this, needed them instead of sitting in this waiting room drowning in my thoughts as I waited for my fate.

"He's been in Texas with Charlie while we dealt with Vincent's partner—"

"Where is he?" Bryson's tone was hard as he pulled Tinley close once again.

"Dead. Eight bullets to the chest will do that to a man. They're transporting his body to the morgue, where they'll gather his DNA so we can close all the cases he's tied to, even the three in Chattanooga. On the positive side this means we don't have to hunt down the bastard's relatives to find a partial DNA match to get a warrant for his."

The squeak of rubber against the floor had me turning,

following the sound. The swinging doors to the operating rooms flew open, and a tall woman in surgical scrubs, face pinched, stepped into the waiting room. Scanning the space, her eyes landed on me.

"The family of Remington Dotson?"

I strode toward her, meeting her halfway. "That's me."

She eyed me. "Husband?"

"Sure."

She sighed and gestured toward the side. "Let's find somewhere to—"

"Oh fuck," I stated, knowing exactly what that meant. "Please, no."

A comforting hand pressed to my lower back while a heavy weight rested on my shoulder from the other side. Tinley and Bryson's comforting presence was lost as my heart hammered in my chest.

"Sir, if you'll just—"

"She's everything," I rasped.

The doctor's features softened. "It was touch and go. She lost a lot of blood, and there was some damage from the knife." I swallowed down the sob that wanted to make my agony apparent to the world. "But she's stable. For now." I slumped, Bryson catching my weight before I could fall into the doctor. "The reason I wanted a room was to discuss.... Her uterus was too damaged. I had to perform an emergency hysterectomy to stop her from bleeding out."

She continued to talk. Thankfully Tinley responded, asking additional questions I couldn't seem to get myself to ask.

"I want to see her," I demanded, cutting off the conversation.

"I'm having her transferred to ICU until tomorrow. You

can see her then. I'll have someone come out and let you know when she's moved."

She turned, but I reached out and grasped her elbow.

Surprised eyes met mine.

"Thank you," I said, a little stronger than earlier. "Thank you for saving her life... and mine."

With a smile and nod, she turned and disappeared the way she came.

Moving to a seat, I folded into the chair and bent forward, holding my head between my hands.

As soon as she woke up, I'd make this right.

Do everything I could to make her forgive me.

Even if I spent the rest of my life on my knees.

35

REMINGTON

An insistent ding from somewhere near my head tugged me awake before I was ready. Groggy as hell, I blinked away the sleep coating my eyes, quickly scanning my too-bright hospital room, searching for Tallon. Four days had passed since I woke up from surgery, confused and so very thankful to be alive. Not once had Tallon left my side, choosing to work from the single armchair in the corner of my suite, sleeping on the rollaway cot they brought in each night.

Except right now, the chair where he normally sat working during the day was unoccupied.

My lips turned down as I took in the laptop sitting on top of the worn cushion.

"Tallon?" I called, wondering if maybe he was in the adjoining restroom.

Instead of hearing him reply, the door leading to the hall clicked open, and a familiar form pushed through.

"Hey there, Remington," my favorite nurse, Dolores, chimed, hurrying to my bedside, arms full. The deep wrinkles adorning her sweet face pulled as she grinned, finding me awake. "Just need to change out this IV bag and that dang alarm will stop. Annoying little machines, but they sure make my job easier. How are you feeling this afternoon?"

I shifted my gaze to look out the windows, the bright afternoon sun blazing through. "Afternoon, huh? I didn't mean to sleep that long."

Her soft hand patted my own. "You need your rest, dear."

I nodded as she fiddled with the machine before changing out my IV bag. Settling against the flat pillow, I stared at the far wall, contemplating where Tallon could be.

"I heard your doctor talking around the nurses' station. Sounds like you'll be discharged tomorrow if you keep progressing like you have. Isn't that great?"

Fucking finally.

Sure, I was stabbed and almost died—well, actually died once on the operating table, though we weren't telling Tallon that tidbit—but I was ready to go home. I missed the comforts of my little house, missed my hectic routine.

My smile grew.

"Do you know where Agent Harper went?" I asked, throat raw.

As if she sensed my discomfort, Dolores grabbed the enormous plastic cup and placed the bendy straw against my lips. With a shy smile, I took down half the contents before pulling back with a relieved sigh.

"Hmm, I'm not sure, dear. He took a call and stormed out of here in an utter fit. But that tattooed one is here somewhere."

The tattooed one being Charlie.

He and Crew arrived two days ago, though Crew hadn't made it to the hospital yet, instead staying at the house with Tallon's sister, Tinley. Who was beyond ecstatic about being an aunt, though we weren't talking out loud about that connection just yet.

Hell, that was the theme of the week.

I hadn't wanted to tell Crew about Tallon, or the fact that I was missing the very organ that bastard Carting wanted to crudely cut out of me, or that I died.

Died.

The missing organ thing had come as a shock, yet I was alive, so I felt selfish being upset.

And yet here I was, about to go home. The familiar feeling of overwhelming emotions swelled in my chest, threatening to drown me, but I shoved it all back down. Not now, later. Later, I'd deal with the emotional trauma from the last week.

Though I was now ready to tackle one major topic.

It was time to tell Crew that Tallon was his biological father. I was ready the moment they arrived in Nashville, but with doctors, my random sleep schedule, and the FBI constantly wanting to talk to me, there hadn't been a chance.

The door to my room pushed open, Charlie stepping through with a bag dangling from his hand with a familiar logo.

"Is that PF Chang's?" I squealed, wincing at the pulling sensation along my lower stomach.

"It is," he said with a smirk. Dolores shot him a glare. "Don't worry. I ordered enough for all the nurses too."

And just like every woman who Charlie directed his attention toward, Dolores beamed, a pink flush now tinting her cheeks. With a quick thank you, she shuffled from the room.

Making grabby hands, I demanded Charlie closer, yanking the bag from his fingertips with my good arm as soon as he was within reach. Holy hell. Actual food, and it smelled amazing. My mouth watered as I peeked inside the white plastic bag.

"Thank you," I exclaimed as I pulled out the various boxes, placing them beside me on the bed. Frustration mounted at only using one hand. The broken bone better heal fast. "Do you know where Tallon went?"

His responding silence paused my hands. I peeked up through my lashes.

Charlie cringed. "What are you going to eat first—"

"Charlie," I demanded. "Where is he?"

"I don't want to tell you."

My heart sank. "Why not? Is he hurt? Is it Crew?"

He held both hands in surrender. "Oh, fuck no. Everything is okay."

"Okay," I repeated. "Then tell me where he is."

"Well...."

"Charlie, you're my closest friend, and friends tell each other everything, so spill it. I'm freaking out over here." Which was the truth. The heart rate monitor beeped in a quicker cadence than it had just seconds ago.

"Don't freak out."

"Too late with your stalling."

"Your parents showed up. At your house."

My jaw dropped. *Oh fuck.* Hunger forgotten, I began putting all the food back in the bag. "We need to—"

"Tinley immediately called Tallon, and he raced over to handle the situation. That's all I know."

"When was this?" I glanced back to the window as if I

could tell the time by the direction of the sun. *Tallon was here when I ate breakfast, wasn't he? Or was that yesterday?* I huffed in annoyance. "I can't remember when I saw him last."

"Hey," Charlie said, moving to sit on the edge of the bed by my feet. A comforting weight settled over my shin. "I'm sure you saw him this morning. He's only been gone for a few hours, and it's around three." His brows dipped as he searched my face. "Did the doctors say how long the short-term memory loss would stick around?"

Mind reeling with the possibilities of Tallon murdering my parents, I nodded. "Should get better and better now that I don't have the overwhelming stress of a serial killer hunting me. Can you call him?"

"Oh look, lettuce wraps," Charlie exclaimed with fake excitement, pulling out a white Styrofoam box.

"Fine. I'll just see for myself," I hissed and shifted along the bed to somehow climb out. A dull throbbing pain radiated from the layers of stitches as I moved. My breathing picked up, a wave of heat making sweat dampen my underarms and forehead. This was a terrible idea, but I needed to know everything was okay. "I'll just go over there and—"

"You'll sit your sexy ass in that bed like your doctor told you to do."

My heart leapt as Tallon strode into the room looking sexy as hell in his dark jeans and black North Face coat. His bright blue eyes latched on to mine, and he smirked.

"What happened? Where are my parents? Are they dead?"

His brows rose higher up his forehead with every question.

"They showed up, and I handled the situation. They are now headed home with their tails between their legs after I told them I'd shoot them both if they ever demanded you come home again." I snarled at that, making his smile grow. "Your soon-to-be ex-husband was not with them."

"Soon-to-be ex?"

Charlie raised his hand as if waiting to be called on by a teacher. "Rhyan has an attorney friend who drew up divorce papers for you. All you have to do is review them and approve, and she'll get those papers served to your jackass of an ex."

I blinked as I looked between the two men.

"Oh, wow."

"And to answer your last question, no, they are not dead, but I promised them death if they ever crossed the state line into Tennessee again."

I fisted a handful of the waffle-pattern yellow blanket. "Did Crew see all this?"

"No, Tinley pulled him inside and distracted him. Though—" He shot a look over his shoulder. "—Crew demanded he come see you." Tallon ran a hand over his too long hair. "And he's very convincing."

I snorted. "Yeah, I know." After putting all the containers back in the bag, I handed it off to Charlie. "Can you put that in the fridge somewhere? I'm dying to see Crew and don't want to wait another second."

"Yep. And I'll give you three some space. Just let me know when you're ready to eat."

Tallon followed Charlie out the door, motioning into the hallway. The stomp of running feet sent my heart leaping in my chest, pulse racing with anticipation. Tears lined my lower lids before he even entered the room.

The moment I laid eyes on my sweet little boy, a sob shook my shoulders, and tears leaked down my cheeks. He smiled and hurried over, his small arms open, ready to wrap me in a hug. Despite the discomfort, I shifted to hug him over the bed rail and squeezed him as tight as I could with the cast.

"I missed you so, so, so much." I sobbed into his hair after a few long sniffs. He smelled different, but beneath it all, it was still my little boy smell.

"Missed you, too, Mom. Are you okay? The doctors said you were hurt really bad."

After they moved me from the ICU, having had a day to process what all happened, I told Tallon I didn't want Crew to know the full details of what went on the last couple weeks. One day I'd tell him everything he wanted to know, but right now, at nine years old, he didn't need that kind of darkness lingering in the back of his mind.

"I'm good now, sweetheart. Especially now that I've gotten to see you. Did you get taller?" Hand on his shoulder, I pushed him away and gave him a full-body sweep. "Yep, totally got taller. I think you're bigger than me now."

"Easy to be." He smirked, then took in my hot pink cast. "Cool cast. Of course, you went hot pink."

"Oh, I missed you." Movement behind him had me glancing at Tallon, who tried to discreetly wipe at his cheeks. "Hey." Taking a deep breath to calm my thundering heart, I pulled Crew close. "Remember all those times you asked me about your dad, and I told you he was out fighting the bad guys?"

"Yeah," he said, already distracted, studying the various tubes and machines. "Hey, what does this one do?"

"Do you want to meet him?"

His full attention snapped to me, cool machines forgotten. "Really?"

"Really."

He chewed on his lip, a nervous habit of his. "I don't... I don't know." His blond brows furrowed. "Did he do this?"

"Oh no. Absolutely not. He's the one who saved me."

His head bobbed. "Good. Because if he hurt you, I get to hurt him back, right? That's the way it works. Don't start a fight, but finish it." A deep chuckle rumbled through the room, but I didn't dare glance over Crew's shoulder to Tallon. "But, um...." He tipped his face down to the floor. "Do you think he'll like me?"

My heart shattered at the vulnerability in his soft tone. My lips parted, but Tallon beat me to it.

"Crew, I already love you."

Fresh hot tears leaked down my face as Tallon stepped forward to stand beside Crew, who tilted his head back up, surprise clear on his face.

"Tallon, this is Crew," I said. "Crew, this is your dad, Special Agent Tallon Harper."

"My dad," he whispered in what sounded like disbelief.

"I'm sorry I've been gone." Tallon dropped to a crouch, putting them at eye level. "But I'm here now, and I'd like a chance to get to know you, if you'll let me."

Crew didn't respond for a second, then softly asked, "Will you leave us again?"

I swallowed down another soul-shaking sob. *My sweet baby boy.*

"I have to travel for work, but no, I won't leave you and your mom again. I want this, want you two."

"Like a family?"

Tallon's smile widened as heavy tears dripped from the corners of his eyes. "Like a family. You good with that, little man?"

Instead of responding with words, Crew lunged forward, wrapping his arms around Tallon's neck in a tight hug.

Tallon stumbled back, catching them both with a single hand to the floor before they could fall backward.

His watery gaze met mine.

A family.

Our family.

Forever.

EPILOGUE
REMINGTON

Cursing under my breath, I continued to search the parking lot of the Little League park for an empty spot. Showing up a little late guaranteed I'd be half a mile from the fields, but that was okay. The freedom of knowing Crew was taken care of, here on time without me stressing to get off work early, was absolute bliss.

I sighed when white lights flashed on a large SUV backing out of a space. Tapping my fingers along the steering wheel, I waited patiently. Not being rushed, Crew's entire world not only on my shoulders, was a welcomed relief.

Since that day in the hospital, Tallon had stepped in helping me, not just Crew. For the first time in my life, I could let go and take a deep breath. Mom guilt sometimes crept in, demanding I feel bad for not always being there for Crew, but Tallon helped me work through it when it reared its ugly head.

He wanted alone time with his son, to get to know him, just them two. And I was grateful.

After parking, I grabbed my jacket and blanket from the

passenger seat and shoved the door open. Spring was in the air, making it slightly warmer than it was just a few weeks ago. Still not warm enough for me not to come prepared with warmer gear just in case; if the wind blew just right, I'd be freezing in the metal bleachers.

Walking up to Crew's team field, I leaned a shoulder against the fence, watching the game for a second. My bag vibrated with an incoming call. Pulling my phone free, I swiped the screen.

"Hey, you," I said.

"Are they winning?" Charlie asked. "You're on speaker-phone, by the way."

"Hey, Rhyan," I said, my grin so wide my cheeks burned. "And I don't know. I just walked up."

"Text me as soon as you know. I think they have them beat. I just know it."

I laughed. "You don't even know who we're playing. Hey, have you guys talked to Jameson?"

We'd tried calling him earlier in the week but didn't reach him. We'd called once a week while he was at Quantico, checking in to see how it was going.

"Yeah, he's good. Rhyan gets updates from the academy instructors too. He's doing great."

"Good. Okay, I'm making my way to the stands. I'm sure all the Karens will know the score, so I'll text you when I find out."

"Are they still giving you a hard time about your tattoos?"

I smirked. "Well, I might have instigated some... controversy."

"What did you do?" Rhyan asked while laughing.

"Put my Fitbit around my ankle so they think it's an ankle monitor."

I pulled the phone away from my ear as their loud laughs roared through the phone.

"I'll text you the score. Bye, you two. Love you."

"We love you too," they said in unison.

Dropping the phone back into my bag, I moved farther down the fence. As I approached the bleachers, a pair of piercing blue eyes locked on mine. Picking up the pace, I didn't hide my wide smile as Tallon's grew.

"Hey, you," I said as I took the space he'd clearly saved for me. Fingers skirted around the back of my neck before tightening. Hauling me closer, Tallon sealed his lips to mine, holding my stare the entire time.

"I missed you, Kitten," he said against my mouth.

Heat rushed to my cheeks. "I saw you this morning."

"Still missed you." I shook my head as he loosened his hold but kept his hand there, fingers brushing along my hairline in gentle strokes. "We're winning, by the way. And Crew is about to bat."

"Oh good." I swept my gaze to where he would be standing taking practice swings. "Tallon, what the hell is he wearing?" I hid my laugh behind a raised fist.

"I told you," he grunted. "He needed more protective gear."

"He's basically wearing what the catcher does... to bat."

He just shrugged, completely uncaring that he was going overboard with the need to protect our son. My heart swelled as I stared at the amazing, infuriating man.

"And we need to talk about switching teams. I saw that fat ass yell at him. Twice."

Reaching down, I gripped what I could of his massive thigh. "Tallon. That's the coach, and he's not yelling, he's coaching. We've been on this team before. He's a good guy." His eyes cut my way. "Not as good as you."

He huffed and dropped his hand from around my neck to grab my hand. He drew it up to his lips and placed a kiss to each knuckle. "I just want to keep you two safe."

It was nice knowing this was all Tallon being Tallon, and not a result of me not being able to have more kids after the emergency hysterectomy. Sometimes I allowed myself to get sad about it, to lie in bed and mourn the choice that was taken from me. But then I looked at Tallon, saw the way he was with Crew, and I knew they were enough.

No, not just enough.

Everything.

"He's up," Tallon said, as excited as a kid in a candy store. Hands cupped around his mouth, he yelled in support. "Let's go, Crew!"

My boy, our sweet little guy, turned at the sound of Tallon's voice and shot him a shy smile. The protective gear really wasn't as bad as I made it out to be, but still, it was a little much. Those blue eyes met mine, and his smile grew wide. Hand raised high in the air, I gave him a big wave.

"We've been working on this," Tallon said like he was giving himself a pep talk. "He's got this. Hit the hell out of the ball, son."

Oh fuck, I think my heart just exploded.

Turning back to the game, I watched Crew swing.

Strike.

"It's okay, Crew," Tallon yelled. "You've got this!"

Crew ignored us this time and tapped the end of the bat against the plate.

Another swing.

Strike.

"Oh fuck, I can't take this," Tallon muttered under his breath. "This is killing me. I want him to get a hit because he's always so proud of himself."

"I know," I said, swallowing down emotional tears that threatened to leak from my watery eyes.

Fuck, what is wrong with me? I cannot turn into a sobbing mess every time he does or says something sweet about Crew.

"One last swing," Tallon whispered, hand now tightly gripping mine.

I winced a little but didn't say a word.

Crew pulled the bat back, elbow up, and stared the pitcher down.

Swing.

Hit.

Tallon jumped up, pulling me right along with him. The ball continued to soar through the air over the shortstop's head.

Jumping up and down, I yelled for Crew to keep running as I watched the ball drop between the center fielder, who was just sitting in the grass watching a butterfly, and the left fielder.

"Go, go, go, go!" Tallon shouted, his excitement palpable as he moved to stand on the bleacher seat in front of us. "Keep going, buddy!"

He rounded second base just as the left fielder picked up the ball and tried to throw it to third, but it went wild.

Clasping Tallon's hand with my other, I gave it a hard shake. "Shit, shit, shit, shit," I muttered as Crew hit third base and bolted toward home.

The third baseman launched the now-recovered ball toward the catcher, who was positioned and ready at home.

"Slide," Tallon yelled, voice clear over all the other cheers.

And Crew did.

Just as the ball hit the catcher's glove.

Dust billowed from the ground. Crew looked up at the ump, who stood just a foot away.

"Safe," the ump roared.

Tallon and I looked at each other before turning back to the field and erupting in shouts.

An in-the-park home run.

"Fuck, I'm so damn proud of him. Did you see that? He's amazing. I knew he could do it. Just so, so proud." Tallon's voice broke at the end, and he wiped at his eyes. "Damn pollen."

"Tallon," I rasped, staring at his handsome face and the happy tears he was clearly holding back.

"Yeah?" he said, watching Crew jog back to the dugout, while giving him two big thumbs-up.

"I'm ready."

Tallon whipped his attention to me. Eyes wide, he searched my face.

"You're ready?" I nodded. "Kitten," he croaked. "You'll marry me?"

"Yes. More than ready."

Grabbing my face between both hands, he pulled me close and sealed his lips to mine.

I melted, the tears I was holding back now streaming down my face.

And just like that my life got even better.

An evil man tried to take this away from me. But I was here, with Tallon, with Crew.

I was alive, and I intended to live.

With them. Happy. As a family.

Together.

ALSO BY KENNEDY L. MITCHELL

In Clear Sight: A Small Town, WITSEC Interconnected Standalone Series

Safe Haven - FREE Prequel

Guarded by the Marshal

Cherished by the Agent

Saved by the Officers

Hidden by the Doctor

Protection Series: A Dark Romantic Thriller Interconnected Standalone Series

Mine to Protect *

Mine to Save *

Mine to Guard *

Mine to Keep *

Mine to Hold *

Mine to Love *

Mine to Share

Mine to Shelter

*Now available in audio!

SEALs and CIA Series: A Navy SEAL Interconnected Standalone Series

Covert Affair

Covert Vengeance

More Than a Threat Series: A Connected Bodyguard Romantic Suspense Series

More Than a Threat

More Than a Risk

More Than a Hope

More Than a Threat Series Boxset: Complete Series

Power Play Series: A Protector Romantic Suspense Connected Series

Power Games

Power Twist

Power Switch

Power Surge

Power Term

Standalones:

Finding Fate - Dark, Captive Romantic Suspense

Memories of Us - Contemporary, Small Town Romance

ABOUT THE AUTHOR

Kennedy L. Mitchell lives outside Dallas with her husband, son and two very large goldendoodles. She began writing in 2016 after a fight with her husband (You can read the fight almost verbatim in Falling for the Chance) and has no plans of stopping.

She would love to hear from you via any of the platforms below or her website www.kennedylmitchell.com You can also stay up to date on future releases through her newsletter or by joining her Facebook readers group - Kennedy's Book Boyfriend Support Group.

Thank you for reading.

ACKNOWLEDGMENTS

Wow. Another book done. I could not, nor would want to, do any of this without so many people. First my amazing alpha readers Em, Chris, and Kristin. You guys are amazing. Thank you for helping mold the story to flow better and make sense to everyone else! I love writing for you three.

Second thank you to my awesome beta reader Darlene. THANK you so much for the detailed feedback and oh so encouraging words. You're a GEM!

And of course thank you to my ARC team. You guys rock. All the posts you share, comment and like to reading I couldn't do any of this without out you. Thank you for helping spread the word on my books and being so damn encouraging. I'm luck to have you.

To the reader who read this book. THANK YOU. You're amazing. Thank you for giving me a chance. I hope I was able to steal you away from reality for a little while with this spicy, suspenseful read.

Happy reading friends.